When the Yellow Mocker Calls

Lila M Beckham

When the Yellow Mocker Calls

Lila M Beckham

When the Yellow Mocker Calls

Sold by Amazon Digital Services Inc.

Cover art: S C Beck

Lila M Beckham

When the Yellow Mocker Calls

Lila M Beckham

Foreword

I was blessed to grow up in a family of storytellers, and when they talked about the days of yore, describing what it was like when they were children and telling stories about their youthful adventures with their brothers, sisters, and cousins- and told stories about their parents and grandparents, I realized they were talking about *my* family- *my* aunts and uncles, grandparents, and great-grandparents; I could have sat there for hours and listened; many times I did and then begged for more- I wanted to know these people. I pictured them in my mind as I listened, and when the story ended, I wondered about the things they didn't talk about- didn't describe- What was their lives like before my parents and grandparents were born?

Although I admired my father and his brother's storytelling ability, they lacked details past the crux of their own childhood memories- On the other hand, my maternal grandmother, Mae, who was born in 1904 was the family historian on Mama's side of the family. She knew things from way back-

She knew the lineage of her and Grandpa's family back to the mid-1800s, and could easily name these people from memory; at least five generations worth; maybe more. She's gone now; been gone since 1986, but her knowledge of her family's history inspired me to learn more about them, and I wanted to know about my father's side of the family.

Lila M Beckham

When the Yellow Mocker Calls

Since her departure, I've dedicated many hours researching-verifying names and records- digging through censuses, military documents, wills, etc., walked though cemeteries and jotted down dates and information. During this process, I've compiled an extensive family tree. Many of the stories I'd heard and the names given me were accurate right down to the T.

The story I'm telling in this book, is from my father's side of the family; it is about his maternal, great-grandmother and her family.

These partly Indian ancestors on my father's side of the family, had many strange beliefs and some odd superstitions. They freely spoke of ghosts- animal and human spirits that roamed the earth years after they'd departed in death. They freely spoke of the existence of unexplainable, dare I say, supernatural occurrences and the connections between the living and the spirit world... And, while some of the adventures in this book actually occurred, others were intricately weaved with the visions I had of how their lives were as I traveled with them via census records, wills, deeds, and military documents. Many of the folks in this book actually existed over a hundred years ago; they were my kinfolk; their physical descriptions come from fading photographs and wartime documents- their manner of speech drawn from the stories told by my ancestors. Some characters are fictitious, plucked from the thin air of imagination as I rode in a wagon along the dusty roads and trails of the early 1800s while listening to family storytellers; any resemblance to actual people is purely coincidental.

Lila M Beckham

When the Yellow Mocker Calls

This book is meant for entertainment purposes only and should not be taken to heart as being factual in all its contents; however, the telling of this story is my way of honoring those folks that came before me. I hope you all enjoy reading their story as much as I enjoyed writing it.

The Author,

Semmes, AL

Mar, 2016

Lila M Beckham

Dedication

This novel is dedicated to the memory of my father's maternal great-grandmother, Charity Finley Gulledge. I will never know everything about her, but what I do know about her life has always fascinated me and sparked my imagination. A strong, courageous woman, she loved thoroughly, endured much pain, and overcame many hardships in life. The stories that traveled down through the generations about her and what I've discovered through genealogy research has inspired me to be a storyteller, a writer; and, they've inspired me to be a better person. I wish I could have known my Grandmother- I can only imagine the conversations we would've had.

Lila M Beckham

When the Yellow Mocker Calls

Lila M Beckham

Contents

Lila M Beckham

18, 1843

1. **The Sign of the Whirlpool Wind**

1. **Escape!**

1. **Cherokee County - Georgia Country**

1. **Canton**

1. **Reunion**

1. **Hank Wheeler**

1. **Spellbound**

1. **The Passageway**

1. **Visions**

1. **Evil Incarnate**

1. **Retribution**

1. **The Hidden Cave**

1. **Behind the Waterfall**

1. **A Georgia Mountain Christmas - Cherokee Co, Georgia Dec 25, 1843**

1. **Interlude**

1. **Paint Me a Mountain - Jacksonville, Benton Co, AL Nov, 1849**

1. **Purgatory**

1. **Jeremiah's Demons**

1. **Noccalula Falls - Black Creek Falls, Cherokee Co, AL March, 1851**

1. **Princess Noccalula**

1. **The Spirits Song**

1. **The Singing River - Gaylesville, Cherokee Co, AL**

Lila M Beckham

When the Yellow Mocker Calls

1. **Acceptance**

1. **The Conclusion - Henry's Letter**

Lila M Beckham

When the Yellow Mocker Calls

Lila M Beckham

1

The Watershed, Spartanburg District
South Carolina
Oct, 1829

Groaning in relief, the young girl squatted behind a huckleberry thicket and emptied her bladder; the tart odor of pine straw saturated with urine filled the air around her. Inhaling deeply, she smiled; not so much from the aroma of the urine, but from the other scents in the crisp October air.

Waking along the watershed usually meant another bland beginning to another bland, uneventful day. And most days, the young girl whose name was Charity, hated getting out of bed in the mornings; she preferred to lie in bed a few minutes moaning, groaning, and stretching before getting up- especially once the weather began to turn cooler the way it had in recent weeks. However, that early October day in the year 1829, fourteen year old Charity sprang out of bed like a jackrabbit ready to run a race with a hare. Something special was going to happen that day; she knew it as surely as she knew her own name- however, she'd also been having a nagging pain in her innards that foretold a warning of some sort; a premonition that everything was not as it seemed.

Hesitating a moment because of another of those nagging aches in her belly, Charity stopped mid-stride to question her feelings before going into the kitchen to start breakfast for her and her grandfather.

Her grandparents had always told her that she had a "gift of knowing," and that she needed to hone in on those feelings when they came to her.

When alive, her grandmother, Mi' Thebe, possessed the same gift. Mi' Thebe was a full-blood- a Cherokee - the daughter of Shooting Arrow, Shaman of the Bird Clan of the South Carolina mountains north of Savannah- the English words for her grandmother's name was, Shadowy Moon.

After stoking the fire, Charity placed a few pieces of bacon in the frying pan and set it on the grate above the fire, then stepped outside the old, log cabin to go to the toilet. Taking a deep breath of the cool, fresh mountain air, Charity bent over and stretched her back to remove the stiffness she felt from sleeping in her not so comfortable bed. Her bed consisted of a cot with a straw-ticked mattress atop a wooden bunk that seemed to become flatter and harder every year as she grew older and heavier.

Her grandfather had built the log cabin some fifty-odd years earlier, as a wedding gift for Mi' Thebe. The bunk and mattress were made for the girl-child that came along some years after they became husband and wife, in a tribal ceremony with all of Shadowy Moon's clan members in attendance.

When the Yellow Mocker Calls

Since clanship is matrilineal, Shadowy Moon's mother and oldest brother served as representatives. And, because her grandfather could not be represented by his mother, which was Cherokee custom, a kindly elder of the clan represented him. First, the couple exchanged foodstuffs, a venison ham from him, symbolizing his intention to keep meat in the house, and an ear of corn from her, which symbolized her intention to be a good Cherokee wife. Afterward, the wedding party danced and feasted for hours.

The priestess of the clan then blessed the sacred spot chosen for the ceremony for seven consecutive days- Once that had been done, the bride and groom then approached the Sacred Fire. They were wrapped together in a blue blanket- sung to and blessed by the priestess, as was all in attendance. Once the priestess was satisfied that all was well, the blanket was removed and they started their lives together.

The girl-child born to them, was Charity's mother, Gige'sdi. Charity's mother had been named Gige'sdi because of the violet color of her eyes.

Being the daughter of an Englishman and a Cherokee squaw, Gige'sdi, had been a raven haired, violet-eyed beauty that turned the head of many a young brave. It wasn't long before she caught the attention of a handsome, young brave named, Ugug Usdi. Ugug Usdi was an old name that meant, Little Owl.

Charity could not remember her parents at all, but often wondered what her life would have been like if they had lived

Lila M Beckham

through the yellow fever epidemic that occurred when she was only three-years-old.

As she grew older, Charity also wondered why she, a small and weak child lived, and her strong, grown-up parents, died.

Nokomis, the Cherokee name she called her grandmother, had always told her that her parents died because it was the wish of the Great Spirit that they join Him in His home in the sky; however, her grandmother's reply did not satisfy her question. She did not feel that saying they died because it was the wish of the Great Spirit, was a real answer to her question.

When her grandmother passed away, Charity watched her for an hour, hoping to see her spirit leave her body to travel to the Great Spirit's home in the sky. When her grandfather noticed her waiting and watching, he asked her what she was doing, when she told him, he said that her grandmother's spirit had left and gone into the Great Spirit's home in the sky, the moment she died.

"Our spirits leave us as soon as we pass away, child. The spirit cannot exist in a body that ain't breathing." His voice broke slightly before he turned and walked outside.

Now that it was just her and Grandpa left, it was a little lonely for her. Charity loved her grandfather, but she missed her grandmother something fierce. She missed her grandmother's scent... her storytelling as they did chores- she missed her cooking, too... And, although she was excited about leaving it, she loved her home- it was the only home she'd ever known. Going into town with her grandfather to get supplies, would be the first time he had ever let her accompany him on one of his bi-yearly trips, and it would be the very first time she had ever left the cabin for an overnight excursion.

She wondered if he wanted her to go with him because he was getting old… Maybe, he just wants me to learn the way of his people, the white men, thought Charity. After all, he had told her that she could not wear her buckskins and that she had to wear the cotton dress he'd given her a few months earlier. The dress came from the Trading Post across the river near the Cherokee settlement of Brownstown; he'd traded some pelts for it.

Charity did not like the way the dress felt against her skin- the material was thin and light; it hardly felt as if she had anything on. At first, she balked at wearing it, but finally gave in because she wanted so badly to go with him.

Wiping the thoughts from her head, she decided that she was not going to worry about all of that dressing in dresses and stuff; not today, today she would get to go on a real adventure. She would see and maybe even get to talk to other people; not, that she didn't enjoy her conversations with her grandfather, but she wanted to meet other people and have conversations with them too. Besides her grandmother and grandfather, and the occasional visitor they had from Brownstown come to the cabin, she'd never talked to anyone. Many times in the last year or so, since her grandmother's passing, Charity had wondered what it would be like to be around other people. Life in the hills of South Carolina, in 1829, was not an exciting life for a young teenage girl.

Just before she stood from behind the huckleberry bush, a yellow-bellied mocking bird lit in it. It stared at her for a moment- its beady, dark eyes burning into hers, before it uttered a noisy complaint and then flew away... The only bird that had ever come that close to her was the small hummingbirds that came in the summertime. A chill ran through her as she stood and made her way back inside to finish fixing their breakfast.

✷✷✷

"Are you ready to accompany this old man to town," asked her grandfather when she walked back inside. She smiled her acquiescence and patted his shoulder. He reached up a rough, age-spotted hand to pat hers, and then said, "We'd better get to moving if we're going to make it to Eli's before dark."

"Who's Eli, Grandpa?"

"Eli is an old friend of mine; he stopped by here to visit once. You weren't knee-high to a grasshopper at the time, so that's probably why you don't remember him. I've known Eli his whole life- Me and his father, Henry, came to these hills over sixty years ago."

"He must live a long ways," mumbled Charity, wondering why he'd only visited once...

"Naw, not that far a'tall," her grandfather responded. "No more 'n about twenty miles down the Savannah. I usually stop off over at his place on my way to and from Fort Charlotte. Sometimes, Eli goes down there with me- when he's in need of supplies, or his woman is in need of cloth or other womanly things."

"Hmm," mumbled Charity. She knew what he meant by women things- she had found out about a woman's curse the year before when she had come of childbearing age, as her grandmother called it.

After finishing up their quick breakfast of leftover biscuits and the bacon she fried, they finished loading the wagon and were driving away from the old cabin by the time the sun was coming up. Charity never looked back as they drove away- she was more interested in what lay ahead than what she was leaving behind. Besides, they'd be back in less than a week, or so she thought…

The first few miles of the trip were uneventful; both were quiet, each, with stuff other than talking on their minds. Even if there had been something new and beautiful to see, Charity's mind was so full of wondering about where they were going and who she might meet that she did not notice anything. She did not notice the beautiful multi-hued mountains or the lush green valleys, the tall, willowy birch trees, or the assortment of animals that watched them pass by.

About noon, they stopped to stretch their legs and eat some of the bread and venison they'd brought with them from home. They had both been quieter than was their usual on this journey; both, lost in their own thoughts and concerns. After they climbed back onto the wagon and traveled another few miles in silence, Charity startled her grandfather when she suddenly spoke; he had to ask her to repeat what she'd said.

"I asked you what they're like, Grandpa."

"What who's like?"

"Your friends; the ones you said we are going to see."

"Well," said Grandpa, hesitating. "They are a lot like us, I reckon. About twenty years ago, Eli married a woman named Nancy. Yeah, it was at least that long ago. They have one son still a living; he's about your age, maybe a year older; his name is Henry. Eli named him after *his* father; my friend, Henry," added her grandfather, reminding her of what he'd already told her.

"What about your friend Henry, where is he?"

"Well, he died a couple years back," her grandfather replied. Charity could hear the sadness in her grandfather's tone.

"Oh, I'm sorry, Grandpa, that's sad… Why did he die?"

"Old age, I reckon…"

"Like when Nokomis died; she was old."

"Yeah, sorta like that, Child. We get old, and we die."

When her grandfather said that, the way he said it, she knew right then that he was feeling his age, and probably fearing that he, too, was about to die - He was trying to get her settled somewhere, before that happened.

"Is that why you wanted me to come along?" she asked, giving him a direct look.

"Huh?" Her grandpa questioned, acting as if he didn't hear what she said. She knew there wasn't anything wrong with his hearing, he heard real well most of the time; she could never slip anything by him.

"Are you taking me to Fort Charlotte because you think you're not going to be around, much longer?"

When he did not immediately respond, she asked, "Are you trying to get me married off or something?"

"Well, now that you mention it," said grandfather.

"I don't want to get married, Grandpa!" Charity exclaimed. "I want to stay with you and take care of you, the way you took care of me, all these years!"

"Well, that really ain't up to you; It ain't up to me either… You see, your mama, she must've known she wasn't going to be around when you come of age; she musta knew that me and your grandma wouldn't be, either. She gave you your name, and a good Christian name at that; my own mama's name, who was her grandmamma.

"She said that with your blue eyes and fair skin, you ought to have a white woman's name… I think she hoped that one day, you could pass for a white woman. She wanted you to have a better life than what the Indians had."

"Is that why you put me in this dress and told me that I

couldn't wear my Asani, Grandpa?"

"Uh-huh, it is," he responded, never taking his eyes off the trail.

"Indians ain't looked upon too fondly in most places- Your Cherokee name, given to you by your father, was Sahani... Do you remember your grandma a telling you all of that?"

"Yes, Grandpa, I remember; I remember everything Nokomis taught me. Sahani means blue- he named me that because of the color of my eyes."

"Yeah, that's right, but we always called you by your Christian name, Charity; your mother and grandmother insisted on it- she could see into the future you know…" he said.

"Uh-huh," Charity mumbled.

"My friend Eli knows you are three-quarter Indian- that don't bother him none- We done talked about this and we both agreed that maybe you and his son Henry will hit it off and want to marry."

After she did not respond, a sideways glance from her grandfather let her know that he noticed her silence. He continued his discourse after pulling off to the side of the trail so they could stretch their legs again, use the bathroom, and eat a bit more of the venison. Charity was quiet and although she got the blanket and basket out of the wagon and served her grandfather, his food, she herself only drank a few sips of water. Her abstention from food and drink did not go unnoticed by her grandfather.

Lila M Beckham

"I just want what's best for you, child. If it means me giving up my last year or so on earth, then so be it- it's what has to be done. I may not last another year; this could be the last chance I get to see to it that you are settled somewhere and taken care of," he said firmly.

Charity did not respond to her grandfather's spew of thoughts- her mind was in turmoil. Both were quiet as they gathered up their blanket and the food basket. Soon, they were back in the wagon and back on the trail. Her heart felt heavy in her chest as she sat beside her grandfather looking dead ahead.

Although sitting quietly, Charity's mind was racing a mile a minute. How Grandpa can do this, is beyond me... Why did she feel as though she had no choice in what was going to happen, even though it was happening to her? Silently, she pleaded in her heart that her grandfather would change his mind and take her back home with him.

"What if this Henry feller doesn't like me, Grandpa," she asked suddenly. "What if Eli and his wife don't like me either," she asked, thinking to herself that she could easily make them not like her, just by being rude and ugly. She could do that, even though it would cause her grandfather embarrassment... Charity didn't want to embarrass her grandfather or to hurt him either, but she wanted to go back to the cabin with him, not stay with complete strangers...

"If they don't like me, can I go back home with you?"

Charity asked.

"Nope," he replied, firmly. "If young Henry doesn't take a liking to you, I'm sure some young buck down in Fort Charlotte will. They're always looking for wives down there."

Charity did not speak, but she didn't have to; her grandfather could tell that she was mad about what he had said.

"You look madder than an old, wet settin' hen," said her grandpa. "I swear, young'un, I can almost see the smoke a spewing out your ears." He chuckled to himself, and then said. "You keep that up, we'll look like we're hauling a tar kettle with us. You need to get yourself straightened up before we get to Eli's house; I would a lot rather see you married to young Henry than to some young buck I know nothing about."

Charity thought about jumping off the wagon and running back home, but she didn't want to leave her grandpa. The last time she snuck a look at him, she noticed that he didn't look so good- he was pale and his skin looked clammy.

"Are you alright, Grandpa?" she asked, as sudden concern for him overwhelmed her thoughts.

"Yes, child, I'll be fine," her grandfather replied. "I'm just getting too dang old for this long trip into town; these old bones of mine ache to high-heaven- I can't handle riding in a wagon all day like I used to. Heck, if'n I remember right, I'm neigh on eighty-two year's old, be eighty-three come December," he said thoughtfully. A sudden, awful aching in Charity's heart almost took her breath away. She looped her arm around her grandfathers and held on for dear life… She didn't know what she would do or how she was going to survive without anyone she knew around…

2

Eli's

The sun was low in the sky behind them before her grandfather spoke again. "We ought to be at Eli's cabin after another mile or so," he said. "We'll get there just in time for some of Nancy's good cooking. No disrespect meant, but I'm tired of eating your and my cooking. I always look forward to visiting with them-" he chuckled. "I never told your grandma this, but I'll tell you; that Nancy, she sure can cook. Her cooking is better than anyone else's cooking I've ever eaten, even your grandma's. O'course, your grandma didn't know nothing but Indian cooking when I married her- which I ain't a saying is a bad thing-"

"Do they know we're coming?" interrupted Charity.

"They ought to know, or at least know that I'm coming," he replied with a sideways glance. "I've come through here about this time of year, for the past fifty some odd years- and the last twenty of those, I've stopped right here at Eli and Nancy's place."

When they topped the next hill, Charity saw gray smoke

rising from the chimney of a small cabin situated in a valley a half a mile below. As they neared the cabin, she caught herself holding her breath in anticipation of the unknown.

When they were within a quarter-mile of the cabin, an old yellow dog come out from under a cedar tree and started barking at them- The front door of the cabin popped opened and a tall man with graying hair came and stood in the entrance. That must be Grandpa's friend, Eli, thought Charity. A small woman whose dark hair was pulled up off her shoulders and twisted into a bun appeared behind him. And, that must be Nancy, thought Charity. Her grandfather waved and they waved back. When they arrived at the front of the cabin, her grandfather pulled the horses to a halt, set the brake, and then got down off the wagon. He turned and reached his hand up to help her off the wagon. Charity was so nervous that when the dress she was wearing caught on the brake lever, she almost tripped and fell over the side of the wagon. Her grandfather caught her and landed her firmly on the ground.

As soon as her feet touched the earth, a strange sensation swirled through her - she had the sudden feeling that she would be there for a very long time...

When she came to herself, she looked around for her grandfather; he had already walked toward his friends- She saw him shake Eli's hand and exchange hellos. She wished she could hear what they were saying, but they were talking quietly. No matter how hard she strained her ears to hear them, she couldn't understand what they were saying. It seemed as though hours had passed since she had gotten down off the wagon; when in fact, it had only been a couple of minutes at the most. The gentle tone of a woman's voice finally penetrated her concentration enough to draw her attention from her grandfather and Eli's quiet conversation.

"Hello, dear, you must be Robert's granddaughter, Charity. We've heard so many wonderful things about you," exclaimed the woman.

It would have been really nice to hear about y'all, too; especially before today, thought Charity. She wanted to stomp her foot in rebellion and run home as fast as she could, however, she had been taught her manners while growing up, and she was brought up to be polite to folks; therefore, she swallowed her fear and irritation and smiled back at Nancy.

"Yes, Ma'am, I am Charity," she replied, standing as straight and tall as her four foot ten inch frame would allow.

When she was younger and acted surly, her grandfather always told her, "Just because you live out in the wilderness, doesn't mean you have to act like a heathen. Wild Indians don't even act that way!"

"I'm Nancy," said the woman, "I'm Eli's wife- we are looking forward to having you in our family. It will be nice to have another female presence around- I've lived in a house full of men so long that I've almost forgotten what it's like to have another woman in the household." She liked being called a woman instead of a child- again, she smiled at Nancy.

Charity had to look up at the woman to see her face; that was when she realized that even though the woman had appeared small when standing in the doorway beside her husband, she wasn't so small after all. She had to be almost a foot taller than Charity was- she was the tallest woman Charity had ever seen- she didn't take into account that besides her grandmother, Nancy was the only woman she had seen, at least that she remembered…

About that time, another figure appeared in the doorway of the cabin. That must be Henry, thought Charity. The young man smiled toward her grandfather and said, "Hello, Mr. Robert. It's good to see you again." He had a slow, gentle voice like his father; it was pleasant to the ear.

Charity could not take her eyes off the young man as he walked over to where her grandfather and his father stood. When he came face to face with her grandfather, he extended a hand and shook hands with him just as his father had done. Henry wasn't quite as tall as his father was; he was maybe about the same height as her grandfather.

His thick, dark hair was the color of his mother's; his eyes were gentle and dark colored like his father's. When he smiled at her grandfather- she noticed that he had a beautiful smile and a dimple on the side she could see.

She wished that he would look at her and smile at her the way he had at her grandfather. *It's like he don't even know I'm here.*

Nancy's voice finally penetrated her concentration and pulled her focus off Henry; she turned to look up at her. It was then that she realized that Nancy was speaking directly to her; her face turned pink with embarrassment.

"I'm sorry, Ma'am, I didn't hear you," she stuttered. "I was…"

"There is no need to be embarrassed. Everything must be overwhelming- especially with this being your first trip away from home. Just relax, everything will be fine. Would you like to freshen up, before supper?"

"Oh, yes, Ma'am, I'd love to," Charity replied, quickly. "If you don't mind," she added shyly.

"Not at all; follow me inside and I'll show you where everything is."

As she followed Nancy toward the cabin, Charity turned to look over her shoulder. The men were still standing, talking quietly. The boy, Henry, was watching her intently. When their eyes met, her breath caught in her chest; looking at him straight on, she could see that he was a very handsome fellow. It sort of surprised her because there was nothing remarkable about his mother's and father's appearance other than their height.

When the Yellow Mocker Calls

Watching the slip of a girl follow his mother toward the cabin, Henry thought that she must be an Indian child from one of the villages- he wondered where she came from. When he first walked outside, he had not seen her. The girl was so small that she must've been hidden behind his mother's skirts; she appeared to be several inches shy of five feet tall. And, even though she wore a cotton dress, he thought she was an Indian child because of her olive complexion and her long, straight and thick, jet-black hair which hung below her waistline; the ends landed about mid-butt-cheek.

At Fort Charlotte, he'd seen Indian children wearing white peoples' clothes before, but not very often- most were orphaned children that were taken in by white merchants who fed and clothed them and in return they did physical labor for the merchants… As Henry studied her from behind, Charity turned to look over her shoulder. When their eyes met, Henry felt as though he had been hit in the gut by a cannon ball! It was a minute before he could breathe again. That is no child, thought Henry; she is very beautiful-

∗∗∗

Although Henry was not as innocent as Charity was; he had not spent his entire life squirreled away from other people- stuck at the homestead as she had, he still lacked intimate discourse with the feminine gender. He had accompanied his father on numerous hunting trips and had gone to Fort Charlotte several times, but he had not had the pleasure of seeing or meeting many young women. And, even though he'd seen plenty of Indians and a few white women in the trading posts and at Fort Charlotte, none looked as pretty as Charity did. Thick dark lashes emphasized the violet color of her eyes, making them bright, even at the distance of twenty feet or so…

***

Stepping through the doorway of the cabin, Charity suddenly stumbled, then looked down in awe when she realized that she was walking on a board floor- she'd never seen anything on the floor but dirt!

"I know it's unusual out here in the wilderness for folks to have wooden floors," said Nancy, "but I told Eli that before I would marry him and move away from my family, that he would have to build me a house; a real house. I wanted wooden floors like the floors my mama had in her house in North Carolina. There was no way I was going to try to sweep dirt off of dirt," Nancy chuckled. "It took him a year to build this place- and like I promised, I married him once he finished. It's been twenty-one years and I've never regretted marrying him and moving here…"

Thinking that Henry must have seen her stumble and nearly fall, Charity was so embarrassed that she actually didn't hear a word that Nancy said.

He probably thinks I'm a clumsy ox, thought Charity, but Henry wasn't laughing and thought nothing of the sort; he was still marveling over her beauty and the color of those beautiful, violet eyes of hers.

"We have an outhouse out back and there's a washbasin, soap, and a pitcher of clean water on the washstand by the back door," said Nancy.

When she saw Charity looking around as if she were in a panic, she said, "Don't be scared, Charity; I realize that you've been raised in a more primitive environment- you'll get used to the differences."

Charity looked into Nancy's eyes- she saw only love and understanding in them; it placed her more at ease.

After Charity freshened up, Nancy said, "Eli tells me you've spent your entire life living on the watershed." Charity did not know exactly what that meant, so she just nodded her head.

Since her grandmother had passed away, Charity had not had a conversation with anyone other than her grandfather, and an older Indian man that came around every few weeks to visit them; therefore, she let Nancy do most of the talking, responding as best she could to the questions Nancy asked. As she talked, Nancy was busy finishing her cooking- she was cooking on a wood burning stove; that in itself was a curiosity to Charity. All they'd ever had for cooking purposes was a fireplace; it had a grate for frying, warmer rack off to the side, and an iron arm that swung out to hang the big iron pot on; she'd never even seen a woodstove before.

Nancy was proud of her stove; she also was proud of the few simple pieces of nice furniture she owned. The stove, an ornate, carved bedstead, and a wooden cupboard was brought from Virginia by a family that was traveling through on their way to Alabama.

Somewhere along the trail, the man's wife had died during childbirth; he and his son were going on to Alabama. Hauling the furniture and iron stove was slowing them down, but he said he didn't want to just dump them out along the trail; they were part of his late wife's dowry. Nancy wanted those items of furniture and stove so much that she had begged Eli to see if he could barter for them. Low and behold, the man took a mule and few sacks of corn for them. The man and his son stayed with Eli and Nancy for a few days before moving on. He left with a lighter load and a promise from Nancy to always take care of the stove and furniture.

3

The Last Supper

Ogling the fine amenities the Gulledge's had that she was not used to seeing, temporarily kept Charity's mind off of Henry and the fact that her grandfather intended to leave her there with them. However, something Nancy had said about her being raised in a more primitive environment troubled her thoughts; she did not know what primitive or environment meant, but the way Nancy had said it, caused her to feel that she was not as good as someone who was not raised in a primitive environment. She would have to remember that and ask her grandfather what it meant…

"Charity, would you mind setting the table for supper-" Nancy stopped mid-sentence when she saw the look on Charity's face. The poor child has no idea of how to set a table, thought Nancy. She smiled at Charity, hoping to ease the anxiousness that was clearly visible on her face.

"It's alright, dear; don't be afraid. I'll show you how to set the table. I am sure you will catch on pretty quick; there's nothing to it." Nancy did not know that Charity's thoughts were on primitive environments and not setting tables.

Charity smiled politely and let Nancy show her how to set a table.

When they had gotten everything ready and on the table, Nancy went to the door and called the men folk in for supper.

Although Charity was hungry, once everyone fixed their plate and began eating, she became nervous; she could barely eat because she kept sneaking glances in Henry's direction. It seemed he had a second sense or something, because nearly every time she peeked at him, he'd be looking at her!

Her grandfather and Eli were still talking about the fur trade and farming. She heard Eli tell her grandfather that he was thinking about clearing off more land and diversifying his crops. He wanted to plant something else besides potatoes and corn. He said that the land was rich and fertile, most anything ought to grow there. Then, he grumbled that he wanted other stuff to eat, he said that he was tired of just meat, potatoes, and corn.

✳✳✳

Charity thought Eli must be picky with his food or something; potatoes were a luxury rarely served in their cabin… There had been many a day that she wished she had some potatoes to eat; there'd also been days when she would have liked to have fresh meat on the table. She couldn't understand anyone grumbling about having too much of something to eat…

✳✳✳

"Be thankful for what you got, son," said her grandfather.

Lila M Beckham

"Since I've gotten too old to hunt, we don't get a lot of fresh meat; and now that the wife has passed, me, and this child have been lacking in fresh vegetables- our gardening skills are lacking."

"Don't pay Eli any mind, Mr. Robert," said Nancy. "He just likes to grumble. I cook more meat and potatoes because that is what I have the most of to cook. One day, I might fry them, the next day, if I find a few carrots in the garden, I'll make a stew."

"Yeah, Nancy's right;" admitted Eli. "I don't have any call to be grumbling about eating… we have more than a lot of folks has, but we was born poor; I reckon we'll die poor," said Eli, and without stopping his string of discourse, added, "I hear the land over in Georgia and Alabama is better for growing cotton than it is here in the watershed. Maybe one day, these youngsters will get a chance to check it out," Eli mused.

Charity and Henry both snuck a quick look at each other. She knew her face must be blood-red from embarrassment- Charity knew what was up because of the conversation she and her grandfather had on the way there, but wondered if Henry had any idea of what his father and her grandfather had up their sleeves.

Eli and her grandfather also talked a little about raising tobacco, indigo, and rice like many of the large plantations around Savannah were doing; both agreed that without slaves or a passel of hardy sons to work the land, it wasn't even worth the discussion.

When the Yellow Mocker Calls

At last, it was time to go to bed; Charity sighed with relief as she lay down. Snuggling as deep as she could into the straw-ticked mattress Nancy had put down for her on the floor next to her grandfather. A sudden fear overwhelmed her emotions; she wanted to cry out. When she reached over to touch her grandfather's hand; he responded by patting her hand. Somehow, she knew that this would be his last time to pat her hand and comfort her…

Charity tossed and turned until she finally fell into a restless sleep plagued by dreams. In one of her dreams, she was running barefoot through the forest, briers stuck deep into the bottom of her feet and thorny thickets pulled on her clothes. Why, am I running, she wondered. What am I running from- what am I looking for? In her dream, she stopped and looked up into the darkening sky. She saw an eagle perched high in the top of a tall pine tree. The eagle looked into her eyes and spoke; it was her grandfather's voice she heard. The eagle said, "Take the long road, child; take the long road." The eagle flapped his wings and flew away. "Grandpa," Charity screamed, attempting to run after the eagle. "What does it mean?"

It was hard to move and as hard as she struggled, she could not move. Once again, she screamed for her grandfather to come back. This time, when she called out to him, she sat straight up in bed and woke; that was when she realized that she had screamed loud enough to wake herself.

In a panic, she began looking around for her grandfather.

Lila M Beckham

She was disoriented, this was a strange place she was in- was she still dreaming? Finally, she saw her grandfather lying there beside her, he had not moved. She did not hear his usual soft snores; his chest wasn't rising and falling as it normally did in his sleep. Charity reached over to her grandfather and placed her hand over his- he still did not move. She shook his arm, trying to wake him. When he still didn't wake, she realized that he was as her grandmother had been the morning she found her dead. Charity began sobbing uncontrollably. In a matter of moments, Nancy was by her side, holding her, saying, "Don't cry child, don't cry." Nancy's arms, although strong and steady, did not comfort her- they were not the familiar arms of her grandmother or grandfather…

Reeling from the loss of her beloved grandfather, Charity's thoughts were rushing in a thousand different directions. He was the last of her family, he raised her. She had never spent time with her father's people, and as far as she knew, they had all moved on by now. The pain in her young heart was almost unbearable. By keeping up a constant stream of chatter, Nancy tried to keep her attention on something else, but Charity's thoughts could not leave him, nor could she shake the dream she'd had just before waking…

Nancy went to the stove and put on a pot of coffee. When it was ready, she offered Charity some; she accepted. The warm creamy mixture soothed her frayed nerves as soon as she drank it. When it was light enough outside, Eli and Henry dug a grave out back of their cabin, underneath a cedar tree to bury her grandfather; it was where Nancy and Eli had buried three of their four children. Three of their children died in the same yellow fever epidemic that had taken Charity's parent's lives.

Her grandfather's funeral was a somber event. All Charity could do, was watch flashes of her life with her grandparent's travel through her mind's eye, and cry softly. Eli spoke a few inadequate words over her grandfather's grave.

Henry stood back, quietly watching this beautiful young girl. After they had most of the grave filled in, he saw her dry her tears, straighten her back, then hold her head up high before she turned and walked back into the cabin. He fell in love with her right then and there.

Helping his father finish filling in and mounding the grave, he marveled in amazement that he had witnessed a girl turn into a strong young woman.

That evening at supper, after Eli and Nancy had firmly stated that she was to stay there with them; citing that it would have been what her grandfather wanted, Charity asked Eli if there was any way they could take her to her grandparent's cabin so that she could get the rest of her things… she did not specify exactly what she needed to get- that was personal. She didn't own much, other than memories and a few trinkets acquired through her short life, however, there were things there that were very dear to her heart; she wanted them very much.

When the Yellow Mocker Calls

Eli nodded his head, but said that it would be a day or so before they could go. He and Henry had to leave before dawn the next morning to check his traps; if left too long, any animals he'd trapped might be ruined; they'd be worthless and he'd have to destroy the pelts - Charity nodded her head; she understood how important it was to check traps- after all, her grandfather had been a trapper too. By the time she woke the next morning, Henry and his father were gone. Charity helped Nancy with the chores, and then went to sit by the cedar tree and visit with her grandfather.

As she sat beside her grandfather's grave, she tried to recall everything she could remember from her earliest childhood as she had a conversation with him in her mind. She did not know how much time had passed when a rustling in the nearby bushes drew her attention to them. Focusing her attention on the bushes, she saw them moving slightly. Expecting the dog, or maybe a rabbit, deer, or maybe even a wild boar to be the culprit, she was extremely shocked when through the bushes came a large brown colored bear!

So taken aback was she, that she temporarily froze, but as the bear neared her, she began looking around for anything that she could use to defend herself. Finally, her eyes lit on a limb, she lunged for it; however, as soon as she moved, she heard a loud explosion!

Turning her attention back toward the big bear, she looked just in time to see him fall; but the huge brown bear wasn't dead-

Lila M Beckham

he was trying to get back up! Charity grabbed the limb and began beating it over the head. She heard Nancy hollering at her, but didn't want to give the bear a chance to recover. Finally, she understood that Nancy wanted her to get out of the way; she'd had enough time to reload the gun. This time, Nancy took careful aim and shot him from a just few feet away. When the black smoke cleared, Charity and Nancy looked at each other, and then at the dead bear- they could not help but laugh!

"I thought surely we were fixing to have to bury you too," Nancy told her.

"I was not going to give up without a fight," Charity replied breathlessly.

"That, I could see," said Nancy. It had been frightening, but now that it was over, they could both laugh about it.

✳✳✳

When Eli and Henry returned from checking their traps, they were quite surprised to see the women skinning the bear. They were full of questions, but Nancy told them they'd have to wait to hear the full story. That if they really wanted to help, to pitch in and make themselves useful. Before long, fresh bear meat was on a spit, and roasting alongside some potatoes. The rest was soaking in brine water to ready it for the smokehouse and for canning in jars. The hide was stretched between several poles. Nancy said the hide would make them a nice warm blanket.

"Or, I might leave it stiff and use it as a rug to put on the floor beside my bed, for the cold winter mornings; I hate putting my bare feet on cold floors!"

That night, after asking the Lord to bless what they were about to receive, they dined on fresh roasted bear meat. Charity listened while Eli talked about his and Henry's day checking their traps. They had come up mostly empty, he said; then turning to look at her and Nancy, he said; "Well, I can tell you womenfolk had a much more exciting day than we men did. I'm anxious to hear all about it," he grinned.

"Me too," said Henry. "I want to know how y'all killed that bear."

"Yeah, I know y'all do," Nancy replied with a grin. Not leaving out any of the details, nor embellishing the story at all, she proceeded to tell in great detail how she and Charity had come to kill the bear all by themselves.

Charity saw Henry look at her in amazement when Nancy told how she grabbed a limb and tried to beat the bear to death after she shot it the first time. She grinned at Henry over her fork, took a big bite of her meat, and then started laughing. Henry laughed too, thinking what a beautiful, playful smile and laugh she had. He liked this Charity better than the quiet, shy Charity he'd first met. Her bravery in helping to kill the bear and playfulness eating it, just made Henry love her more and want to get to know her better.

Lila M Beckham

Before they finished supper, Eli spoke up and said that she and Henry could take her grandpa's wagon the next morning and go to fetch her belongings. He said that he knew it would take them at least two full days to make the trip, one day going there and one day coming back.

"Thank you, so much! Are you sure it won't be any trouble," a surprised Charity questioned.

Eli said it would be no trouble at all. He said that he could do without Henry for a day or two; but he couldn't leave Nancy there all by herself for that long. To which Nancy ruffled up and replied, "I think I've proven that I can take care of myself quite well, thank you," she said, refuting his statement.

"Yeah, that I can see," mumbled Eli, taking another bite of roasted meat.

4

The Trip Home

The trip home in the rickety, old, bone-jarring wagon was hard. Each turn of the wheel seemed to tighten a vice around Charity's heart that caused it to feel heavier and heavier. For the first few miles, she sat quietly, thinking exclusively about her life with her grandparents. She thought about how they had always been a part of her life; her earliest memories. She had no memory of her mother and father- all she really knew about them was what her grandparents told her. Her grandmother and grandfather were the only parents she'd ever known. After seeing Eli, she had a faint recollection of seeing him sometime before, maybe when she was small. And, other than Tokola, the old Indian man who came often to the cabin, they were the only people she'd ever interacted with until her grandfather took her with him to Eli's. Charity was deep in thought when she finally realized that the wagon had stopped moving and that Henry was speaking to her.

"I'm sorry; did you say something? I didn't hear you- I was thinking about… Grandpa," she said.

"It's alright, I understand," Henry replied. "I was just asking, which way to go now. I see a fork in the trail up ahead and I don't know which way to go."

Looking up the trail, Charity was taken aback. She did not know which trail led to the cabin. She didn't remember the fork in the road either.

The squawk of an eagle drew her eyes to a tall pine tree. Suddenly, she remembered the dream she had the night her grandfather died. She looked to the eagle atop the tree and remembered her grandfather's voice saying, take the long road child; take the long road.

"Grandpa," she whispered.

"What?" Henry asked.

"I don't know which way to go!"

"Well, I certainly don't know," replied Henry. "I've never been to Mr. Robert's cabin."

Hushing him, Charity said, "Just hold on and let me think!" Glancing around, she tried to remember and retrace the trip backwards from the day she and her grandfather had traveled through on their way to Eli's homestead. She still had no recollection of the trail forking. Just then, the wind picked up. The wind blowing through the pines seemed to whisper- take the long road.

Frantically, she gazed around, that was when she noticed that one trail curved not too far down it; the other trail, was long and straight. She could see the road going a long way.

"Take that one," she pointed, "Take the long road."

Henry smiled and then geed to the horses. After several

miles, she began to recognize some of the features of the land. Smiling to herself, she whispered, "Thanks, Grandpa."

About an hour later, they stopped alongside the river to stretch their legs and eat. Neither spoke barely ten words during the time they stopped. Anxious and thoughtful, Charity was not in a talking mood; Henry experienced a shy streak that made him tongue-tied when he did try to talk.

The sun was about to set when they reached the cabin. Charity was surprised to see smoke coming from the chimney. She knew that her grandfather had made sure to extinguish the fire the morning they left. She ran to the door and jerked it open, half-expecting to see her grandparents there, but it wasn't them.

"Oh!" she said in surprise. When I saw the smoke, I didn't know who was in here. How are you, Tokola," she asked, suddenly wondering how she was going to tell him that her grandfather, his old friend, had passed away…

In broken English, Tokola replied, "I fine." In expectation, he peeked around her to the front door and asked, "Where's Robert? I go help him."

With a heavy heart, she stopped Tokola from going out the door and told him, "Grandpa has gone to Tsusgina'I, the Ghost Country, which lies in Usunhi'yi, the Darkening Land to the west."

A look of great sadness crossed Tokola's face; Charity could no longer hold back her tears. She cried for Tokola; she cried because she was home; she cried because she had lived her entire life there, and she cried because she knew that it would be the last time she would ever set foot inside *her* home. She cried because the scent of her grandparents surrounded her and she could not hug them to her chest. She wanted to hug Tokola to her and hang onto him for dear life- he was familiar, someone she was *used* to.

"It is sad day for Tokola, too," he said, and then without saying another word, he turned and walked out the door and into the forest. Her eyes followed him as he disappeared into the rust colored, forest vegetation that was bathed in the yellowish-orange glow of the end of the day, which quickly faded into the bluish - blacks of the night after he vanished through the trees.

Tokola had always walked slowly, with a hitch in his step; his limp, gotten from an injury many years earlier. Watching him disappear into the forest, Charity wondered what happened to him- then she remembered a story her grandmother had told her about her grandfather and Tokola.

She turned from watching Tokola walk away, to see Henry, quietly, watching her, as though he was seeing something for the first time.

"Is there something you want to say, Henry?" she asked tartly.

"No," he replied. "I thought I'd get in a couple of sticks of firewood, it gets a bit chilly at night."

"Good. You do that, and I'll fix us something to eat."

They ate quietly, neither saying much at all. After supper,

Lila M Beckham

Charity went to her corner of the one-room, squared cabin, and pulled a small, handmade trunk out from under her bed. She opened it up and tenderly pulled out her mother's "hahl'tawoja" which was the Indian word for hair comb, and "gilusti" hair pins. She did not want to lose them; they were all she had left of her mother. Also, retrieving her Asani; Asani was what the traditional, feminine dress of her people was called, and her "tsulawa", moccasin boots, she lovingly placed them all back into the trunk, for she would also be taking it with her. She did not want to forget her people. She knew that even though she was going to live in the white man's world, she would always be Cherokee.

Sitting by the fire, leaning back in her grandmother's rocker, she turned to Henry and asked, "Henry, have you ever wondered what it's like?"

"What, "What's" like," he responded. "I haven't ever considered what its like to die or anything like that."

"I was not talking about dying, Henry; I was talking about other places. Before Grandpa brought me to your house, I had never been anywhere."

Henry sat quietly, chewing on a twig. At first, she thought maybe he didn't understand her question. When she was about to ask him again, he started to speak in that slow drawl of his.

"Yes, I've wondered, too," Henry replied, thoughtfully. "One of my uncles lives over there in Alabama; he writes to my father about once a year or so. I've thought about going there;

hope to go one of these days."

After his response, they both just sat there quietly and thought about things… A little while later, Charity told him that she was going to lie down, and that he could sleep on her grandparents' bed if he wanted to. Henry nodded his head, but did not move to the bed; instead, he got up and walked outside. Charity tossed and turned for a while before she was tired enough to fall asleep. Just before she dozed, she heard Henry come inside and lay down; his presence comforted her.

✳✳✳

The next morning, Tokola was outside when they awoke. Charity told him that she wanted him to have all of her grandfather's things. She was taking just one thing of his, a small, hand-carved eagle; she was leaving the rest behind. It was not that she did not want to take everything with her; she did. If possible, she would have stuffed the entire cabin into her trunk to take with her- but she knew it wasn't possible- in the back of her mind, she thought that maybe one day in the future, she could return. She told Tokola that he was welcome to stay at the cabin for as long as he wanted- her grandfather would like that. He'd often asked Tokola to live there with them. When Tokola stayed only a day or two and then left, her grandfather would joke about Tokola's wandering bone.

As she packed what few belongings she could into the small trunk, Charity was thoughtful. When finished, the trunk, along with the rest of her belongings was placed into the wagon. There was a patchwork quilt that her grandmother had lovingly made by hand. She said she started it when she was just a young woman and over the years, had added to the quilt using different pelts she had soaked in a wet wood ash solution and then tanned and softened. When spread out, you could see the different scenes she'd worked into the quilt. Charity remembered that her grandma use to call the scenes, her "Seasons of Life," when looking at the quilt. It would now be Charity's responsibility to treasure it and to make sure that she told her children and grandchildren about her grandmother. And she would tell them all the stories she remembered from her grandmother's telling of them; she wanted to keep them alive through the telling of them over and over.

Taking a last long look around the dilapidated old cabin, Charity's heart felt so heavy she wondered if it would keep beating. When she was finally able to move, she walked to the door, then stopped to look once more at her home- Above the mantle hung a painting that her grandfather said his mother, her namesake, painted when he was a boy- it was of Heath Mynd, a mountain near his village of birth, Norbury, which he said was in Shropshire, England. When her eyes left the painting, they landed on her grandmother's old corncob pipe lying on the mantle. She went over and picked the pipe up. Lovingly, she fingered it, feeling the smoothness of the bowl and stem from years of use; she dropped it and the pouch of tobacco in her coat pocket. She thought she might just take up smoking it, the way her grandmother had.

After making sure that everything she wanted to take was in the wagon, she hugged Tokola tightly and then took a long look around the outside of her home. She wanted to remember every crack and crevice; she figured she would probably never see it again. She then walked over and climbed up onto the wagon. She sat up straight and never looked back as she and Henry drove away. Charity knew that if she ever looked back, she might never leave…

After they'd traveled several hundred yards, Henry chanced a sideways glance at her. What he saw broke his heart, it also made him admire her more. Silent tears slid gently down her cheek…

Quietly, they drove for several miles before Henry got up enough nerve to start a conversation with her.

"You know, they say the land in Alabama is rich and good for farming." When she didn't immediately respond, he turned to look at her.

She smiled and said, "It Sounds like you've been thinking on that some."

"Yep," he replied, "been thinking on it a lot. Here-lately, I'm thinking that maybe I want to go there one day and see it for myself."

"What do you think your ma and pa will think of that," she asked.

"I reckon, I ain't rightly said anything about it to them, yet," he grinned. "I'm near about grown; I can make my own choices; so, if I want to go, I'll go."

Henry was still grinning; she couldn't help but to smile back.

They rode along, each talking about their lives -before the last few days events- happened, it was a sort of, "get to know one another" conversation.

When they ran out of talk, they rode quietly. Unlike her first trip down the Savannah, Charity noticed everything, taking in the surrounding beauty and hugging it deep into her memory in case something happened and she never saw it again. She voiced her thoughts aloud to Henry.

"You know something, Henry. When we traveled through here a few days ago, I didn't even notice how we followed the river all the way down. Nor did I notice how beautiful it is along here."

"Yes, it is beautiful country we live in," Henry replied. "Some of the plantation owners have begun planting rice along the banks of the river because it's easy to divert water for it to grow in."

"Rice grows in water- you mean like water lilies or reeds do?"

"Yeah, sort a like that- they call them rice paddies. It's starting to become almost as important a crop as cotton, tobacco, and indigo. Especially here, along the Savannah River."

Charity suddenly pointed to a big plant in the sandy soil. It had fan-shaped fronds. "What kind of plant is that," she asked.

"Why they're palmettos," Henry replied. "You mean no one ever told you what they were before..."

"I never wanted to know before- if I had, I'm sure Grandpa would've told me. I know what cotton and tobacco are, but what is indigo and rice?"

Henry told her that rice was a grain, sort of like wheat, you could boil it and eat it, and that it was really good with tomato gravy when tomatoes were in season. He told her that indigo, was what blue dye was made from.

"My grandma always called it, wodi."

"Whoa dye, huh?"

"You have to say it a little faster, wodi; we boiled it down to color thread and stuff- I wouldn't a wanted to eat it though," she giggled. Both of them laughed at the thought of eating indigo.

It was nearing dark when they topped the same hill that she and her grandfather had the first time she saw the little cabin.

"I sure hope your Mama has supper ready, I'm about to starve to death!"

"Me, too," said Henry - they looked at one another and began laughing.

5

The Census Taker

Spartanburg Dist. South Carolina
Late Oct, 1829

While they were eating supper, Eli asked how things were at the cabin. Charity told him that when they arrived, her grandfather's friend, Tokola, was there awaiting her grandfather's return, and that it broke her heart to have to tell him that her grandfather had died.

"How is Tokola?" he asked, saying "I haven't seen him since... the year before last, I think it was. Over the years, he's traveled through here many times with your grandfather, headed down to Fort Charlotte. "

"He took it kind a hard, Mister Eli, but he seemed to be doing better by the time we left this morning."

"That's understandable," said Eli. "He and your grandpa have been friends for fifty years or more- I reckon his being Shadowy Moon's brother, he and Robert was probably more like brothers than friends- of course, Tokola was just a boy when they married."

"What!" Charity's mind immediately remembered a story

her grandmother told her a story she called, 'blood brothers.' "I did not know he was her brother? Why didn't they tell me that he was family," she asked.

"Most likely, they figured you already knew," said Eli.

Charity felt sad. If she had known that Tokola was family, she would have hugged him even harder before she left him. He was her granduncle, a living, breathing relative! She went to sleep that night, trying to think back through the years to all the times Tokola had been in their cabin. It seemed that as she was growing up, he was always around.

In fitful sleep, she dreamt dreams of Indians, palmettos, cotton, tobacco, rice, indigo, and eagles flying through the skies calling to her, telling her to take this trail or that, and her reaching up, trying to catch them before they flew away. The next morning, she helped Nancy build a fire under the big, black iron pot out back of the cabin and then fill it with water so they could wash clothes. About an hour later, as they hung the first of the wash on the line, they heard a rider coming up the trail that led down to Fort Charlotte.

"Well, I know it ain't Eli or Henry," said Nancy, "they rode off to the North Country, this morning."

Both watched the rider come into view, once he rounded a thicket of dogwoods. In tow, was a pack mule that looked to be loaded with supplies.

"Who you reckon he is," asked Charity.

"No telling who it is, but he looks like one of those,

Government fellers."

Charity didn't know what a Government feller was, but he was the fanciest dressed man she'd ever seen.

"Good morning ladies; my name is Harrison Williams," said the rider, tipping his hat before he dismounted his horse.

"Morning, Mister Williams," both replied.

"I am here on behalf of the Federal Census Bureau," Mr. Williams informed them.

"Oh, is it 1830 already," Nancy exclaimed.

"No Ma'am, it's not," replied Mr. Williams, "I started early this time around, seeing that the population is ever growing. Folks are spreading further south and west and it's going to take longer for me to cover my area- I have been assigned to census the Ninety-Six District. Is your husband home?"

"No, sir, he ain't," Nancy replied, adding, "They should be back directly, though. He and our son went to check a few traps."

"Well then, Ma'am," said Mr. Williams, pulling a wooden box out of his pack, "I will just have to get the information from you two ladies. I will need to know, the head of the households full name and age. How many men, women, and children are in the household and their ages? I will also need the number of slaves owned by the head of household. Also, any free persons of color that may live in the household." His eyes traveled to Charity when he said the last. Mr. Williams' glance toward Charity did not get past Nancy's notice.

"Well, now, Mister Williams," said Nancy, placing her

hands on her hips. "It looks to me like you could use a good meal and something to drink first."

"I'd be much obliged, Mrs.?"

"Gullege," Nancy replied. "The last name is Gullege, been that for nearly thirty years now, it use to be-" Charity didn't hear the rest of what was said, she was too busy checking out the census taker and debating whether to speak up or remain quiet and let Nancy do the talking. She decided on the latter.

Nancy headed toward the cabin; Mr. Williams followed closely behind her. Charity wavered a moment and then followed them into the cabin. Mainly, she was curious about Mr. Williams. In her short life, she had never seen very many other humans, other than her grandparent's, the Gullege's and Tokola; and this feller here, was a real dandy!

He wore a funny little hat, spectacles over his eyes, and he had a big wooden, square, flat box that he carried into the cabin with him. Charity watched in amazement as he unlatched and then unfolded the wooden box; it had legs and a surface like a small table. He called it a portable desk. He opened a compartment and took out a large book. As he flipped the pages, she saw that many of them were mostly blank. He then took out a small bottle, removed the stopper, took a quill, and dipped it into the bottle, and then made marks on a sheet of paper in the big book! She had seen marks and drawings like those before; they were in several caves that were near her grandparent's cabin; however, the marks in the caves were made with charcoal.

Charity had only seen a couple of books in her lifetime, and the marks he made on the paper, were the same type of marks that were in the books. She was always warned to be very careful, and told not to touch the books. So, to say the least, to see this man actually making marks in one, was awe inspiring…

***

Charity did not know how to read or write; and, before this day, had never given it much thought, but now, her curiosity was piqued. She wanted to learn the mechanics of it. From watching Mr. Williams do it, she didn't think it looked all that hard to do.

Mr. Williams sat at his little desk and continued to ask Nancy questions, and she continued to answer him, as best she could. He asked her, her husbands first and last name. "His name is Eli Gullege," Nancy answered.

"How old is he?" Mr. Williams asked.

"I reckon he is about 47 now, cause he is a year or so older than I am."

"Are their any other men in the household?"

"Our son, Henry- Come springtime, he'll be 15yrs old," Nancy responded.

"What about slaves?"

"What about 'em, Mister Williams- Do we look well off enough to own slaves?" Mr. Williams glanced at Charity.

"No, she ain't, and no, we don't own any. Never could afford any even if I took to slavery- my folks owned a couple-"

"What is your age, Mrs. Gullege," interrupted Mr. Williams.

"Well, I'll be 45yrs of age come April," she answered.

"And the girl," he asked, nodding toward Charity.

"She turned 14 a couple of months ago," said Nancy.

Her reply, brought a quick head turn from Charity. She was stunned! How could Nancy know how old she was, when she herself didn't even know for sure. Birthdays were something that her grandparents had never made any fuss over. Charity made a mental note to ask Nancy about it, as soon as Mr. Williams was gone. In the meantime, Nancy had been slicing some of the bear meat and some bread, which she placed on a plate and handed to Mr. Williams, along with a glass of buttermilk. He ate the meat and bread as if he was starving to death. He must not have eaten in a while, thought Charity, watching him devour the meal. He's awful thin for a man.

When he finished the last sip of buttermilk and ate the last crumb of bread, he told Nancy that it was delicious and he really appreciated the food. He said that he'd had nothing but hardtack to eat for days.

Charity had eased up pretty close to Mr. Williams as he ate and talked with Nancy- she was trying to get a closer look at his book. When he noticed her straining her neck to look, he said, "Come here and I'll show you."

She walked over to his portable desk, as he called it, and he showed her his papers. The book wasn't bound like the other books she'd seen, his pages were bound together with strings. Along the top of the page he was open to, something was written in sections that were squared off.

"Can you read at all?"

"No sir, but I'd like to learn," Charity replied.

"This is a Census Schedule - Along the top of the page it reads, - Schedule of the whole number of persons, within the Division allotted to Harrison Williams. It's divided into columns, for names, genders, land owned, and such as that- The squares and lines, with these marks and writing is where I notate the number of each and so on." He looked up at Charity- she smiled at him. "These words written at the top of the columns says: FREE WHITE PERSONS, MALES, FEMALES, SLAVES, FREE PERSONS of COLOR, INDUSTRY-"

Charity was about to ask him what 'industry' meant, when Nancy spoke up saying, "Charity, will you please go check on the clothes in the pot. I'm sure we need to get those into the rinse water, wrung out, and hung up, else wise, they will never dry before nightfall." Charity thanked Mr. Williams for showing her his book, and then went outside to tend the clothes pot.

Using the big stick she'd tried to kill the bear with, Charity was moving the clothes, piece by piece, from the boiling pot into the rinse pot, when Nancy and Mr. Williams came out of the cabin. Mr. Williams was walking toward Charity, holding something out to her. It was a smaller book; he called it a journal. This one was blank. He told her to write things she felt were important in it and then smiled as though he was handing her the world. Although Charity did not know it right then, he was.

While she and Nancy finished the wash, they talked. Charity asked how Nancy knew how old she was; Nancy's reply surprised her.

"Why, I remember when you were born," said Nancy. "Henry was just a tiny thing himself, just learning to take a few steps, when Robert and Tokola came through on their way to Fort Charlotte. Your granddaddy was so proud to be a grandpa! He bragged about how pretty a little thing you were and that like your mother, you had inherited eyes that were the color of his mothers."

Charity wished her grandfather had talked more about his family; however, he wasn't much of a talker about family and such. She wondered what and who he'd left behind when he came to America- Now, that her grandfather was dead, she would never know...

6

Blood Brothers

After they finished washing clothes and had supper started, Nancy saw Charity fingering the pages of the tablet the census taker had given her.

"If you'd like, we can start doing some lessons each day," said Nancy.

"Oh, yes ma'am," exclaimed Charity, "I would like that very much." Nancy could see that Charity was going to be an eager student, and as quick witted as she was, she should be a good one.

She was right. Charity took to schooling, like a duck to a June bug; she soaked up learning like a sponge. Within a week, she knew her numbers to one hundred, and with the help of Nancy and Henry, She was learning the alphabet, and how to write her name. Charity was determined to learn to read and write words like the ones she saw in Mr. Williams' census book.

Paper was scarce; therefore, to conserve the ever-so-valuable, paper, she and Henry took to doing her classes outside, using sticks to write in the dirt. Nancy had several cherished books she'd kept with her from her youth, and one that had been a gift from the man they traded for the stove and furniture. Each night, after supper, she and Henry took turns reading aloud to everyone. Other than having the ability to write his name, Eli had never learned to read nor write nor had he any interest in learning- however, he too, seemed to enjoy their nightly, literary get-togethers.

As for the books they read from, according to Nancy, the most important book was called, the Holy Bible; she said that it was a biography, written hundreds of years earlier to bring Jesus Christ the Lord to peoples attention and to tell of his great works on earth- Nancy said that it was written by various Disciples of Jesus Christ- she then had to explain how Jesus was the Son of God, born of a human, the Virgin Mary, and that his Disciples were followers of His teachings to Charity who'd never known of this man- the Great Spirit's Son and his miraculous work on earth. The Bible stories were very interesting stories, and they taught many important lessons; however, Charity and Henry much preferred reading and listening to the story read from the book Nancy had about a man named Robinson Crusoe. The story of being shipwrecked on an island was mysterious and thrilling. Stories of pirates and shipwrecks piqued the imaginations of their young minds much easier than the book of Leviticus did. It was not that Charity didn't enjoy the Bible stories; she did, and they, too, had mysterious happenings that stirred her curiosity, but she'd grown up in the home of a storyteller. For as long as she could remember, she'd listened to Nokomis tell *her* stories.

Occasionally, her grandfather would tell a tale or two, but it was hard to get him to reminisce and tell stories of his growing up years. On the other hand, her grandmother could start at breakfast and talk and tell stories until they lay their heads down at night.

The stories her grandmother told about her parents and grandparents, and about when she was a child in an Indian village, were told in such a manner that Charity could envision every detail, even placing herself in the story in her grandmother's place. When she listened to Nokomis talk, she *was* that child in the village; and, in her mind, she could see her ancestors as if they sat there in front of her. She also loved how her grandmother had told her the ways of her Indian ancestors, emphasizing the importance of her Indian heritage.

Nokomis told her she must *never* forget who she was and where and from whom she came...

As Charity became more comfortable with her new family, she shared some of her grandmother's stories, including the one about how her white, English grandfather, had come to win the heart of her Indian grandmother.

Nokomis told Charity that at first, her father, who was the chief of their tribe, did not trust the Englishman- (her grandfather). And, that he was accepted as a friend to the Indian on a probationary basis. Her father, the Chief, said that the young Englishman would have to prove his character as a human being before having the honor of being a friend, to Shadowy Moon's father and the Indian peoples. When Charity could see that

Nancy, Henry, and Eli all wanted to hear the story, she channeled her grandmother's spirit, and stood up in front of the table to begin. At first, she was a little nervous, but their 'anxious to hear the story faces,' gave her confidence the boost she needed to begin.

"This is the story Nokomis told me about Blood Brothers -

"One day, many years ago, while out hunting for meat to feed the tribe, her brother," (who Charity now knew was Tokola) "and my grandfather, the young Englishman, had gone miles away from camp, trailing a deer. Nokomis said that it was a *lean* year because the previous winter had been very cold. Tokola and the Englishman knew if they could catch up to the deer, and then kill it, that it would feed the entire tribe for several days.

"After trailing the deer for over a day, they had gotten far away from the camp and low into the swamplands. By then, the cold winds of winter had begun to blow. Thinking the deer might be joining others of its kind to winter in the swamps, they continued to trail it. They were walking down a rise above a creek bank, when, suddenly Tokola was swallowed up by the earth!

"You might be thinking quicksand, but it was not quicksand, nor mud, no…" she paused dramatically, her eyes wide the way Nokomis used to do, letting them absorb her words.

"It was not quicksand, no. Mother Earth had opened her mouth and swallowed Tokola - he had dropped thirty feet, into the bowels of the earth, and landed in a deep wide cavern!

"Grandfather, had become good friends with Tokola, he knew he had to rescue him, but he had no rope. He heard his friend moaning in agony and knew that he was alive; but he knew that if he did not get to him that he would surely die. Being a resourceful, quick-thinking man, his quick mind, thinking ahead of the man, was cutting lose the smaller vines that held tight, the mighty wisteria vine to the largest live oak trees. He soon had enough cut loose to drop into the mouth of the earth and down to his friend." Again, Charity paused in her telling, to look each in the eye, as her grandmother had always done.

"Grandfather gathered, dried moss, small limbs, and twigs that he knew would not injure Tokola when dropped into the mouth of Mother Earth. He soon had all he needed to provide light and warmth in the belly of the earth. He tied together all the vines; then, he tied one end to a tree and dropped the other, along with the bundle of small limbs and twigs he'd gathered in the opening and then climbed down to where Tokola was. He started a fire, using his flint rocks and dried moss; then, he placed the small twigs and branches on it to keep it burning. Once the fire was built, he could see that his friend was greatly injured. Tokola's hip was broken, the thigh bone snapped into like one of the little twigs. But, grandfather feared not the broken bones; he knew what he must do. He knew what herbs he needed to ease Tokola's pain." Charity paused, looking at their faces. Each seemed to be engrossed in her story.

"Grandfather placed Tokola near the fire to warm him and

Lila M Beckham

then, he climbed back out to retrieve his pack. Next, he needed to find a white willow tree; once he found one, he peeled some of the bark off a limb. He knew this would ease Tokola's pain if he could get him to chew it.

"He returned to the cavern to find that Tokola was drifting in and out of consciousness; he could not chew the bark. Grandfather, climbed back out, went to the creek and filled his bladder with fresh spring water. A light snow began to fall; it melted as soon as it touched the ground.

"In his pack, he had enough flatbread for a couple of days; but he knew that without meat, his strength would not last. It was fortunate he had a tsulaski in his pack; a tsulaski, is a small cooking pot made of earth. He would use this to brew a tea of the willow bark. He found a straight limb, the length of Tokola's leg; one that he could use, to set the break. When he returned to the cavern, he tried to make his friend comfortable, and as soon as he thought the tea was strong enough, he got him to drink it.

"After a while, he could see that Tokola had grown drowsy, a little later, he was unconscious. Grandfather pulled the bones back into place, the best he could and then strapped his leg to the limb, using young, limber vines."

Charity looked at each of them, to make sure they were paying attention.

"When he woke, Tokola was wracked in pain. Grandfather had only the willow tea as medicine; it provided only a little relief. Having woven a fish trap from thin, willow branches and wisteria vines, Grandfather would leave his friend only long enough to search for food. He was able to catch a few minnows and small fish, which he broiled over the fire, the minnows and smallest fish, he used to make a broth which they both drank- it supplied them with nutrition and strength. With Grandfather's care and willow bark tea, Tokola began to improve; however, the world outside the cavern had grown colder.

"When Tokola healed to where he could sit up, he worried that he would never be able to pull his weight up the vine and stick ladder to reach the top, and that if he fell, he would re-injure his leg or he could die... He and Grandfather both agreed to wait longer- Grandfather feared that the creek would freeze over and he would not be able to catch more minnows and fish.

Tokola urged Grandfather to leave him there and save himself, but Grandfather would not leave him there to die. Tokola told Grandfather that he was his, "Danitaga", which meant blood brother. After which, they cut their palms and mixed their blood to claim the close friendship each felt for the other; they mixed their blood so that they would forever be as one. Each would carry within them the other's life blood, a part of their soul, wherever they journeyed.

"It was now the month of the cold wind moon. It had turned bitterly cold, with snow falling heavier than Tokola could ever remember it having fallen here before. As the days drifted by, Grandfather had managed to fasten together a sled, on which he planned to place Tokola for the journey back to the village; he planned to leave as soon as the weather broke.

"Tokola's father, was Chief Skwalaguta, he was to eventually be Chief of the AniTagwa, the tribe of the Catawba. During their time in the cavern, Tokola had given Grandfather the Cherokee name of, "Asuhiski," which meant fisherman. Grandfather climbed out of the cavern with Tokola on his back. It took him three moons, pulling Tokola behind him, to get back to where the tribe's camp was." Again, Charity paused, looking each in the eye.

"Chief Skwalaguta was happy to see his son returned to the tribe alive, when they had given them both up for dead, that he gave grandfather, Shadowy Moon to be his bride. Nokomis said that she was grateful her father had given her to marry Grandfather- she was already in love with him, and she was proud to be the "udalii," which meant wife, of such a strong and brave man. That was the end of Nokomis' story - but now, I can tell you that Shadowy Moon and Asuhiski lived a long and happy life together- they loved each other deeply and I never heard an unkind word pass between them. The end;" Charity smiled with pride, as they clapped.

7

Fort Charlotte, South Carolina

Early March, 1830

When trapping season ended, Eli planned a trip into Fort Charlotte so that he and Henry could trade the beaver pelts they'd collected, the bearskin of the bear Nancy and Charity killed, and some deer skins.

At the fort, they could trade them for ax heads, knives, awls, fishhooks, cloth of various types and hues, woolen blankets, linen shirts, kettles, jewelry, glass beads, muskets, ammunition and gunpowder. You could even trade for brandy and rum at the fort. Every year, Nancy asked Eli to get a bottle of rum, which she used in her canning and for making rum cake on special occasions; not to mention it was also good for colds.

This year, as Eli planned his trip to the fort, Nancy let him know way ahead of time that she and Charity would be making the trip with them. She said that there were some items that she couldn't leave to the men folk to pick out, especially cloth.

"There's no telling what type of cloth you'd come back with," she told Eli. "I need to make Charity a couple of dresses and I don't want to have to make them out of burlap sacks."

Because the trip would require an overnight stay, Eli and Henry had to pack the tent and enough supplies to last the length of their trip, plus the furs and other stuff they wanted to trade. They also need space for four people to ride. That would be quite an undertaking for one wagon; therefore, since they had inherited Charity's grandfather's wagon, they decided to take both wagons; Eli and Nancy would ride in one and Henry and Charity in the other.

"Did you know that Fort Charlotte is a historic fort," Eli asked Charity, when she inquired how far it was to the fort and how long it had been there, etc. Charity shook her head and told him that she did not know much at all, other than her numbers she'd learned, how to read a little bit, and what she had been told in stories by her grandparents, and, what she had learned since living with them.

"Well, then, let me give you a little history lesson tonight," said Eli. "Fort Charlotte is a historic fort, because its seizure, by a troop of mounted, South Carolina Rangers was the first overt act of the Revolutionary War in South Carolina." Charity was 'all ears' as she listened. She knew nothing of wars, revolutionary or otherwise; however, by the time they went to bed that night, she knew that all the white men in America weren't born there- they or their ancestors were born in other countries and then came there by boat, either freely, or as indentured servants to earn their passage. She also found out that Nokomis and her ancestors were already in America and that the white men that came had taken their lands and made them move further west... Charity did not think that fair at all and as she lay in bed trying to go to sleep, some of her grandmother's sadness as she told her stories, like the one of her parents and others being forced off their original lands before coming to where they were now, made more sense to her.

The next morning, as they readied to leave, Charity was very excited about the trip to Fort Charlotte; but sadly, it brought back memories of how her first trip with her grandfather, had ended. She did not dwell on the past pain and heartache long though; she knew her grandfather would not want that. And, as Henry geed to the old horse and as they followed Eli and Nancy's wagon toward the trail to Fort Charlotte, she began to feel excited again. She was finally going to get to see some of the rest of the world!

The trail to Fort Charlotte was a little bumpy and overgrown for a few miles; Charity could tell it was not well traveled, but about two hours out, the trail they had followed from the homestead joined another trail and the road became wider, smoother- it was well-traveled and much better.

Charity talked nonstop, asking Henry questions about everything she saw- not that there was much to see; the vista consisted mainly of flowers, plants, trees, and the occasional sporadic animal that jumped out of the woods, saw them, and then ran the other way.

Occasionally the road ran alongside the Savannah River for

a spell before it veered away again to go around backwater swamps or dense forested thickets. Henry was very patient answering her questions, and every once in a while, he'd chuckle at her enthusiasm over simple things. They may have been nearly the same age, but Henry was more worldly; he had not been quarantined to the homestead his entire life as she had.

About midday, they pulled the wagons to the side of the road, got down to stretch their legs, use the bathroom, and to eat the lunch Nancy had packed for the occasion. Charity was still in talk-mode, Henry was still patiently answering her- but mostly just letting her ramble; neither of them noticed Nancy and Eli's eye exchange as they watched the two youngsters. Yes, the pairing of the two was going to be the perfect blend of personalities; their life together should be a happy one.

***

When they neared Fort Charlotte, the traffic along the trail became more congested. They had traveled three-quarters of the day without seeing another soul, but after the last intersecting trail they had been passed by three buggies and several lone riders on horseback- Charity closely examined each as they passed. She never knew there were so many different looking people in the world! The fort came into view around four o'clock, and when Charity saw there were Indians camping around the fort, she was even more surprised.

When she saw all the Indians there, she sort of expected to

see Tepees like she'd seen in a book; instead, there were several clay and wood lodges that had thatched roofs and there were small mounded mud huts scattered around. When she asked Henry what type of structures they were, he said they were, 'Asi' houses, explaining that many of the Indian's wintered in them because they were smaller and easier to heat. They were made of wattle and daub.

When Henry saw that she did not know what he meant, he explained that the Indians there were mostly Cherokees. They made their houses from wattle, which was stakes driven into the ground and interwoven with twigs and branches to form the frame for the house. When the framework was complete, they covered it with a mixture of mud, clay, straw, leaves, and even dung.

I bet that's smelly, thought Charity.

"They can probably withstand the elements better than our cabin can," said Henry. "If your grandfather and Tokola had been stranded atop the land instead of in a cavern, he could have built one of these for them to stay in- it would have been easier to warm than just sitting by a campfire."

Just before they entered through the gates of the fort, Charity noticed a very old Indian man sitting cross-legged on the ground in front of a campfire, chanting. Every now and then, he would sprinkle something into his fire, causing blue flames to leap from it. The old man had a blanket wrapped around him that was woven of many bright colors, colors Charity had only seen in the sky, the flowers of spring or among the tree leaves in the fall. Upon his gray head, he wore a leather-skin band with two turkey feathers dangling off the side. When he looked up at her as their wagon passed by, she saw that his eyes were the color of the snow falling down; his eyes seemed to follow her. His eyes were in such stark contrast to his overly sun-darkened skin- that his white-eyed stare somewhat unnerved her.

"Who he is?" she whispered.

"Oh, that's just old, Two Feathers," said Henry. "I think he's some sort of shaman or something; I've always heard that he went blind during a snowstorm, although I don't believe it."

"Why don't you believe it," asked Charity, saying, "I saw his eyes; they are the color of snow."

"Indians tell all sorts of tales; most of them are hard to believe -" Henry stopped, when he noticed the look on Charity's face.

"Are you mad at me?" he asked.

His words sent Charity deep in thought, thinking of all the stories she had listened to with such enthusiasm all her life. That he had the nerve to say something like that... Of course, it made her mad, but it was more hurt feelings than being mad.

Nancy broke through her thoughts when she told her to get down off the wagon and go with her to the Mercantile so they could start looking for the things they needed to buy, while Eli and Henry traded the skins; some of the skins they would get paid money for; some, they would use for bartering.

Charity was not listening to Nancy's chatter; her thoughts were still with the old Indian man; his face and eyes would not leave her thoughts. She had decided that as soon as she could sneak away, she was going to go and have a conversation with him.

Once again, Nancy intruded into her thoughts when she touched her arm and said, "Charity, are you listening to me?"

"I'm sorry, but no ma'am, I wouldn't- my thoughts were elsewhere."

"That's understandable; there's a lot to take in. I was asking you what you thought of this patterned material." Charity looked down at the two-tone drab colored cloth Nancy held in her hands. "Feel it- it'll make a fine everyday dress," Nancy suggested.

Charity touched the material. "It's alright," she replied, trying to act as if she liked it, although, she actually did not have an opinion of it, other than it did not feel as good as her deerskins did. She would much rather wear her Asani than the dresses Nancy was talking about making for her. However, she knew that she needed to dress as Nancy wished her to; it was what her grandfather had wanted…

Nancy placed her order for the material and several other items, knowing that Eli would pay for it when he got paid, and then she and Charity walked out of the mercantile.

"Come, let's get back to the wagon and get supper started; come supper-time, the men folk will be starving to death."

Charity stepped off the stoop first because she had walked

out the door ahead of Nancy. Immediately, they were nearly run over by an Indian Scout on a big, buckskin horse in full run. The horse stopped by planting its front feet into the earth and sliding almost close enough for her to touch its nose. It suddenly reared up onto its hind feet and nearly threw its rider, who in turn, let out a string of profanities in Cherokee that Charity fluently understood.

When she started laughing at him for being such a rushing idiot, wishing he had been thrown off the horse, he narrowed his eyes and stared at her; his eyes were hard and mean looking.

With disgust in his voice, he called her a, "gayh go gi AniYvwuyu, a liar to her people." She flung Cherokee words back at him, trying to sound as vicious as he did. "Nihina, nihinahv- What about you," she said, "Ahutsi agateno, yonega, ayosgi, - You're just a captive scout, of the white soldiers?"

After glaring at her a moment longer, the Indian scout laughed loud and hardy, before riding off at a gallop.

This has been a terrible day, thought Charity. If it wasn't bad enough already that Henry had hurt her feelings, the way he talked about Indians, now this Indian Scout had called *her* a traitor to her people. She was so mad she wanted to scream!

During the walk back to the wagon, she had time to cool off; the old Indian with the white eyes returned to her thoughts.

When she and Nancy made it to where they were to set up camp, Henry and his father had already secured payment for the skins they brought and had begun setting up their camp; it was located in a spot just outside the gates of the fort. Nancy immediately got busy starting supper. She had brought ingredients for a stew, which she intended to cook in an old, iron pot, which she hung on a rod over the campfire.

"I don't have to cook like this very often; I'm a little rusty," she said. "Hopefully, it will be fit to eat once I get done with it," she laughed.

"Don't worry, woman," said Eli. "I can't speak for the rest of 'em, but I'm so hungry I could eat the north end of a south bound hog!" Nancy chuckled at his joke and gathered her fixings and began adding them to the pot.

Charity hung around a few minutes, totally ignoring Henry because she was still a little mad at him. After Eli and Nancy were busy and not paying attention to her, she eased her way over to the old Indian's camp. He was still sitting cross-legged by his campfire. She caught herself wondering just how long he could stay in that position. As she neared him, she lost some of her bravado, becoming more nervous the closer to him she got.

When she was about fifteen feet from him, he said, "Death rides a pale horse. I beheld death. Because I was brave, He did not take my life; he took my sight, because I was blind."

A gasp escaped her mouth.

The old, white-eyed Indian man chuckled softly, saying, "I seem to have that effect on people."

"How did you know I was here?" Charity stuttered.

"I am blind, not deaf," chuckled the old man. "For one so

slight, your footsteps are heavy; a burden, you must carry."

Ignoring his statement about her heavy footsteps, she asked, "Why did you say that about death and a pale horse?"

"That was your question, was it not? You want to know what happened to my eyes. Why they no longer hold color, as yours does?"

"Well, yes, it is… what happened to them," Charity asked.

"Sit down," said the old man, "And I will tell you how my eyes came to be the color of falling snow."

Stunned by his words, Charity wondered if he could read her mind- Did he know her thoughts. She crossed her legs and then sat down.

8

Death Rides a Pale Horse

"I have heard the stories that go round 'bout how I lost my sight; few, are brave enough to ask. You, Little One, are braver than those who claim to be brave." Charity did not respond; she was busy studying his face. She could tell that he was a handsome man at one time; now, not so much. His skin appeared to have the texture and appearance of the underside of a dried boar's hide- his face, trenched with deep fissures, reminded her of the lines on the map she saw hanging by the door on her way out of the Mercantile.

"When I was a young warrior I was too self-important to have the sense of a turkey. A turkey will fly a mile with an arrow through his heart and not even know that he is dead," he said, pausing to let her absorb what he'd said.

"I was raised with other young braves and taught to track, hunt and fish by the women of the tribe; we was taught to be warriors by the warriors of the tribe- all of our teaching was taught us so we could protect the tribe.

In my twenty-first year, our tribe was 200 strong, mostly women and children- Heavy rains that year caused floods and ınd storms that came out of the sea. When winter came, blinding, snow storms came too- Ela was not good to the 'Earth People' that year- food was naught- our gardens did not grow- our animals did not reproduce- nor did the animals of the forest…"

Sitting cross-legged by the fire, Charity listened intently. If anything, she had a thirst for knowledge of any sort and hungered for stories told by her ancestors; stories told by the elders were the best stories of all.

Instinctively, she knew that she must pay close attention and concentrate on what Two Feathers was telling her- it was important. After the pause, when he knew that she had absorbed the depth of his words, he continued.

"Our tribe was starving- dying by the day." Charity momentarily wondered if his tribe was the same tribe Tokola and Nokomis belonged to. "We had eaten all the roots, dried meat, grains and nuts we had stored for winter. We had eaten all the rabbits, eaten all the squirrels, deer, possums, coons, snakes, and even the dogs… it was not enough- that winter was the longest and coldest the elders could remember. Then, we had to eat the horses."

Pausing again, appearing deep in thought, he let her absorb his words.

"You must never have to eat the horses," he said, "It should not go that far." He appeared thoughtful. "If we young bucks had not been so cocky and full of piss and vinegar, we would have been able to look ahead, to be prepared.

"During a break in the weather, on the night of the wolf, a full moon night, we left camp to search for food. We left on foot- we thought the worst was over. The moon was so bright, one could see as day. There was ten of us in our party, no longer proud, strutting peacocks. Too hungry to lay and wait for the return of the animals, we headed to the river to try to catch some fish; it was frozen over- It has to be mighty cold to stop Old Man River from flowing…"

Pausing again, either giving her time to absorb his words or to gather his thoughts, he then continued. "After a full day's hunt and having found no game, we traveled on. Having no recourse, and with a little strutting rooster still in us, me and two others, Running Horse and Tutolaka, said we were brave. We told the others that we would cross the river, go into the white man's village and get food for our people.

"Before daybreak, we crossed the frozen river and snuck into the village of the white people only to find that they too, were starving. No food did we find there. Death was rife in the village- bodies stacked, awaiting the ground to thaw for burial - the white people had not been prepared at all…

"Heads hung low; we turned back to the river. Halfway there, I saw a scrawny deer at the edge of the forest; I raised my hand to stop the others. We each took aim with our bows and let loose the arrows, each, finding our target. The deer felled dead and bleeding to the frozen ground. We rejoiced and drank of the warm blood, for strength…

"We trussed the deer so that we could carry him back to camp. As we again headed to the river, carrying the deer, I sensed a strange feeling- something was coming for me… It was not my first time to have such feelings. Hearing a grunt and long-drawn-out breath, I turned and witnessed a large, black bear followed by a big, pale horse come from the forest into the clearing. The bear growled, rising to its hind legs; the horse reared up in indignation, snorting at us for being in his presence."

Charity was holding her breath in expectation, neck-deep, and completely immersed in the story he was telling her, she was right there beside him, facing the bear and the pale horse as they charged him.

"The bear started toward me- the pale horse, ran behind him, caught him, reared up and trampled him. It was a fierce battle until the horse reared again and stomped the bear, killing him. I thought it was over and the pale horse would move on and we could take the bear back to our camp. Then, with his blood-red eyes, the pale horse looked to where I stood. Running straight at me; he charged- He did not see me- he looked through me as he come full speed." Two Feathers paused once again, giving Charity time to breathe. When the old man did not immediately begin speaking again, she asked, "What did you do?"

"I froze- I did not know what to do- by the time my mind started working, I did not have time to raise my bow. I pulled my knife and lunged at him… In that moment, time froze- our eyes met. In his eyes, I saw him running, and on his back rode, Death, and Death looked me in the eye.

"You think death is a thing that happens when someone's spirit leaves the body behind, but Death is an embodiment- He comes to claim the spirits of those that pass into the firmament of the Heavens…

"When I looked into his eyes, I could not move; I could not release my eyes from his. As our bodies crashed together, the last vision I had, was of Death on a pale horse. The world turned as black as a starless night- the darkness entered my mind, my soul shook with fear, and then my eyes could no longer see… Never again, have they beheld light or the beauty that is, Ela, our Mother Earth. Even the familiar darkness, we see when our eyes are closed is no longer there." When he paused, Charity exhaled and then took another deep breath, listening intently, as he continued his tale.

"I lay in Death's arms; writhing in feverish pain, my stomach drawn tight from hunger. I talked with the Great Spirit and asked him to take me and release me from my torment, but he said it was not my time. He said that I must learn to see, not with my eyes, but with my heart, my spirit within.

"He nourished my body with the blood of the bear, which gave me strength, then said, that because I was brave, I would live. I was to teach my people of his ways. The Great Spirit told me that when the yellow mocker called, and I lay in death's final arms, that I would again be able to see," he paused, looking into his fire. Charity's thoughts went immediately to the yellow-bellied mocker she saw the morning she and her grandfather set out on his final journey- was the yellow mocker telling her that her grandfather would die that day- did he come to warn her?

"Did I die?" asked Two Feathers thoughtfully. "I do not know, but I *was* dead in the darkness. For how long; I do not know. When I awoke, my sight was gone. They whispered of my eyes, saying the snow had taken my sight. I told them that *Death*, had taken my sight. That Death rode a pale horse and was chasing the bear, and when we smashed together, death caught me and tried to claim my spirit.

"Running Horse and Tutolaka did not see the pale horse, or death. They say that I fall down. That I was ill and talking out of my head. That it had been two moons ago and they could not carry me and the meat, so they had stayed with me. For that, I know they were my friends.

"Why was I chosen? I do not know. I only know that I must tell every one of the Great Spirit's ways, how he saved me from Death, and how we should care for one another. We should prepare for our days ahead, build stronger homes and plant crops so that we will have shelter from the storms and food to feed our peoples.

"I tell you, Little One, to always be prepared. To build a sturdy home, plant crops to feed your family, be kind to fellow peoples, but beware, for Death rides a pale horse. You cannot outrun Death…" he paused.

"Change is all around us- even in the coolness of your shadow, the earth changes… The white man has come; they are filling up our lands. If you are lacking in strength, they will overrun you- If you are blind to disparity, you become uncaring- you lose those things you do care for… We cannot be blind to the changes around us, Usdi Sa'quo, Death can judge harshly. You may die, you might live, or, you may have to continue on as I have, without sight or hearing. You may not be able to walk or to speak, but you must strive to do what is best for your people… your children," he paused and looked up from his fire to face her. When he spoke, Charity felt that he could actually see her.

"What is this burden that weighs down your spirit, Little One?"

Once she decided to answer him, it was as if a floodgate had opened. Charity told him about her parents' deaths, and about being raised by her grandparents. She told him about her grandfather's death and how she came to be living in the white man's world. She told him about the dream she'd had the night her grandfather died, and about the fork in the road. She told of how she now knew that Tokola was her grandmother's brother, and how she had had dreams and visions her entire life that she did not understand.

He in his wisdom, told her what his interpretation of her dreams meant. When he sprinkled his powders in the fire, it caused blue flames that leapt high and bright. He told her that one day, she would journey far, far away. He told her that she would have many sons and daughters and that she would suffer much pain and heartache. And that she would endure many other hardships in this new land. She could not avoid this journey; it was inescapable. When he finished telling her this, Charity tried to get to her feet, but they were numb from sitting so long in that position.

Standing on her tingling, half-numb feet, she asked him how he could sit so long in one position without hurting. He laughed and said, "Endurance, Little One. You will soon learn, is essential to life…"

Making her way back to camp, Charity thought about all the things the old Indian man had told her and took them to heart, because, he, like her grandmother, appeared very wise; he seemed honest and humble; she liked that. She turned to look back at the old man; she wanted to see if he would be looking in her direction, but there was nothing there. Charity could not believe her eyes- The old man was gone, and so was his colorful fire! There was not even a reminder of what had been there.

When Henry saw Charity walking back to camp, he watched her turn and look back; he, too, looked and was surprised to see that old Two Feathers and his fire were both gone. Only minutes before, he saw the two of them sitting by the fire, talking…

"I told you he was strange," said Henry, when Charity was near enough.

"I wouldn't call him, strange- he's just different. He seems very wise."

"I wouldn't know; I've never actually talked to him- I was surprised to see you sitting over there with him."

"I felt drawn to him- almost as if he willed me to come to him- He knew I was coming. He said I had a destiny... The last thing he told me was, not to let yesterday, use up too much of today."

"Yep, sounds wise to me too, I reckon," grinned Henry.

"Don't make fun of me, Henry Gullege- I just might change my mind," Charity said sternly, turning her back to him.

"Change it about what," asked, Henry, trying to maintain a straight face.

"Since there is a preacher here, I was thinking about marrying you. Now, I'm not so sure," she replied, slipping a peek in his direction. After a momentary look of shock crossed his face, Henry grinned from ear to ear and quickly gathered her in his arms and swung her around.

"That would make me the happiest man in South Carolina," he exclaimed, kissing her cheek, and then hugging her tight.

Nancy and Eli, who were nearby, listening to the exchange, smiled at one another- they, too, were happy that Charity and Henry were ready to marry. Nancy could not wait to hear the patter of little feet running around their home. She had come to love Charity as if she were her own daughter and welcomed the union. Eli smiled and cut off a chunk of tobacco and put it in his mouth- he'd learned it was best just to keep quiet when womenfolk were openly expressing their feelings. Eli's thoughts went to Charity's grandfather- *Looks like it all worked out; you got what you wanted, old friend- she'll be taken care of.*

Charity and Henry married before the family left Fort Charlotte. Charity knew it was her destiny to marry Henry. She knew, even without Two Feathers telling her it was… and, it was what her grandfather had wanted. He had virtually handpicked Henry for her husband, which was why he took her to them before he died… Looking into Henry's loving eyes and saying, I do, as they stood before the minister, Charity realized how much she truly cared for Henry- he was her soul mate, her other half- the Great Spirit had brought them together and he would see them through.

9

Endurance

Life on the Gullege farm was hard- much harder than it had been living with her grandparents', however, there were also many good times too; and being with Henry made the hard work worthwhile.

Charity was happy. Henry was a loving and gentle husband, but living in such close quarters made it hard for them to explore their newfound love as much or as often as they wanted to, and with all the chores that needed doing, come nighttime, they were tired and sleepy.

Oftentimes, early in the morning, before Nancy and Eli woke, they would take a blanket and slip off into the forest for an hour alone. It was for those precious 'alone moments' that the two of them got through the rest of the day.

Their love was very fertile, so within a few months, Charity was big with child. Once Henry realized she was to bear a child, he worried that she was too small of stature to birth something as large as a baby. He went to his mother with his concerns. Nancy told him not to worry and assured him that Charity's hips were built for childbearing and she should not have any difficulty when her time came. Even though Nancy had assured Henry of Charity's childbearing ability, she *was* slightly concerned about her small size, especially the further along she got.

Celebrating Thanksgiving with Henry's family, was the first Charity ever knew of the event- however, once Nancy and Henry explained why it was a celebration, she understood that it was a white people's celebration. And, once she had her first ever taste of what Nancy referred to as, dressing with the roasted turkey, she knew it would be her favorite time of year from then on. The dressing consisted of cornbread mixed with turkey broth and drippings, rich with sage, sautéed onions and sweet green peppers, and served with the roasted turkey and creamy gravy. Her grandmother had made something similar, however, she did not think it had the peppers; instead it had corn and meat; but it had been so long since she'd had it that she could not remember exactly, nor could she remember the taste… There was also a sweet thick preserve made from tart, red berries that Nancy served with it. Henry and his father collected the berries each year from a bog high in the mountains where the weather was cooler. Charity decided that each year, she would cook such a meal for her husband and children…

* * *

A week and a half after Thanksgiving, Charity knew her time had come- Nancy had been watching her with a keen eye- noticing how low she was now carrying the baby. Watching her waddle around the kitchen, setting the table for supper, Nancy thought that Charity might become frightened the closer her time come- Nancy had, to the best of her ability and personal knowledge, explained what happens and what to expect when the baby came.

At first, wide-eyed over Nancy's telling, Charity was a little apprehensive, but then, as if he were right there beside her, she heard the old man's voice whisper in her ear, "Endurance, Little One. You will endure." After that, she had not let it worry her, at least not until the first contraction wrapped around her uterus and not so gently squeezed her tightly. Charity grabbed a hold of the table and nearly dropped the plates she was carrying. Nancy had told her there would be *binding* pains, but hearing something and experiencing it is two different matters.

"You might need to go lay down," said Nancy, taking the plates from Charity and setting them on the table.

"No, I'll be alright- you told me that the pains will be spaced out at first and then get closer together. You said it could take up to a day for the baby to come; I don't want to spoil our supper together. Henry and his father have been gone for five days- what sort of homecoming would that be for Henry to come home and find his wife piled up in bed this time of day! See, the pain is already passing; they should be here anytime now."

"Okay," said Nancy, "but, remember what I told you, the pains are only going to get harder and more painful the closer to the time of the baby's birth. You let me know if you need me."

Charity nodded her head, muttered "Yes, ma'am" and then resumed setting the table.

With the food in the warmer, Nancy and Charity waited Eli and Henry's return from Rutherfordton, where they had gone to pick up what they suspected to be no more than a wagonload of possessions, belonging to Eli's uncle and his wife, who had both passed on within the last year. A mail carrier had come bearing a court-sealed letter to Eli- it contained his uncle's last will and testament and a letter from the judge of that district declaring Eli the sole beneficiary, once his uncle's debts was paid off. Eli had not seen his kinfolks in nearly ten years, and felt ashamed that he had not taken the time to make the two day trip to see them. He told Nancy that there probably wasn't much to collect, but since his aunt and uncle never had any children of their own, he felt obligated to go and collect what there was…

When five o'clock rolled around and the men folk had not returned, Charity decided to take Nancy's advice and get off her feet for awhile. They had begun to swell the last several days; it had both her and Nancy worried. Her labor pains had become steadier, but were still nearly a half an hour apart. Her back had a steady ache and her feet felt as if she was walking on spongy prickles. Once she lay down and closed her eyes, she immediately went to sleep. What seemed like hours later, Charity woke to find Henry lying beside her; he had his arm gently draped over her. She felt the need to relieve her bladder, but when she tried to roll over to get out of bed, a sudden sharp pain contracted low in her stomach. When she stood, she felt her bladder empty onto the floor between her bare feet. As hard as she tried, she could not stop the flow. Embarrassed, she cried out in frustration. Henry immediately jumped out of bed and ran to her side. Hearing the commotion, Nancy and Eli also came to see what was wrong. When Nancy looked down and saw the puddle of water around Charity's feet, she let out a nervous giggle.

"Oh, my dear, I am so sorry," said Nancy, placing an arm around Charity's shoulder. "I slap forgot to tell you about that." Nancy's arm was comforting. She had become a replacement for the mother that Charity did not remember from her childhood.

"That's just your water breaking- it means the baby is close to birthing. We should get you back in the bed. I've had water boiling all day, and I've got a good collection of rags, my scissors and thread, everything is ready, I'm ready, and I think this baby is ready too," she said, palpating Charity's stomach as she talked. "He feels as though he has turned downward and is headed out- Everything should go smooth once he starts coming."

"How do you know it's a he," asked Henry.

"Oh, it's just a guess, but I believe I'm right," Nancy replied. "Have y'all settled on a named yet; I know there were several you had in mind."

Henry looked from Charity to his mother. "Yes, ma'am, I believe we will name our first born son, Uriah, after your father."

Eli, who had stood back quietly watching, now spoke up. "Looks like that sawmill equipment we inherited from my uncle is going to come in handy. We need to build another room onto the house. That's something we can work on over the winter."

A cramp low in her stomach that wrapped around her back and twisted something in her private place, suddenly caused Charity to grab hold of Henry's arm, "I think it's trying to come out," she exclaimed, trying to contain the terror she felt inside from making it into her voice.

"Just stay calm, dear, and everything will go smoothly," said Nancy. "I'm not saying it's not going to hurt, because it is, but it's nothing you cannot bear," she said firmly.

Nancy's words immediately brought the old Indian, Two Feather's, image to mind and his words to her, that day in Fort Charlotte.

Three hours later, an exhausted but happy Charity, birthed her and Henry's first child, a son, whom they named Uriah, after Henry's maternal grandfather. Lying in bed, looking at the tiny bundle nursing at her breast, Charity and Henry smiled in adoration of each other and what the two of them had created.

"Isn't he perfect," she said to Henry, as she pulled the blanket back and examined Uriah's tiny feet and hands. "Do you want to hold him?"

"Yes, he is, perfect," said Henry. "And I'd like to hold him, but, he looks so tiny and delicate, I'm afraid I'll break him."

"I thought the same thing when he first came out, but your mama said that babies are more resilient than they appear."

"I'm just trying to figure out who he looks like- he looks a little like you," said Henry, "maybe, a little more like me-"

"He favors my father," said Nancy, who was standing in the doorway. "His head, neck, and shoulders are shaped just like my father's…"

Charity looked toward Nancy; the sadness in her voice tugged at Charity's heart. "He knew you loved him, Mama Gullege," she told Nancy. She didn't know why she said it, but felt that she had to.

"Yeah, I suppose he did," Nancy said softly. "I just regret that I never had the chance to see him or my mother after Eli and I married and moved here." She smiled at Henry. "You would have liked him," she said. "Oh my, look at me getting all misty eyed." She wiped her eyes with her apron, which still had Charity's blood on it. "I wasn't saying that I regretted marrying your father and moving here- don't ever think that, son. I love you and your father more than anything in this world and I wouldn't change my life here with y'all for anything. Now, let me get into the kitchen and get us some breakfast started. The supper we fixed last night was plumb ruined by the time you and your father got home - you both must be starving."

"Well, I don't know about Henry or Papa Gullege," said Charity. "But I am starving to death. I didn't know birthing children was such hard work!" Henry leaned over and kissed her on the forehead.

From the doorway, Nancy smiled at the scene before her, then turned and went into the kitchen to start breakfast.

Lila M Beckham

***

Fall 1834

Charity often thought of the old man and his words over the next several years, as did she her grandfather and grandmother. She made it a point to remember her Cherokee language, even speaking it to her babies in song as she nursed them. If she had known beforehand that her grandparents were going to die when they did, and if she had known that Tokola was her uncle, there were many things she would have said and done differently- she loved Henry with all her heart and other than her grandfather's death, would not change a thing about her life since coming there. However, there were some days she just couldn't get her life with her grandmother and grandfather out of her thoughts. She knew that wistfully looking back on her past would only hinder her appreciation of the day and usually tried to get out of her reminiscent moods as soon as she possibly could.

***

In 1831, when Charity and Henry had their first son, Henry and his father built a room onto the small cabin. A year and a half later, they had another son, whom they named John. The one extra room had sufficed, but now that Charity was expecting her third child, they were making ready to build on another room to allow the family room to grow.

Nancy and Eli were very proud grandparents- Charity often felt that her babies were getting all the love and attention they would have given their own children had they not died during that horrible yellow fever epidemic.

Over the last three years, Nancy had taught Charity how to put together a good meal, oftentimes having very little to work with as far as ingredients go. They gathered herbs from the herb garden, picked vegetables and dug potatoes from the spring and fall gardens, and even ventured out into the forest to gather different things at different times of the year that did not grow in their gardens; nuts, berries, bay leaves, wild sage, greens, and even medicinal herbs that they either preserved or dried, according to what it was. And, Nancy taught her how to care for her family, other than feeding them and making sure they had clean clothes and beds to sleep in.

She taught Charity to be gentle, yet firm with the children, and showed her how to stretch their provisions, to make them last longer and go further. She often saw Nancy wait until everyone else was served before she fixed her own plate- to these things, Charity paid close attention.

Nancy taught her how to make quilts, not from the hides of animals they way her grandmother had, but from cloth; flour sacks, cotton and flannel material bought from traders, or from the Fort, even to use old worn out clothes when available. Some of the quilts they made were colorful with many different pieces of cloth- solid and patterned. Some of the quilts were plain, with maybe a solid color, and starburst of varied colors in the middle. They had made her and Henry a large quilt and they had made a quilt for each child; both started while they were still in the comfort of her womb.

"What a blessing it is to have a home you can be proud of. It don't matter whether its two rooms or a dozen, you want to keep it clean and welcoming, something you can proudly hold your head up and say, "I did this myself!" Nancy told her as they sat across from each other over the quilting rack sewing on another quilt, this one, for the unborn child Charity was carrying.

"I wish we could get a hold of some pretty patterned material for this quilt- I think this baby is going to be a girl," said Nancy.

"You think so," said Charity. "You're probably right; this baby does feel different; it moves slower and has been easier to carry."

"I know I'm right," smiled Nancy. "Your hips have spread out with this one; with the other two, you were out front."

Charity looked at Nancy and then smiled. She would be happy to have a daughter- she could teach her all the things Nancy and her grandmother had taught her. She just hoped that she could be half as good a teacher for her daughter as they had been for her...

✳✳✳

Nancy was right- Charity's third child was a daughter; they named her Martha Jane, after Nancy's mother.

Lying in bed, surrounded by her children, telling them a

story her grandmother had told her, Charity knew that all the lessons Nancy had taught her would be lessons that she was going to teach her daughters. However, she did not want to forget her Cherokee heritage, nor did she want her children to forget theirs either; it was an essential part of their being. Although they were toddlers, she took them on short jaunts though the woods to look for berries and wild plums, to dig sassafras roots, and to find chinquapins; she even took the boys with her when she went to hunt squirrels- teaching them how to search out nests for the best hunting spots. They'd look for rabbit pellets to find rabbit trails- and, even though she took them with her, when she hunted- she didn't let them shoot her musket- she felt that just as her Cherokee ancestors had reared their children- her duty was to teach them to hunt barehanded- it was their father's responsibility to teach them to be warriors.

Her children would know about her parents and grandparents; she would tell them all the stories her Indian grandmother had told to her as a child, but, she would also add to those stories. She'd make sure they knew that Tokola was their uncle and she would describe him in great detail as she would her grandfather and grandmother. She would also tell them of her first adventures away from her grandparent's cabin and meeting their father and their grandparents, and she'd tell them about her one and only trip to Fort Charlotte. She'd also tell them about the dreams of her grandfather and the stories he had told her. She wanted them to know about Two Feathers and how she had met him, and she'd tell them what he had told her.

Her children were part her and part Henry, they were life itself. Everything she'd ever experienced was essential to whom she was. Events molded her. Her past was an integral part of her being…

***

As 1840 passed and another federal census came and went, Charity could tell that Henry had grown restless. His restlessness did not get past Eli and Nancy's notice either- they could not help but noticed the change in their only child. One day, while the older children were playing and the younger ones were napping, Nancy took Charity aside for a woman to woman talk. And as they sipped their afternoon coffee, they talked. Coffee was a luxury that Charity had grown to love. The dark and rich hot drink soothed and relaxed her. Aside from sassafras tea, it had become her favorite drink. Sassafras tea was one of the things Charity had introduced, into her new household.

When she first went out into the forest and dug some roots and prepared it for her new family; she could not believe that they did not know about the root of sassafras tree and what a wonderfully aromatic and delicious drink it made, when boiled, strained, and mixed with sugar and fresh spring water. She always served it cooled, for the children, but sometimes she preferred hers, still warm. Sassafras was good year-round. The roots could be gathered in the cold of winter, that was when the sap was the richest- and then it could be dried to preserve it to have the rest of the year. She had also taught them about different herbs that could be used for common ailments such as aches, pains, and fevers. Nokomis had taught her all of this when she was very young.

As she and Nancy sat down, Nancy said to her, "Me and Eli noticed that Henry seems to be getting restless; I wanted to ask you if he has said anything about what's been on his mind?"

"No, Ma'am, he hasn't said anything," replied Charity, "but, I can tell something's on his mind. I was just waiting on him to speak on it, which I figure he will do in his own time. You know he is a thinking man; he has to mull things over and chew on them a while before he makes up his mind. When he figures it out or decides to tell us, we'll know," she assured Nancy.

Charity was right; however, that time would not come until the spring of 1843. She had just recently given birth to their seventh child, another daughter. They now had four sons and three daughters; the house was virtually bursting at the seams. Then, at supper one evening, Henry announced that he was moving the family west to Alabama.

At first, Charity was concerned about leaving Eli and Nancy there alone; however, Nancy assured her that she and Eli were about ready to be by themselves for a spell. Saying they were getting on up in age and that it would do them good to be alone with each other, that they hadn't had any alone time since they first married.

Lila M Beckham

Charity sensed they were putting on a brave front- because they wanted their son to be happy and at peace with himself. However, Eli and Nancy understood their sons need to be his own man and make his own decisions. When they first married, they had struck out on their own, settling in the small valley to build their home and raise their children- they had never regretted it and could not deny their son the same opportunity. However, both agreed that she and Henry had better write them every month to let them know how she, Henry, and the children were doing.

And, so it was, the decision had been made that she and Henry, both under the age of thirty, with seven children ranging in age from a newborn to twelve years of age, would over the next several months, whittle down their belongings to only what they absolutely needed to carry with them; it all had to fit onto and into two wagons. This, Henry and Eli both agreed, would be all she and Henry could manage between the two of them, and then set out on a journey that would take them a little over six years to complete.

The journey would take them through some wild and perilous times that before complete, had both her and Henry doubting that the move west was what they had thought it would be.

Remembering old, Two Feathers words about endurance, Charity knew that they must prevail, for this too, must be part of her destiny.

When the Yellow Mocker Calls

The Old Spartanburg District they had grown up in, borne their children in, and in its rich black earth, buried the remains of loved ones, no longer held what was meant for them or their children.

Before they left that morning, Charity stood back to get a good look at the wagons and to take one long last look around the place she had come to call home- she would soon be twenty-seven years old. She had been married nearly half her life. She had borne seven children and still looked like a young girl herself. Her two oldest boys were already taller than she was as were the older girls. The oldest, Uriah, was almost thirteen. Next, come John, Martha Jane, Charles, Nancy, then Aaron, and baby Mary. Her emotions were torn every which way- hugging Nancy, crying because they were leaving, and feeling excited to be going all at the same time- she hadn't felt this way since she and her grandfather had struck out for Fort Charlotte fourteen years earlier…

Henry helped her up onto the second wagon and into the drivers spot, then handed her the reins, clinging briefly to her hand, squeezing it, and smiling his excitement. He instructed Uriah, "Help your mama if she needs it," and then the small wagon train set out for Alabama.

After traveling about four hours, they came to the fork in the road that led to her grandfather's old cabin. Henry stopped the wagons and looked back at Charity; she nodded her head.

Lila M Beckham

When the Yellow Mocker Calls

Even knowing it would be nearly dark by the time they reached it, he turned his team onto the trail that led to her old home. He wanted her to have one last look around and say goodbye to her memories there, before they headed off to Alabama.

When the trail to the cabin came into view, they could see that the trail had not grown over. This surprised Henry, he hollered back at Charity and told her that squatters might have taken up residence in the cabin, so she needed to prepare herself for that.

As they pulled up in the yard, the front door opened. They were both overjoyed to find that Tokola was still alive and living in the cabin! He was so happy to see Charity that he practically hopped across to the wagon, as she was climbing down off it.

They spent the night and had a wonderful visit with her uncle, who told her children of an adventure he'd had as a young brave, and how he had met the great, Cherokee Silver Man, Sequoyah, and how Sequoyah had taught him about the white man's, "Talking Leaves," and how Sequoyah had created a Cherokee Syllabary so that the Cherokee could communicate by writing on paper the same as the white man did. Charity said she wished he had told her that story before she met the census taker, then she might not have felt so ignorant about his writing on paper.

From that day forward, Charity would fondly call writing on paper as "talking leaves."

Lila M Beckham

The next morning, as they drove their wagons out of the yard of her former home and headed west, Charity, although trying to be brave, could not contain the single tear that eased its way down her still beautiful, cheek…

The tear did not get past the notice of her two oldest sons that sat beside her on the wagon seat. Each looked at the other, and it was as if a silent vow passed between them. If at all possible, they never wanted to see that again, and each felt their protective ire rise up in defense of their mother.

10

Crossing the Savannah

Augusta, Georgia Country

May 1843

After traveling northwest along the Savannah River for a few days, the small caravan came to a crossing into the Georgia city of, Augusta. After paying the tow fare and crossing on the ferry, they were all in awe of the hundred year old city. The most populated places either had ever been was Fort Charlotte. Neither Henry nor Charity had ever even been to Savannah, although Charity had always wanted to go there and had imagined what it would look like from descriptions Nancy had told about when telling her about it.

The children were very excited and asked many questions about the stores and people; they were curious about the cobbled streets. Neither charity nor Henry had seen cobbled streets before.

The delicious aroma of food being prepared, made all their mouths water; several of the children licked their lips, trying to savor the aroma; however, Charity had not noticed or she would have gotten on to them- Her mouth was also slightly ajar, but it was over the beautiful houses, carriages, and the fancily dressed men and women. Even in her dreams, she had never envisioned it this way. Hers, had been a simple life, filled with the simplest of pleasures.

Henry drove on through town and she followed; they set up camp on the western edge of town in a thicket of willows near a creek. While Henry went to check out the town and see what it was going to take to replenish their supplies, Charity had the boys gather firewood so that she could get started fixing supper. None of them, including the young'uns, had had anything to eat all day except cold, leftover biscuits they'd had for supper the day before. By the time Henry returned to camp, Charity had a pot of potatoes cut up and boiling and was making biscuits. Henry was very excited.

"Guess what I found out," he exclaimed.

"You know I'm not good at playing guessing games, Henry. If you want to tell me something, just spit it out. It must be something good, you look like you're about to bust a gut," chuckled Charity.

"I found out that they're having a land lottery over in the central and western part of the state, what use to be the Creek and Cherokee's land. All we have to do is make it to each of the counties in time to get our name in the hat. If we're lucky, we will get our land for free," he said excitedly.

Charity felt her dander rise at the mention of land that used to belong to the Creek and Cherokee Indian's. She'd heard all about how they were driven from their lands and sent out west somewhere. She could not help the anger and sarcasm that were in her voice as she replied, "You mean land that they straight-out stole from the Indians, don't you Henry." Her ire and sarcasm did not seem to affect Henry. "What about Alabama? I thought that was our plan."

"We can still go on to Alabama if we don't get picked in the lottery," Henry replied. "But, it's at least worth a try if we can get the land for free. Just think, Charity, we could be land owners," Henry implored.

"We could've stayed in Spartanburg County and been land owners, Henry Gullege." Charity didn't look up from her biscuit making, but she could tell that her words weren't affecting Henry at all. He was just too fired up over the thought of the free land in Georgia that was up for grabs.

"Henry, I'm your wife. Just tell me what the young'uns and me can do to help you? I'll do everything I can to help you; you know that."

Although not happy about Henry's land-chasing of late, she could not help but smile, when Henry smiled and let out a huge sigh of relief. However, a few minutes later, Charity's thoughts were not about getting free land, they were on what had happened to the poor Indian families that once lived on the land the government was divvying out on a first come first served basis. Where were they now? How were they being treated?

Charity knew all about the 1831 through 1838 removal of

the Five Civilized Tribes, starting with the Choctaw Nation and finishing when the final tribe of Cherokee Indians who were stripped of their rights and forced to move many thousands of miles away, hundreds of them dying along the way. *On what would come to be known as, 'The Trail of Tears.'* She had read all about the *Removal* in the newspapers that Nancy had Eli and Henry pick up when they went to Fort Charlotte- Nancy used them in Charity's continued schooling; they'd also used some of them in her children's studies.

After supper, Henry, Charity, and the children took a walk and explored the city of Augusta. While talking to several old men outside the Mercantile, their third oldest son, Charles, inquired about an old dugout canoe he saw leaning against the side of a building. The men said that the area was first used by the Indians as a place to cross the Savannah River. The most well dressed of the two men, told them that after the city of Savannah was founded in 1733, its founder, James Oglethorpe, sent a detachment of troops on a journey up the Savannah River in 1735, with instructions to build at the head of the navigable part of the river. This part of the river was on a fall line; that made it a good location for water mills, grist mills, and sawmills. The settlement thrived, and Oglethorpe named it Augusta, in honor of Augusta, Princess of Wales.

"A real princess!" exclaimed Martha Jane.

"Yes, little miss, a real princess," replied the man. They all smiled at Martha's enthusiasm.

The next morning, they set off again; this time, they were headed to Washington County, where Henry heard that a land lottery was being held. It took them several days to get there; Henry was disappointed because of how slowly they had to travel. He left Charity and the children setting up camp and went to the land office; he came back with his head hung low. Charity could tell he was deep in thought.

"Are we going to Alabama now, Papa?" Uriah asked.

"No!" Henry snapped, hurting Uriah's feelings.

"He's just a boy, Henry," Charity admonished. She knew what had to be done if Henry was ever going to get this 'free land' thing out of his system.

"Henry, me and you need to talk," she said.

Henry turned to look at her; she had that same steeled look of determination, he witnessed the day they buried her grandfather. She reached out and took his hand. "Come and take a walk with me."

As they walked hand and hand beneath the willows, alongside the creek, Charity was quiet. She was deciding on just how she would put her idea, to Henry; she was also giving him time to think about his harsh manner of answering Uriah. After a few minutes, Henry stopped. "I shouldn't have snapped at the boy like I did; I'll apologize when we go back."

"Yes, you should... They're out of their normal surroundings, but they're also excited to be on this journey-they've heard Alabama so much that it is all they want to talk about as we're traveling along. However, I have something else that I want to discuss with you, Henry." Charity looked up into his eyes; she felt her heart flutter- but knew it was what had to be done.

"I have an idea how you can get to the lotteries sooner." She saw Henry's forehead furrow. "I know how much getting the land means to you. I think that it would be better for all of us, if you took the saddle horse and a few provisions and traveled to the next lottery county alone."

"Alone…" Henry stammered. "No! I'm not going to leave you and the young'uns by yourselves!"

"It's the only way, Henry; don't you see that," she implored calmly. When he didn't speak she continued. "Charles, John, and Uriah are all three plenty big enough to help me. They have already gathered up the firewood. They know how to fish. Uriah and John can drive one of the wagons and I'll keep driving the one I'm driving, I'll just get in the lead. And, you know that I'm a good shot with a musket. We won't go hungry," she said firmly.

Henry's eyes were searching her face.

"This spot here is a real good place for us to camp awhile. There's this creek right here and the town is less than a mile away. All you have to do, once you get the land, is double back here and get us," she explained.

Henry looked deep into Charity's eyes; he knew she was right. He would definitely stand a better chance of making it to the next county in time for the lottery if he went alone; however, it meant leaving her and the children alone and having to fend for themselves. They were miles from home; they didn't know a soul; he did not want to leave his family alone, but he wanted his own land to build his family a home on... With a little more persuasion from Charity, he finally agreed.

Between the two of them, they decided that Henry would leave as soon as he and the boys had chopped some wood and dug a few fishing worms. There was also a good patch of young willows nearby that they could use to make a couple of fishing traps.

That afternoon, they were all busy as bees. Henry and the boys were busy as beavers gathering their allotment of things, while Charity cooked a pot of brown meat stew. Her browned meat stew was just browned meat, onions, potatoes, and a few seasonings, cooked down with thick brown gravy that they could sop up with biscuits. She and Aaron milked the cow so they had good fresh milk to go with their supper.

After all the young'uns were asleep, the dishes done, and the leftovers put up, she and Henry snuggled close and held each other tight, not wanting to let go, even to make love. Once Henry went to sleep, Charity tossed and turned... Morning came way too soon; she had coffee brewing before daybreak. She packed Henry a bucket of leftover stew, some biscuits, and some dried jerky to take with him. She then lay down beside him and woke him gently using her lips and fingertips... her gentleness soon turned urgent with need. In gentle, yet passionate abandon, they made love, clinging together long after their needs were sated. Once Henry had the horse saddled and packed, she kissed him long and hard. At first light, he rode off to the north…

11

Georgia Country

"Well," said Charles excitedly. "I caught myself looking down as I was walking alongside the creek and that's when I found it!"

"Found what?" asked Uriah and the other children, immediately gathering around him to see what he'd found. Charity was busy with the baby, but could hear the excitement in his voice as he began to tell them what he'd found.

Wondering what he'd found, Charity turned again to look in his direction. She was curious as to what had him as excited as the children were. He was surrounded by his brothers and sisters, each trying to scrooch closer to him, to get a better look at what he held.

"What did you find, Charles?"

"This!" Charles exclaimed happily, holding a clay pot and several arrowheads up where she could see them. From a distance, the pot looked to be in nearly perfect condition.

"Bring it over here where I can look at it."

As she held the pot and turned it in her hands, she could see that it was indeed in near perfect condition. Although she was unfamiliar with the markings, she was pretty sure it was Creek, especially, since they were the Indian tribe that previously lived in the area.

"Martha Jane, Nancy, y'all watch the baby and Aaron. Charles, Uriah, John, y'all come with me. Charles, show me where you found these things; maybe we can find some more." She could not contain the excitement in her voice as they struck out toward the nearby creek bed where Charles said he found the pot and arrowheads.

She and the children spent the next several hours exploring the creek banks looking for treasures. They would spend many more days, exploring the areas around the campsite. It gave the children something to look forward to, and it gave Charity a little time away from worrying about Henry.

The boys had gotten good at trapping fish; however, Charity and the children were getting tired of eating fish every meal. They'd been begging for some brown meat stew for several days...

At supper that night, she told the children that when they woke up the next morning, to stay at camp- and not to wander away for any reason; not even to go to the creek.

"Why?" they asked in unison.

"I'm going to get up before daylight, take my musket, and go out and see if I can kill us something to eat besides this dang bony fish," she said, setting her plate down while making a face. "By the time I pick all the bones out so the babies can eat it, I'm too aggravated to fool with picking me some."

"I want to go with you," said both Charles and Uriah.

"No," she said firmly. "I need y'all here, to take care of the little ones."

"But, *Mammma!*"

"Ain't no buts about it, boys" she said. "When your daddy gets back, and he sees fit, he'll teach you boys how to hunt. Right now, I need y'all to watch out for your brothers and sisters."

"Are you sure you can shoot that musket, Mama, I ain't never seen you shoot it before," said Charles.

Charity gave him a stern look. "Y'all remember that story about me and your granny killing that bear?"

"Yeah," they all answered.

"Well, your father took me out right after that and started teaching me how to load, aim, and shoot - later on, he bought me that musket a trip to Fort Charlotte, and I've had plenty of practice using it. Don't y'all worry- I'll get something for us to eat, even if it's just a scrawny old jackrabbit."

＊＊＊

When the pale light of dawn rose in the east, Charity was about a mile south of their camp, squatting in a thicket next to a meadow. She had found this spot while they were exploring the creek banks, looking for relics from the past. The tell-tell signs of animal traffic, let her know that it would be a good spot to kill something to feed her family when the need arose.

When the Yellow Mocker Calls

She had been there nearly an hour- she'd loaded the musket right away. She did not want to be caught off guard should something present itself; however, her legs and feet had started to cramp from squatting in one position for such a long period of time. She wore the most muted color of dress she had, hoping to blend in with the thicket once day broke.

She could have worn her buckskins; they would not have stood out at all, here where all the animals lived; but she was afraid she would get mistaken for a wild Indian, and shot, or worse, sent off on the Trail of Tears and never see Henry or her children again. Those were the thoughts running through her mind when she heard a rustling in the bushes, about twenty feet behind her. After watching and listening for a few minutes, she figured that whatever it was, it had undoubtedly gone the other way.

As she was repositioning herself, something hit her hard in the back, nearly knocking the breath out of her. Simultaneously, it seemed that it hit the ground with a thud, about five feet in front of her. To her surprise, it was a large white-tailed buck! Hitting her must have thrown him off balance, causing him to fall. She jerked up the musket and took aim, just as he was trying to get up. He looked stunned; but when he saw her, he turned to make a run for it. Although, Charity could hear her heart pounding in her ears, she tried to hold the barrel steady so she could shoot the deer. Easy, she told herself, as she took aim and squeezed the trigger.

Lila M Beckham

Boom! The old musket fired, but she couldn't see a darn thing for all the black smoke in front of her. She didn't know whether she had hit him or not.

"You got him, Mama, you got him!" she heard a voice yell.

Surprised, she turned to see Charles, her explorer and most curious son, right there, about thirty feet behind her!

"What are you doing here?" she asked. "Didn't I tell you to stay at the camp with your brothers and sisters? What if I had mistaken you for a buck?" Charles was coming nearer as she scolded him. "That might be you lying there, kicking and squirming on the ground!" She was furious with him, but had to smother a smile, when he said:

"He ain't kickin' or squirming around no more, Mama. You shot that sucker graveyard dead!"

Sure enough, the deer was no longer moving. She pulled the big knife she'd brought with her, out of her waist belt, and said, "Well, since you're here, you're going to have to help me gut him, bleed him, and truss him up. I can't throw him over my shoulder and carry him the way your daddy would. Come on, I'll show you where the scent glands are, we have to be careful not to cut them when we dress him out, or it will ruin the taste of the meat."

"I know that, Mama; Papa's been showing us how to dress 'em out."

"Well, good- that'll be less work for the both of us," she grinned. Her heart was still beating fast, but it wasn't pounding in her ears any longer.

After they gutted the deer and bled him out, they fashioned a truss from a fallen tree branch, then tied the deer's legs together and slid the pole through them. She took one end and Charles the other. This made it a lot easier to carry their prize back to the camp.

Charity was still piqued that Charles had blatantly disobeyed and followed her out of camp- next time, she would pay better attention when she left camp- However, she was thankful that he was there to help her; she would have had a heck of a time trying to drag the deer back to the camp, alone.

Following Carter's Mill Creek, Charity and Charles made it back to their camp; they got there before the younger ones had awakened. Uriah was perturbed that Charles had gotten to help his mama carry the deer back to camp; but got over it once he realized that he'd get to help dress out the deer.

It took them a little better than an hour to dress out the deer. She told the boys, "You boys did a fine job; your father would be proud of you- I'm proud of you too." And she was proud of them. She could see that they, too, were proud of their accomplishment.

***

Meanwhile, several counties over, Henry was about to get into some mischief, of his own. The last name had been drawn out of the hat and again, he failed to make the cut. This was the third county he'd gone to, with no luck. He was growing more and more discouraged. He felt that he was letting his family down. When the grizzled old man offered him a drink of whiskey, he took the jug and swigged down several big gulps. Henry had never imbibed spirits before; the hot liquid sliding down his throat and into his stomach felt good after the initial burn. And, after several more large swigs, so did Henry.

He and the old man sat and drank for the greater part of the afternoon. Henry drank, bemoaning the fact that he still had not been drawn in the land lottery, and the old man, was just thankful for some company.

The old man seemed to become louder and more belligerent, the drunker he got, while Henry just got more and more quiet and depressed. Some of the men who were also camped there were getting fed up with the old man's loud, vulgar mouth. They started to complain to the pair, and then asked them to leave camp, saying they needed to take their whiskey somewhere else to drink it. The old man didn't like it very much. He jumped up and took a swing at the leader of the protesters, Henry was right behind him. They lit into the crowd, with a furry! The old man, driven by drunken pride, and Henry, driven by shame and a rage that even in his drunkenness, he did not understand.

The town sheriff fired several shots in the air and stopped most of those fighting, except Henry who turned and punched the sheriff right in the jaw. The last thing Henry felt was a hard whack to the back of his head, and then everything went black.

12

Sandersville

Charity fried some of the fresh venison to go with the leftovers from the night before. After everyone ate their fill, she cleaned up her cooking area and then told the children that she was going to walk into town to see if she could trade some of the fresh meat, for some flour, lard, and beans. She took the back-strap, which was the tenderest part of the deer, and the two hind-leg-quarters, hoping they would be enough to get the supplies that she needed in order to keep her children fed. To help carry the meat, she took Charles with her, leaving Uriah and John to watch the girls and Aaron. It was a long, hard walk carrying the fresh meat, which was heavy.

When they finally made it to town, she didn't waste any time, she went straight to the mercantile. The proprietor's name was Benjamin Butler. He was a kindly man, with a warm, friendly smile. She explained what she wanted to do, and although sympathetic, he said that most folks either raised or hunted their own meat, so he really didn't have much call for venison.

Holding out the tenderloin toward Mr. Butler, Charity asked

if he was sure he couldn't just trade a couple of pounds of beans for the back-strap so that she could feed her children... Seeing the tenderloin she held out to him and the desperation in her eyes, Mr. Butler took pity.

"Alright, Ma'am, I'll tell you what- I'll give it a try, maybe folks will buy the meat- I'll give you twenty pounds of flour, ten pounds of beans, and five pounds of meal. I'll also throw in three pounds of sugar, and the wax you'll need to seal your canning jars so's you can salvage the rest of that meat."

Charity was so thankful that she wanted to hug him; so she did. He laughed and said, "That was a first. Most folks usually get mad about how much stuff cost these days!"

Charity wanted to hug him again when she saw him slip six licorice whips into one of the bags. After leaving the mercantile, she got one out, pulled it in half, put half in her mouth and handed Charles the other half. He grinned- it had been a long time since they'd had any candy.

Walking along the main road, red dust puffed up behind their heels and settled atop the palmetto bushes that lined both sides of the road. Toting the heavy bags had become quite burdensome, so Charity stopped and equally divided the bags of foodstuffs into the two burlap sacks Mr. Butler had given her to lessen the burden on her back and put a little more onto Charles' back.

Dragging the heavy burlap sacks behind them, Charity glanced up to watch a Carrion crow as it soared above them.

Although no one had ever told her anything about crows delivering bad news or anything, she knew that the low-flying crow was an omen of some sort; and a bad omen from the feel of it. Its soaring overhead, forebode something bad was coming her way; she just didn't know what was coming.

"What's wrong, Mama?"

"I don't know yet, son, but whatever it is, it will soon present itself." As soon as she said that, the Carrion crow sailed south and away from them. In seconds, it was out of sight.

After rounding the next curve in the road, she and Charles came face to face with two, rough-looking men on horseback. One was a white man- the other, a large Indian the likes of which she'd never seen. Even among all the Indians she'd seen at Fort Charlotte, Charity had never seen an Indian that looked like him. He was big and hawk faced, with just a strip of hair that ran right down the middle of his head. She didn't like the way they were looking at her, especially the white man. His stare made her very uncomfortable. She'd never had anyone look at her the way he did. Instinctively, she looked down to see if her dress was open or something. The white man's eyes and expression gave her the willies. She felt exposed and vulnerable.

Just after they passed, Charles said, "Did you see that, Mama? That Injun shore was funny looking."

"Shush!" she said, almost loosing grip on the croaker sack as she reached to cover his mouth with her hand. "He might hear you, and come back and scalp us! He sure looked like he'd enjoy doing it."

"Yeah, Mama," Charles whispered, "He was one mean looking Injun, that's for shore. I can't wait to tell Uriah and John about him!" Charles' voice was filled with excitement, but tinged with fear.

Charity was apprehensive; she had a feeling she'd never felt before and strange visions, swept through her mind. Suddenly, she realized that the men would have passed their campsite- her children… she needed to hurry!

As they neared the campsite, they saw that most of the children had come out to the road to wait for their return. In a wave, they all ran to meet them. Little Aaron, trying hard to keep up with his siblings, fell and bumped his nose in the dirt. Charity undone the string she had tied the croaker sack with and began handing off the bags of supplies so that she could see to Aaron- however, he had already jumped up and grabbed one of the bags from Charles who had done the same and was trying to carry it back to camp. It was a comical sight. The bag of sugar was nearly as big as he was; the sight of him trying to be as big as his brothers brought a smile to her face, temporarily relieving thoughts of the strange men from her mind as they followed the trail off the main road back to their campsite. After they reached the camp, Charity pulled the licorice whips out of one of the bags and divvied them out to the children. She then began separating the bags; she wanted to cook some of the beans for supper, and was looking for them.

Lila M Beckham

Uriah sensed that something was bothering his mama. And, as soon as he saw that she was alone, he went over to her. "What's wrong, Mama?"

Charity told him that it wasn't anything for him to be concerned about, but Uriah did not accept that and voiced his concerns.

"Since Papa is gone, I'm supposed to help you look out for trouble, and take care of my brothers and sisters."

Hearing the angst in his tone, Charity looked up from digging through the bag and saw her oldest child with a different set of eyes. His staunch appearance and the love and admiration in his expression, showed his loyalty to her and to his family; she realized that he was all grown up.

"On our way back from Sandersville, we ran into two men on horseback. They looked mean; it scared me a little bit; that's all."

"Don't worry, Mama," he said firmly. "I'll help you watch out for any sign of trouble," he assured her.

Charity hugged him to her and told him that she was proud of him.

"Mama, how much longer you reckon Papa is going to be gone?"

"I don't know, Son. It could be awhile. In the meantime, we have got to keep the family fed and keep ourselves safe."

Her hand on Uriah's shoulder, she felt his muscles tense under her fingers,

"You're growing up so fast that I don't know what to do," she said softly. "Now, help me and let's get this stuff put up so I can put on a pot of beans."

For the time being, she and the children were safe and they had plenty of food now that she'd killed the deer and traded some of it to replenish the larder. Charity made a mental note not to go anywhere without the big hunting knife tucked into her waist belt.

✻✻✻

Watching the children play while she washed the beans and put them in a pot that she hung over the fire, Charity decided that since she had sugar, she was going to make a gallon jug of sassafras tea and some sweet-cakes as a special treat for the children. She dug through the wagon until she found her bag of sassafras roots and retrieved her tea jug. Her plan would require two cups of the cherished sugar, but it would be worth it to see them enjoying the treats with their supper.

She boiled several of the sassafras roots until the liquid was dark and thick and then strained the liquid through a piece of cloth. As soon as the roots began to boil, her surprise treat, was no longer a surprise. The aroma of the boiling sassafras filled the entire campsite, immediately drawing the children over to her cooking area. Charity laughed and told them to go and play, they were going to have to wait until supper for some of the delicious drink. Once she had mixed the sugar with the hot liquid and stirred it well, she picked up the jug and headed toward the creek where she kept the milk and such that needed to stay cool; the water should be cold enough to cool it down before supper.

By the time she fed the children and got them into bed that night, she was worn slap out. She thought for sure that she would sleep like a log, but then the dreams of Henry came. In her dreams, his head was bleeding, but for some reason, although she knew he was hurt, she also knew that he would return to them. In her dream, when he returned, he was smiling and happy. That dream suddenly ended and she began a different dream. This dream was about the man and the Indian she had seen earlier that day; it was not a good dream; she woke in a cold sweat, a scream at the back of her throat. She knew the demons she was fighting in her dream, would soon become reality…

Exhausted, Charity tossed and turned, trying to go back to sleep to get the rest her body so badly needed; however, when she finally dozed, the dreams returned. This time, she was in the middle of a valley. Across the way, she saw a huge, white buffalo come charging from the forest. Shots rang out; the sound vibrated and echoed across the fields. The mighty buffalo, fell to his knees and skidded across the ground, its nose digging into the soil, much like Aaron's had when he fell on the road. She saw it all play out in slow motion, every frame more painful than the last. She ran to the buffalo, it lay bleeding, struggling to raise its head, dirt and blood clogged its nostrils. She wiped the blood and dirt from its nose; it gasped for air and then snorted, blowing dirt and blood onto her arm. Gasping in more air, its breathing came easier. Then, it spoke to her in her native Cherokee.

"Go to, Tsalagiyi," (In Cherokee, it meant, "A Place called Cherokee.") Somehow, just as she had with the eagle, she knew that the buffalo's spirit was that of her grandfather.

"But Grandfather," she replied, "I cannot leave here; it is where Henry knows we are. Here, is where he will come to find us."

The buffalo said one other word before its nose dropped back into the dirt. It said, "Donadagohvi," It meant, "we will see one another again."

"Please, don't leave me, Grandfather," screamed Charity, tears filling her eyes; the buffalo was dead. Charity awoke, wet tears clinging to her cheek.

"You okay, Mama," asked Uriah, concern in his voice. Her moaning and crying had awakened him.

"It was just a dream, Son. Go back to bed- tomorrow is going to be a long day and we don't know what tomorrow may bring.

✳✳✳

When Henry regained consciousness, his head felt as though it was the size of a pumpkin; the pain was so intense that the little bit of sunlight that managed to sneak through the barred window, sent sharp pains through his eyeballs and deep into his brain.

"Well, it looks like you are finally back with the living, son," said a man that when Henry looked at him, knew he was the sheriff he'd seen the day before. The sheriff, walked over to where Henry lay and kicked him several times in the ribs. The impact of the sheriff's boot to his ribs caused Henry to gasp for breath, while wincing and moaning in pain.

Henry's actions only seemed to irritate the sheriff, who acted as if he were going to start kicking Henry again.

"Now, why don't you just leave him be," said a voice from somewhere behind Henry. Henry recognized the voice as being that of the old man he was drinking with after the lottery.

"If you don't shut your trap, Old Man, you're gonna get some of the same," said the sheriff through gritted teeth.

"Well, go ahead then- it just ain't right, kicking a man when he's down," mumbled the old man, whom Henry figured must not be too far from him.

"I need to get back to my family," mumbled Henry.

"Well, said the Sheriff. "You can bet your lily-white ass that ain't gonna happen for quite awhile. I got you on a drunk and disorderly charge, and on an assault charge. Do you remember what happened?"

Henry moaned as he tried to roll over and sit up. "Can't say as I do," he mumbled.

"Yeah, that's what I figured," said the sheriff, bending down to look Henry in the eye. The sheriff's face was beat up. "It was me you assaulted; you're lucky you're alive- lucky I wasn't alone with you after you were brought in last night, or they'd be burying you this morning…" With the sheriff's words, Henry vaguely remembered taking a swing at somebody.

"You fella's better enjoy today- come tomorrow morning, you'll be tried and sentenced." Henry was glad when the sheriff walked out; he sighed with relief and promptly passed back out.

The next day, him and the old man was dragged up in front of the judge. The sheriff and several others testified against Henry and the old man.

"How do you plead," asked the judge.

They both answered, "Guilty." There was no denying they'd been drunk.

"Can either of you make a bond," asked the Judge. Both answered, "No," since neither owned land; you had to own land to bond, or have lots of cash.

"In that case, let's continue," said the judge. The judge sentenced both Henry and the old man to one year hard labor, in the Walton County prison.

This was like a final blow to Henry's ego. All he had ever wanted was to be a man of his own and to be a good provider for his family. *What's going to happen to my family with me locked away,* wondered Henry. This time, he'd really messed up- he had failed Charity and the children. With a sad and heavy heart, Henry plopped back down on the bench when the jailer led him over to it.

13

Echo's in the Dark

Halos surrounded the angel's head; Charity stared in awe at the lovely painting. It gave her a peaceful, serene feeling to gaze upon the image.

"Is there something I could help you find?" asked Mr. Butler.

"Yes, Sir, there is. Do you know of a place called Cherokee?" she asked.

"Well, Ma'am, as a matter of fact, I do know a place called Cherokee. It's about a hundred and fifty miles, due north of here, up there in the mountains- it's smack in the middle of the Cherokee Indian Territory. They've been clearing them Indians out for years, but there's still renegades running loose. Why do you want to know; if you don't mind my asking?"

"You've been good to me and my young'uns, so, no, sir, I don't mind you asking," she answered. "I'm supposed to meet my husband there," she lied.

"I didn't know you'd heard from your husband."

"I didn't, Mr. Butler. We talked before he left, and he said that if he was not back by the end of the month, for me and the young'uns to go to Cherokee. I just forgot to ask exactly where it was, that's all."

"The name of the town is Canton. That's what you need to ask for, if you get lost along the way. There's a large lake there, called Allatoona by the Indians. It'd be a good place to set up camp, once you get there. Just saying, incase you hadn't thought that far ahead," he said.

"Thank you, Mr. Butler. That's good to know." Charity was thoughtful. "If somehow, we happen to miss one another and Henry shows up here, would you mind letting him know where the children and me were heading."

"Of course, I don't mind, Ma'am. Are you interested in trading that Indian pot you're holding for more supplies?" he asked, noting that Charity was holding the pot that Charles found near the creek. Charity glanced down at the pot she held in the crook of her arm and stepped forward.

"The Indians broke or buried most of the pottery they wouldn't able to take with them. That one looks to be in good shape," Mr. Butler explained.

"Yes, it really is," Charity sighed. "I hate to part with it, but I need some more flour and meal before we set out for Cherokee."

"I'll do you a fair trade for it," the proprietor promised.

"Thank you, Mr. Butler- I greatly appreciate it."

So it was that Charity got the supplies she needed, before she struck out for Cherokee. She knew Mr. Butler gave her much more in trade than the pot was actually worth. For the clay pot, he traded her ten pounds of flour, five pounds of cornmeal, five pounds of dry beans, and a slab of smoke-cured bacon. She would never forget Mr. Butler. He had been very kind to her family.

The children really hated to leave the place that had become like a home to them. They liked exploring the area and looking for treasures; but when their mother explained that they were going to Cherokee Indian country, they became very enthusiastic about leaving, especially the boys.

She lied to them, the same as she had to Mr. Butler; by telling them that their father had told her to meet him there. She didn't like to lie, but she didn't want to tell them the truth- that her grandfather came to her in a dream and told her where to go, and that from her previous experience with dreams of him, that she knew to follow his directions... She didn't feel the children were old enough to understand. It would be several months before she realized that they understood much more than she realized they did.

Lying on her pallet, trying to go to sleep, Charity could hear the lonesome call of a whippoorwill, somewhere in the distant night. She wished she could shush him; his lonesome call was a reminder of how lonesome she was without Henry there. She had also heard the whippoorwill's call just before dark, although he'd been further away. Growing up, her Indian grandmother had told her that hearing a whippoorwill calling before dark meant that someone you know will soon die and you should tie a piece of cloth in a knot to choke off its call of death. And, although she had done this when she heard the whippoorwill, it still preyed upon her mind as she tried to fall asleep, causing her to toss and turn for nearly another hour before she finally dozed.

When she finally slept, she did not know she was sleeping. For she was wandering through the foothills of a strange land of darkness, and in the darkness, she came upon an even darker place, and became lost… It did not matter which way she turned, or how far she went in any direction, there was nothing except the darkness.

In desperation, she called out to her grandfather to help guide her, but there was no response, only her echo's in the darkness. Her own voice returned over and over, calling out her grandfather's name. Still, she called out again and again, but there were only the echoes.

The firm pressure of Uriah's hand on her shoulder, shaking her, woke her.

"Mama, wake up," he said firmly. "You was calling for your grandfather. Why were you calling for him, Mama?" Uriah asked curiously.

"It was just a dream, Uriah. Go back to sleep."

"But Mama, you sounded scared," he said.

"I was scared," she said. "But still, it was just a dream. I was lost in the darkness and I thought he was there, so I was calling for him."

Lila M Beckham

"Why did you think he was there?"

"Because, he comes to me in my dreams and helps guide me. He has, ever since he died. I was about your age when he died.... Now, you need to try and get some sleep. We've got a long, hard day ahead of us tomorrow and every day after, at least for a while."

Uriah lay back down and after a few minutes, she could tell that he was asleep, but for her, sleep was elusive. After awhile, she got up and put coffee on- then she sat down next to the fire and wrote Nancy and Eli a letter. She wanted to let them know that they were all right and was going on to Cherokee. She dared not tell them that Henry had gone off on his own, trying to win land in a lottery. They would be worried about him; her and the children too; especially her and the children, left to fend alone.

As soon as the sun began to rise, she woke the children, fed them and then they packed everything back into the wagons. She and the older boys harnessed the teams and then they struck out, due north, which took them back through town. Charity dropped the letter off, to be mailed when the post ran.

As she was getting back onto the wagon, she saw the two men she'd seen several days earlier; the white man that ogled her and big, hawk-faced Indian.

The white man tipped his hat toward her and smiled his smile she disliked; Charity gave him a hard look, letting him know that she didn't appreciate the way he ogled her- the Indian, gave her a mean, hard look, as if he despised her. I wonder what I ever did to make him dislike me so much, thought Charity as she grabbed the reins, geed to the horses, and then headed her team out of town. Uriah, John, and Charles followed in the second wagon.

Charity hoped to make it at least twenty miles a day. She had cooked a big batch of biscuits and a pan of cornbread. Those, along with some of the sowbelly and the deer jerky they'd made, should sustain them for several days, before she would have to stop earlier in the day, to do some more cooking.

✳✳✳

Over in Walton County, Henry stood with his back to the room, looking out the barred window of his jail cell, feeling sorry for himself. Wishing he could go back and rethink his decision to go off on his own, chasing rainbow dreams of owning free land.

"Why don't you quit feeling sorry for yourself and sit down awhile! Standing, staring out that window, ain't gonna get you outta here any faster. Tomorrow, they're supposed to be taking us over to that Walton County Prison. After a day there, you ain't gonna feel like doing nothing, at least for a week- your ass'll be dragging son. They work ya ta death over there, busting big rocks, down at little pebbles. They get ye up afore daylight, throw some pig-slop in front of you for your breakfast. Then work you till dark thirty, throw some more slop to you for your supper. By then, you try ta sleep, but ye are too tired- it takes a while ta get used to it. It took me nearly a month, the last time, just ta be able ta sleep at night," grumbled the old man.

"Last time," Henry asked. "You mean you done been in there, before?"

"Well, no, not that one; but they's all the same. I done my fair share- been in several of 'em over the years and I can pretty much say, they was all the same," replied the old man.

That night, Henry tossed and turned, worrying about Charity and the children. Although, he didn't have any doubt that she could take care of herself and the young'uns, he knew she didn't have any idea of where he was. She might even think that he was dead... Would she just stay, where he left her? Was it even allowed for her to camp there that long? That might be considered, squatting... As it was, he wouldn't rightly sure what she might do, or where she might go. What if she went back home? What if she went on to Alabama?

Henry stood and looked out the barred window. Slowly, he raised his eyes toward the heavens. "Lord, why did I have to take a swing at that sheriff?" Henry asked aloud.

"Well son, I ain't the Lord," said the old man with a chuckle. "But, I figure you done it because you was tanked up on whiskey!"

"Don't you ever shut up, Old Man?"

"Ain't nothing wrong with talkin', son; it helps ta pass the time a day."

"I'm worried about my family- worried they ain't gonna make it without me..." Henry turned and sat down on the floor and put his head between his knees. The old man gazed over at him and shook his head.

"Ain't much use in worrying, son; they ain't a dang thang you can do about it, as long as ye stuck in here."

Henry slid on down and laid down, almost in a fetal position. Tears of frustration stung his eyes.

"Ain't no use cryin' bout it either, ain't gonna change nuthin'."

Henry sighed.

14

Dancing Rabbit Creek

Having only stopped twice, because she wanted to travel as far as they could that first day, Charity halted the wagons just before dark at what looked to be a good camping spot. It was a nice grassy area in the bend of a good-sized river, which she thought it might be the Oconee River she saw on the map at the mercantile; however, she was not certain if it was; and, she did not know how far they actually traveled that first day.

She had tried to memorize the map at the mercantile, but seeing it on a two foot by three foot map hanging on a wall and actually traveling it, were two entirely different realities.

At first, she tried to stay due north, but it was not possible unless they plunged the wagons off into the river; she opted to follow a well-traveled road that stayed alongside the river- she knew it had to go somewhere important; that was what Henry had done to get them as far as they'd come. He said, "Well-traveled means it goes somewhere."

She and the children immediately began setting up camp. It consisted of getting out the bedrolls, the coffee pot, a frying pan, biscuits, cornbread, and hauling some water up from the river.

She fried a little of the bacon for supper so they could have it with their bread; she had to admit it made a good supper and didn't take that long to prepare, which was good because they were all bone tired, especially the youngest ones. Aaron fell asleep with a bite of biscuit in his mouth and the other two little ones were asleep before their heads hit their pillows. The older young'uns wanted a story before turning in. They loved to listen to the stories their mama told them. She told stories that were passed down from her grandparents, Nancy and Eli, and even some that she had no remembrance of where they came from. The children loved the ones about the Indians the best. So that night, Charity told them the story of her other grandfather; her father's father. His name was Kawa'ha, which was an old name that meant "lost."

His parents had named him this when he was a toddler. He often wandered off on his own and got lost. So the name kind of stuck.

With her five older children sitting cross-legged around the campfire, still eating their supper, Charity began her narrative.

"When Kawa'ha was a young brave, he had to prove his worth as a warrior. This was the custom of most all Indian tribes. Before a male could marry and have the privilege of being called a warrior, they must go out into the wilderness alone to meditate. And, before their return, they must make a brave kill to prove that they could provide for their families and for the tribe.

It was said that Kawa'ha was gone for a long time. At first, they feared he had not survived; but when he returned, he had a tale that most did not believe." Charity looked to her boy's faces as their eyes lit up in anticipation.

"Kawa'ha walked miles from camp, where he came upon a creek that shimmered in the moonlight, as most shimmer in the sunlight. He decided that this would be his place of meditation. He prayed to the Great Spirit to let him prove his worth as a warrior; and, he prayed that he'd make a grand kill, the likes of which had not been done before by his tribesmen.

After meditating through the changing of two whole moons, he said the Great Spirit came to him. The Great Spirit told him to prepare many arrows, to make them with small arrowheads.

When he questioned the Great Spirit as why he should make them so small, the Great Spirit did not reply. "They will not fell a mighty buck," yelled Kawa'ha, rebelling against the Great Spirit's plan. The Great Spirit became angry with Kawa'ha; lightning flashed from the clouds landing at Kawa'ha's feet. Chagrinned, Kawa'ha done as he was told to do. He gathered many fine, straight branches to use as arrows, and then gathered many small, smooth stones from the creek which he sharpened into arrowheads.

Once this task was completed, the Great Spirit said to him, "Now, you must wait by the shimmering creek; be patient, Kawa'ha."

Kawa'ha, again did as he was told. He waited and waited and waited, then began doubting the Great Spirit's plan; however, he knew he could not question the Great Spirit again or he may never prove his worth as a warrior.

After sitting all night, watching the creek, Kawa'ha had grown tired. Just as the sun began to rise, the creek appeared to start dancing, but it was not dancing; it was trembling from the movement of hundreds of rabbits that suddenly appeared out of nowhere- running toward the creek.

Kawa'ha raised his bow and began shooting the arrows he'd made. He shot until he had none left, not even one. When he gathered the rabbits his arrows had pierced, he accounted for them all. He had fifty arrows and now he had fifty rabbits. That would be plenty enough to feed his entire tribe. He knew then why he had to make all the small arrowheads.

The Great Spirit had sent him the rabbits.

When he returned to his people with the freshly killed rabbits and told his story around the campfire, he was marked as a great warrior, and the creek where he killed all the rabbits was named, "Ulisgisgu tsi sdu ama awaya; which is Cherokee for, Dancing Rabbit Creek."

"Jumping Jehoshaphat," said John. "I wish the Great Spirit would send us a bunch of rabbits! I shore could go for some rabbit, fried up or roasted, right about now." The other children laughed.

"It's not nice to poke fun at the Great Spirit," Charity chided. "In one way or another, the Great Spirit provides for us all, and maybe soon, he will provide us with some rabbits."

While telling her story, Charity remembered that her grandmother used to make rabbit snares to catch rabbits. It was an option she had not thought of before, but one that she and the boys could easily accomplish. All they would need was some willow branches and some vines. "We need to get some rest. I want to leave very early in the morning."

"I liked your story, Mama," Charles said. "Maybe one day, I can go off on my own and meditate about being a great warrior…"

Charity looked at her third born son and smiled- his heritage showed as clearly as did her own. His hair was straight and as black as night. His eyes were dark. Not the brown of his fathers, but the black of his Indian ancestors. "You will one day, Son. In my eyes, you're already a great warrior." Charles smiled happily- neither Uriah nor John mentioned wanting to be warriors, but they looked more like their father's people, therefore their mindset might have been more of a white man's intuition than that of an Indian.

She lay for hours it seemed, trying to fall sleep; her mind was traveling everywhere but to sleep land. When the sky to the east pinked, she woke all the children; they were on the road before the sun was up in the sky good. Again, they traveled, until about an hour before dark only stopping twice to let the children stretch their legs and use the bathroom. They again made camp by the river. This day, however, Charity has left the boys setting up camp, while she took the old musket and walked up along the river.

It wasn't long before they heard the "boom" of the old musket. A few minutes later, they heard another boom. Their mother came back toting a rabbit and a squirrel in one hand and her musket in the other. She set the boys to cleaning the wild game while she dug through the wagon for her cooking supplies and frying pan. That night, while they dined on fried rabbit, squirrel, potatoes, and batter bread, fried a golden brown, she told them the story that old Two Feathers had told her about how his eyes came to be the color of the falling snow. After the oohs and aahs over the story, and with full, satisfied stomachs the children soon fell asleep.

Charity cleaned the dishes and put them away, and then got her a clean dress out of the wagon and walked down to the river. The sugar-white sandbar glowed in the moonlight. Quickly, she washed her body in the frigid water, washed her dirty dress and then wrung it out real good before she dried her body and donned the clean clothes. When she returned to the camp, all the children except Charles were asleep; he wanted to know more about the old Indian with eyes the color of falling snow. She lay down beside baby Mary and snuggled her close. She told Charles that she did not know very much about Two Feathers and had only met him that one time in Fort Charlotte.

"I hope I get to meet him one day," Charles whispered excitedly.

"Who knows, maybe you will," Charity mumbled, already

dozing. This night when she lay down and closed her eyes, she immediately went to sleep.

***

Tossing and turning in his bunk, Henry tried to get into a comfortable position; his back and arms ached from swinging the heavy pickaxe all day. Although he swung and busted rocks all day, his mind was on Charity and the children. He had decided that as soon as he caught him a chance to go, he was going to make a run for it. He had the pickaxe; he could easily bust the chains off his ankles and then make a run for the woods.

"I know what you got on your mind boy," said the old man, "and you best not try it. I've seen better men than you, try to escape and fail."

"Well, maybe, they didn't have what I have," said Henry. "I have something worth trying for; my family needs me."

"We've all got something worth trying for, Son, be it a woman or a bottle a whiskey, but that don't mean we can make it outta here," the old man mumbled something that Henry couldn't hear. "They'll hunt you down like a dog; that's if they don't shoot you in the back, whilst you're a running away. Didn't you see those armed guards on horseback- they very proficient with those rifles they's a totin'. You had better give up that notion boy, and try to stay in one piece, til ye time is up. Then, they'll let ye jest walk right on out the gate, and not say a dang word about. I did it several times already, so I know what I'm talking about.

"Here, chew on this willow bark. It'll help ease the pain. I done been in this situation afore; it'll get easier as the days go by. Soon, your appetite will come back and you'll be able to sleep at night. You'll even get use to the hard labor. You'll be lean and as strong as an ox, when you get outta here!"

Right then, Henry wondered if he would even be able to live long enough to get out, surviving on the grub they were feeding them; he'd never had to eat slop like a pig before. He sure hoped that Charity and the children were eating better than he was. He had taught her how to shoot the musket he bought her right after they married; he knew she was a good shot. The boys knew how to fish, but he had not started teaching them to hunt yet... Henry wasn't much of a praying man, but said a prayer, that the Lord would provide for his family in his absence and keep them safe from harm, until he could get back to them.

15

Asgaya Gigagei - Spirit Lightning

Leading the small caravan, Charity was ever watchful for things that might benefit her family or that could place them in danger. So, when she brought her wagon to a halt, Uriah, who was driving the second wagon, also brought his wagon to a halt. After a moment, he stood up to peer over her wagon to see what was holding them up. When he could not see directly in front of her, he hollered, "What's wrong, Mama?"

"Nothing's wrong, son," she hollered back. "The road forks up ahead and I'm trying to decide which way to go."

After studying both roads, Charity then looked toward the sun. The fork to the left, looked more to the north, but she could not see as far down it as she could the other road. She did not know which way to go. "Oh, Grandpa," she sighed. "I wish you had come to me last night?" With a heavy sigh, she yelled, gee-haw to the team to get them started and then turned the team down the road to the left, saying a silent prayer that it was the right way to go.

They traveled for several hours before Charity realized that with each mile they seemed to be getting further and further away from the river. After driving several more hours, and the road still had not rejoined the river, Charity began to worry that they may not find a water source close enough to camp beside. It was a good thing the wooden kegs they kept on the back of the wagon for the stock, were still about half full of water. However, she knew that by the time she watered the stock, there probably wouldn't be much left for her and the children. Just about then, she noticed the vegetation changing to the, tell-tell signs, of water nearby; she was almost certain that in the three days they had been on the road, they had probably covered at least sixty or seventy miles, maybe more. The days were getting longer and the weather was getting warmer; she would have sworn that it had reached nearly seventy degrees that day. It was getting into mid-March; the milder weather should make it easier on her and the children, or at the least, so she thought. When the ground turned sandy and she saw palmettos growing alongside the road, she knew they were near the water; she began looking for a place for them to make camp.

After several more miles, she caught sight of a river shimmering through the trees. She pulled the wagon off the road and down toward the river, so they could set up camp in a small clearing that was next to a thicket of willows. If she failed to kill something with the musket, she and the boys would make several snares and see if they could snag a few of the jackrabbit's that were usually numerous near swamps.

When they finished staking out the teams to graze and

watered them, she figured there was at the least, two good hours of daylight left- Charity told the boys to take their fish traps and go down to the river to see if they could catch some fish for supper. After she fed the baby, she told Martha Jane to watch her and the younger children; she took her musket up river, to see if she could kill a couple of squirrels or rabbits. This is a nice place, thought Charity, as she gazed around; we could stay here a day or two and rest up. She knew the children were restless and they were tired of sitting in the wagons all day and not being able to run and play.

Just before dark, the skies darkened with steel gray clouds; the sound of distant thunder rumbled in the distance. It had been a long time since it had last rained. The ground was as dry as a powder keg; the rain would help settle the dust.

Just before dark, the boys caught several good sized catfish. They hated skinning them; but the meat was some of the best tasting fish you could eat. Charity killed a couple of squirrels and gathered some herbs and a few fresh greens while she was out. The sage and bay leaves she collected would be a great accompaniment to any meat or fish she cooked. The bay leaf was also good flavoring for a pot of stew. She thought she might get up the next morning and start a big pot of browned meat stew and cook a fresh batch of biscuits. The loudness of the thunder jarred her from her reflections. She set about frying the catfish so that they could eat before the rain set in. She told the children that as bad as she hated it, they all were going to have to sleep under the wagons. Even though a storm was imminent, there was just too much stuff packed into the wagons to allow room for any of them.

"We will have to sleep under the wagons tonight; we can't set everything out of the wagons in this weather- it'll ruin. We're going to have to let down the flaps and sleep side by side. The flaps won't keep out any running water, however it looks as if we're in a good spot- it's not too flat here. Y'all hurry up and eat so we can get prepared."

They finished eating and put things away five minutes before the first of the rain started. Charity suspected that it might get rough, but the night ahead, was much worse than she could have ever imagined it would be. Thunder shook the ground; from the vibrations, they could hear things rattling inside the wagons. When the rain let up a moment, the boys came crawling in under the wagon with Charity and the girls.

"Boy, this shore is a mighty bad storm, ain't it, Mama," said Charles.

"Yes, it is Charles. It may calm down in a bit," she said, trying to soothe their fears. However, the storm didn't let up; for hours, lightning popped all around them; she could hear it and feel it when it hit a tree or the ground. The horses were uneasy in the stormy weather; Charity was glad that she had overseen the staking out of the horses; she would hate it if they got loose and ran off. Moments later, they heard a tree splitting as a lightning bolt tore through it. The horses whinnied loudly. The youngest, baby Mary was very scared; Charity could feel her little body trembling when she snuggled her close. Even holding the child tightly against her, she still trembled. Uriah and Charles were peeking out from under the flaps trying to see the storm. Charity wanted to look too, but knew her child needed her close.

"Hey, Mama, look," hollered Uriah, of course she had to look to see what he was hollering about. When they peeked out from under the flaps of the wagon, they saw blue lightning, dancing around on the ground.

The lightning floated just above the grass. It rolled and twirled above the ground as if it were the sound of music generated by an orchestrated symphony. It would roll and swirl right up to the wagons, and then it would run and twirl in the opposite direction. The horses sounded as if they were going crazy; she could hear them stomping their feet and jerking at the ropes that were tied to a guy wire that was stretched between two elm trees. Again, she prayed they didn't get loose.

"Why is the lightning doing that?" Several children wanted to know.

"It is the "Asgaya Gigagei," said Charity, remembering a tale her grandmother had told her when she was a small child.

"Nokomis said that blue lightning came from the Lightning Spirit. She said the Lightning Spirit will send it to dance around you, while judging your character; he also uses it to test your courage. If you are brave, he will let you live, but if you are afraid, lightning will strike. So you must not be afraid," she told them.

"But, I am scared, Mama; I can't help it!" Little, Nancy's voice trembled as she said it; therefore, Charity knew that she was truly frightened.

"It's all right Nancy, you are young; the Spirit recognizes that. You will not be judged harshly until you have reached the age of knowledge."

"Have I reached the age of knowledge," several of the children asked at the same time.

"No, not yet," Charity answered. "Not yet."

∗∗∗

In Walton County, Henry felt beaten down and defeated. The seemingly endless days of swinging the heavy pickaxe and worrying about his family were taking a toll on him. He was so depressed that he did not want to get out of bed, much less follow orders, which led to him getting pushed around by the guards, who were quick with a kick or a punch to the kidneys.

The old man tried talking to him and gigging him to get him to get with the program and do what was expected of him. "If you don't get yer ass in gear, Son, they gonna be toting you out in a pine box and a burying ye out back!"

"Maybe I'd be better off in a pine box, anyways," mumbled Henry.

"Keep it up and you want ever see that family or yourn again!"

Henry grumbled and rolled over to face the wall. While he slept, Charity came to him in a dream. She lay cuddled in his arms and whispering in his ear. At first, he could not hear what she was saying, but then he began to hear and understand her whispered words of encouragement and her endearments of love. She told him that he must be strong; that she and the children were fine, and that she was on her way to a place high in the mountains. And, when the time came for them to be together again, he would find them in a place called Cherokee. Before she left, she made gentle love to him, kissed and caressed his sore aching body. He woke to the feel of her naked body pressed against his, but when he tried to embrace her body, she was no longer there. Was it just a dream, he wondered; it seemed so real. It felt real... The feel of her body pressed against his and her words of encouragement lingered in his thoughts as he drifted back to sleep.

When Henry awoke the next morning, he jumped right up; the old man could see a big difference in his cellmate. Henry got up with a new mindset as to how he was going to serve out the rest of his time. Like the old man said, the better he followed orders and conducted himself, the better off he was going to be. He had to make it through this in order to return to his family whole, not broken and beaten down; he needed to be able to properly support his family.

He was physically weakened from the days of hard work and not eating. When the guards brought their breakfast, Henry tore into the slop like a starving hog. He had decided he would eat everything they put in front of him in order to keep up his strength; he would need that strength; moreover, Charity and the children would need that strength!

16

Dewa's: Better known as flying squirrels

With the feel and taste of Henry's lips still lingering upon hers, Charity stretched lazily and smiled. Was it really just a dream, she wondered; she could almost feel his arms holding her tight. His touch seemed so real, as did her floating through the night winds going to where Henry was. It felt as if she were flying, gliding through the night winds as if she were an eagle.

When Charity pulled back the canvas flap to crawl out from under the wagon, she was surprised to see the sun had been up at least an hour!

"Oh Lord, I'm being lazy this morning," she mumbled aloud. She hadn't slept this late since she was a young child. *It must've been the late night, combined with the rain, the wonderful dream, and then the darkness underneath the wagon that let me sleep so soundly.*

After she crawled from under the wagon, all the children started waking up and crawling out from underneath the wagon. All were rubbing the sleep out of their eyes, stretching and yawning. When they looked to their mother, they saw that Charity was facing toward the river, studying it.

Suddenly, she turned toward them and asked, "Did you boys remember to tie the fish traps off to a tree, before you left them yesterday?"

"O'course we did, Mama," answered Charles, "we ain't stupid you know."

"I never said y'all were stupid, Charles- I was just looking at how the river is overflowing the banks down there; that was a lot of rain last night- the river is half-way up to where we are. I'm glad y'all remembered to tie them off. We didn't lose them to the flood, but we won't be able to get to them until the water recedes; that might take awhile."

The children all looked toward the river.

"We need to see if we can find some more firewood boys. I don't think the wood ya'll gathered up and put inside the wagon yesterday, is going to be enough to cook a pot of stew and a fresh batch of biscuits."

"Oh boy," exclaimed Aaron. "I've wanted stew for days and days, Mama!"

"Days and days, huh," Charity smiled. Several of the other children chimed in with, "me too, Mama."

"Well, if the Lord's willing and this water doesn't rise any higher, we will have a pot of stew before the day is over- that is, if we can find enough dry firewood to cook it." Several of the children took off toward the woods to look for firewood.

"Mama," yelled Uriah.

When she heard him yell, Charity turned to see that Uriah

was down toward the river; she figured his yelling for her had something to do with the fish traps or firewood, but as she went toward him, she could see that he was very excited about something and sensed that it had nothing to do with fish traps or dry kindling.

When she reached him, Uriah excitedly pointed toward an old dead tree that had toppled down during the storms of the past night. "Look Mama! What are they, Mama," he asked.

"Oh my," she exclaimed in a whisper. "I haven't seen any of those in years! They're called Dewa's; they are flying squirrels."

Charity smiled, remembering the tiny gray squirrel she toted around in her pocket when she was a little girl. She had named him, "Gulega", which meant Climber. By now, all of the children had gathered behind her and Uriah.

"Can we catch one, Mama?"

"Sure we can," she replied, "they make excellent pets. Go get one of the small blankets from the wagon and we'll try to catch several of them." All of the children were easing pass Charity, trying to get a glimpse of the tiny dewas.

"If I'm going to stand a chance to catch any of them, y'all must be very quiet and not get too close yet," she whispered. "Dewas have very good ears and can hear really well." The children stopped and turned to look at her.

"I will show you older boys how to catch one and then, it will be your turn to catch one; but I must warn you," she whispered hurriedly, emphasizing her next words, "Go after the smallest ones; they will be easier to catch and tame, and they don't bite nearly as hard as the older ones do. I know they all look tiny, but some are fully grown, and some are not."

She then told them all to stand back as she took the blanket Mary had brought her and eased toward the felled tree. Some dewas that had been on the ground hunting food, had run back to the tree and into the holes in it, where their nests were. That is, all but a few, whose nests must've been on the side that landed on the ground. She saw at least six to eight of them that were huddled down against small broken branches of the rotted tree.

Two dewas huddled close together, beside a small limb; they had sensed her nearness and were trying to hide. She threw the blanket over them, then grabbed it, and swept them up, limb and all. She took them to where the children waited. "I want one, Mama," begged Aaron. She told him to open his shirt pocket. She reached her hand into the bundled blanket, felt around, and caught the smaller one; it was squirming, but did not bite her. She put it into his pocket, keeping her hand over it to calm the tiny animal within.

"What do I do, Mama?" he asked.

"Keep your pocket buttoned, and for a while, you'll need to cup your hand like this, and hold it over him to keep him calm. Just be gentle with your touch when you rub him; you can also talk to him," she told him. "He will come to enjoy your touch, and your pocket will become his new home."

She gave the bigger of the two dewas, to Martha Jane and

Nancy, telling them that they would have to share it and tame it together. She had her reasons for wanting them to work together and share in the care and taming of the dewa. She felt it would bring out their motherly instincts and teach them to be more compassionate. Then, she helped the older boys catch them one. She told all the children that their dewa would be their responsibility to take care of, and that they needed to gather up foodstuffs, like small nuts, berries, and seeds for the squirrels- "Don't forget that they also need water to drink," she told them, "they become thirsty just the same as you and I do."

After all the flying squirrel catching was over, Charity started the pot of stew for their supper. They ate the leftover fish from the night before, along with some buttered grits, for breakfast; it would hold them over until the stew was ready and the stew would be enough to feed them the rest of the day. She had decided that where they were camped was a good place to stay a few days.

After breakfast, she left Uriah in charge of watching over the younger children and also with helping Martha Jane keep an eye on the pot of stew, while she took one of the smaller horses and rode him barebacked up the road, to take a look around the area.

About a mile and a half up from where they had camped, she came to a spot where the river crossed the road; what appeared to be a structure of some sort, maybe a covered bridge or something, was visible on the other side of the channel. It could have been an outbuilding from a farm forced into the river by the force of so much rain falling at once…

Seeing the water over the road, Charity gauged the depth of the rising river, by marking a spot on the structure with a tree on shore. From living near the Savannah River all her life, she knew that once the river crested, it would eventually begin to recede. How long that took; depended on how much rain had fallen upriver. She decided she would ride back later that afternoon to see how much higher the water had risen, or hopefully, receded by then.

Riding back to camp, she saw fresh tracks where a deer had crossed the road. She would come back later and see if she could kill one. If so, it would supply them with meat for a long while if she could preserve it.

After checking on the children and the stew, she and John walked down to the river's edge to see if they could see the boy's fish traps. She'd hate for them to lose them after all the hard work they'd put into making them. Of course, they could make more, but those were special because they were the first they'd done on their own.

One of the traps was barely visible, bobbing up and down, about fifteen feet out from the bank. Their camp was a good hundred yards above the river and Charity was pretty sure it was safe to stay put; however, she was worried about how they would ford the river, if that structure she saw torn apart and floating in the river, was the bridge that use to go across it.

"I can swim out there and get that trap," said John. "All's I got to do it cut the rope and haul it back to the bank."

"Don't let the water fool you," she told him, "just because it is up in the trees along the bank and looks pretty calm, it is still very dangerous- the undercurrent can be very swift and sweep you under, entangling you in the underbrush so that you'd drown. Don't ever go into a river or creek that is rain-gorged- Grandpa taught me that when I was a child. He said he had a friend that drowned in such a situation."

John was solemn and quiet- apparently he was thinking of what she'd said; he nodded his head but didn't say anything. After a minute or so, they turned and went back to camp.

When the stew was done, Charity fried up some cornmeal fritters to go with it for their supper. The bay leaf added a wonderful flavor addition to the rabbit stew. For an added bonus, because of having a good day and catching dewas, she made a gallon of sweetened sassafras tea to drink with their supper. An hour after dark, the children were all fast asleep, with their bellies fully satisfied, but Charity wasn't asleep; she was restless- She got up and walked down to the edge of the river. Overhead, the moon was round and bright- its reflection wavered eerily in the water that flowed around the trunks of the birch trees along the bank. She sat down on a log, closed her eyes, and thought about Henry. In her mind, she went to him and told him about their day and how much the children were enjoying the place where they were camped.

***

Lying on his bunk, Henry was having a wonderful dream. In his dream, Charity and the children were running and playing along the banks of a river; their smiling faces warmed his heart. Just as he focused on Charity's face and was walking toward her, someone banging on the bars of the cell he shared with the old man awakened him. It was time to get up and go back to work.

Henry sighed heavily. The old man, whose name he learned, was Jeremiah McClure, had been sick for several days; Henry had been trying to do the work of both he and the old man and it was getting the best of him.

Jeremiah, he learned, had been born in St. Augustine, Florida. He said that his folks had come to the Americas from Ireland, as indentured servants. When Henry questioned him about his raising and how he came to be where he was, the old man seemed to welcome the chance to talk about it.

"My first memory of childhood," he said, "was picking up scraps off the floor, from around the master's kitchen table, and eating them."

He said that his mother was too scared to hand him anything to eat, for fear she would be accused of stealing it and be punished; therefore, she'd drop things while she was working so that he could pick them up and eat them- "I didn't mind it a-tall; it filled my stomach and sometimes she'd even drop a little sweet-cake. I reckon my folks was good, honest, hard-working folks," he said. "I surely would be ashamed for my pa to see me now," added Jeremiah.

"How old are you anyway, old man?" Henry had asked.

"I was born, right afore the Revolution," he said. "I'm gonna be sixty-eight come June, if the good Lord's a willing, that is."

"For a promise of freedom, my old man fought in that there war, but he never lived to see his freedom; he was kilt in 1779 during the siege of Savannah; I was four years old. I don't remember him a'tall, but I was always proud of him for what he done, bringing my maw over here the way he did and all- Conditions was bad being a servant, but she said they was much worse where they'd come from…

"After my pa died, Maw was released from servitude- but we didn't have nowhere ta go. Folks weren't hiring servants; they could get all the indentured servants or slave labor they needed. After a spell working the streets, she got in with a no good piece a shit, bastard that beat her daily- and even though I was just a little feller, he beat me too; I reckon just for the hell of it, or because I took up space and breathed air. For a long time, I held those beatings he give me against my maw, never intending to forgive her- I even had it in my young mind that she was responsible for my pa a dying- I didn't figure it out until I was gone from there… I reckon she'd be dead by now…

"As soon as I was big enough to hold my own agin him, I decided I wouldn't gonna take no more beatin's - I put a knife in his gizzard and left him lying on the floor in a pool of his own blood. Even after I gutted him, that sum-bitch was still a trying ta git up… I been on the run ever since," he finished.

Even though he was a man, Henry had never been around anyone who used as much colorful language as Jeremiah did, but he didn't mind it too much- As a matter of fact, he was growing quite fond of the old man. That was why he had taken on his share of the work. Jeremiah was becoming like a grandfather to him. He had looked after Henry when Henry was sick; and, when he was down, he had encouraged him to keep moving, to keep fighting to stay alive… He was also good company to have around. And, Henry really needed a friend…

17

Wind Walker

With the barrel of her musket propped firmly on the limb of a tree, Charity took steady aim at the deer. The medium-sized buck was grazing at the edge of a thicket of wax myrtles, near where she saw the deer tracks the day before. John and Uriah were squatting in the bushes behind her. She had brought them along to help with the bleeding out of the deer, should she kill one, and to help her carry it back to camp. They could then dress it out and help her prepare the meat for making jerky and so forth. She also hoped to can some of the meat in jars so that it would last a lot longer. She was glad that Nancy had shown her how and taught her how to preserve food in glass jars- it was much better than having to dry it all into tough leather strips… Taking careful aim, Charity squeezed the trigger, while saying a quick prayer that the bullet would hit its mark. She was worried that she wasn't close enough to the deer, but if she had tried to get any closer, the deer would have seen her and ran off into the woods.

The old musket was not very accurate at far distances, and she really needed this kill in order to keep her children fed. Once preserved, the meat would last them a good while.

It took the black smoke a good minute to clear. Even before it cleared, she heard John exclaim, "You got him, Mama!"

"I knew she would," said Uriah.

"Alright, boys," she chuckled, "We got him; now, let's bleed him out and carry him back to the camp."

When they got back to camp, they dressed out the deer; she cooked up a good bit of the meat that day, putting it into jars and sealing them with wax the way Nancy taught her to. The rest of the meat was packed in salt brine water so the next day she could smoke it. She told the boys to take the ax and go see if they could find a few hickory limbs to use for smoking the meat.

The children enjoyed playing with their little flying squirrels; the tiny critters were becoming tame and no longer tried to jump out of their hands. When she last checked the road near the river, the water had risen a good two feet. She hoped that the river crested soon, or else she may have to move their camp. She could not go forward, because the road was under water, and she darn sure didn't want to go back to where she had come from. She also didn't want to get too far off the trail, because she feared they may get into trouble.

All the children seemed to be fine and healthy, however, the last day or so, Charity had been feeling kind of poorly. She wasn't exactly sure what was wrong with her- she felt awfully tired and had to lie down before dark. She told the older boys to watch the little ones and to make sure all of them were under the wagons before dark. She could tell they were worried, probably because they had never seen their mother sick before. She could not remember ever being sick, except once or twice as a child…

For hours, or maybe it was days, Charity wasn't really sure- she was barely conscious of anything except the vague whispers of her children and of Uriah trying to get her drink to something. She dreamed that she was running from the river, but the water kept catching up to her and pulling her under. It was so real that she could feel the water burning her nostrils and filling her ears and lungs. As she fought against the rising water, a giant eagle suddenly scooped her out of the water. In its talons, she hung as limp as a rag doll. The tree tops, brushed against her body, tearing at her flesh and her clothes as he flew- Suddenly, he dove downward and she thought that he might land, but then he flew upward, higher and higher into the sky, carrying her along with him as he soared.

After coughing the water out of her lungs, Charity called out to the eagle, asking him, "Where are you taking me, Mighty One?" He answered that he would show her the secret of her gift.

"What secret- what gift?"

"It will soon be the moment of the Equinox," said the eagle. "You will walk upon the wind. Your spirit shall leave your body and travel within the parallel dimensions of place and time. The wind will take you wherever you want."

"But, this cannot be- it is not possible!"

"Ah, but it is possible, little one," said the eagle. "Your gift has many possibilities- It has happened many times before. Now, you must learn to guide your spirit when it leaves its earthly body behind."

"How?"

Ignoring her question, the eagle asked, "Where shall we go?"

"Are you my grandfather?"

"Yes," he answered. "I am, Adastiyuali Tsitsalagi!"

She knew that he said, "I am Shooting Arrow, I am Cherokee!" Shooting Arrow was her maternal great-grandfather, he was a Medicine Man, or a Shaman as some prefer to call. She remembered Shadowy Moon, her Nokomis, speak of her maternal grandfather; his name was Shooting Arrow! Suddenly, she felt as light as an eagle's feather. High above the mountains, they soared through the air- the eagle's talons, no longer held her; she soared alongside her great-grandfather, Shooting Arrow, the mighty eagle.

Her first instinct was to travel home.

In an instant, she soared over the Savannah River and over the old cabin she shared with her grandparents. Tokola come out into the moonlit night to stand in the clearing. His head back, eyes staring up into the night sky, he smiled a large smile. With fisted-hands raised toward the heavens, he shouted, "Galieliga, Eladildasdi'nole, galieliga!"

What he said was, "I am happy, Wind Walker, I am happy!"

When the Yellow Mocker Calls

Swooping low, she dusted him with love before turning south. Soon, she was gliding over Eli's and Nancy's cabin, but they did not know it was her- they only saw an eagle. Henry suddenly came into her thoughts- to him she flew. When she reached him, she saw him lying on a cot; it was the same as her dream a few days before. "Oh, Henry," she sighed. "My poor darling- he looks so tired. I know I shouldn't wake him, but I need him so much.

She lowered herself gently to his side and cradled him in her arms. Ever so gently, she kissed his forehead, his eyes, his neck, and then his mouth. He returned her kisses, gently at first, savoring the taste of her lips and then becoming urgent, needing. Gently, she made love to him; her own body as urgent and needing as his- she kissed him deeply, passionately, her lips and fingertips, lingering on his face. It was now the month of the Windy Moon, she felt a cool breeze float over her naked body; it causes her to shiver. With one last, gentle, lingering kiss, she left him- his lips still pursed in a kiss…

She walked the wind again, this time, soaring back to where her children lay beneath the wagons; most were sleeping. She saw herself writhing in agony, filled with sickness; she could not let her body die- After lowering her spirit back into her body, she slowly woke. No longer sick; her spirit felt strong, renewed. Rising to her knees, she crawled out from under the wagon. After stoking the fire, she started breakfast. The children would love some batter-bread pancakes for breakfast; some of the coveted butter and syrup atop them would be a special treat. She also fried the last of the slab of bacon- she wished she had some eggs and buttered grits to go with it. Moments like this, made her wish she was at home with Nancy.

As Charity gazed across the field, away from the river, she saw tiny flowers opening up, reaching for the morning sun. Yes, spring is here…

***

When Henry woke, he could still feel her lips, upon his flesh. Still taste her, smell her scent; slowly, he opened his eyes. Disappointment filled him- he was still in the prison- he heard the old man chuckle.

"What are you laughing about you old coot?"

"You, that's who, Lawd have mercy that must've been one hell of a dream, you was having," said the old man.

"Whatdayamean?" Henry asked

"When I woke up awhile ago, you was all puckered up, and had a big ole smile on your face."

Before Henry could respond to Jeremiah's gigging him, the guards started banging on the bars with their small head-knockers. Henry jumped out of bed, he too felt rejuvenated and content. He didn't question why; he knew why; it was because Charity had come to him. Even though they were miles apart, she had found a way to be with him.

Cheerfully, Jeremiah said, "Ye better eat your slop and use

the pot boy; we got a lot of big rocks ta bust inta little rocks, today."

Henry was glad the old man was feeling better. He would hate it if something were to happen to him. The prison had them clearing a swath of land twenty feet wide of rocks, underbrush, and trees, in order to build roads. To Henry, it seemed that he and the old man was the target of most of the swift pops of the whip that came from the head guard, Jack Wright.

The old, fat and lazy head-boss-guard, Jack Wright, was always sitting in a buggy with a whip in his hand, watching them as they worked. He was quick to slap it across some poor, souls back every now and then, and he was constantly preaching about how, 'This country's a growing, and they're going to need good roads to get where they're a going.'

On this day, he was in an even more 'slap the whip' mood than usual. Henry wished he could pop him just one good time with that whip of his, just to show him how it felt to be whipped.

What Henry couldn't see were the scars underneath old Jack Wright's coat. Scars that no one had ever seen, except his wife, his ex-master, who also happened to be his father, and that damn Yankee overseer his father employed to keep his niggers whipped into shape… Yeah, Jack Wright knew what the whip felt like; that was why he'd kept it with him all these years and probably why he liked to use it- The last time he'd felt it, was thirty-five years past- It was the day he jerked it out of that Yankee overseer's hand and whacked his head off with his cane cutting machete. It was the day he took leave of his father's plantation and struck out along the Mississippi River, putting as many miles as possible between him and his misfortune of being born to a quadroon woman instead of a white one on Samuel Wright Parker's plantation.

Yeah, he'd left all that behind him, choosing the surname of Wright over his previous Parker surname. He had never returned to Louisiana nor did he plan to. There, it didn't matter if you appeared to be as white as the driven snow- if you have just one drop of Negro blood, you're considered, a "nigger" and the property of a white man...

18

Jack Wright's Old Place

On the night of the crescent moon, there were only two visible stars. They shined brightly, flickering back and forth as if they were communicating with one another; almost like lovers, flirting, thought Charity as she lay watching them. A deep void cavitied within her soul; it would only etch deeper as the days passed. She was sure that Henry should have found them by then.

After waiting nearly a week for the water to recede far enough for them to proceed, they were finally able to continue their journey. They had traveled and camped another week and still had not come to a town or a settlement. She was very much afraid that she would completely run out of supplies before they found another town where she might replenish them… The last several days, all they'd had to eat was squirrel meat, fish, and what few edible greens she gathered along the way. There was very little in the way of flour, meal, or other necessities she needed to feed her children well.

The previous night, she had walked the winds again, lying in Henry's arms as long as she could; it helped ease her loneliness and strengthened her, but traveling alone with just the children was beginning to take its toll on her nerves. And now, today, she was faced with another trial- how was they to cross this damned creek that was in the middle of a swamp!

They had run out of passable road nearly a week back, and had been blazing their own trail through the underbrush. The road they were on had crossed the river, but where there must've once been a bridge, now was only pilings. She had immediately thought of the structure she'd seen in the river after the flood. She'd be damned if she was going to turn around and go back the way they had come, so they blazed forward. Every time they encountered an obstacle, she'd had to find a place for both wagons to cross. At the end of the day, it was up to her to make camp, feed her children, and make sure they were all safe. So far, she'd managed, but this obstacle in front of her seemed impassable- it was the first time they'd come to a creek surrounded by a swamp the size of this one- she doubted she'd be able to cross it without help...

Exploring the area, checking to see if she could find another way through it, she stepped across the slow moving creek only to have her boot sucked off her foot by the thick mud and aquatic plant life. If it does this to me, I can imagine what it would do to the horses and the wagons, thought Charity. However, the trees and undergrowth were not quite as thick here was she was. The surrounding area was marshy and reeked of dead, decaying leaves left over from the fall and winter months as spring etched its way into summer.

As she explored further, she saw that most of the ground was covered with thick, green moss that when she stepped on it felt like a thick padded rug beneath her feet. *This moss might prevent sinking too deep.* Wisteria vines frapped the trees; a gray haze hung heavily over the forest. After she crossed the creek and made it through the swamp to where the forest ended, she took a look around; she let out an enormous sigh of relief. Smoke, rising from a chimney, whose top was barely visible over a hill to the west, was a welcome sight. Hurriedly she crossed the creek and excitedly told the children what she saw.

The creek she had been so afraid of crossing for fear that they might get the wagons stuck, did not give them any trouble at all; they crossed the creek with hardly any effort at all. The children were excited, and became even more so as the small band made their way toward the distant smoking chimney.

About two o'clock in the afternoon, they topped the hill and she could see that the smoke wasn't coming from a chimney in a town as she first thought; momentarily, she felt disappointed. However, her disappointment didn't last long when she realized that it was actually a good-sized farmhouse and that it had several outbuildings as well as pastures and a large garden area. Usually, wherever there was a farm, there should be a town somewhere nearby, at least within a day's ride…

As she drove the wagon toward the farm, Charity wondered just exactly where they were and how much further they would need to go to reach the place called Cherokee. She pulled the team to a halt in the driveway, about fifty feet from the main house.

A woman of small stature, but broad of hip, came out onto the porch. In her hands, she carried a musket that was nearly as long as she was tall. After looking them over for a minute, she must've decided they weren't a threat; she set the gun down and leaned it against the door frame; still within reach.

"What brings you folks out to these parts?" asked the woman.

Charity, explained that they were on their way to Cherokee.

"Well, you folks done got off the trail a little ways," the woman informed her. "This here is Walton County, Georgia-Cherokee is northwest of here, probably another hundred miles or so. You're welcome to set up camp and stay awhile. My husband is at the prison, he works there. He won't be home til the end of the month. There's hay and grain for the horses out yonder in the barn… We don't get much call to socialize too often out here in this godforsaken wilderness. I'd appreciate the company."

Thankful for the invitation, Charity left the boys to unhitching the wagons under a large oak tree while she went inside to talk to the woman of the house. She soon learned that the creek they just crossed, was called Sandy Creek, and that they would still have to cross the Alculachee River and the Yellow River before getting into Cherokee County. The woman's name was Marilee Wright.

"Since I wasn't expecting company for supper, I'll just have to whip up a batch of bacon, eggs, taters, and catheads for your supper," said Marilee.

"Ma'am, I don't want you to feel obligated to feed me and my young'uns but you just don't know how good that sounds; we haven't had eggs or bacon in nearly a month, and its been much longer since we've had any potatoes."

"Well, as you could probably tell from the smell of all those pig waller's out there, I got plenty of bacon- bacon, sausage, ham, jowls, and nearly any other part of the pig you'd want to eat."

"You wouldn't think it to look at 'em, but my young'uns eat well and they can eat a lot," said Charity.

"Well, they're a growin' and needs a lot- don't you worry, I got plenty… speaking of children, they sure are a quiet bunch."

"That's because they know they better behave." The children had finished their assigned tasks and were sitting on the front porch, waiting politely.

Marilee walked back out onto the front porch where they were at and told the boys that they were welcome to do some exploring around the farm. "I had better not hear y'all a hell-hacking the animals, though. If I do, I'll be out here with a limb to your butts. Y'all understand that?"

"Yes 'um," they replied simultaneously. They could tell by the tone of her voice and the stern look in her eye that she meant business. They took off running, anxious to look around the farm

and explore. "You girls want to follow the
come inside with your ma and me?" Of
go inside. Marilee handed one of ther
dust rag and told them to make ther
baby Mary.

Marilee made a pot of coffee and she and Charity
kitchen sipping coffee, sweetened with cream, as they peeled the
potatoes for supper. Mary sat on the floor and played with dust
particles that floated in the streams of sunlight that came in
through the windows; for the time being, Charity was content. It
was wonderful to be in a place that had a roof over it and to have
another woman to talk to; Marilee was a great conversationalist.

When Marilee suddenly asked, "Where's your man," It
caught Charity by surprise; she didn't want to admit that she
didn't know exactly where Henry was, and although she hated to
lie, she fibbed a little by saying, "He's in Cherokee. He went
ahead of us to get us some land they're giving away in the land
lottery, so he's waiting on us to join him."

"Shucks," grumbled Marilee. "The government has been a
giving away those Indians land, left and right. They are trying to
get folks to settle down hereabouts; the bad thing about it is all
them Indians ain't gone yet. Some of them are hidden out in the
mountains. You and those young'uns will be traveling right
through the middle of them on your way to Cherokee. "

"They're not really savages, though, are they?"

"Depends on what you call savages," said Marilee.

Lila M Beckham

ing to change the subject, Charity asked, "What about
ss Marilee; how do you make it with your husband
ng off from home like he does. I know it has to be hard
h him being gone so long and all?"

"Nah, not so much… he may only come once a month, but
he sends me help in the form of a prisoner or two at least once a
week. They come out and does whatever work needs doing, stuff
that I ain't able to do myself. Or don't want to do," she chuckled,
"You know the heavy stuff, like butchering, plowing and planting
and sech as that."

"With a place this size, I would have figured that you'd
own a few slaves to help take care of it."

"Noam; the mister hadn't never took to owning niggras.
Besides, we don't need 'em; the prison is never empty, so we
have prisoners out here year round. They're free labor- it helps us
and it helps the prison. Most of the stuff that's grown out here is
sold to the prison…"

"You aren't afraid, being out here alone with the
prisoners?"

"Shucks, no," said Marilee. "He only sends prisoners that
ain't dangerous, and while they're out here, he sends an armed
man to watch over 'em; mainly, to keep them from running off.
All of 'em seems to enjoy it- I cook them a big tasty meal-
something they ain't used to getting- Before the day is over with,
they're really respectful - they'll do whatever I need them to do. "

It was nice in Marilee's house, but after learning where she was and how much further she needed to go, Charity was anxious to be on her way. She enjoyed the good food, the soft bed, and the wonderful warm bath and head-washing she had, as did the children. Marilee was great company; she fed them well and seemed to be genuinely worried about their welfare, but Charity was determined that they only spend a couple of days at Marilee's.

Marilee also seemed to really enjoy having the children there. Charity was finally bold enough to ask her if she'd ever had any children. Marilee shook her head, saying that when she and the Mister first married, she had one child and then a year later had another- both died shortly after birth. She said of course it was just her and her husband- he helped with the delivery, but the children died right after being born.

"He buried them before I could see them. He said that seeing the babies would only make it harder for me to let go of them… I reckon he was right," said Marilee. "It would have been hard to bury my babies if I had gotten to hold them… After the second one died, the mister started staying away from me- he said he didn't want to cause me and undue worry or pain- I tried to change his mind, but he was determined that we quit trying. The mister seems alright with it, and after a couple of years, it was fine with me, too- I never did like all that intimate stuff."

Charity felt sorry for Marilee- sorry for the loss of her babies, and sorry that she might never know how wonderful those intimate moments could be…

Lila M Beckham

The next day, when they began loading the wagon with the supplies Marilee had given them, Charity thought Marilee was going to cry- she felt sad for Marilee, but she was anxious to be on the trail.

Marilee had given them plenty of supplies, including several chickens and a rooster so they could have fresh eggs on the trail. Charity and the boys had to build a coup and strap it on the back of one of the wagons, to hold the chickens…

"Growing young'un's needs eggs to eat," said Marilee, "it might take those chickens a while to start laying regularly; they'll get used to moving and eventually start laying," She said that her mother and father had done that when she was a little girl when they moved from Virginia to South Carolina.

Once the wagons were loaded, she and the children each gave Marilee a hug and then climbed aboard. When they reached the end of the driveway, she headed in horses in the direction Marilee told her to go. Standing on her porch, Marilee waved to them as they left- Charity looked back once she reached the road; she saw that Marilee still stood on the porch, watching them go- For a brief moment, she felt an urge to turn and go back- but she brushed the feeling aside, she needed to keep going.

***

Finished for the day, Henry and Jeremiah were sitting around the bonfire, exchanging stories of what led up to their current predicament. Henry told Jeremiah that before the day he got locked up, he had never in his life drank whiskey; never even had the desire to drink.

"My paw ain't a drinking man," said Henry, "but I did see some drunken men down in Fort Charlotte a couple of times over the years, they were whooping and a hollering... It looked like they was a having a good ole time, same as you did that day... I reckon that might've been why I drunk it. I was feeling about as low as a snakes belly the day you offered me that jug. I reckon I took that first swig, thinking it'd make things better."

"I know what it's like boy; I had me a wife once too," said Jeremiah. "She was a pretty little thing. I found her up in Tennessee. Her pa owned a trading post, in a little settlement high on a bluff overlooking the Mississippi River. That little settlement is now known as Memphis.

"We soon married and I dragged her off to Missouri with me. The year was 1802. I was a young buck and wanted to join in on the movement west... my wife ended up dying about a year and a half later, when a yellow fever outbreak occurred in a place called, Cape Girardeau. She died first... then a couple of days later, the baby died- it might've made it if I'd a knowed how to take care of it..." his voice drifted off and he was lost in his remembrances...

They had been sitting there, quietly enjoying the night, when a guard named Flanagan, come walking up to them. He told them that they had been chosen by the boss to go out to the

Wright farm the next day. They were to do the chores that needed doing and bring back some supplies to the prison. He said that he would be taking them out there, and that they needed to go ahead and hit the sack because they were leaving at first light.

"Yes sir, Mr. Boss Man, sir!" Jeremiah said smartly. "We'll be up and ready with bells on our toes, ready ta go."

Flanagan gave him a dirty look, then turned and walked away…

19

Shape Shifter

Charity and the children left Marilee's amid warm hugs and wishes for a safe journey. The girls, especially, were reluctant to leave. They enjoyed being at Marilee's, having the luxuries of a roof over their heads and not stuck riding in a wagon all day. Charity figured that being there, reminded them of being at home with Nancy. Right away, Marilee had taken them under her mother-hen wing, by giving them chores to do and then she took them into the kitchen with her to *help* her cook. The boys weren't mopey at all- they were raring to go; they enjoyed camping out and being on the trail. To them, it was a grand adventure. The last couple of years, the older boys had gone with their father and grandfather to check the traps. And, they had even gotten to go to Fort Charlotte a time or two. But the girls had always been right up under her and their grandmother, Nancy; therefore, they had become little homebodies.

Charity drove the teams pretty hard that first day, trying to make up some of what she felt was lost time. They had to make camp that night without the benefit of a creek or river nearby. Charity was glad they had filled the water barrels before leaving

Marilee's; at least she had water for the stock and for them to drink. By the time she stopped to set up camp, the children were bone-tired and so was she; she was glad she didn't have to cook. Marilee had fried several chickens and packed them some beans and biscuits to go with it. They filled their bellies and were asleep, before it was good and dark out.

Charity awoke just before daybreak to the sound of a wolf's howl. She was used to all sorts of wild critters, but there was something about a wolf's howl, that always gave her an eerie feeling. She peeked out from under the wagon flap, but it was so dark that she couldn't see five feet in front of her. She decided to wait a little while to get up to use the bathroom and make coffee.

As soon as day broke, Charity crawled out from under the wagon and headed to stoke up the fire so that she could make her coffee. She hadn't gone ten feet when she comes face to face with an older Indian man. She let a small gasp escape, but other than that she was too stunned to even speak much less scream for help. He looked at her strangely, then turned, dropped down on all fours, and ran away, turning into a wolf as he went! For some reason, unknown even to her, in that moment, she yelled, "Come back!"

When she yelled, all the children came crawling out from under the wagons, asking, "What's wrong, Mama?"

"It's nothing," she said. "I must have still been asleep and dreaming."

"You weren't dreaming, Mama," exclaimed Aaron, "I saw

him too!"

Good, she thought to herself. At least, I'm not going crazy...

"Exactly what'd you see?" asked Uriah.

"It was an Injun; he got down on all fours and turned into a wolf!"

"Did that really happen, Mama?" asked several of the children.

"Yeah, I reckon it did. Me and Aaron both saw it- him," she replied.

"What was he, some sort of wolfman?" Charles asked.

"When I was a little girl, Nokomis told me stories about them," Charity replied. "Nokomis called them, Shape-Shifters. She said they can change from a human into the form of an animal. It was told to me that some of them are, "yvwigisgi", man-eaters!" The children all gasped, in surprise. "We need to keep a watchful eye in case he comes back. Don't any of you children go off by yourself even if its to relieve yourselves; take one of your brothers or sisters with you," she said firmly.

After all the commotion, it took a few minutes for all of them to settle down and she saw that they all asked a brother or sister to go into the woods with them to relieve themselves. She made her coffee- definitely needing it after running into the Shape-shifter. When the children finished their necessities and morning chores, Charity gave them the leftover chicken and biscuits to eat, but hurried them to eat quickly so they could leave. She wanted to get as far away as possible; she felt her children's safety was at stake.

She loaded the old musket and kept it propped beside her in the wagon. And she told the boys, to keep the machete within reach and to keep a watchful eye out for anything out of the ordinary.

They maintained a steady pace and after several miles, relaxed in their seats. By late-afternoon, they had come to a wide river. That must be the Yellow River that Marilee had told her about, thought Charity. She could see that they would not be able to cross it; at least, not without a bridge of some sort or a ferryboat; it was just too wide and too deep…

Up ahead, the trail forked. One road stayed along the river and the other road, branched off to the right. She decided they would set up camp there for the night. By morning she should be able to decide which road to take. She needed to relax her nerves and unwind a bit; she also needed to cook them something. It would have to be something simple because she just wasn't in the mood to cook.

The boys wanted to explore along the river and she told them to go ahead, but to stay within earshot and to stay together. She started a fire, and then decided that she wanted a cup of coffee, since she didn't really get to enjoy her coffee that morning because of the Shape-shifter. She had just started supper, and was drinking her coffee, when the boys came running back into camp, hollering, "Injuns, Mama!"

"Indians," she corrected.

"Where were the Indians?" she asked.

"Over yonder," Charles said, pointing to a trail into the forest.

"It was a whole camp full of 'em," added John.

"Did they see y'all?" she asked.

"I don't think so," said Uriah, "but Aaron was making a lot of noise," he grumbled. "We tried to hush him up, Mama, we really did, but you know how excited he gets."

As if on cue, Aaron yelled, "Look!" and pointed toward the woods.

Following his pointed finger, Charity looked toward the woods. Standing at the head of the trail, calmly watching them was a large wolf. Charity caught, and held the wolf's gaze, determined not to flinch or look away; she wanted him to know that she wasn't afraid of him.

They held each others gaze for what seemed like a long time, and then, suddenly, his eyes left hers and turned to her left. Following his eyes, she turned to see Uriah is holding her musket, aiming it toward the wolf.

She screamed, "No!" just as he pulled the trigger.

The wolf yelped when the slug tore through his left shoulder; he then tried to run away, but couldn't. He fell to the ground, and then started trying to get back up. Charity ran over to the wolf. Stunned, she stared in awe as he began changing from a wolf into a man!

Lila M Beckham

"Shape Shifter," she exclaimed under her breath.

Realizing what was about to occur, she suddenly turned and yelled, "Bring me a blanket, quickly!"

Martha Jane came running with a blanket. Charity took it and hurriedly draped it over the man, who was now trying to sit up.

"Indians!" screamed Nancy, who then grabbed her little sister and crawled under one of the wagons to hide. Charity looked up and saw, five Indian braves coming out of the trail the wolf had come from.

✳✳✳

Meanwhile, back in Walton County, Henry and Jeremiah were in a prison wagon on their way out to the Wright farm, where Charity and the children had just spent two days and had taken their leave from, barely twenty-four hours earlier… if they had only known…

✳✳✳

"What all we gots ta do out to this here farm, Mr. Boss-man, Sir," Jeremiah asked, Flanagan, who was driving them out.

"Don't worry bout it," grumbled Flanagan. "You just do as you're told, old man, and you and me, will get along just fine."

"Well, damn, Flanagan, I was jest a wondering, if'n I was gonna have ta milk any cows," he said, working his hands as if he was milking a cow. Then he said, "Moo, Moo," and winked at Henry, while chuckling at his own jokes.

Lila M Beckham

Henry couldn't help but to grin back; he admired the old man's gumption; he kind of reminded him of Charity's grandfather; not just in looks, but in his mannerisms too; they both had the same light-humored gruffness about them.

They arrived at Jack Wright's Farm about midmorning. Marilee Wright came out onto the porch, she was smiling. Henry decided right then and there, that he liked her. Her rosy cheeks and friendly smile showed she was genuine and a kind-hearted person.

Flanagan puts them to work chopping hickory wood to smoke the hams while he and Marilee went to pick out the hog's they were going to slaughter. A little while later, they saw Marilee go back into the house; Flanagan sat down in a rocking chair on the front porch, laid his rifle across his lap and then propped his booted feet on the railing. He appeared to be watching them chop wood, but they suspected he was dozing.

About noon, Marilee stepped out and rang the dinner bell that was mounted on one of the porch columns. While they were working, they had smelled wonderful aromas coming from the house- they were definitely ready for something good to eat - even if it wasn't as good as it smelled, they knew it would be an improvement over the slop they were used to being served at the prison.

Flanagan motioned for them to come to the house. Marilee told them to wash up first. They both washed their hands and faces at the well, and then went into the house. She had the table set for them. It was piled high with fried chicken, taters, and some other good-smelling vittles.

"Lawd have mercy, look a here, Henry!" exclaimed Jeremiah. "We's done died and gone to heaven, ain't we?

"Ma'am, I can't speak fer Henry here, but I ain't seen vittles like this in a month of Sundays- you've done gone and outdone yourself, Missus!"

"If you think this is something, y'all should've seen it the day before yesterday!" said Marilee, with implied satisfaction. "I had me a young woman and her seven, yes, I said seven, little young'uns for company! If you think you men folk can eat a lot, you ought to see a bunch of growing young'uns tear into a table of food," she smiled big, her cheeks even rosier if possible.

Henry and Jeremiah quickly looked at one another. Jeremiah chuckled, and said, "Set down boy and let's eat this fine grub the missus done been a cookin' for us."

Taking the old man's lead, Henry sat down, but his mind wasn't on food; it was full of questions he wanted to ask Marilee about the woman and children- he was sure it must have been his wife and his children.

"Ma'am, I don't know nuthin' bout feedin' a passel a young'uns, but I don't think they could out-eat this old man- I'm hungrier than a bear that's been a hibernatin' all winter!"

Marilee chuckled, then said, "Eat up, Mister McClure, you're gonna need a good belly full a food to keep up with the work that needs done around here the next couple a days!"

"As long as you keep feedin' me like this, I'll work my tail off," said Jeremiah. Flanagan gave him a gruff look, meaning for him to shut up and eat.

✳✳✳

Meanwhile, over at their Yellow River campsite, Charity was shocked to see that the Indians had their hatchets drawn as if they intended to attack her and her children. Her fear did not last long- she knew if they were going to attack, they would have done so immediately. One of the Indians even had a musket that was almost identical to hers. She figured he probably traded something for it. Even at the distance she was from him, and her limited knowledge of firearms, she could tell that his gun was broken; it was missing several parts and he clearly didn't have any ammunition.

"Stop," John hollered, grabbing the musket from Uriah and pointing it toward the Indians. "Don't move," he yelled, when one of them took a slight step toward Charity. The older Indian among them stuck out his arm to halt the others. Charity, could tell from his feathers and his staunch demeanor, that he was a man of importance.

"Please," Charity pled, "We meant no harm, mean no harm either. He scared us because he was a wolf - he scared my children!"

"We take him," said the old man as he walked over to the

Shifter and grabbed him roughly by his uninjured arm. He jerked him up off the ground, grabbing the blanket from around him, leaving him standing there naked. He then handed the blanket to Charity. She was so surprised that she didn't think to insist he keep the blanket and return it later. The old man gave her a hard stare- the Shifter appeared to be embarrassed.

She was unsure of the old man's manner. He turned to his group and motioned for them to take the injured man with them. He then turned to face Charity, still looking gruff and mean.

He spoke in Cherokee, saying, "AniTsalagigatohi," Which she knew meant, "This is our land, given to the Cherokee."

"Tsitsalagi" she told him - which meant - I am Cherokee".

After a momentary look of surprise, he said, "You are welcome to stay," then added, "You will have no more danger. I am, 'Alisgia Waya,' Dancing Wolf, son of Two Feathers, 'Duyugodv Ayosdi,' the Truth Seeker."

"Two Feathers!" exclaimed Charity, surprised to hear his name spoken after so many years. "Oh, my goodness, I thought he'd be dead by now- he's not in, "Wudeliguhi" the Land of the Dead?" she questioned.

She knew not, whether it was from her use of Cherokee, or of her exclamation of his father's name, but he looked extremely surprised, and then asked, "You know my father?"

"Lord, yes," she said. "I could never forget him if I lived to be a hundred and one- I met him in Fort Charlotte when I was a young girl. He told me about endurance and the story of, Death

Rides a Pale Horse," she said, smiling because of the memory.

Dancing Wolf's warm smile erased the troubled look from his face. "My father is very old. He would be glad for the company of an old friend."

"I would truly love to see him, too," she said, asking when she could.

"Tomorrow, I come get and we go," he bowed slightly and then turned and vanished into the forest.

That night, Charity had trouble going to sleep; the Shape Shifter had unnerved her. That someone could actually turn themselves into an animal was beyond belief. When her grandmother had told her about Shape Shifters, she had accepted it as truth- but then, as she grew older, she doubted it was possible, and figured it was just an embellished tale... Remembering her own experiences of late, like walking the winds and animals talking to her, guiding her, she had to laugh at herself for being so close minded. After what she had experienced, she should not question what some perceive as impossible...

After waking early, Charity walked down to the river to bathe and wash her hair. The water was still very cold, but the bath she had taken at Marilee's, had been two days ago. After she bathed, she brushed out her long hair and then braided it before twisting it into a bun and pinning it at the nape of her neck- She then scrambled some eggs, fried up a batch of hoecakes, then fed the baby when she woke. By then, the older children were up and ready to eat. She was sitting down, enjoying a cup of coffee, when Dancing Wolf suddenly appeared beside her. He seemed to have materialized from out of nowhere. She did not see him at all until he was standing right beside her.

"Lord, have mercy; you scared the living daylights out of me!"

"Who this Lord?" he asked.

"Never mind," she said. "It's just a saying that white people have."

"Are you ready to see my father?" Dancing Wolf asked, adding, "He is waiting for you."

She told Martha to get the baby and for the children to come with her.

"You want me to stay here and keep an eye on things, Mama?" asked Uriah, eyeing Dancing Wolf suspiciously. She could tell he thought the Indians might steal their things while they were away from camp.

"No," she replied. "You're going with me- everything here will be fine. I am like a proud little hen- I want Two Feathers to see all of my children."

They all followed Dancing Wolf to his camp. Charity wasn't at all surprised to see old Two Feathers sitting cross-legged by the fire, chanting, and sprinkling powders into it.

"Why does he do that," she asked Dancing Wolf.

"My father is a Truth Seeker," he replied.

"Oh" said Charity, still not quite understanding exactly

what a truth seeker was. Dancing Wolf, sensing her confusion said, "He is what white people call, a holy man."

When she stood in front of him, it was as if she was the young curious girl that had stood in front of him fourteen years earlier. His eyes were still the color of snow falling down, and it looked as if he still was wrapped in the same, brightly-colored woven blanket that he was wrapped in, in Fort Charlotte.

"Hello, Little One, I am happy to see you," said the old man, whose voice she remembered so well from so long ago.

"And, I am happy to see you, too," she exclaimed, adding, "When I didn't see you in Fort Charlotte, I wondered what happened to you."

"We were herded here by the soldiers. They say we will stay here for a spell and then they left. We live here on the, "Egwani'dalonige." What you call, the Yellow River. Our life is good here, but the Fire Spirit says the soldiers will come again…" Charity felt a sadness that was weighty and deep… she wondered if it was what Two Feathers was feeling.

"Little One, you now have many little ones. I see you have learned endurance," he said thoughtfully.

"Yes, I have, Two Feathers; these are my children," she said proudly, waving a hand to encompass the small group as if he could actually see them.

"Let me see them, one by one," he said.

Charity called them to her and told them to go one at a time, to stand before Two Feathers, beginning with the eldest.

"But, Mama, why do I have to go; he can't even see me," said Aaron, her youngest son.

"Shush," she said, giving him one of her you better behave looks. "He can see you as good as I or anyone else can. Now, be quiet and wait your turn."

After Two Feathers had visited with each of the children, he told them that they could play with the others, adding that it was good for them to visit with family. He then called Charity to his side.

"You have fine offspring, Little One, but the little man, he will bring you much heartache in a great war of the white man. I am sorry Little One; he will not survive to give you grandchildren."

Charity looked to where little Aaron was laughing and playing with the other children; her heart ached...

"Why?" she asked. "Why will this happen?"

"I do not know why, Little One, only that it is," he replied. "The rest will give you many fine grandchildren..." he was quiet a moment.

Swallowing a large lump in her throat, she decided that she would have to think about what he told her about Aaron later; she could not face it right then.

"There is danger following you, Little One."

"You mean the Shifter- I don't think-"

"No, Little One- the one who follows is evil- but evil will not prevail; you will be safe once you leave, Tsalagi."

"What happened to the Shifter; is he okay?" she asked.

"He is my son, he will live. He is, "Nu dahn tv at," said the old man.

"Oh, I see, he is crazy, huh?"

"As a loon," said Two Feathers. "The Great Spirit wasted a fine gift."

"I wish I had that gift- I'd not waste it."

Ignoring her remark, he said, "My son was curious about you; he thinks you look like your mother."

Before Charity could respond, he said, "You must go now, Little One. You must reach the place of the Tsalagi; your man will find you there."

When Two Feathers was lighting his pipe, she saw his fingers trembling as if he'd grown feeble; she wondered if she'd ever see him again.

"Not in my human form, Little One," he said, as if reading her thoughts. "My friend, the Yellow Mocker, calls my name- it is almost time-"

"Almost time for what- and who is the Yellow Mocker?"

"He is my friend- he sits in yonder tree," he said, pointing a feeble finger toward a tall tulip poplar, abloom with yellow flowers. After searching the tree with her eyes, she saw a yellow-bellied mockingbird.

"Are you referring to that yellow-bellied mockingbird in the tree?"

"Yes, my friend, the Yellow Mocker; he is here to guide me

to the Great Spirit. He has been calling my name; he is waiting until I am ready."

"How do you know he is here for you and not someone else?

"He is my familiar- my spirit guide- I recognized him when I was a young warrior… You will recognize your familiar when he looks into your eyes, Little One- do not be afraid- he is your friend."

"But…"

"You must go now, Little One. When the Great Spirit claims my inner being, my spirit will soar over you, to say goodbye."

✳✳✳

Henry and Jeremiah finished eating and were back to the wood pile chopping hickory for the smokehouse- however, both had been quiet because Flanagan was within earshot; they did not want him to hear what they had to say. When Flanagan finally left the porch to go to the outhouse, Henry stopped chopping wood and turned to Jeremiah.

"Did you hear what she said? That means that my wife and children were just here," Henry said excitedly. "If I leave now, I can catch up to them in no time at all."

"You're forgettin' one thing, boy," Jeremiah reminded him.

"What's that?" asked Henry.

"Well, for one, whether you like it or naught, you are still chained to me, we's stuck together. Her and them young'uns has a team of horses a pulling them along. All's you'se got is your feet, and another thing, dumbass, you don't have any idea of which way she was a headed. You need to cool your heels and we'll see if we can get some more information, from the missus."

"All right," said Henry, "Since you seem to know what needs to be done, I'll leave it up to you; but I ain't a going back to that prison. One way or another, I'm going after my family- straight from this farm!"

"I don't hear no chopping going on out there you two- Just because I'm in the shitter don't mean y'all can slack up!"

"Yes, Sir, Mister Boss Man," yelled Jeremiah; both went back to chopping.

Flanagan had them helping to kill hogs when they finished the wood. Before suppertime, they had killed three hogs, dressed them out, and had them hanging in the smokehouse.

Marilee cooked a fine supper, complete with a cobbler for desert. Henry eyed Jeremiah, wanting him to do the questioning, he was supposed to do. Jeremiah knew Henry was getting antsy, but he was waiting for the right moment to bring up Henry's family, without letting on that it was his family.

"I bet cha them young'uns you was talking about would've liked this here cobbler, Ma'am- it's delicious." Jeremiah grinned at Marilee.

"Yep, I reckon they would've," Marilee replied, a tinge of sadness in her voice. "I tried to get their mama to stay a few more days, but she was bound and determined to get to Cherokee and in a hurry to do it, too. She said she was supposed to meet her man up there. They were trying to get some of that Injun land, the governments been giving away to settlers."

Flanagan cleared his throat, letting Jeremiah know that he wanted him to quit asking questions. Marilee gave Flanagan a stern look and spoke up. She said, "Flanny, this is my house, and even if these fellers are convicts, they're still human beings. I don't want folks sitting around my table and being quiet while they eat. Heck, being out here by myself all the time, I get enough of quiet. I'm enjoying Mister McClure's conversation-it's a heck of a lot better than yours!"

Flanagan appeared surprised by her words and slightly embarrassed.

20

Yellow River

Georgia Country
April 18, 1843

The children really enjoyed playing with the Indian children- the boys were learning how to make bows and slingshots and the girls were learning new things too watching the girls and women in camp- they wanted to stay longer with the Indian's at Two Feather's campsite, but Charity told them they had to be moving on; their father would be expecting to find them in Cherokee. Reluctantly, they settled in for their last night in the Yellow River camp they had made. Early the next morning, they broke camp and got back on the road.

She had decided to stay on the road that ran parallel with the river instead of the one that veered away, somehow, feeling that her intuition would guide her in the right direction. She didn't get to talk to Two Feathers again- if so, she might have questioned him further; she didn't have time to worry about or decipher his meaning about the danger following her. Nor did it sink in what he'd said about his Shape Shifter son thinking that she looked like her mother, not until the next day when she was on the road again and had plenty of time to think… How did *he* know what her mother looked like; she didn't even know what her mother looked like other than the description given her by Nokomis. As for the danger- she had felt that since leaving Sandersville and had a pretty good idea of what or rather who it was.

They traveled most of the day without incident. Then, late in the afternoon, they came to a river crossing. The man that operated the raft said that he charged two bits a wagon to cross. Charity was disheartened; she had run out of money not long after Henry left. When the raftsman spied the chickens in the back of the wagon, he licked his lips and said, "Now, I just might be willing to exchange passage for one of them there chickens."

Charity was quick to jump on that. She asked, "Both wagons?"

"Yes 'um, I reckon that'd be fair enough," he replied.

"What do we need to do?" she asked.

"You ain't got to do nothing, Ma'am, except drive the wagons onto the raft, one at a time. Then, I'll take y'all across, one at a time; that's all it'll hold."

Charity hollered back and told Uriah, to make sure he kept a tight rein on the team, especially after he got them onto the raft.

The raft carried her wagon across the river and then crossed back over. She was on the opposite shore, nervously watching as the raft brought Uriah, the boys, and the other wagon across. She was relieved when they made it across without incident. The raftsman took one of the hens for his pay, and told Charity to stay on the trail to the northwest, and she should get to the town of Canton in a couple of days.

About an hour before dark, they came to a creek; she stopped to make camp for the night. Taking Charles and John with her, she went to the creek; each carried a bucket to fill with water for the stock, and for cooking. The pebbles and sand in the creek bed were unusually shiny in the late afternoon sun. Charles asked, "Mama, you reckon this here is the creek where Kawa'ha killed all those rabbits with his arrows?"

"I wouldn't be surprised," Charity replied, "but, I always thought it was in the Carolinas, for some reason."

Just then, John hollered, "Charles, Mama, come look at this!"

"Go ahead," she told Charles, "I'll be there in a minute." Charity was scooping up a bucket of water when she saw something yellow, shinning on the creek bed. She reached down and scooped it up in her hand. There was lots of it, all in the creek… She had heard about gold before, so she was pretty sure that is what it was. "Charles, run and get me, my dishpan," she said.

When he returned with the dishpan, she carefully skimmed it along the bottom of the creek. "Now, you boys get the water for the stock. We'll come back first thing in the morning, and see if we can get some more." They grumbled a bit, wanting to stay and get more of the shiny metal pebbles, but she told them they had chores to do and she had to fix something to eat.

After supper, with all her children except baby Mary gathered around her watching, she added some water to the pan, swirled it around, and then picked through the sand and sludge in the bottom of the pan separating the yellow pieces from the rest. She put each little fleck and pebble of the gold metal into a small bowl. When finished, she had maybe a quarter cup full.

"If we can find enough, we can buy some land," she said excitedly.

"Mama, I don't think I can sleep," Charles mumbled.

"We all need to get a good night's sleep. We will stay here and find as much of the gold as we can, before we leave to go to Cherokee."

After they all laid down, Charles kept asking questions until she finally told him that if he didn't be quiet so they could all go to sleep, that he would have to stay at camp and not help find the gold.

She was as bad as Charles, though; her mind was too active and she was having a heck of a time going to sleep. Sometime later, she drifted off to sleep, but it was not a good sleep; she was in and out of dreams.

Dreams of Two Feathers, Kawa'ha, and the Shape Shifter filled her night. Then she dreamt of Henry and little Aaron. She dreamed they were being shot at by men in blue uniforms. They had huge guns on wheels that shot slugs as big as cantaloupes! She woke in a cold sweat, crying and frightened. In her dream she saw Aaron; he lay dying, calling her name.

Suddenly, she sat up as she realized that he actually was calling her; he had crawled in under her wagon and was lying beside her on her pallet. She reached over to soothe him; it felt as if she could fry an egg on him; he was scorching hot! She got out from under the wagon and stoked up the fire, so that she could see to him. She then got a pan of cool water and sponged his body, trying to cool him down. She knew she needed to get some quinine water down him to bring his fever down, so she dug through the wagon where she kept her medicinal fixings until she found it. She boiled some of the water that they already had in the barrels, just in case the creek water was contaminated.

It was too early in the year for yellow fever. Fevers, such as malaria and yellow fever, usually didn't show up until the very hot weather months, of July and August. By daybreak, her four youngest children were burning up with fevers. They complained of stomach aches, headaches, and that their throats hurt when they swallowed. She nursed them all through the day and that night.

The next day, while sponging the children with cool water, she noticed that their fever was breaking. She killed one of the chickens, plucked it, washed it, and then dropped it into boiling water. She remembered Nancy doing that when the older children were sick one time. After the chicken was done, she drained a good bit of the broth off for the sick children. With the remaining broth and chicken, she mixed up some flour dough and dropped spoonfuls of the dough into the pot to make dumplings for her and the older children. By the end of the day, she saw that they all had small red spots on their stomachs and backs. These soon spread to the rest of their body.

✳✳✳

Still chained together, Jeremiah and Henry were locked into a shed that first night after they finished eating supper at Marilee's.

"Just unchain us, Flanagan," said Jeremiah, "Hell, ye a locking us up ought to be enough! At the least, we'd be a mite more comfortable, if'n you'd jest unhook us from one another!"

"Just shut your trap and get some sleep old man," Flanagan replied, as he turned to go out the door. "Y'all got a lot of work to do tomorrow," he hollered through the closed door, and then they heard his footsteps walking away.

"Damn it!" said Henry, "We won't be getting out of here tonight."

"Just relax, Son, and let me think about it," grumbled Jeremiah.

"But, she's already got a two day head start,"

"Well if we was still at the prison, you wouldn't even a knowed where she was," Jeremiah reminded him. "At least this way, you now know they're alright and ya know where she's headed."

"I'm going to get out of here, Old Man; I ain't a going back to that prison!"

"What about old, Flanagan, huh, what you gonna do about him?"

"I don't rightly know right now; if I have to, I'll knock him in the head!"

"Well, ye just might have to- We might can bust these chains off with the ax tomorrow while we're a choppin' wood," suggested Jeremiah.

"What if we've chopped enough wood already; then what? We won't even get near an ax, if that's the case."

"Well," said Jeremiah, "Maybe some other opportunity will present itself. Right now, I want to get a little, shuteye. This old man be tired after all that wood-choppin', and eating them good vittles makes a belly content. I can hardly keep my old eyes open. It's been a long day, son."

Sweat-soaked, bone-tired, dust-caked and staring down the barrel of uncertainty, Henry was chomping at the bit, wanting to go after Charity and the children. He drifted in and out of sleep, dreaming, dreams of Charity and the children. He dreamed he was running through a heavy rain, trying to follow the wagon ruts left by their two wagons, when he ran off a cliff and fell- he kept falling and falling, and falling…

21

The Sign of the Whirlpool Wind

All four of the sick children were covered head to toe, with dozens of small red spots that soon turned into blisters. The blisters even spread to their mouths, eyes, and private parts. Charity knew they were in misery; she felt so helpless. She was trying her best to doctor them, but nothing seemed to help.

In a moment of calm, she suddenly remembered being sick when she was a little girl. She had a red, itchy, rash that spread all over her; she was in misery until Nokomis dried some black-eyed Susan's, then mashed them up into a powder that she rubbed all over her body. It had helped the itching and dried up the rash. There were a few wildflowers growing where they were camped, but she did not see any black-eye Susan's anywhere.

Powder, hmm, thought Charity, that reminded her of when Eli had gotten poison oak... Nancy rubbed cornstarch on his arms for the itching. Nancy said to never scratch a rash, because it would cause it to spread.

She put socks on the children's hands and then tied cloth strips around their wrists so they could not scratch the blisters. Then, she rubbed each child down with a mixture of cornstarch and the juice from a succulent plant her grandmother used on everything from bug bites to sunburn. After several hours and another application, they seemed better. To keep their minds off of their itching bodies, She told them every Indian story she could remember, however, they seemed to be getting very restless just lying around; therefore, she decided that the next morning they would get back on the trail.

During the time the children were sick, the older boys had been picking gold out of the creek. They had added to Charity's first find and now had nearly three quarters of a cup full. She did not know how much it was worth, but hoped it would help them buy some land. Somehow, she knew that Henry did not get any of the "Free" land that was given away- and she had to admit that she was glad; she could never have enjoyed living on land that was taken from someone, no matter who it was.

That night, the weather was so nice that she pulled their pallets out from under the wagons and they slept under the stars. When they were all settled in their blankets, she extinguished the lamps and slipped under the cover. After extinguishing the lanterns, they noticed how bright and clear the night was. The stars were so bright that you could almost see as clear as day.

As Charity lay gazing up at the night sky, she saw a shooting star streak across the heavens. It reminded her of another story from her childhood. Then, she saw another, and then, another! She called to the children and told them to look up at the night sky.

Lila M Beckham

"Wow, Mama! Why are there so many shooting stars," they asked.

"Many, many, thousands of years ago," she replied, "The Great Spirit went out bear hunting."

"Bear hunting?"

"Yes, bear hunting- do you see those stars over there - the ones that form a drinking gourd," she asked, pointing toward the southern sky.

"Uh huh," they replied.

"Well, the Great Spirit saw a bear and just as he let loose his arrow, he saw that it was a mother bear; following close behind her, was three cubs. His arrow pierced the mother bear's heart, killing her instantly."

"Aw…" moaned the children.

"The Great Spirit's heart was broken by what he'd done, so right then and there, he placed those stars in the night sky to always be a reminder to hunters, to not be too quick to let loose their arrows. He did it to remind them to be patient and not to kill in haste," she finished.

"So" said, Charles. "Does that mean that maybe the Great Spirit is hunting rabbits tonight, like Kawa'ha?" All of them laughed, including Charity.

"You never know," she chuckled. They then lay for an hour or so, picking out different groups of stars that looked like different animals and such.

"Hey, look!" little Aaron called excitedly, "Those stars over yonder look like a man-horse to me. Do y'all see it?"

"No it don't!" refuted older brother John.

"Yes it does," Uriah said firmly, pointing out the outline of the man-horse.

Martha Jane spoke up and said, "Ya'll boys are just plain dumb. It's a man riding a horse, not a man-horse," she exclaimed.

"Yeah," Nancy chimed in- "it's a man on a horse and he has a bow and arrow raised to shoot something- Oh, it's the Great Spirit!" she exclaimed.

"Is it, Mama," several of them asked at once.

"I'm not sure," Charity mumbled, marveling at the wisdom of a child.

***

Twenty miles away, old Two Feathers saw in his mind's eye, an entirely different sign. What he saw was the sign of the Whirlpool Wind; he was worried about Little One and her children… He could not yet go on his journey.

***

Charity was happy her children were doing better; she smiled to herself, enjoying the sibling rivalry. Soon, she drifted off to sleep. However, it was not a good sleep- her dreams never seemed to be good dreams anymore- When she woke briefly, she longed for her days of youth when her nights were filled with tranquil dreams…

The next morning dawned dark and gray; she almost

changed her mind about leaving, but figured it would soon blow over; she was wrong…

They ate, packed the wagons, hitched the team, and had been on the trail for a couple of hours, when all hell broke loose. The wind blew swiftly and a large dark cloud suddenly dipped down toward the ground and began swirling around. Charity had never seen clouds act like these before, and it frightened her. She didn't exactly know what to do or if there was anything in particular she needed to do. Although the swirling cloud was still a good ways off, it looked as if it was headed their way. That's when she saw several other clouds begin spinning downward and forming a tail that dropped even further into the trees. It looked like a whirlpool except one of wind, not water.

"Unole, waguli!" exclaimed Charity, when the trees started to snap, twist, and break as the funnel cloud dipped into them. The trees broke apart and then flew up into the dark funnel- It scared the living daylights out of her.

"If it can do that to a tree, I'd hate to think what it can do to us," she thought aloud. "We need to get out of the way," she hollered back to Uriah and the boys. "Follow me," she yelled, as she headed the team toward the foothills, off to her right.

As they neared the hills, she saw what appeared to be a trail between two big rocks. It turned out to be a small, boxed in area, just big enough for the two wagons to fit up into and turn around. The whirling wind was closing in; Charity had never been so frightened for her children's safety. She was trying to get the girls out of the wagon, when the boys ran up beside her wagon.

"Mama, there's a cave over there!" John hollered, pointing.

"Y'all run," she said, grabbing the baby out of Martha's arms.

✱✱✱

Henry woke from his dream just as he hit the jagged rocks at the bottom of the cliff. Whew!" he mumbled, "It was only a dream." Was it some kind of warning, he wondered? Maybe, Charity and the children were in danger. Or, was it he, that was in danger?

He lay there thinking for a bit and then dosed off to sleep; he went straight back into the dream he was having before he woke. He was falling, forever it seemed, and then hit the jagged rocks at the bottom. This time, though, he didn't wake up, instead, he floated up out of his body. He could see his body lying bloodied on the rocks. Flanagan came running up, bent over his lifeless body a moment and then stepped back and nudged him with his booted foot. He said, "I told ye not to try and make a run for it ye scalawag. Now, look what you've done gone and done- ye kilt your stupid self!" Henry snapped awake.

When morning came, Henry was worn slap out from dreaming. And after failing so many times in his dreams to escape, he felt defeated.

Jeremiah said, "Gosh dang, Boy, what's gotten into you overnight, huh? You was raring ta go last night - I told you that I was gonna sleep on it- Well, I did, and I have decided the best time for us to make a run for it, is whenever old Flanagan ain't a looking. After breakfast, he'll set us to doing something, like he always does after we eat- and then he'll head to the outhouse to do his business. We'll jam the door shut and haul ass out through them woods behind the smokehouse. I can get ahold of some kind of tool ta break these chains a loose- and we'll go," Jeremiah explained.

"After that dream I had last night, I figure there is only two ways to get loose. One, I can figure out a way for us to overpower him and lock him up, in outhouse or this here shed, don't matter which to me. Or two, I can just outright kill him; but if I kill him, then we'd have to kill Miss Marilee too cause she'd be witness to it- So you decide which way it's going to be, Jeremiah. Frankly, I'm prepared to do either- come hell or high water, I'm getting loose today and going to find my family!" said Henry.

22

Escape

The strong winds nearly picked little, Nancy up off her feet as they entered the cave. If it had not been for John and Uriah grabbing her arms and dragging her inside, the wind would have siphoned her right back out the cave entrance as it seemed to do with all the air in the space.

A moment later the air returned and they could breathe, but then they heard hellacious noises coming from outside the cave as the whirlwind wreaked havoc around them. The noise level was deafening; it seemed to put pressure on their eardrums so that they couldn't fully distinguish between the sounds - It was a roaring, grinding wood sound, that was extremely loud at times, and definitely scary; especially for the younger children.

"I think we're safe in here," she told the children.

"But what about the wagons and animals, Mama?" asked Uriah, the most logical thinking of her sons.

Right about then, it became quiet. The sounds of the winds seemed to suddenly die down. They all went to the front of the cave. There were branches and other debris covering the entrance. They cleared them away as they made their way outside

- their belongings were scattered on the ground and one of the wagons was lying sideway's against the walls of the canyon.

"Where did the horses go?" John wondered aloud.

"I've heard of the whirlpool winds, but I haven't ever seen anything like that," Charity told the children. "I've heard that along the coast, in places like Savannah, they have hurricanes that come in off the water and blows hard winds that tear things up, I remember a tree blowing down near my grandparent's cabin when I was young, but this was different."

"Mama, listen!" exclaimed Nancy. "I hear chickens."

Soon, they had rounded up most of the animals. Outside the narrow passage into the small canyon, they found the other wagon. It sat upright, completely intact, with the team still harnessed to it! Charity was very thankful; it was the main wagon they needed; it held all their foodstuffs and bedding.

Most of the stuff from the tumbled wagon was salvageable; even the wagon. Her and the children picked up all their stuff they could find, then shooed all the loose animals into the boxed canyon; they then dragged a fallen tree across the entrance hoping to keep them contained.

Charity told John and Uriah to search the surrounding area for the other team of horses. By the time the boys returned with the horses, and the cow, she and the smaller children had straightened and sorted most of their stuff.

"Did you boys see a creek while y'all were searching; we need to get some water for us and the stock."

"There's water in the cave," said Charles.

"Is there?"

"Yes, Ma'am; I heard it when I was exploring the cave," he replied.

"I don't want any of y'all going in there without a lantern," she scolded. "It's not safe. Remember what happened to Tokola," she warned.

"But the earth swallowed him up," reminded Aaron.

"Yes, that's right, it did; right down into the belly of a *cave*," Charity reminded him. "Let's take a couple of lanterns in with us so that we all can explore the cave. I think it's best we go ahead and make camp here tonight- it's too late to try going further today- besides, we don't know which way that whirlpool wind went and I wouldn't want to meet it again today."

"At least, the wood has already been chopped," said John, "that whirlwind made a quick task of it."

"It looks like it cut a trail through the woods. I wonder where it went?" asked Martha Jane.

"I don't know," answered Charity. "I just hope that it keeps going- it can go anywhere it wants as long as it's not the direction we need to go."

When they entered the cave, this time with lanterns, they saw that the cavern was huge! It smelt damp and musky. It was also very cool inside.

"Can we live here, Mama," asked Charles, adding, "It would make a great place to live, wouldn't it!"

"I don't know about living here, but we can definitely spend the night," she answered. "Right now, we need to find water. Our water barrels all spilled out when the wagon overturned; our stock needs water and so do we."

"There's a pool of water back here," yelled John, from somewhere deeper in the cave.

The pool was crystal clear along the edge, but a little way out from the edge, it was as black as smut. To Charity, that meant that it was probably deep.

"Y'all don't get too close, it looks to be very deep," she said, reaching down and scooping up a handful to taste.

"It tastes kind a funny, like it has iron or minerals in it, but it's not too bad," she said, adding, "I think it will be alright for us and the stock to drink."

Late in the afternoon, it clouded up and began to rain. This time, taking no chances, they brought all the animals into the cave, tying them off between several tall posts that Charity thought must have crusted over with rock. She had no idea of what stalagmites were. The boys managed to tie the chicken coop back together; that kept the chickens confined. Charity figured it would be several days before they settled down enough to lay eggs again. There were a lot of strange things in the cave, even a few ferns grew close to the entrance. She also saw several small plants growing that she had never before. The boys brought in some wood and started a fire near the entrance so that she could fix them some supper. Once the fire burned down at bit, she raked the coals over, and prepared a simple supper, of salvaged eggs, ham, and hoecakes. It wasn't much, but it was enough to fill their bellies.

Just before Charity drifted off to sleep that night, she heard the rain and wind pick up in intensity outside. She dreamed she was flying through the air to Henry, but everywhere she looked, he wasn't there. A panic consumed her. Then, suddenly, she was standing beside Tokola. She knew she was dreaming.

"Why are you in my dream," she asked him.

"I have gone to the land of Anis'gina, with the Ga'nodu;" he replied, adding "I no longer walk among the living, Wind Walker. Come, Wind-walker, let me guide you to where you search."

Away they flew; and, in a split-moment of time, she saw Henry, chained, and locked away in a shed. Without any hesitation, she went to him.

✸✸✸

Henry felt her presence. He called out her name, awakening Jeremiah.

"What" asked the old man? "Who are you a talkin' to, boy?"

After Jeremiah woke, Henry could no longer feel her presence there.

"Damn it, Jeremiah!" Henry exclaimed. "Why'd you have to go and wake up old man; you messed everything up!"

"Well, Son, you might jest be glad I did," Jeremiah whispered, "cause I done come up with a plan to get us out of here!"

"Okay old man; if you have a plan, then spit it out, because I'm ready to get to my family," said Henry. "They need me."

"Instead of waiting until after breakfast and losing half the day, as soon as old Flanagan opens the door ta let us outta here this mornin', we'll rush him. After we overpower him, we will shove him in here, gag him, tie him up, and then lock him in," Jeremiah said smugly.

"What about Miss Marilee?" Henry asked.

"What about her?" responded Jeremiah, "I figure we'll jest see what happens. We will threaten her if we have to, I don't wanna have ta hurt 'er or nothin', she's a good woman. We can tie her up if we have to; it won't matter if we do; when we don't return to the prison tomorrow evenin', you can bet your boots they'll be sending someone out here ta see what the heck is a going on."

"That sounds better than having to hurt them," Henry told him. "I don't really want to hurt anybody, if I don't have to."

"Me neither, son; me neither."

Henry and Jeremiah were wide-awake come daylight, listening for the tell-tell signs that Flanagan was up and about. He would usually moan and groan several times, then grunt and fart really loud before he crawled out of bed.

"Now, remember, son. You grab him, jerk him in here, and

then we'll both tackle him and tie him up," instructed Jeremiah. Henry nodded.

At the first signs of daybreak, they heard Flanagan begin stirring. After his usual grunting and farting, they heard him come out of the adjoining building, and then head to the outhouse. They knew that very soon he'd be coming to open up the shed they were in to let them out. Henry and Jeremiah lay in wait. The sudden sound of thunder in the distance worried them- if it rained, it'd be easier for someone to track them…

✱✱✱

Charity woke with a start, wondering what woke her. "Oh my… Henry… I almost touched you; then something happened," she whispered into the darkness. She rose up and looked around; she was still in the cave. She heard the storm raging outside. The sound of running water could be heard over the outside sounds from somewhere at the back of the cavern. They should be safe as long as they were near the entrance, she thought.

She then remembered Tokola and him telling her that he had died; she cried. Not because he had died, but because she didn't get to spend much time talking to him in her dream.

As she lay there thinking, the sound of the wind died down; the quietness was eerie. She wondered how long it had been since she fell asleep. She got up and lit one of the precious candles she had brought in from the supply wagon. As she neared the entrance of the cave, she realized that it was still night, but she could see outside very well. The storm had let up; there was a full, bright moon. The moonlit night beheld the day's destruction. Felled trees and debris was everywhere. She never would have thought that hurricane winds could get that far inland from the coast. That was undoubtedly, what it was- a hurricane- although it was awful early in the year, for such.

"Mama?" Hearing her name being called, Charity turned to see Charles walking up behind her.

"What are you looking at?" he asked.

"Nothing, just outside - I was thinking about your daddy," she said. "I hope he doesn't have any trouble finding us."

"Don't worry, Mama," he said. "Papa can track real good; he won't have any trouble finding us." Charity smiled and put her arm around his shoulders. She loved her children.

Henry's finding them wasn't Charity's only worry; she was also worried about feeding her children. Supplies were getting low again. If they did not get to a town where she could trade some of the gold for supplies, she was going to be scrapping for food; her ammunition and powder were also low... She was thankful that the whirlwind did not destroy everything and blow off what food they did have. She was even more thankful that none of them were injured.

She decided that if the weather stayed clear until after daybreak, they would get back on the trail as soon as they could get everything loaded and the teams hitched to the wagons.

"You need to go on back to sleep, Son. We are going to

need all the strength we can get in the morning. With all these stopover's we've been doing lately, we're getting behind."

Sensing something more, Charles asked, "What is it, Mama?"

"It's nothing, son, I'm still thinking," she replied. In reality, she was thinking of Henry, chained and locked up somewhere that seemed familiar, yet different. Although she knew he was locked up, she had a feeling that he wouldn't be for long. Henry would find her soon and they would be together again; that was all that really mattered…

As soon as the sun peeked over the eastern edge of the earth, Charity rousted the children from their dreams and told them to get up and stretch… In the darkened cavern, they would have slept all day.

"Let's get everything packed up so we can get on the trail again. Time is a wasting," she said cheerfully.

Soon, all the children had eaten and were loaded and ready to go. Then, Nancy started crying; in all the confusion of the past day, she had lost her flying-squirrel. Uriah gave her his, to settle her down; she was satisfied.

Charity knew the cow needed milking, but it would have to wait until they camped for the night. After an hour on the trail, it clouded up and began to rain a slow misty rain. Of course, it was the month of the "Ka'wani," (the Flower Moon,) There would soon be grass for the stock and wildflowers for the girls to pick and exploring for the boys to do. About an hour and a half before dark, they came to a small creek; it would be a good place to make camp.

She checked their supplies to see if she would need to go hunting; Marilee had supplied them with several smoked hams and some cheese and butter; but she was running awful low on staples, salt, flour, cornmeal, and sugar. She cut up the rest of the ham they'd eaten for supper the night before and breakfast off of that morning and made a pan of biscuits that would serve for their supper and breakfast. She cut up a couple of potatoes, boiled them down, then added the ham, some butter, milk, and a little flour to thicken it. The children liked the impromptu ham and potato soup; they ate every bit of it and then sopped their bowls clean with their biscuits!

That night, she was asleep before her head hit the pillow good; soon, she was in dreamland. She was driving the wagon alongside a long, wide river when she came to a well-traveled crossroad; she didn't know which way was the right way to go. Her grandfather suddenly appeared beside her on the seat- she turned to him and asked, "Which way is the right way?"

"Remember what I taught you, Child; follow the North Star," he said, "It will guide you where you need to go."

"Please, don't leave me, Grandfather," she begged. "I feel so tired; sometimes, I just want to turn around and go home."

"I know child, but this is your future. It has been chosen for you; you must stay on course."

"But, why, Grandfather? Why must I go one way and not

another? Am I wrong to question the Great Spirit?" she asked.

"No, Child; you are not wrong. There is no wrong or right; we all question the course we're on; however, if you stay true to yourself and stay the course, your questions will be answered."

When she turned to face him, he was gone. She looked to the North Star and turned her wagon in that direction. Soon, she was no longer in the wagon; she was walking the wind in search of Henry. She found him asleep under a Scuppernong thicket. She went to him and held him close. He roused in her arms; she made love to him; cradled him, and covered his face and lips with tender kisses. When she left him, she told him to follow the North Star, it would guide him to her.

✳✳✳

Henry awoke when she left him; he could still feel her touch on his skin. The events of the day ran through his mind. Old Flanagan never suspected a thing. He and Jeremiah tackled him when he opened the door; they subdued him, tied him up in the shed, and then made their escape without a hitch. The only thing he worried about was that Jack Wright would still have them hunted down like dogs and dragged back to prison.

Henry thought it not fair that they were sentenced to prison in the first place. They'd done nothing terrible enough to warrant such a strong sentence as six months hard labor. He figured it was just a way for them to get free labor. He looked over at Jeremiah, wondering why the old man still wanted to stick with him once they were free. Once they made their escape, he could have gone in any direction he pleased... Henry felt that maybe the old man needed a friend as much as he did- he would never leave him needing; his friendship was such a small price to pay - he felt he at least owed him that much.

Now that Charity had come to him in his sleep, he was sure that he could find her and the children. He woke Jeremiah just before daybreak and told him that they needed to be heading north.

"Well, I'd a thought we'd be a heading west, toward Alabama," said Jeremiah grumpily.

"Nope, not yet, Old Man; we got to catch up to my family first, and they're headed north, toward the mountains."

"We'll catch 'em boy, don't you worry none," said Jeremiah. "This old man ain't a gonna slow ye down none. I still got a lot a spunk left in me."

"That's good to hear Old Man, because I ain't wasting any time getting to where I'm going," Henry smiled. He felt he could take on an army of prison guards if he had to, to get back with his family!

***

A few miles away, old Two Feathers sat cross-legged in front of the Sacred Fire, chanting and sprinkling powders into It. Suddenly, he stopped chanting, and a smile came to his old wrinkled face; he then took a final breath...

Lila M Beckham

23

Cherokee County

Georgia Country

Gasping for air and pushing an invisible 'something' away from her face, Charity sat up with a start and began gulping air into her lungs. It felt as if all her breath was suddenly squished out of her lungs. It was not a scary feeling. She remembered a dark shadow hovering over her, then consuming her, momentarily, smothering her. At first, the shadow radiated love, compassion, and understanding- feelings that returned once she could breathe again.

Charity lay there a minute and then got up to pee. As she walked toward the woods, she looked up at the moon- a halo surrounded it, but in the center, there appeared to be the shadow of a man... She stared at the moon a long time, trying to separate the man's figure, from the other shadows- He was as clear as day, but then he merged with the shadows. A sort of eeriness settled over her, but she continued to the edge of the forest and used the bathroom. When she stood, she felt unbalanced and woozy. What a mysterious feeling this was- it was as if her body was not her own... She had never felt this way before...

Even though, she felt odd, it was as if she could see more clearly than ever before. Even in the darkness, she could define each limb, every branch, leaf, even the blades of grass growing from the ground were brilliantly clear to her…

She returned to the wagons and stoked up the fire. As it caught and blazed to life, she sat cross-legged and gazed deeply into the flames. Within them, she saw Two Feathers sitting by his fire just as she was setting by her fire. He called her name and she answered. He spoke of the visions he had and how they came to him. He told her of his powers of observation and how he used them to foretell future events, the futures of human beings- her future. He said that she too could see these things if she opened herself to them. They conversed for a long time; how long, she did not know, just that it was and they did; they were connected in a way that they could speak to one another without talking.

The sound of the children talking roused her from her dreams. She rose to find that she was still underneath the wagon lying on her pallet. This is strange, thought Charity- I was just sitting by the fire talking to Two Feathers… She shook the thoughts from her head and stood to stretch- her body felt relaxed, not stiff. She went over and stoked up the fire, feeling as if she had just done that- she resisted the urge to sit cross-legged to see if she'd go back to where she was before the children woke her… She then set about preparing breakfast. As she listened to the children going about their morning rituals, while laughing and talking, she felt normalcy return. She looked toward the forest as she usually did and saw squirrels and birds busily foraging for food; that too, was normal. She came to the conclusion that she must've dreamt the entire thing with Two Feathers; however, it still felt very real…

When she finished cooking, they ate, and then resumed their journey.

The day had dawned bright and sunny. It was as if the storms had never come, and it was as if a new season was upon them. They were getting closer to the mountains; it was prettier country than they had been traveling through. There was less red clay, but the terrain was rockier.

They traveled all day, each mile taking them higher into the mountains. Several times that day, she saw a yellow-bellied mockingbird alight in a tree, then watch them until they passed. When next she saw one watching them, she looked directly into its eyes- the eyes staring back at her were friendly, familiar. Two Feathers' words came to her of meeting his spirit guide… A yellow mocker was his spirit guide- was he also hers?

Late in the day, they came upon what she could tell was once a fine cabin; it overlooked a deep ravine. It looked to be livable, but she could tell that it hadn't seen life in a long time. It reminded her of a larger example of her grandparent's cabin. The children wanted to explore for treasures; she easily gave into their wants, because she herself, wanted to explore the old cabin.

The front door opened into the main living area of the cabin- which was maybe 20x20 ft and consisted of a kitchen, a dining room, and a sitting area; there was a loft above. A homemade table took up at least an 8ft by 4ft section to the left of the front door. The kitchen was in the center and the seating area was to her right. The large fireplace in the middle of the room was for cooking and for heating. The chimney went up through the middle of the loft area; she thought it was built that way maybe to warm the loft...

Looking around the cabin she decided that if she had the room, she would take the table with her when she left; it was just the right size to fit her family's needs. Off of the dining room was a back room; a curtained doorway separated it from the rest of the cabin. She knew before she even opened the curtain, that death had visited this place.

When she drew back the curtain, she could make out a homemade, lodge-pole bedstead in the middle of the room. The light coming through the small window gave the room a murky appearance. Upon the bed, under several layers of quilts, were the skeletal remains of the cabin's former owner. Before she even got near the bed, she knew it was a woman.

As she stood beside the bed, the woman, made herself known to Charity; visions of the woman's life ran through her mind. A barren, but loving life she and her mate had shared while alive- maybe even in death, for they shared a deep love for one another. Charity knew what it was like to love someone like that and for that love to be returned in the same manner. She and Henry loved like that, and her love for her children knew no bounds…

Standing beside the bed, she was witness to the woman's life. She saw clearly where the woman had buried her love, gently covering his body with stones because she was unable to dig a proper grave for him. Then the woman went inside, lay down on the bed and gave up on life…

"Don't fret none, ma'am; me and my strong son's will make sure you and your love receive a proper burial," Charity said aloud, wishing she knew the couples names so she could mark their graves. Standing there beside the dead woman's bed, she decided that this was where she would wait for Henry; he should catch up to them soon. Charity wrapped the skeletal corpse in the bed linens that were on the bed, talking to her the entire time as if she were alive. Charity told her about herself, about how she was raised and about her grandparents. Then, she told her about Henry and his folks, and then she told her about her children, telling her each of their names and what their personalities were like. When she finished, she tied it snugly using the corners of the sheet; she then got the older boys to help remove it.

After they removed the woman's body and buried her out back beside her husband, Charity turned the straw-ticked mattress over and remade the bed with linens she found in a chest at the foot of the bed.

While she, Charles, and Martha swept and cleaned the cabin of spider webs and dust, she sent John and Uriah, since they were the eldest, out to explore the surrounding area to see if there were any people living nearby. They came back about an hour later, very excited.

"Mama, there's a whole town down there," they said, pointing in the general direction of northwest, exclaiming, "It has a church and everything! We didn't go all the way down, but you can see it from the bluff above the river."

It was getting late, so she decided to wait until the next day to go into the town to check it out. "That's wonderful," she replied, relieved that she could replenish their supplies. "We'll check it out tomorrow after we finish our chores. Y'all pitch in and help your brother and sister clean while I fix us something to eat."

Charity cooked their supper that night, the same way she and her grandparents always had; in the fireplace. It was nice to have a roof overhead, although before they could really make themselves at home, she would have to see what she could find out about the folks that had lived there. She was almost certain they had no family around; the corpse would not have still been in the bed if they did.

That night, they all piled into the little two-room cabin to sleep; the older children slept in the loft and Charity and the younger children slept on the bed.

After a dreamless night in the comfortable bed, morning arrived before she was ready to rise. She sent the boys to milk the cow and chop wood while she fixed a breakfast of eggs, ham, and hoecakes. Suddenly, the door flew open and Charles came running, calling for his mother to come help.

"Uriah's bleeding real bad!"

She ran outside to find John holding Uriah down on the ground and little Aaron, trying to hold his brother's foot still. After she was able to get his boot off, she saw that only half of his left foot was intact; His toes had been near about chopped off! She ripped off the bottom half of her slip and tied it tightly around his foot.

"Am I gonna die?" asked Uriah.

"No," she replied sharply, "Don't even think such a thing. We just have to get you to that town to get some help." I sure hope they have a doctor, she thought to herself as she gave the children instruction on how to help her get Uriah into the wagon and make him comfortable.

✳✳✳

Henry and Jeremiah were making their way as fast as they could; they had gotten as far as the Yellow River, near where Charity and the children had camped. It was also near Two Feathers campsite. They both knew their empty bellies were slowing them down.

"Boy, you and me ain't a going to be able, ta keep up this pace lessen we get some grub in our bellies," said Jeremiah. "I'm so hungry, if ye laid a steak atop my head, my tongue would slap my brains out, a trying ta get to it!"

"What brains, Old Man," teased Henry. "Sometimes I

wonder if you even got any. Besides, you ain't the only one that's hungry; I'm hungry too. I could probably eat the ass end outta a billy-goat myself... We're going to have to find something to eat, that's for sure."

Jeremiah mumbled, farted, and then his stomach went to growling. "I thank my belly-button is done stuck to my backbone," he grumbled as he sat down beneath a willow tree.

"You know, we could probably make a good fish trap out of some of these willow branches and a honeysuckle vine," said Henry. "That'd probably be the quickest way to get something to eat. You start digging some worms and I'll gather some thin branches and vines."

"Give me the dirty job, huh."

"Well then, you gather branches and vines and I'll dig- unless you wanna chase down that jackrabbit over yonder."

"We'd play hell catching that jackrabbit!" grumbled Jeremiah. "What we should' a done was took Flanagan's gun."

"No, we shouldn't have," said Henry. "If we had gotten caught, that would've just given those scoundrels more to use against us."

"Well, either way, old Flanagan ain't a gone tell them the truth as to how we got loose the way we did," Jeremiah said angrily. "He's probably gone tell them all kinds a bawl-faced, lies, like we robbed him, or we stole his gun. We may as well a done it as get accused of it," said the old man. "At least then, we'd had a way to kill us some grub ta eat!"

"Quit your jabbering old man. Dig some bait while I weave a trap; we can chunk it in the river and catch us some supper instead of just standing here grumbling about how hungry we are!"

24

Canton

After John harnessed the team to the wagon, he, Charity, and Charles loaded Uriah into it. She and Charles then headed to town with him. She left John and Martha Jane to watch over the younger children, with strict orders that they had all better be on their best behavior until her return. John was nearly twelve; she figured he ought to be capable of watching the little ones.

Even with the rags tied tightly around his foot, it was still bleeding profusely and had soaked the rags a deep, dark red. Charity worried that Uriah might go into shock from losing so much blood. She saw it happen to a neighbor of Eli and Nancy a couple of years back. The neighbor fell in a field he cleared and a splintered tree trunk punctured his thigh causing him to lose lots of blood- By the time she and Nancy got to him, after his young son came seeking help, he was in shock; he died minutes after they reached him…

The trail from the cabin down to the town was steep, and it was several twisting, miles long. To Charity, it felt hours long as she held to her eldest son's foot, trying to apply pressure to his wound.

Near the bottom of the mountain, the trail ran into a more, well-traveled road. It was then another bumpy mile to the bridge that crossed the river, into town. Charity spotted the Sheriff's Office and told John to head straight to it. She knew that the sheriff should know where the town doctor was; that's if they even had one. When the wagon came to a halt, she jumped down and ran into the sheriff's office.

"I need a doctor quick; my son's toes have been chopped off in an accident- he bleeding bad!" she exclaimed.

"Lord, Ma'am, I'll take you to him. It's right down yonder, at the end of the street; you just follow me!"

She climbed back on the wagon and the sheriff ran ahead of her, clearing the street. When he reached a house at the end of the street, he ran in and got the doctor, who came running out to the wagon.

"Let's get him into my office so I can see to him," said the doctor. The office was actually just a couple of rooms in his house. He and the sheriff each grabbed an end of Uriah and carried him into the doc's house.

"He's lost a lot of blood, Doctor…- Charity realized they hadn't been introduced. "I was afraid he'd go into shock," she told the doctor.

"Yes, Ma'am, you have a right to be scared," the doctor replied. "That happens a lot. In a case like this, it's the shock caused from loss of blood that kills most folks, not the wound itself," he said.

They laid Uriah on a table, then the doctor unwrapped his foot.

"Near about cut them clean off, didn't he," observed the sheriff.

"Ma'am, you have done good, trying to stop the blood by cauterizing the wound, but this'll never heal the way it ought to, now that the flesh and bone has been burned. I have to finish the job by removing that part of his foot."

"Are you saying that I made it worse?"

"Now, I didn't say that- Under the circumstances, you did the best you knew how to do. It's what most farmers, Indians, and lay people would 'a done out in the wilderness to try to stop the bleeding."

"Can you save him?"

"I have to take those toes off- Look, I can give him some laudanum to ease him some, but it's not going to kill all the pain, just dull it little."

"You do what you have to do; I'll help anyway I can," Charity said. "Just please, don't let my son die."

"I'll do everything I can, Mrs.?"

"Gullege," said Charity. "I'm Charity Gullege, and the boy on the table is my son, Uriah. The other boy is my son, Charles."

"Ma'am, I'll do everything in my power. You might have to assist me, if you've got the stomach for it," he said, adding, "The sheriff and your other son can help hold him down."

"Now wait a minute a dang minute, Doc!" exclaimed the sheriff. "You know I'm not good at watching this kind of stuff, much less a helping with it!" the sheriff protested.

"Please, Sheriff," begged Charity. "We need you're help; please…"

The Sheriff couldn't resist the pleading in Charity's voice, or the look in her eyes; he agreed to help with the amputation. There wasn't much holding them on, except a little flesh on the bottom of his foot, and a couple of small bones that weren't cut clean through. The doctor walked over to a cabinet and then came back with a two bottles of something, a teaspoon, and a small rag. He poured something from one of the bottles on the rag and then placed the rag over Uriah's mouth and nose.

He then handed her the other bottle and the spoon.

"You stand by his head, Ma'am. Even though he'll be unconscious, we need to get a couple of spoons of this laudanum down him, before I start the operation," he said. "If he starts moaning or rousting up, cover his nose with the rag," he instructed. The rag had a pungent odor.

Charity did as told and dosed Uriah with the laudanum, then placed her hands firmly on his shoulders to hold him should he try to rise up. It only took the doctor a couple of minutes to cut Uriah's toes the rest of the way off, and to cauterize the tissue on the remainder of his foot.

"If you can keep gangrene from setting up in it, he should be alright; however, he's going to have a limp the rest of his life," said the doctor. "Just keep him off of it a week or so and keep it clean and dry. Change the bandage every day- he's young and healthy, he ought to heal fine."

The doctor handed her the bottle of the laudanum, saying he wished he had something stronger to give her; he told her to give Uriah a spoonful every couple of hours, to ease the pain. He then mixed up a poultice of alum, sulfur, and mineral oil for her to put on Uriah's foot.

"Use this once the bleeding completely stops," he advised; adding, "It needs air at first; this might clog it up or cause bloody pus to excrete."

The Sheriff and the doctor loaded Uriah back into the wagon, making him as comfortable as possible. Then the doctor asked her where they were staying, so he could ride out in a day or two, to check on him. She told him they were traveling through, on their way to Cherokee, and had come upon a cabin that was up the mountain above and across the river. She also told them about finding the remains of a woman and burying her.

The sheriff spoke up, saying, "It's probably the old Finley place. I haven't seen them in town in nearly a year. If they're dead, I don't see any reason y'all can't stay there as long as you want to. There don't seem to be anybody else in a hurry to claim it. If they were, they would've been there.

"Did you say, Finley?" Charity asked.

"Yes, ma'am, least that was the name they were known by."

"My grandfather's name was Finley- I wonder if they were

kin…"

"That'd be something you'd have to ask your grandfather-the man's name was Thomas; don't know what his wife's name was- some said she was Indian. By the way, Ma'am, this here is Cherokee. Least ways, it's Canton, and that be in Cherokee County," he said, and then asked, "Where in Cherokee was you planning to go?"

"As a matter of fact," said Charity, quickly hiding her surprise, "I was to meet my husband in Cherokee, in a town that is near a lake the Indians call, Allatoona? I think is what he said."

"Well, ain't that something," the sheriff grinned. "It looks like you in the right place then, don't it." The doctor smiled in agreement and nodded.

✳✳✳

Henry and Jeremiah had come to the place where the whirlwind had caught Charity and the children. They found the cave; they also found a few damaged items, they left behind. Henry was worried about their safety, but Jeremiah pointed out that you could clearly tell from the wagon tracks that they got it all back together and headed toward the northwest.

"And from the looks of them tracks, we are only a day or so behind 'em. We can follow their tracks and catch right on up to them."

"I sure hope you're right, Old Man, It has been way too long, since I saw my family; I miss my wife; the children too."

"How old'd you say them young'uns of yourn was?" asked Jeremiah.

"Uriah, he's the oldest; he's thirteen," said Henry proudly. "Next in line, is John; he's twelve. Charles is ten, nearly eleven. Martha Jane, is eight, no nine. Nancy is seven. Aaron is five, and the baby, Mary, is almost two years." Henry smiled, thinking of the love he and Charity shared, conceiving their babies. He missed that closeness with her; he missed them all, terribly. He vowed to himself to never get into trouble or separate from his family again.

"Sounds like you got yourself a pretty good set of stairs, there boy," Jeremiah said, "But, you and the missus must a started mighty young."

"I reckon so," said Henry. "We was fourteen and fifteen when we married; but Old Man, let me tell you something; I wouldn't change any of it, for nothing in the world. I reckon I was just meant to be a family man. Come on, we'd better get to moving if we're to catch up to them before they get to Alabama!"

25

Reunion

As Charity drove the wagon out the east end of town and headed back toward the cabin, she was shocked to see two riders riding toward her. She recognized the pair immediately; it was the same scary looking Indian and the dubious looking white man that had given her the heebie-jeebies back in Sandersville. When they got closer to her, she saw that white man was leering at her the same way he had the other time she saw him. The large hawk-faced Indian was still just as scary looking as the first time she saw him.

The white man tipped his hat toward her, but the Indian's eyes never veered from his line of sight, which was straight over his horse's head.

She couldn't help but feel a little scared. What was the chance that they would happen to show up right there where she was? Had they been the cause of her uneasiness these last few weeks? Their journeys would have had to run almost parallel, in order for them to show up in Canton at basically the same time she and her children did. She would be glad when Henry got caught up to them, which she knew, would be in a couple of days.

She headed the team on toward the bridge that led the way back to the old cabin. Charles too, recognized them immediately. Even as young as he was, he could tell that his mother was afraid of these two and he knew he should be wary of them too.

"Mama, that's the same Injun and white man we saw back in Sandersville, ain't it?" he asked.

"Yes, Son; it's them," she replied.

"I wonder what they're doing up here?" he asked.

"I don't know, Son, but you don't be a worrying about them," she said, adding. "Anyways, your daddy will be here in a couple of days, then we won't have anything to be concerned about."

"Really!" Charles exclaimed. "How'd you know that, Mama?" he asked.

"I can feel him getting closer," she replied. "Now, you look after your brother. Make sure he's comfortable, but keep his foot off those bags of flour, meal, and sugar- we wouldn't want them getting ruined."

Feeling eyes on her, she glimpsed over her shoulder, and saw that the leering man had stopped and was watching them go. She geed to the team to hurry on, putting as much distance between the men and her wagon as she could. She probably drove them harder than she should have, but she was in a hurry to get back up the mountain to check on her other children. She was glad everything appeared normal as she neared the cabin. Several of the children ran outside to greet them.

Lila M Beckham

"Mama, there was two men that come by here," said John. "One of them was a big, funny looking Indian, like the one Charles told us about in Sandersville… He was an ugly, mean-looking sucker!" exclaimed John.

"Y'all quit worrying about those two men," she said. "We need to get your brother unloaded and into the house, then I can fix y'all some supper."

It was a rough night, for both she and Uriah. She had put him in the bed with her, so that she could keep him dosed with the laudanum and to be able to keep a close watch on him through the night. The laudanum helped, but she could tell that the pain never completely left him.

As soon as day broke, she went out and gathered some white willow bark and wild hemp, which she rendered down to a syrupy broth, then mixed one part laudanum to two parts of the concoction she'd made. She was going to give it to Uriah. The two together, ought to be enough to dull the pain.

She knew that the medicine could become addictive and that as he healed, she would have to wean him off the mixture. She also decided to ask John what, if anything, had the leering man and the Indian said when they stopped by.

✸✸✸

"The Injun-" said John; "Indian," she corrected. "The In-di-an, never said nothing, Mama, but the white man wanted to know where my pa was."

"What did you tell him?"

"I started to tell him it wouldn't any of his business, but you taught us to be polite, so I told him that he was on his way home. That man shore acted funny, Mama; he gives me the willies."

She knew something wasn't right about those two; now, she knew they were probably following her, but for what reason, she didn't know. She'd have to worry about that later, right then, she needed to get ready for Henry's homecoming. While in town, she had bought supplies using a small amount of the gold she and the children had found. The store proprietor acted as if he wanted to ask her where she got the gold from, but she remained cool and aloof letting him know that she wasn't receptive to questions.

In the supplies she bought, there was a quart of fresh blueberries. The next day she gathered everything she needed for what she had planned- she cooked the blueberries down with several cups of sugar, until they were thick and sweet, then dropped in flour dough dumplings, to make what Nancy called, blueberry cobbler; it was Henry's favorite dessert. He loved it the way Nancy served it warm with a little rich cream whipped up and spooned over it.

While the blueberries were cooking, Charity washed and cleaned a pot of greens she gathered from the Finley's overgrown garden- she intended to cook them with a chunk of ham in them. In the meantime, she killed and roasted one of the chickens and cooked two cakes of cornbread to make a pan of chicken and dressing. Her and the children gathered sage, wild onions, and other spices for the dressing. These dishes were not only Henry's favorites; they were foods her whole family enjoyed. Charity wanted to prepare a feast for Henry- she knew that he would be there by supper-time the next day.

As the hours passed, she could tell that Uriah's pain was lessening. She was relieved there was no sign of infection; thank the Lord, is what Nancy would have done, so that is what she did. She was grateful Uriah lost only his toes and not his life.

The sound of them dropping into the bucket beside the operating table and the smell of his burning flesh would be with her for the rest of her life.

"It smells like Thanksgiving in here!" said Charles; the children all agreed.

"We will be giving thanks," she said with a smile, "Your father is coming home - y'all need to go out and gather some pine cones and boughs to make it smell even fresher in here. I'm sure it will please your daddy to come into a good-smelling place, especially since we will be calling it home for awhile."

Dr. Jackson Lane came out to the cabin that afternoon to check on Uriah, he seemed surprised that his patient was doing so well, so soon. Charity told him that she had added a recipe of rendered willow bark and hemp, to the laudanum medication to make it stronger.

"That'll be fine," said Dr. Lane. "Just be sure to wean him

off of it slowly; we don't want him to suffer withdrawals by taking it away too soon. I'll be back out in a day or two to check on him." She stood in the doorway and watched the doctor ride away, wishing the time for Henry to arrive would hurry and come; she needed him home…

Henry and Jeremiah had been following their wagon tracks from the place of the whirlwind for a day and a half; the terrain becoming more mountainous had not affected them much, but had slowed them somewhat causing Henry to grumble- Jeremiah knew he was slowing Henry's progress and he felt bad about it, however, he felt Henry had more to worry about than how fast or slow they were traveling. Shrewd, old Jeremiah had noticed something that Henry had not. There were two sets of shoed, horse tracks, carrying single riders that were also trailing the wagons.

He was hesitant about telling Henry, because he didn't want him getting all hotheaded or overly worried. However, at the end of the second day past the box canyon, where the whirlwind happened, he decided he would go ahead and tell him so they could devise a plan, in case trouble waited ahead.

Henry was appreciative of the old man's knowledge. He'd been around a lot longer than him and was more experienced at noticing things like that. Yep, the old man had been all over the country, or so it seemed, and although he'd practically crawled into a whiskey bottle the last thirty years or so, he still was a shrewd character.

As they talked, Jeremiah said, "I think I'm gonna give up whiskey dranking," adding, "You know, I ain't had a drop of whiskey since we been locked up and I feel better today, than I've felt in years."

Old Jeremiah had not had anything or anyone in his life to care about, not since his wife and baby died; but now, he had Henry. And, although he had never met them, he had Henry's family. Just hearing all about them from Henry, he felt he knew Charity and the children...

Jeremiah had come to care a great deal about Henry. Henry was the first person that had acknowledged him as an equal or shown him any respect in years. If he had a son, he would've wished him to be just like Henry... Yep, thought Jeremiah, he would just hang around awhile to make sure Henry's life didn't take a turn for the worse, the way his had.

Mid-afternoon on the third day- they topped a rise and through the trees they saw smoke rising up from the chimney of an old cabin...

✳✳✳

Charity could feel Henry's nearness; she went to the door of the cabin to look out. Her eyes were drawn toward the southeast trail that she and the children had come up when they found the cabin; she saw two figures on foot, walking toward the cabin.

"Henry," she whispered, and in anticipation took a step out the door.

Henry saw her in the doorway. He broke and ran as fast as he could to her. When he reached her, he swept her up in his arms and swung her around and around and then kissed her deeply. A mutual need rose between them.

The old man hung back, not wanting to interrupt their reunion. He was misty-eyed as he watched them embrace. Moments later, all the children were coming out the door. Even from the distance he was, he could see how excited they all were- he could hear their excited voices and saw that they were all trying to hang onto their father. It warmed his old heart, but caused an ache in his chest; he wished that he had been able to see his child grow up and be as excited about seeing him come home, as these young'uns were to see Henry.

After a few moments of hugging and kissing Charity and the children, Henry sighed in satisfaction. Charity turned to look at Jeremiah then took Henry's hand and asked, "Are you going to let your friend stand out yonder all night or are you going to invite him into our home?"

He liked the sound of that… "Our Home," he repeated.

"Oh Lord," said Henry, "In all the excitement, I almost forgot about him; that's Jeremiah. We've sort of been traveling together the last month or so."

Charity smiled, "Tell him to come on and join us- supper will be ready soon." Henry motioned for Jeremiah to come to the cabin.

When Jeremiah reached them, Henry grinned big and proud and said, "Old Man, I want you to meet my family."

"Ma'am, I feel that I already know you and these young'uns- y'all is all Henry here can talk about- I be Jeremiah McClure, Ma'am."

Charity smiled at him and took his offered hand.

"This is my wife, Charity," said Henry, completing the introduction.

Jeremiah could see why Henry could fall so deeply in love with just one woman; she was a beautiful girl, apparently she also had a good head on her shoulders. Any woman that could do what she had done on her own these last couple of months deserved love and respect.

Like a proud papa bear, Henry introduced each of the children, except one. Noticing the absence of his oldest son, he asked. "Where's Uriah?" Charity then told him about the accident Uriah had while chopping wood.

Uriah was awake when his father came in and sat down on the bed.

"Papa, I'm sorry I messed up. We found another ax in the shed out back, so we figured we could get more wood chopped if we both chopped- John's ax slipped off a log and nearly took my foot off; we didn't know it was that sharp. It was an accident Papa, please don't blame John, he didn't do it on purpose."

"I know he didn't, son; it was an accident, plain and simple.

It ain't anybody's fault really. You boys are young and didn't know to separate yourselves far enough apart to keep something like that from happening. I'm home now and we're going to be fine. You'll be up and about in no time at all."

"I think I'm ready to get out of this here bed; Can you help me up to the table, Pa?" asked Uriah.

"Sure, I can, if you think you're up to it," said Henry. "We just don't want you to rush it too fast and have to pay for it later."

"Are we still going to Alabama, Papa?"

"Yes, Son, we're still going. Georgia hasn't shown me enough to keep me here for long; we'll head to Alabama as soon as your mama is ready. She likes this place here- she told me the sheriff said that we can stay here as long as none of the Finley's kinfolk come and claim the land. It won't be ours, though, unless we file claims to it and I don't think that will happen. I don't want to sink too much time into it, if you know what I mean."

"Yes, Papa, I understand. A man that has his own land and a family, has something worth working for, right?"

"That's right son; he sure does," Henry smiled. "Now, let's get in there and eat, before your mama gets mad at us for making her wait any longer." As Henry helped Uriah into the dining room, he said, "The best part of this day is that we get to eat all them fine vittles, your mama's been cooking for us."

Before Henry and Jeremiah arrived, Charity had already set the table, using Mrs. Finley's plates and utensils. She was sure that Mrs. Finley wouldn't mind. She definitely seemed to be enjoying having a houseful of children around. Charity had observed her spirit walking around the cabin, smiling at the goings on. It didn't bother Charity seeing Mrs. Finley's ghost there. Neither did the spirit of the young woman that had followed Mr. McClure inside.

Since meeting Two Feathers at Yellow River, she had seen several ghosts, and was getting quite used to seeing them. They were just spirits, they meant no harm; they just weren't ready to cross over...

"Ma'am, this is a mighty fine table you've set before us this day."

"Well, thank you, Mr. McClure."

"Please, Ma'am, just call me Jeremiah. And, if'n you don't mind, I'd like ta be the one ta ask the blessing this evening."

"No Sir, I don't mind at all," Charity replied, "We'd be honored to have you ask- for we have truly been blessed this day."

"Yes'um, we sure have, ain't we," Jeremiah agreed.

For some reason, Jeremiah reminded her of her grandfather. It was not so much that he favored him, and the tone of their voices and manner of speech was nothing alike- Maybe, it was because he was old and gray bearded like her grandfather was or because they were both wise with age; either way, she decided she liked Jeremiah very much and was glad that Henry had found a friend in him. Speaking of beards, thought Charity, Henry is going to need a good bath and a shave before he would look like his old self. But even if he returned to looking like his old self, she didn't feel that he was the same sweet, innocent Henry that had ventured off in search of free land two months prior; however, she also realized that she wasn't the same, either- time and events change people...

That night, Charity felt content; she enjoyed having her entire family together again. The children were happy; they were laughing and talking, each needing their father's attention after his prolonged absence. She loved the loving looks Henry was giving her over the tops of their children's heads. And their newest family member, Jeremiah, who was grinning from ear to ear as he told tall-tales to the boys about his adventures, seemed to be making himself right at home...

∗∗∗

Yes, they're the picture of a perfect family, thought Hank Wheeler, as he spied on them from the edge of the forest. What he wouldn't give to have him a woman like that one in there. He'd wanted her since first laying eyes on her back in Sandersville. He'd seen some mighty-fine Indian flesh in his years of traveling about and he'd had his share of them, but that one in there was especially pretty with those big, violet-colored eyes of hers.

Yep, he wanted her mighty bad. The only thing that had held him back, was his scout, Unegadihi- Unegadihi had gotten the name of, "Unegadihi," from the Cherokee; it meant, "white-man-killer". The two of them had been together as partners, for nigh on twenty-five years- way before the relocation of the Georgia Indians started was when he had taken him on as a scout for the army.

For years, Hank Wheeler had him a little squaw named, Ugugunega, which in English meant, White Owl. He'd traded her father half a dozen fine horses for her- but she'd died twelve years earlier in a smallpox outbreak. Since then, he hadn't replaced her- he'd just taken what he needed whenever he needed it and Unegadihi had never interfered. He didn't know what it was about this little half-breed squaw, but whatever it was, for some reason, Unegadihi had stood firm on him not taking her and doing as he pleased with her. Unegadihi usually never said a word about who he took or what he did to them; but this one here, was different. The Indian had been acting strange- so strange that he even had him a little on edge. Maybe he wants her for himself, thought Wheeler. Yeah, that's probably what it is… Well, thought Wheeler, he's got another thing coming if he thinks that's going to happen.

***

Charity could sense that Wheeler was out there watching them; she felt his eyes on her and her family, but she was determined not to let it bother her. Not tonight, she thought to herself as she smiled at her husband. She had her Henry back home and her son was recovering; that was all that mattered right then.

After supper, she cleared the dishes while Henry and the children got caught up and became reacquainted with one another. She knew that later on, he would be all hers.

She heard Henry, laughing at their pet flying squirrels as they crawled in and out of his pocket. Even the old man couldn't resist the little critters, and soon, he, too, had one in his pocket. He laughed and told Henry that he could see why they were only good to have as pets. "It'd take a dozen of them little critters to make a decent meal for one man," he chuckled as one of them climbed atop his head then scrambled down into his shirt pocket.

At bedtime, they moved Uriah into the front room and made a place for him to sleep. Jeremiah opted to sleep near the front door. He said, that way, he wouldn't be disrupting their sleep; he said that since he was getting older, he needed to get up and go out more often. The real reason he wanted near the door was in case someone tried to sneak in on them…

Charity was thankful the cabin had a loft for the children; that way, she and Henry had the back bedroom all to themselves. It had been months since they had been entirely alone in a room with an actual bed- they could strip off naked and truly enjoy their reunion. But as the time came for them to close themselves off from the world, both felt a little shy- It's almost like our wedding night, thought Charity as she gazed at Henry.

She heated water and filled the bathtub so that she and Henry could bathe- she had intended for them to bathe separately; that was how they had always bathed, but Henry stripped off naked and crawled into the tub before she could suggest otherwise. When he asked her to wash his back, she obliged- Lovingly, she soaped and washed every part of him that was above water level. When he finished, she shyly slid her dress off and stepped into the tub. He soaped the washrag and gently washed her back, arms, shoulders and neck. She thought he was going to wash her breasts the way she had washed his chest, but he released the rag and let it slid down her chest. She finished bathing and then stood to dry off.

While she was finishing her bath, Henry had put on his nightclothes- she was at a disadvantage. When he stood to dry, she had adverted her eyes, but not Henry; his eyes took in every inch of her body while lying in bed waiting for her to join him. Timidly, she dried her body and then donned her gown, before walking to the bed. She had butterflies in her stomach as she stood beside the bed waiting on him to extinguish the lamp; however, he had no intention of smothering the flame.

After a moment, she slid her gown off her shoulders and let it drop to the floor in a puddle at her feet. She saw his body respond to her nakedness as she climbed into bed and lay down beside him. And, even as hungry as they both were for each other's touch, they took their time to rediscover each others body and fully enjoy their reunion. Henry's touch was soft and gentle as he took her into his arms and held her a moment before they kissed.

As they kissed and explored the others body, their earlier

shyness left them. Henry's lips and tongue left her mouth and found their way to her breasts; tenderly, he suckled and teased before moving down to her stomach and thighs. Her back arched to his touch as he pleasured her slowly and gently before mounting her and thrusting himself deeply into her womanhood. He stifled her moans with his lips and tongue to keep her from screaming out in pleasure. After only a few precious moments, neither could hold back any longer; they succumbed to the moment of most intense pleasure, luxuriating in the waves of dissipating passion... they soon fell asleep in each others embrace. Morning came way too soon. Charity would have loved to stay in bed another hour, but duty called. Reluctantly, she crawled out of bed and dressed. Henry was sleeping so peacefully, she quietly slipped out and left him to sleep a few more minutes, before the children would noisily arise.

26

Hank Wheeler

When Charity awoke the next morning, the wonderful aroma of brewing coffee filled her nostrils. It reminded her of when she was a little girl and woke in her grandparent's cabin. After dressing and going into the front room, she stopped short at seeing Jeremiah sitting at the table; for a moment, his gray hair and beard caused her to think he was her grandfather. For some reason, Charity had forgotten they had company. She quickly twisted her hair into a bun and pinned it, making herself presentable.

"Hope you didn't mind that I helped myself to making some coffee, Ma'am," Jeremiah said sheepishly.

"No, sir; I don't mind at all, as long as you made enough for me too," she said, smiling at him, and saying, "Good morning."

He grinned at her and said, "O'course I did, Ma'am; and a good mornin' ta you, too. It's been a few days since I had a good cup of coffee; I was a startin' ta have the jitters and a mighty big headache to boot."

✳✳✳

Jeremiah could tell from the looks of her that Henry had done right by her, the night before. Yes, sir, she looks like a satisfied woman this morning, thought Jeremiah, accessing her relaxed features. Many men do wrong by their womenfolk. Lots of 'em don't take into account that women enjoy being intimate too, as long as you're gentle and let 'em enjoy it. Otherwise ye leave 'em frustrated and grumpy; he didn't like frustrated and grumpy.

He'd learned about pleasuring women from a wealthy woman down in New Orleans who a healthy appetite for male companionship, back when he was in his mid-thirties... He'd spent four of the easiest years of his life, in the bayous of Louisiana... until war carried him away from there. Life, as a guest of the Viilliere plantation's mistress, was everything a man with a taste for good rum and a healthy libido could want, until the British came ashore intent on capturing New Orleans. General Jackson saw to it that that didn't happen, but still, their capturing the plantation disrupted his days of leisure there...

✳✳✳

At first, Charity was a little shy around Jeremiah; however, his easygoing nature set her at ease.

"Ma'am, I would've started some breakfast, but to tell the truth, I ain't much of a cook."

"That's alright, Mr. McClure. I'm just going to fix some flapjacks and sausage this morning. I was able to get some maple syrup while I was in town the other day; it will be a real treat for Henry and the children; you and me too," she added. Pouring herself a cup of coffee, she set down at the table with Jeremiah.

"I want to thank you for keeping an eye out last night, Mr. McClure. I was able to get a good night's sleep knowing that you were sleeping in here by the door. I know you slept there so that you could watch out for us."

"Well, Ma'am, it weren't no trouble a'tall… And, I wouldn't gonna bring it up so soon, but quite frankly, I did want ta talk to you about those two riders that's been a'follerin' you and them young'uns."

"To be honest, I don't know why they seem to be following us, Jeremiah. The first time I saw them, was back in Sandersville. One of them is a white man that wears his feathered hat, askew. He plumb gives me the heebie-jeebies the way he looks at me… The other one is a big, hawk-faced Indian. He's scary looking too, but don't bother me like the white man does," Charity told him.

"Does the Indian have jest a patch a hair that runs right down the middle of his head?" asked Jeremiah.

"Yes, he does; how'd you know that?"

"Because, I know those two men," said Jeremiah, with a curl to his lip. "That's Captain Hank Wheeler and that Indian scout of his. Wheeler ain't right in the head; he ain't right at all! I have been a knowing of him, since the Red Stick War, of 1814. Yep, I fought with Wheeler at the Battle of N'Orleans…

Lila M Beckham

He's always had him a thing for Indian girls; even back then, he was raping and pillaging Creek Indian maidens. He'd even grab him a slave girl outta the fields if he took a fancy to her… He'd have his way and then leave 'em for dead most of the time. Many of us didn't like what he did, but they was some of 'em that did- those of us that didn't take to it, mostly avoided it and kept our mouths shut. Wheeler's never done nothing but take what he wanted. He might've set his sight's on you, Ma'am- I saw him march a hunnert infantry, forty miles off the track we was headed just to get at one little gal…"

Charity understood then why she felt so eerie lately and why she saw such awful visions flash through her mind when Wheeler was near.

"I can tell you one thang for shore, Ma'am; that's not gonna happen- If I have breath in my body, it ain't ever gonna happen to you; not on old Jeremiah's watch. I ain't afraid a him the way I was when I was younger. You keep your eyes peeled and let me know about any strange going's on; and, I'll do the same. Have ya told your man, yet," he asked.

"That coffee sure smells good," said Henry as he walked into the room from the bedroom. "I can't believe I was still piled up in bed, with the sun done a coming up- it peeking through the window was what woke me."

"You looked like you were resting peacefully, so I didn't want to wake you," Charity said, getting up from the table and walking into the kitchen area. She poured Henry a cup of coffee

Lila M Beckham

and handed it to him. He kissed her on the cheek and patted her on the hip. She blushed and then busied herself cooking the flapjacks and sausage for their breakfast.

She knew that as soon as the children smelled them cooking, they'd be up and running about. Uriah stirred on his pallet; she wondered if he was hurting in his sleep. He hadn't had any of the laudanum mixture since he'd gone to bed the night before.

Jeremiah noticed her looking over toward Uriah; he said, "Ma'am, I hope you don't mind, but I gave the boy a dose of the medicine an hour of so b'fore you got up this morning. He was starting to moan a little in his sleep. I took it upon myself ta doctor him and not wake you up."

"No, Mr. McClure, I don't mind at all. When he stirred, I felt a little guilty at the thought that I might've neglected him," she replied.

"You ain't got anything to feel guilty about," said Henry.

"No, Ma'am, you sure don't- you've done a fine job a doctoring him and that foot of his."

"Yes, you have," assured Henry.

While eating breakfast, Henry asked Charity, "You're sure the sheriff said there wouldn't be a problem with us a staying here for a while, right?"

"I'm sure," she replied. "He said this place belonged to the Finley's and that unless some of their kin showed up and laid claim to it, we could stay here as long as we wanted to."

"Well, I'm not sure how long we'll be staying, but we may as well fix it up and make it more livable. Jeremiah, do you mind helping me and the boys do some repairs on the cabin after we eat?"

Jeremiah replied, sprightly, "I'm ready when you is, Henry- I bet I can work circles around you and those boys!"

"As soon as y'all eat your breakfast, you can have at it. We're going to need some more wood chopped," she added, her voice barely above a whisper. She felt a pang of guilt in her chest over Uriah's foot.

"Don't worry bout the, would've, should've, and could've been's, Ma'am," said Jeremiah. "Who's to say that it wouldn't a happened even if you or his pa had been right there with him? Some things are just meant to be."

"I know," Charity said thoughtfully. "But, now, he'll be crippled the rest of his life; it's gonna be hard on him."

"Maybe not as hard as ye think… there's a lot worse that could…" his voice trailed off and Charity realized that he'd lost a child. By then, the children were all awake and clamoring for their father's attention. Henry tried his best to talk to each one as they were asking a dozen questions at a time, and in return, each one was telling him about their adventures. All the children and adults talking at once made it quite noisy in the small cabin.

"Maybe we can go back and scrape up some more of that gold," Henry chuckled, adding if he'd known when he and

Jeremiah came through there, he would've looked for it.

Jeremiah quickly told him that he might not want to do that. "Ain't nothing worse than getting a fever for that stuff!" Jeremiah exclaimed, adding, "It'd be worse than that land fever, you had."

"Yeah, I reckon you're right, Old Man, but it'd sure make things a lot easier having a pocket full of gold nuggets."

"Yep, but ain't you ever heard, that anything worth havin', is worth fightin' for," Jeremiah said.

"I thought it was anything worth having, is worth working for," Henry replied with a raised brow.

"Yep, that too - fightin', workin', it's all the same- it requires effort," said Jeremiah, then he and Henry both stood up from the table.

"That was a mighty fine breakfast, Ma'am- I appreciate you a havin' me," said Jeremiah, rubbing his full belly.

"Yes, it was delicious, Darlin'," said Henry. Then he, Jeremiah, and all the boys except Uriah, walked outside.

Charity turned to Uriah and asked, "Do you want to go outside, Son?"

"No Ma'am, not right now," he replied, and then added, "Maybe tomorrow."

"It's alright," she said, smiling at him. "You can keep me company while I clean up the dishes and straighten up in here."

✳✳✳

Not far away, Unegadihi was studying his long-time

companion. He had never thought much of Hank Wheeler. As a matter of fact, he was one white man he'd enjoy killing; however, since the wars and the removal of the Indians, it had been to his advantage to hang with the Captain. At least, it had kept him well fed and off of the reservation… However, he knew that Wheeler was up to his wicked ways again; he did not have the stomach for it; not this time.

27

Spellbound

After months of camping under the stars, it was nice to have a roof over their heads; however, Charity was becoming restless. She didn't like being cooped up inside the cabin, day after day. She has never lived close enough to a town to visit often- in fact, she could count on one hand the number of times she had gone to a populated place- and two of those times were Fort Charlotte, which wasn't actually a town... She wanted to go into town and walk around it the way they had done in Augusta; she also wanted to explore the area around the cabin. Heck, she just wanted to get out and do something!

The last time he came out to check on Uriah, Dr. Lane had told her that there were a lot of caves around the area, also Lake Allatoona was nearby, and above the lake, a little higher in the mountains, he said there was a beautiful waterfall that she might want to go see.

While Henry, Jeremiah, and John were working on the exterior of the cabin, she decided to go out and explore near the cabin. Both Henry and Jeremiah tried to dissuade her from going off on her own, but Henry could tell it would be of no use in arguing, because she had her mind made up.

She told them that she had her knife and that she was taking the musket with her. "I'll be fine!" she exclaimed. Begrudgingly, Henry gave in, but told her to be very careful.

So that Henry wouldn't worry as much, she decided to take Charles with her; he loved exploring as much as she did; besides, she figured he'd sneak and follow her the way he had the morning she went hunting and killed the deer.

She and Charles were both excited as they followed a well traveled trail down the mountainside. She figured it must've been forged by Mr. Finley during the years he lived there. She was a lover of nature, and it did not take long for her to accustom to her surroundings; Charles too, seemed to tune right into nature. They could hear a gugutsa talala pecking at a tree, and searched for him with their eyes. Spying him about fifty yards away in an old water oak, Charity pointed him out to Charles. It was a Pileated woodpecker; He was large, probably eighteen inches in height, with a red crest atop his head.

"Boy, that shore is a big woodpecker, ain't it Mama?"

"Yes, Son, he is, and he is magnificent, isn't he!"

Charity could feel the eyes of the forest upon them as they made their way further down the hillside. They were disturbing the animals daily routines; she felt a twinge of guilt for doing so, but her guilt about disturbing them was not strong enough to cause her to return home.

The wind swayed the trees gently, as sunlight flickered

through the late spring leaves. It was exhilarating, traipsing through the musky, smelling woods, listening to the sound of nature.

They soon came upon a small, obscure trail that veered off the main one. Both looked at each other, grinned, and then broke into a run for the new trail. It was slightly overgrown from not being used often, but she could tell that it had been used a lot at some point in time.

It was downhill all the way, which gave momentum to their already fast pace. The trail ended at a clearing. Charity stopped short, but Charles barreled right on into the middle of the clearing. When he noticed that his mother was not with him, he turned to look back. She was just standing there, awestruck, gazing around the clearing.

The look on his mother's face caused Charles to also look around. He wondered what she was looking at; he didn't see anything but a clearing amid the forest. He could tell that she saw something, but what, he didn't know.

"Mama, what's wrong," asked Charles, however, she did not respond. It was as though she could no longer hear him. As though she was rendered motionless, held spellbound by whatever it was that she saw.

Without answering or acknowledging Charles, Charity walked to the center of the clearing where once there would have been a fire burning, but now, was a barren spot on the ground.

Charles watched her as she crossed her legs and then sat

down Indian style. When she began to chant and then speak in Cherokee, making motions with her hands, he walked to his mother's side, sat down as she had, and then closed his eyes and listened. They sat, for how long, neither knew, but then, both awoke, as if from a dream.

"Mama, what just happened?" asked Charles, adding, "I remember some of it, but it was like a dream and I can't remember all of it."

"It was old Two Feathers," she replied. "He is no longer with the living."

"What did he want?"

"He called me to his side and we talked. He wanted to pass along to me his earthly knowledge and some secrets of the spirit world. We will talk about it later," she said, getting to her feet. "For now, we must hurry and get home before your father gets worried and comes looking for us." Charles did not speak, just followed his mother as she started toward the trail. "We're at least three miles from home; it will be dark soon."

Lost in their own thoughts, neither said a word, as they left the clearing.

Charles was thinking about what he could remember from what had just happened. He remembered leaving his body and rising up into the air along with Two Feathers and his mother; their spirits he supposed, because he was definitely not in his body. They floated on the wind, the way an eagle soars, weightless, carried upon the current as they floated above the clearing. It was such a wonderful, peaceful feeling- he could have stayed there forever.

As they floated, Two Feathers and his mother, talked. And, although he did not know what they were saying, Charles could feel the importance of their conversation. The experience left him with a better notion, a greater grasp of his mother's role in life. He knew she was special, but in what way, he couldn't yet fully understand… He hoped one day, to earn the right to know what her role in life was, and what part he would play in that role.

When they reached the trailhead, they came face to face, with the big Indian, Unegadihi! His big, hawked-face, showed concern and then relief at the sight of them. He spoke a few words to Charity, in what sounded like broken Cherokee, and then he turned and ran off down the trail.

"What did he say, Mama?" Charles was eager to know.

"He told me to beware the "dahudigisgi", that means, Captive Catcher."

"What did he mean by that?"

"I don't know, Son, but we need to get going; it will be dark soon."

All the way back to the cabin, Charity was thoughtful; she was also a bit leery, after what Unegadihi had told her. After saying the words, captive catcher, he said, "tsulstanuyi," which meant, he has a beard. To her, it could only mean that he was warning her about Captain Wheeler, but why would he warn her about Wheeler? Weren't they companions- they were always together... She thought they were close, but undoubtedly the big Indian felt the need to warn her, but again, why? She saw a foreboding aura surrounding Wheeler back in Sandersville, and from the first, she knew, "u'ne'go'tsoduh," that his soul was dark, blackened with evil. Nokomis had called it, "Soul Sickness" when she talked about a band of people that came through her village when she was a little girl- she'd said they were surrounded by a floating dark gray mass and that their eyes were lifeless, the pupils shaped like those of a viper when they narrowed them at you... Unegadihi rode with Wheeler, had for years according to Jeremiah; therefore, she assumed that he, too, was evil. Maybe, because they were together, the aura had covered them both; but not this day. This day, when he was alone, she saw a gentle and kind soul... This gift of hers was so confusing at times! She hoped that she would understand before too much longer. Two Feathers said that she would soon know why she was the Chosen One - Telling her, "Eti, gasuyeu, so qua, egahi Ganenu tlv I," Since long ago, you are The Chosen One, Little One, you're the light, The Passageway. I'm the passageway to what, exactly? Chosen for what, exactly, she wondered. Maybe soon, she'd understand...

***

After seeing the violet-eyed one, Unegadihi breathed a sigh of relief, and then made his way back down the trail to where they were camped. When the Captain disappeared earlier that morning, he had feared for Charity's life. The Captain was a "geya kanati," a woman hunter. Once he caught them, he did horrible things to them; and when he tired of them, which could last from a few hours to several days. He would butcher them and leave them for the buzzards and wolves to consume, leaving no evidence of his carnivorous lust behind. Even when the Captain had White Owl for a wife, he would go off on a hunt, sometimes he'd be gone for days, off alone somewhere doing the things he did in his rituals with whoever he set his sights on, captured and then held captive.

On several occasions, Unegadihi had witnessed the carnage first hand, when the Captain could not contain himself long enough to wait to be alone with the young maiden. He'd seen him, bite some of them so hard that it'd tear their flesh. Unegadihi knew that he must protect the violet eyed one from the Captain at all costs; she was special, she was gifted by the Great Spirit. Not many were fit to receive gifts such as hers…

His protectiveness of the violet eyed one was not for himself, but for all human beings. She was a light to the passageway.

Although he had left his people many, many, years ago, his teachings as a young brave were etched deep into his soul. His own love of his first maiden on their wedding night had been a tender love, as taught by his people. He had not had a love for many years now. He missed that human closeness.

"Where have you been off to?" Wheeler asked, suspiciously as Unegadihi walked back into camp.

Unegadihi simply grunted and gave Wheeler one of his, "None of your business, looks," crossed his legs and then sat down by his tack. He leaned back and closed his eyes as if to meditate…

28

The Passageway

"You young chunk head, quit being such an insolent, whippersnapper," grumbled Jeremiah toward John, who had been pestering the tar out of him for the past hour or so. Jeremiah had had enough of him acting like a know it all.

"Leave Mr. McClure alone before I take you out back and switch your bottom with your pa's leather strap!" Charity told John in a firm voice. "There's no sense for you to keep annoying Mr. McClure with all this foolish nonsense. John hung his head, said, yes ma'am, and then went outside.

"Yep," exclaimed Jeremiah, "That's the only thing I hates about watching young'uns grow up. It seems all of 'em knows more'n you do, when they get about his age- makes you want to smack'em upside the head. Heck, I remember being that age myself... When I was about the same age as John, I popped off at my stepfather; he smacked me across the head with a stick of firewood." Charity smothered a smile- she was in for another of Jeremiah's lectures on child rearing- She really didn't mind the lectures and she usually enjoyed the stories that came with his advice. "When I woke up, I remembered why, I was a crawling up offend' the ground. Yeah, I respected the old man after that, and I never smarted off at him again. I finally realized that he would always know more'n I did, because he'd been around a lot longer'n me," said Jeremiah with a satisfied grunt.

"I never remember being like that with Nokomis or with Grandpa," said Charity. "I treated them with the same respect they showed me... Maybe one has to have brothers and sisters, to act like that..."

"Nah, I didn't have any, and I acted like that- maybe it's a boy thang, spoutin' off ta manhood sorta thang... seen it happen some with the Injuns too- those young bucks rebelling against the elders, wantin' ta war when the elders was tryin' ta keep it peaceful..."

Charity looked at Jeremiah- she saw that he was thoughtful.

"Jeremiah, you've been around a lot of different people, haven't you?"

"Sure I has. I been around a long time- done lots, been a lotta places."

"Do you know anything about Indian culture?" Charity asked.

Jeremiah looked at her kind of funny and said, "What kinda Indians- I thought you was at least half Indian."

"I am three-quarters to be exact; but I only know about the Cherokee."

"Well, as a matter-of-fact, I lived with the Iroquois for a spell. I know a little sumpthin about different tribes- why do you ask?"

"I was wondering about the big, hawk-faced Indian, Unegadihi. I saw him a week or so ago, and he spoke to me. It was that day me and Charles went exploring while you and Henry were working on the outside of the cabin. Do you know what kind of Indian he is? He spoke to me in broken Cherokee."

"I believe the ones with scalp-locks, or a crest like his, is called Mohawks, the "man-eaters." They've been called cannibals by some; but I ain't never seen any of that kind a going's on. It probably stems from somewhere way back there in time," he said, then continued. "In their own language, they call they-selves, "Kanienkehaka," which means, "People of the flint." You know how those stories gets passed along from generation ta generation- some of it true, some of it stretched a mile… though, I do know that their womenfolk are the clan leaders. Like most civilized tribes, the womenfolk make all the decisions concerning the clan, excepting for wars o'course, that'd be men-folk business, sort of like you run your household, Ma'am- Henry, he leaves most a the disciplining to you; he takes care of the handy work, don't he, " Jeremiah said.

Charity looked at him long and hard, then asked, "Have you ever heard anyone called a Passageway before?"

"A Passageway, huh?" Charity nodded her head in affirmation.

"Yep, I heard of the passageways, from the Iroquois peoples. Did your folks ever tell you about the different worlds and the passageways to them different worlds?" he asked.

"No, I don't think so; if my grandmother ever told me anything about them, I don't remember, and I am sure I would have remembered." Charity poured herself and Jeremiah a cup of fresh coffee.

"Well," said Jeremiah, pulling himself up straighter in his chair. Charity noticed right away that he seemed sharper than usual and not as uneducated as he led people to believe he was.

"There are all sorts of prophecies, myths, and legends told by the Elders of the tribes that don't change much from generation to generation, or tribe to tribe, so there must be truth to 'em. I've heard several elders describing these passageways between the worlds. Most say it occurs by going up through a reed and entering that world through of a pool of water.

If you close your eyes and think about it, you can see the symbolism and the beauty of this 'water purification' in your mind; its sort a like the Biblical baptism- a rebirth. A person must make a journey upward, through the reed with their eyes closed, thinking only about their destination, climbing to a higher, more compelling level of consciousness. That's the next world," he explained, adding, "I've heard other Indian creation stories that describe the entranceway between worlds, as occurring through a hole in the sky. Either way, most tribes believe that each person's path is predestined and their devotion to it, determines where they are in their spiritual journey to the next world," Jeremiah informed her.

"What about the Chosen One; have you ever heard that phrase?"

"Well, now that you got me ta thinking on all such as that, I reckon there's a lot of stuff a coming back ta me. The Chosen One, if I recall, is, 'He who goes forth shining, or he who let's his light shine;' something to that effect.

There's another way into the next world that I remember hearing that says if you can latch onto someone who's on their journey into the next realm, you can hitch a ride with 'em into the next world, that next higher level of consciousness, without even having earned the right to go there- that'd a be cheatin' your way in… and things don't always go as planned when that happens- Are you a asking all this because you run up with that big Indian, Missy, or is there more to it than that?" he asked curiously.

"I didn't realize that you knew so much about Indians, Jeremiah," said Charity, "but, to answer your question, the old Indian with eyes the color of falling snow, his name was Two Feathers, and my great-grandfather, Shooting Arrow, and my great-uncle, Tokola, all said that I was the Chosen One. And now, this big Indian, Unegadihi, told me that I am the Chosen One, the Light to the Passageway… they all said it, but none have explained what it means to be the "Chosen One" or what I am supposed to do to light the passageway or how to find it; it has me greatly confused. I know that I can travel the wind, and I've even, upon several of the journeys, changed shape, into that of an eagle." She wondered if Jeremiah thought she was crazy. He was thoughtful, but so far, had not spoken. As she sat there waiting, she felt that he believed her.

"Not many are given these gifts; only the chosen one's, so to speak," said Jeremiah. "You'll just have'ta accept it, Missy; there ain't nothing else you can do. This gift you've inherited from you're ancestors is given to you to use and to guide the ones that ain't capable of guiding themselves- If the gift is as powerful as I think it is, you'se can use it for protection too- sort of a protective shield against evil... I *can* tell you one thang- I feel a lot better a knowing that Unegadihi thinks so highly of you. If need be, he'll protect you with his life. Those Mohawks respects the feminine gender much more than other tribes does, more'n most white men do, and that's a shame. Like I said, their clan is ruled by their womenfolk, but so are the Cherokee and several others."

Henry walked in, looked at their serious faces and asked, "What are you two up to?"

"We was just talking, boy," said Jeremiah. "Why? You a gettin' jealous of an old man," he grinned.

"Hell nah, I ain't jealous of you, you old coot! You ain't anything to be jealous of," he said, wrapping his arms around Charity from behind and hugging her gently.

Enjoying their friendly banter and feeling the love radiating from Henry's heart, Charity smiled before turning to kiss him squarely on the mouth.

"Mama's kissing daddy," Nancy hollered. Then, Mary

chimed in, "Mama's kissing daddy, Mama's kissing daddy," she repeated; they all laughed.

Hank Wheeler didn't like the change he saw in Unegadihi. The big, dumb bastard must be in love with that little half-breed squaw, thought Wheeler, as he sat watching him. He was going to make sure Unegadihi got to see what was left of her when he finished with her. Wheeler licked his lips in anticipation- He couldn't wait until the culmination of his plans came to fruition. He'd never waited this long or put this much time and effort into one of his hunts, but he had a feeling that she'd be worth it in the end. It made his mouth water just thinking about it. Yes, he thought, shooting daggers toward Unegadihi, she was going to be a delectable little sweetbread…

Unegadihi knew what Captain Wheeler was thinking about. He could tell from the look on his face and the way he licked his lips every once in a while, that he was thinking about what he wanted to do to the Chosen One. Unegadihi was just biding his time, waiting until the captain made his move. He would then have to act. He was ready, willing, and able to do whatever it took to protect her from Wheeler's grasp.

At the cabin, Charles begged his mother to go on another

exploration. He and his brothers had explored some, but all his brothers wanted to do was to walk into town to look at girls! Ugh! Even Uriah had hobbled along on their last trip to town. He'd been eyeballing some yellow haired girl named Jane, and John was looking at a blue-eyed gal, named Mary; or visa versa. Girls didn't interest Charles that much; he'd rather explore the mountains with his mother, the way they did that day they met the bid Indian on the trail.

"Please Mama, we won't stay as long as we did last time, please," he begged. Charity looked into his pleading eyes; she couldn't help but to say yes.

"We'll go," she said, "but it will have to wait until tomorrow morning. We'll leave after we finish breakfast and chores. I have too much to do today and there's no one to watch the little ones."

"Okay, but we'll go early right?" Charles asked.

"Yes, Son, we will go early," she assured him with a sincere smile. Charity tried to shake it off, but over the last several days, she had been having an eerie feeling that persisted; it just would not go away no matter how she tried to assure herself that all was well...

29

Visions

The morning could not come early enough for young Charles, who awoke before anyone else in the small cabin had roused from sleep. At first light, he noticed that the sky was dark and dreary when he returned from the outhouse. Bluish-black, weighty clouds hung low on the horizon and thunder rumbled in the distance. In his mind, Charles saw him and his mother walking through a storm- it was thundering and lightning; rain fell so heavily, they could barely see five feet in front of them. Crestfallen, Charles surely thought it was going to be a stormy, rain-swept day as he waited on the front porch for his mother to wake and the sun to continue rising. When it did, the dark clouds dissipated and the sky turned brilliant blue. A very mild breeze blew; with it, it carried a bouquet of honeysuckle, Ligustrum, and crepe jasmine… It was going to be a beautiful day on the mountain; Charles smiled.

Noise from inside the cabin drew him indoors to see if his mother was awake. To his disappointment, it was only Jeremiah; he was making coffee.

"Youse is up early," noted Jeremiah as Charles walked to

the table and sat down with a plump. Charles sighed, but said nothing.

"What's the matter? Why is you a dragging around like a gopher turtle carryin' around a fifty pound shell on his back?"

"I'm just wait'n on Mama to get up, so we can go exploring."

"She'll be up as soon as she smells the coffee," chuckled the old man.

"I wish we were leavin' now," said Charles. "It was thundering before the sun come up- it might come back and start raining and then we won't be able to go as far as we wanted to."

"Don't you worry, Son; that rain'll stay away if your mama wants it to," assured Jeremiah. They both heard a noise and turned to see Charity coming from the bedroom; she was fully dressed, right down to her walking boots.

"Let's go to the waterfall that Doc Lane told us about, Mama!" exclaimed Charles, excitedly, jumping up from the table and nearly toppling his chair.

Charity smiled at his excitement- she, too, was anxious to go, but she had certain duties to attend to before they could leave for their day of explorations. "Doctor Lane said that it was on the other side of the lake, about ten miles north of town," she replied. "Let me see if your daddy can do without one of the horses today, if so, we can ride double. He's worried we won't make it home before dark; if we take a horse, we'll make better time."

Henry came from the bedroom; worry creased his brow.

Charity had already told Henry where she was planning on going. He was concerned that she and Charles would run out of daylight, before they could return home.

"If it gets dark, we can camp out under the stars, like we did coming here- it'll be fun, won't it, Mama!"

"I can look after the young'uns," offered Jeremiah.

Charity turned to Henry. "If we don't make it back before suppertime, there are enough leftovers to feed you, Jeremiah, and the children."

"I can cook," said Jeremiah with a grunt. "And I'm a good'urn!"

"What about you and Charles?" Henry asked, "What if you get stuck out there all night; what will y'all eat?"

"I'm taking some biscuits, dried meat, and a jar of peaches. If that don't do us, I'm sure I can manage to scrape something together for us to eat," she said, giving him an impish grin. Charles' excitement had rubbed off on her; she felt vibrant and restless all at the same time; she too, was ready to get going.

"Be careful;" said Henry, "there are all sorts of dangers on the trail." Charity smiled and said, "We will, Henry." She could not help but think of all the weeks she and the children were on their own on the trail- they'd managed fine- she knew how to watch out for danger. Henry was just being overprotective. Charity hurried to fix breakfast and make sure the other children had what they needed before she packed a hamper to take with her and Charles. By the time they were ready, the sun was atop the trees to the east and Charles was even more fidgety than he had been earlier.

"On your way through town," said Henry, "would you stop by the mercantile and tell Mr. Reed that I'll be in later on today to pick up those supplies, he ordered for us."

"I will," Charity said, bending down from where she sat astraddle the barebacked horse. She kissed him soundly; their lips clinging for a few moments. She looked up to see Jeremiah blushing; she had to laugh. She never would have thought an old man like him would be embarrassed over a kiss.

As she and Charles cantered off down the hillside toward town, she started to feel the excitement of being away from her duties and out and about; however, the closer to town they got, the eerier she felt. When they crossed over the river and into town, there was a flurry of activity going on.

"I wonder what's up," Charles asked over her shoulder.

"I don't know, Son, but something definitely is," she replied.

As they neared the Mercantile, Charity started having visions. Horrible visions of a blond-haired girl being savagely raped and mutilated...

The visions blinded her temporarily and she pulled the horse to a halt, right there in the middle of Main Street.

"Mama, what's wrong?" Charles asked.

She mumbled an incoherent reply, and he asked, "Ma'am?"

She couldn't stop the visions; they just kept coming and coming. Suddenly, she *was* the girl in the visions! She could feel him plunging his fingers deep inside her, his teeth biting into her breasts. She tried to look at him, but could only see the top of his head. When he raised his head, his grinning lips were covered in blood. He took his bloodied fingers and smoothed back her blond hair from around her face. He then traced her lips with his finger and stuck it into her mouth, trying to make her taste her own blood- Charity was repulsed by his actions and tried to turn her head- he grabbed her face and made her face him. His features were gruesome and he had an evil grin.

Suddenly, her eyes locked with his and she could not pull them away from him. As he gazed into her eyes, he gasped loudly and drew back momentarily, as if shocked by what he saw…

She did not know that what he had seen was *her* eyes staring back at him.

Charity heard Charles saying, "Mama, what's wrong? You're bleeding," he said excitedly. Blood ran down her legs and soaked into the hide of the horse; her breasts were bleeding too, the bodice of her dress was also bloody.

Charles jumped down off the horse and began hollering for Doctor Lane, who he saw down the street. Charity felt arms wrap around her, and then she was lifted down from the horse and being carried. She raised her eyes and saw that it was the big Indian, Unegadihi, who carried her. She heard Doctor Lane saying, "Bring her in here and lay her on the table." It was the same table they had laid Uriah on, when his toes had to be amputated. As if distanced from herself, she heard someone calling for Henry, and then realized it was her that called his name.

"What happened to her?"

"I don't know, Doc," Charles replied, "She just stopped the horse, froze like she'd seen something and then she started bleeding!"

"Lord, this whole day has been crazy- First, Jane Reed goes missing out of her bed, and now Mrs. Gullege- Lord, help me!" exclaimed Doctor Lane. "You should go get your father," shouted the doctor.

That was the last thing Charity heard, before her world went black.

"She's coming around- Charity, can you hear me?" She could hear, but couldn't find her voice to speak. "Charity, can you hear me?" This time, she managed to mumble Henry's name.

"No, hun, it's me, Doctor Lane... Charity, are you with child?"

"No," she mumbled.

"Hmm…" he mumbled, thinking to himself.

Someone asked, "What's wrong with her, Doc?"

"I don't know," he replied.

Everything went dark again as Charity slipped into unconsciousness.

As soon as she lost consciousness, she was back in the dark, dank place with the bloody-faced man. He kissed her very hard, bruising her lips; the irony taste of blood overpowered her other senses. In his fervor, his tooth cut her lip. He released her mouth, but began suckling and slobbering on her body again.

"I can't explain it," Doctor Lane said to Henry. "It's like she's been violated, and then, there are those bite marks on her breasts- I know its bites because you can see where the teeth dug into the flesh! Now, bruises are appearing on her arms that look like somebody was squeezing them real hard, and it looks like, somebody punched her in the jaw too. Your boy said they left your place and rode straight here... He said she was fine until she stopped the horse. According to him, she just stared off into space and then started bleeding! I ain't ever seen nothing like it in my life!" the doctor exclaimed.

Tears welled up in Henry's eyes when he saw Charity.

"Who could've done such a thing to her," he mumbled to himself. Anger rose up in him something fierce and involuntarily he balled up his fists. Noticing this, Doctor Lane gave him a hard look.

"Oh God, no, Doc- I would never lay a hurtful hand on my wife; she is my whole life. It just makes me so mad that someone could do this to her!"

Disoriented and in a lot of pain, Charity was slowly coming

to.

"No," she mumbled, "the blond haired girl, you have to save her Henry!" Henry looked at the Doctor and the Doctor looked at him.

"She's probably just delirious," mumbled the doctor. "The whole town's been out looking for Jane Reed this morning; she probably heard us talking about it."

"Maybe," said Henry, as he bent down over Charity, taking her hand gently in his. With his other hand, he brushed her hair from her face.

With the stroke of Henry's hand on her hair, a flood of memories came to Charity. "She's still alive," Charity said. "Henry, you have to save her!"

"Save who," asked Henry.

"The blond-headed girl; Wheeler has her; he's hurting her, not me."

Henry and the Doctor both looked at each other.

"What's wrong with her, Doc?" begged Henry.

"You know, I read about something like this in a medical journal a long time back. It said that some people have the ability to feel another's pain, even bleed for them. I think it's called 'stigmata' or something like that. Like Christ on the cross, some people have been known to bleed out the palms of their hands or they'll bleed out their side, as if their side was pierced by an arrow." After taking Charity's hands to check for puncture wounds and finding none, he mumbled, "Hmm, this entire thing is strange, that's for sure!"

Jeremiah, who had been standing back, looking and listening, not wanting to get in the way, mumbled, "She's an Empath," then stepped out the door. Unegadihi, who had carried Charity from the horse to the doctor's house, was also waiting nearby. Jeremiah made a beeline, straight for him.

"Where's Wheeler?" he demanded.

"I do not know," Unegadihi replied. "He left camp sometime during the night. I came into town thinking he might have come to town."

Jeremiah could tell that the Indian was telling the truth, so he asked him if he knew of any place where Wheeler might go to be alone.

Unegadihi told Jeremiah that he'd seen Wheeler entering a cave at the bottom of the mountains, and that he'd also seen the Captain above the lake, near the cave that's behind the waterfall.

"Can you take us to them if need be?"

Unegadihi nodded his head.

"Let's get the Sheriff and head up there," said Jeremiah, gruffly. "He's up ta no good out there, a doing something that ought not to be done to anyone!" Just then, Henry appeared in the doorway of the doctor's house. "We've got ta find the Sheriff!" snapped Jeremiah. "Then we can go find the bastard!"

30

Evil Incarnate

Several men that hung around Doc's house after seeing the big Indian carry Charity inside, stepped up and told Jeremiah that the Sheriff, Mr. Reed, and several others were conducting a search of the outbuildings and storerooms around town, looking for Jane Reed; saying she was still missing.

Someone voiced their opinion that she had run off with a boy.

"We know she's missing," Jeremiah grumbled, "We might know where to find her. Y'all help us find the Sheriff!"

Doctor Lane was staring at Charity and rubbing his chin with his hand. A habit he had when he was worrisome over something and this was worrisome. This is perplexing as hell, he thought to himself.

Mercifully, Charity had slipped back into unconsciousness. He called his wife in to sit by Charity and tend her so that he could take a much-needed break. He walked into the other room and started fingering through his medical journals. He was trying to find the article that he had read a few years earlier; it was written by a German doctor whose name he could not pronounce much less remember- however, he did remember the article. In it, the doctor said that he had examined a Roman Catholic, Augustinian Nun, in some place over *there*. This nun, besides being famous for bleeding from her hands and feet, out of wounds that one would expect to have occurred during the Crucifixion of Christ, was also something of a practitioner of medicine. It said that sick folks came to her and that she "somehow," knew what their ailments were and what type of disease or whatever they had was, and that she prescribed cures for them. The doctor called it a stigma, something or other... Stigmata - Maybe that was the name he was searching for. He needed to look for that word in the title.

When he finally found the article, he sat down with a cup of coffee, lit his pipe, and began to read. The German doctor whose name he could not pronounce wrote that some people, mostly women, can believe and feel something so strongly that it leads to the individual embodiment of the contemplated pain… *That has to be what is going on with Charity Gullege.*

After finishing the article, he mumbled aloud, "Well, I might just have me a case of the Stigmata, right here in Canton! I need to make a record of this; it's surely something that you don't see everyday." He heard his wife calling from the other room. And, as he walked into the room and was walking toward Charity, he saw a mark appear on her face; stunned, he watched as her cheek started to bleed. It was as if some invisible knife had cut her!

"Damn!" he exclaimed under his breath. "What the hell- I haven't ever seen anything like this before," he muttered to his wife.

Mrs. Lane was scared half to death; her eyes were as big as saucers. Slowly, she backed away from Charity. When her husband looked at her, she asked, "Jackson is this some sort of witchcraft or devil possession?"

"No, Martha; this ain't the middle-ages and we don't burn people at the stake anymore." Still thoughtful, he said, "I've been reading up on it, and there has been a few more cases like hers. There seems to be a direct link of some sort, between her, and… someone else that is suffering for some reason. He had almost said Jane Reed- but he did not want to add to his wife's fright. And, although it was probable, he was not positive that Jane was Charity's direct connection.

"Do you think its Jane Reed," asked Mrs. Lane.

"Well, who else could it be," he declared. "Other the fact that they are both women, I don't know why she would be connected to Jane- but she kept saying that we had to save the blond-haired girl- Jane is blond-haired, and she is missing- it's as if this woman is connected to Jane by an invisible tunnel, a passageway… Lord help us, if the wounds she's suffering are replicated from Jane and she is suffering the same violations- good Lord, she's just a child!"

Henry, Jeremiah, and Unegadihi had finally located the

Sheriff and Mr. Reed. Unegadihi was leading them to the cave that was located above the lake, where he saw the Captain checking it out. It would still take them an hour and a half of hard riding to get there. By then, it could be too late to save Jane.

***

Even though she wanted to escape the pain, Charity could not pull herself from Jane; she feared that if she left her, the girl would perish at the hands of the sadistic Captain Wheeler. Wheeler was euphoric. He seemed to be taking extreme pleasure in inflicting pain on Jane. *Maybe it's me he thinks he's hurting; he sure seems to like getting right in my face and staring into my eyes.*

Charity felt his teeth sink into her breasts and although she was in excruciating pain, she could not take her eyes off his as he stared into her eyes.

Every time Wheeler looked into the girl's eyes, he no longer saw her eyes; he now saw those violet-blue eyes of that little half-breed he'd been following. *This is almost as good as having the real thing.*

Wheeler looked deep into her eyes again; the pain and fear he saw there gave him immense pleasure. Um, damn, this is what she was made for, thought Wheeler, staring into her eyes as he plunged himself in her and bit down on her nipple harder, trying to make her scream… *Why won't she give in, most do before it's over.*

Although it was extremely painful and unnerving, so far, Charity had been able to distance herself from what was happening to her body, Jane's body; Jane's mind had left long ago... Charity felt utter disgust and loathing for him and his sadistic lust; she'd never known nothing but gentleness and pleasure when she and Henry made love- but this is not making love- this is pure evil desecration. She knew that with every bite, he was thinking of her, not Jane.

I'm not weak like Jane, she thought to herself; I can survive this, she can't. *I am strong as an ox, wasn't that what Grandpa used to tell me-* and with that thought, she felt her strength growing. Instead of lying there slowly dying, she began to fight back, but the more she fought, the stronger he seemed to become!

After trying to fight him for a few minutes, she changed her tactics; her meager, physical strength was no match for his physical prowess.

Thinking back to the first time she saw him, she remembered how smug and aloof, he acted sitting atop his horse- *He thought he was the epitome of manhood. Maybe that will work.*

Charity started to moan as if he was pleasuring her greatly. It was not that hard to do, it seemed to ease some of the pain she felt.

"Oh, so now you like it, huh," he rasped. He stopped and got off her for a moment. "Well, let's just see how much you like it," he said with a twist of his mouth. He took her again; however, this time he turned her over and began biting her buttocks and sodomizing her with his tongue. When he had finished humiliating her, he turned her back over and then suddenly took a knife and cut her across her cheek. He then licked the blood from her cheek and began wagging his tongue at her.

With blood trickling down her face, Charity glared into his eyes- she had never been in the presence of such pure evil; never knew that such could even exist the world… If Wheeler had a soul, it was blackened, rotten and putrid. Momentarily, she wondered what could have made someone become so vile. Was he possessed by some sort of demon?

✳✳✳

The small posse was riding hard and had reached the first cave, only to find it empty, with no evidence that anyone had even been there recently.

"Are you sure this was the cave," Jeremiah asked Unegadihi.

"It is the one," Unegadihi replied.

"There are lots of caves around this area," said the Sheriff. "I know where several are within a mile of here; my sons used to play up here all the time when they were young boys."

The sheriff's eyes followed Unegadihi as he bent down, looked at some tracks on the hard surfaced ground. "A rider has been through here, maybe a few hours ago. Carrying extra weight, from the depth of the tracks," he said.

"Now, just how would you know that," asked Jane's father.

"Sweat stains on the ground- not be there if long ago."

Henry wondered if the Indian was biding time, taking them in the wrong direction, giving Wheeler time to get away; however, when he saw Jeremiah look at the spot and then nod his head, he figured the Indian was being straight.

Unegadihi mounted his horse. They all climbed back on their horses and followed him; he looked to be following the tracks. About a mile from the first cave, they spied the entrance to another cave; Unegadihi raised his hand and halted them, then signaled for them to be quiet. They tied their horses off to a few willow branches and then eased toward the entrance. They stopped outside the entrance to listen, but could hear no sounds coming from inside.

"The tracks enter the cave there," Unegadihi whispered, pointing to them in the sandy soil.

"We ain't got any lamps!" Mr. Reed exclaimed, in a whisper.

"Hell, it'd take three hours round trip, to get back with lanterns" said the Sheriff, despair in his voice.

"Heck, all we need is just a few fat-lighter pine knots," said Jeremiah.

"He right," Unegadihi agreed. "They burn good."

They all looked around- Jeremiah spied a stand of Longleaf pines, about a quarter-mile from where they were.

"Me and Un'e here will go and get some. Y'all three stay

here and keep your eyes peeled for Wheeler; we's a be back in a jiffy," Jeremiah assured them.

He and Unegadihi lead their horses a good piece away before mounting them and riding toward the stand of pines.

"If Jane's in there, I ain't waiting!" Mr. Reed said through gritted teeth.

"You got to, Sam; you don't have any other choice," said the Sheriff, grabbing Sam Reed's arm to stop him. "Hell, you go in there without any light, you're liable to end up at the bottom of a hundred foot drop," said the sheriff.

"But that's my little girl, in there," Sam Reed cried mournfully.

Seeing the pain on Mr. Reeds face and hearing the anguish in his voice affected Henry to the bone; he was beginning to feel as if he hadn't done anything but bring bad luck to the town after escaping prison and coming there… *was he and his family being punished for his wrongdoing?*

Shortly, Jeremiah and Unegadihi returned with five, fat-lighter pine knots.

From his pouch, Unegadihi produced a flint rock and a shard of hard metal. With just a few flicks of his wrist, he lit the pine knots.

They were all anxious to get into the cave. And, as they eased forward into the cave, they heard the soft flutter of a horse's nostrils as he blew the dust from them. Going into the dark cave from the bright outside light, they were at a huge disadvantage. It would take their eyes several moments to adjust to the dim light of the cave. The narrow entrance opened into a gallery that was about twenty feet across. Stalagmites rose from the floor of the cave; some, reaching the ceiling that was at least twenty feet high, and even higher toward the back of the room. The room was empty except for the horse that whinnied upon seeing them. Jeremiah rushed over and shoved a plug of tobacco in its mouth to calm him, then patted him to keep him from making more noise and alerting Wheeler as to their presence.

With their piney knot torches in hand, they could see that there were at least three other entrances or exits that led out from the room.

"Me and Henry will take that one-" Jeremiah started saying; however, Unegadihi cut him off with a raised hand, as he examined each entrance/exit from the gallery- he was looking for signs of human traffic.

The floor of the cavern was moist and damp, which made it almost impossible to see footprints, if there were any; however, Unegadihi was an excellent tracker, he was almost certain they had gone through the exit to the right of the main entrance.

"We go this way," he said sternly.

"Well, y'all can go that way if you want to trust that Injun, but the Sheriff and I are going down that one," said Mr. Reed, pointing to the larger opening at the back of the room. They all looked at one another and nodded...

31

Retribution

Writhing in pain, Charity shifted from herself to Jane, until the pain became unbearable, then she would have to shift back. Hank Wheeler was a savage! He would stare deep into her eyes as he took her. Taking his time, baring his teeth at her, letting her know what was coming next. If they did not find them soon, she feared, neither she nor Jane would survive this attack…

Henry, Jeremiah, and Unegadihi watched as the Sheriff and Mr. Reed disappeared into the passageway in the middle. They then began easing their way down the opening to the right. The opening was so small that it only allowed for them to enter single file. Jeremiah, then Unegadihi, followed by Henry, entered into the creviced passage. They took their time, trying to be as quiet as possible, not wanting to announce their arrival, to Wheeler.

They had gone, probably twenty feet, when they heard whimpers and moans coming from somewhere ahead of them. Jeremiah stopped and whispered that they should extinguish the pine knots and let their eyes adjust to the light that should be ahead in the cavern.

"They're up there; I can hear noises ahead. We must be as

quiet as church mice, if we are going to get a jump on him," Jeremiah whispered.

Jeremiah is first in line; he is also the first to get a peek into the cavern. He would also be first, to bare witness to the carnage that was taking place inside the room. He could see the Captain's boots, sword, and side arm laid over his neatly folded clothes.

Jeremiah had been in many a battle. Saw men blown apart and gutted like swine. He had witnessed massacres of women and children during the Creek Wars. However, what he saw in the middle of the dimly lit room turned his stomach. He thought for a moment that he'd lose his breakfast.

The Captain had stripped off all his clothes; he was naked as a jay bird. He had the girl spread out on a blanket, also naked. Wheeler was on his knees, over her, teasing her with a knife. Then he bent lower and began biting her nipples; he bit them hard enough that it brought blood! The girl whimpered in pain.

Jeremiah quickly tried to size up the situation. From what he could see, Wheeler had only the knife to use as a weapon; his firearm was not within easy reach. Jeremiah backed up, backing Unegadihi and Henry with him. When he thought they were far enough away, he stopped.

"We need to try to draw him away from the girl; he has a knife in his hand and his firearm in near enough that he could lunge for it… I have an idea, but I'll need to take my shirt off. I'll ease in there and draw his attention. When he heads for me and swipes at me with the knife, I'll try and wrap it up with my shirt.

The two of you can then tackle him and knock him to the ground. Kill the bastard if you have to," he whispered.

All three of them eased back down to the mouth of the passage; Jeremiah took off his shirt. He then snuck into the room and when he thought he was close enough, he made a noise to attract Wheeler's attention.

Wheeler jumped to his feet and lunged for his sidearm atop the pile of clothes. Jeremiah ran in, drawing his attention. Unegadihi had his arms outstretched, holding Henry behind him. When Wheeler turned and lunged at Jeremiah with the knife, Unegadihi dove forward, toward Wheeler, drawing Wheelers' attention to him. Jeremiah lunged with his outstretched shirt, wrapped it around Wheeler's knife-hand.

Suddenly, a loud boom exploded behind them and half of Wheeler's head blew off! Stunned, Jeremiah and Unegadihi both turned to look toward the passageway. There stood Henry, still in a cloud of smoke.

"What'd you go and do that for? Hell, I about had him!"

"He needed to die," Henry stated, nodding his head toward the girl.

"Yes, he did," Unegadihi agreed.

"Well, you ain't gonna get any flack from me. Retribution, is what I call it," said Jeremiah.

The soft whimpers of the girl drew their attention away from Wheeler. Jeremiah looked around for her clothes; they were near where she lay.

"You gents turn yer backs," he said, "And keep her Paw out of here, till I can get her dress on'er and wrap her up in that there blanket. I don't think her paw ought to see the extent of her injuries, do you?" he asked.

They both looked at the girl on the ground and shook their heads.

Jeremiah knelt down beside her, and then tried to pull her nightgown over her head. She began to moan in pain, maybe thinking it was Wheeler about to inflict more pain on her. As gently as possible, Jeremiah dressed her, then wrapped the blanket around her and tried to get her to her feet. She was too weak to stand, and he was too winded to pick her up.

"I need some help now," he said.

It was about then, that Mr. Reed and the Sheriff made it to them. Mr. Reed ran straight to his daughter, but the Sheriff had stopped to quickly assess the situation.

"Did you have to kill him?"

"Yeah I did, Sheriff," Jeremiah replied without hesitation. "He came at us with that knife!"

Henry opened his mouth to say something, but Unegadihi elbowed him, so he kept his mouth shut- *why the heck, is Jeremiah' taking the responsibility for killing Wheeler?*

"Thank you, Mr. Jeremiah," Mr. Reed exclaimed. "Thank you all," he said, before bending down to pick up his daughter up off the floor; he held her in his arms and with a humbled expression, turned toward the passageway out of the cavern.

"Someone please lead the way with a light," he said, "I need to get my daughter to the doctor at once."

"One of you help Sam; the other two, stay here with me," said the Sheriff. "You go, Henry," Jeremiah said firmly. "Me and Un'e here will help the Sheriff. Now, go on and git. You need to get back to Charity; she needs you."

Henry guided Mr. Reed out of the cavern and then helped him put Jane on his horse in front of him; she was in no condition to hang on from behind. It would take several hours to make it back to town.

The sun was already low in the west. Henry feared they would run out of daylight, before they made it back to town. He wanted to get back to Charity, and he was worried about the children, who were home alone.

He knew the older boys were capable of getting the food out of the larder and feeding themselves and the younger children; but they had never been completely unsupervised for any length of time; they always had their parents or grandparents' home with them.

"If we can make it to the main road before dark," yelled Mr. Reed, "there should be enough moonlight to see the road."

"I sure hope so," Henry replied.

✳✳✳

Waiting between her world and the girls, Charity had drifted into a semiconscious state of mind. When she opened her eyes, she was sitting cross-legged in front of Two Feathers fire. He, with eyes the color of the falling snow, was studying her intently. It seemed that several minutes passed before he spoke to her.

"This gift you have been given by the Great Spirit, this ability to cross between the worlds, can be a curse, as you have seen. You must learn to shield your spirit from the evil that lives between our worlds, Little One.

"This place between the worlds, is the Tsusgina'I, it is neither here nor there- it is Nether; it is where the tormented ones go when they leave their earthbound bodies behind. You are a Ganenutlv'I, a Passageway between these worlds. When you travel between our world and their's, you must beware the Nvnehidihi, the Pathkiller. When your spirit leaves your body, your body is weak. The Pathkiller kills in the path; he is usgasetiyu, self-same, dangerous. The Nvnehidihi, they are the Anigateno, the ones who look around, hunting the Ganenutlv'I- the Passageways- they want to stop them from helping lost souls cross over; they wish to keep the tortured souls captive between the worlds. Beware the Yellow Mocker, Little One- when he calls, you must leave netherworld. Now go away, tsilihu, I am sleeping."

32

The Hidden Cave

Although it had only been a day, it seemed a lifetime to Charity before she was released from the spell that had overcome her upon riding into town. Weak, trembling, and chilled to the bone, her teeth began to chatter.

Someone said, "She's coming around."

As she struggled to awaken, she remembered the blond headed girl and what Wheeler had done to her; she began to shake violently.

"Is she cold?" a female voice asked.

"I think it's just a reaction to coming out of this state she's been in," said a male voice that seemed vaguely familiar.

From somewhere deep within her, came a vision of Two Feathers, and she remembered their conversation. She tried to speak, but only mumbled.

"What dear," asked the female voice?

Again, Charity tried to speak, but her tongue felt thick and dry.

"I'm sorry, but I cannot hear you," the female voice said. "I think she's thirsty; is it okay to give her some water?"

"Of course it is," said the male who she now realized was Doctor Lane.

After a moment, she felt a hand slip beneath her head to help her rise up; a cup was pressed against her lips. She was indeed thirsty, and drank her fill.

After she drank, she tried to speak again. This time, she was able to tell Doctor Lane that they were bringing Jane to him. Then, she asked Mrs. Lane for a cup of strong coffee. After Mrs. Lane left the room, she turned to the doctor.

"Jane is very weak, both physically and mentally - she will need great care; she has been horribly mistreated. I will easily heal, but she will not. Please, Doctor Lane," she begged. "Tell no one the extent of her injuries or all that she has endured. It will be more than her mind can handle, if everyone knows."

Doctor Lane nodded his head that he'd abide by her wishes.

A few minutes later, Mrs. Lane brought her the cup of coffee she had requested; Charity sipped it slowly. The hot liquid soothed her throat and calmed her frazzled nerves.

Doctor Lane asked if she'd like a spoon of laudanum- she declined.

"Are you sure you don't want a dose of laudanum, Mrs. Gullege- I am sure that it would help the pain and help you relax."

"Yes, Sir, I'm sure," Charity responded. "I'm feeling much better," she assured him. It was the truth; she did feel fine. As a matter of fact, the wounds she received were almost completely healed- they weren't actually her wounds; they were only conceived of the images within her mind, therefore, they weren't actually real wounds at all and were quickly fading.

***

Another hour or so passed before Henry and Mr. Reed arrived with Jane; Doctor Lane was ready for them. Mrs. Lane had already heated a pot of water, and Doctor Lane had pain medication and salves waiting.

When Mr. Reed brought Jane in and placed her on the table, her face was a visage of pain and misery; shame and humiliation; Charity's heart went out to her - the poor girl was only thirteen years old- just two years older than her own Martha... She knew exactly what Jane had gone through at the hands of Hank Wheeler; she'd occupied the girl's body, heart, and soul.

Henry's relief at seeing Charity alert and talking was very apparent to her; she greeted him with a weak smile and a hug; she too, was relieved that he was okay. She wanted to collapse in his arms and let him soothe her - carry her home so that she could see her children and know that they, too, were okay; however, she knew that she could not yet leave- she needed to be there for Jane.

"Henry, can you wait for me outside- Jane needs privacy." Henry nodded his understanding and headed toward the door.

She heard Doctor Lane tell Mr. Reed that he would have to

wait outside, assuring him that he would let him back inside with Jane as soon as he had checked her over good.

"She's all I got left, Doc-"

"I know, Sam, and I'll take real good care of her, but you're going to have to step out of here so that I can do my job," he said firmly. Begrudgingly, Sam Reed stepped outside with Henry.

After Mr. Reed stepped outside, Charity went to Jane's side and took her hand in hers and leaned closer to her. Slowly, Jane raised her eyes to meet Charity's; a questioning look came to her eyes before recognition set in.

"No one but you and me will ever know exactly what he did to us- we will be fine," Charity whispered to her. "You and I have nothing to feel ashamed about or no reason to be afraid. He is dead; he will never bother us again!"

Jane smiled weakly and said, "Thank you."

Charity squeezed Jane's hand and then kissed her on the cheek.

When Doctor Lane came near the table, Jane's hand began to tremble.

"Could you give me just another moment," Charity asked. The doctor nodded and stepped away. Charity then leaned to whisper in Jane's ear.

"He wasn't a man, Jane- Men are not like he was; he was a monster; a masquerader pretending to be human.

"The love between a man and a woman is not like what he did to *us*," she told Jane, making sure to include herself- hoping that Jane would realize that she was not alone with Wheeler. "The love a man and woman share, is a beautiful thing to experience; don't be afraid of all men; men can be kind, gentle, and loving. Never be afraid to give your heart to the right man…

"I will wait right here and hold your hand while Doctor Lane tends your wounds." Jane squeezed her hand and smiled weakly. When Doctor Lane came back over, she closed her eyes and clung to Charity's hand.

When Doctor Lane gently cut Jane's dress away so that he could tend her wounds, Charity saw the shocked look on his face. She averted her eyes- she could not look at Jane's body without feeling Wheeler's touch- as if she were back in the cavern with him.

Doctor Lane gave Jane a spoonful of laudanum and then began to tend to her wounds. Afterward, he dressed the wounds and then his wife handed him a cotton nightgown to put on her.

Although Jane's external wounds had been tended and would eventually heal- Charity knew the internal wounds Jane suffered would take much longer to heal, if they healed at all- she prayed that they would and that one day, Jane would find love.

It was nearly daybreak before she stepped outside the doctor's house. She was just in time to see the Sheriff, Jeremiah, and Unegadihi ride into town; Wheeler's body was draped over his horse.

Charity walked straight over to the undertaker's shop, which they had stopped in front of. She grabbed a handful of

Wheeler's blood-caked hair and raised his head so that she could get a good look at him. She wanted to be sure that he was, indeed, dead. Vacant, death-glazed eyes stared back at her; she spit on what was left of his face and then let loose his head which flopped down alongside his horse's side.

None of the men, including Henry, said anything or interfered.

After a moment, Charity turned to Henry, and in a calm voice said, "Henry, I'm ready to go home."

✳✳✳

In mid-July, Charity realized that she was expecting another child. She had wanted so badly to leave Canton; it held so many unpleasant memories- Uriah's foot, Jane, Wheeler… Now, they'd not be able to leave- it would have to await the birth of her child.

After telling Henry about the expected event, they made plans to leave as soon as she and the baby were able to travel; which, by her estimates, would be late March or early April of the following year. Henry thought it too strenuous for her and their unborn child to sit on a jarring wagon seat all day.

Sitting on the front porch rocker, sipping coffee, and occasionally puffing on her grandmother's pipe, the late summer months crept at a snails pace. Mrs. Finley's ghost had become quite proficient at appearing out there with her- Sometimes, they'd sit quietly, just enjoying being there; other times, they'd talk for an hour or more…

Uriah's foot had healed, but was still a little tender; however, his broken heart would take more time to heal. His heart was broken because he cared for Jane and her father had sent her away.

Charity heard that Jane's father, who was a widower, had sent Jane to Marthasville to spend a few months with his sister. Marthasville was an up and coming railroad town. (Marthasville, would later be renamed to Atlanta)

Still wanting to explore the area, Charles had begged her almost daily, to go to the waterfall above Lake Allatoona; however, for the time being, she was content to sit right there, talk with Mrs. Finley, and watch fall arrive.

With the help of the older boys, Henry and Jeremiah had made repairs to the cabin and planted a vegetable garden. Henry and Jeremiah also began trapping to make the money needed to buy the things they couldn't raise or kill.

When September arrived, and the weather cooled, Charity became restless. From her calculations, she had about four months to go before the baby arrived. She told Henry that she had to get out and do something, before she went stir-crazy. Eventually, she talked him into taking her and Charles to the waterfall above the lake.

"We can take a wagon and camp overnight," said Henry. "That way, it won't be too much for you at one time."

Jeremiah agreed that she needed to get away for a night or two; he said that he and the young'uns could handle being by themselves a day or two.

They left bright and early the morning of the Autumnal Equinox, arriving at the waterfalls, just before noon.

"It's beautiful up here- I wouldn't mind living right here. I'd never get tired of looking at this," she said, spreading her arms wide to encompass the view of the falls.

"Me neither!" Charles said, looking around.

"Look, Mama!" he said, pointing toward the waterfall.

Both Charity and Henry looked to where Charles was pointing. The sun seemed to beam a ray of sunlight, directly to a certain point in the waterfall; it caused a rainbow to appear.

"It looks like a cave behind the falls," said Charles, excitedly.

"It does look like a cave behind the water, doesn't it, Henry!" Charity said excitedly. "Can we go see?" she asked.

"I will have to check it out first to make sure it's not slippery. I wouldn't want you to fall down," he said.

"Hurry up!" Charity felt the excitement building.

"Just give me time, woman," Henry said with a chuckle. "Charles, you stay here with your mama while I go check it out."

"I wanted to go to," Charles said, disappointed.

Henry walked up to the falls which ran off of the Little River. He checked for a way to the hidden cave. When he reached the area nearest the water, he could plainly see that there was a well-traveled path that led up to and disappeared behind the waterfall.

Retracing his steps back to the wagon, Henry made sure there weren't algae or slippery moss on the pathway that could cause Charity to slip down.

"It looks pretty safe. We shouldn't have any trouble getting up to it. Let me secure camp before we go; that way we won't have to hurry," said Henry.

Soon, they were making their way up to and behind the falls. Henry lit one of the torches they had brought from home; they entered the cavern.

"What in the tarnation," exclaimed Charles.

"Wow," said Charity, gazing around- "this is not what I expected."

33

Behind the Waterfall

Looking around, they were amazed at all the beautiful colors that caused the rocks to look as if they were ablaze. None had even seen anything like it.

"Look, Papa; that column goes all the way to the top!" Charles exclaimed.

The cave was nothing like neither the cave they stayed in after the whirlpool wind nor the one they found Wheeler and the girl in; this one had pockets of very colorful rocks. There were crystals of lavender and orange, and different shades of umber; from gingery, yellow brown to a dark reddish brown color- some were pink and white; there were even some that were so clear that you could almost see through them.

Delving deeper into the cavern, they began to feel a cool breeze coming from a tunnel at the back of the cave. They seemed to travel down hill as they made their way to the back of the colorful cave.

"You might have trouble going back up," Henry said to Charity.

"That's what I have a strong, handsome husband like you for." Henry was pleased to see her happy; she had not been her

usual self since the incident with Hank Wheeler. The
the tunnel was roomy as they started in, but then it
slightly, and then narrowed some more, twisting this way, then
that. By now, they were single file, with Henry taking the lead,
followed by Charity and then Charles.

They walked what seemed several hundred feet and then
came to a wider part of the passage that had water running
alongside it.

"Watch your step," Henry advised. "It's a little slippery
along here." He stopped and held the lantern higher. Across and
above the little stream was a cavernous, deep opening.

"I'd hate to fall off into that," said Henry. Charity and
Charles both tiptoed to see what Henry saw, before they
continued following the passageway.

About fifty feet past where the water ran alongside them,
Henry suddenly stopped and asked, "Do y'all hear that?"

A flutelike noise could faintly be heard above the constant
din of the other noises.

"I hear if, Papa," said Charles.

"Maybe it's just the wind passing through the rocks," said
Henry.

The further they traveled through the passage, the stronger
the breeze felt and the louder the flute noise sounded.

After they walked about twenty feet more, the passage
turned sharply to the right again, and after a few more feet they
saw daylight ahead.

"We found a way out!" said Charles, excitedly.

The flutelike noise was quite loud by then and not knowing what lay ahead, Henry suggested that they quietly ease their way to the light.

Suddenly feeling a heightened sense of awareness, Charity felt a familiar presence. "Unegadihi!" she whispered. She knew that he had been close since Wheeler was killed, but had not felt any concern.

"Where?" Henry asked.

"He is near," she said.

When Henry called out to him, he appeared from behind them.

"What are you doing here?" Henry demanded.

Unegadihi looked toward Charity.

Suddenly understanding why he had stayed near and why he followed them into the cavern, Charity said, "He is protecting me."

"Hell," Henry huffed. "I can protect my own wife!"

"Be calm, Henry!" Charity scolded. "He means no harm and he is not trying to take your place. I think he feels it's his duty," she said.

"Well, it's not- it's my duty to protect you!"

"He sees me as a Passageway to the Great Spirit; that is why he feels he should protect me. It will be alright," she added soothingly.

Remembering how Unegadihi had helped them hunt down

Wheeler and find Jane Reed, Henry gave in. "I reckon it's alright," he said, "but you ought not to sneak up on folks like that; make your presence known, man. You could get yourself shot, sneaking up on people that way!"

Charity and Unegadihi exchanged looks; his expression said that he had let himself be known, because she knew that he was near.

Resuming their mission toward the light at the end of the passageway, they soon saw the tops of trees ahead. "Damn," Henry said over his shoulder. I wasn't expecting that. What's weird, is that it seems as if we've been going down hill ever since we entered the passage and now, we're sky-high!"

The tunnel passage they'd been traveling down widened out into another cave; this one had a much larger opening that faced outward; the entrance looked to be forty foot across and at least twenty feet tall. The inside dimension of the cave was maybe fifty-square. The cave was definitely not a mystery cave- by the looks of it- it had entertained numerous guests.

There were some small animal carcasses piled near one wall- undoubtedly, the remnants of several meals. The remains of long burned out camp fires centered the room.

"Someone stayed here for a good while," observed Henry, pointing out the dozen or so skeletons lying around the room.

As soon as she entered the cave, Charity fell into a trancelike state; she saw what the others could not see; the spirits that remained in the cave…

Since the night on the trail, when the spirit, that at first felt loving, had come and entered her body and she'd had the smothering sensation, she had seen many strange things and many spirits of people she did not know. The spirits in the cave were older and much wrinkled. There were a dozen or so ghosts there; they appeared to be scared or worried, maybe. However, it soon became apparent to Charity that they were lost. They were stuck between the first world and complete death.

After expressing his observations of the room, Henry turned to look at Charity. He saw that her mind was elsewhere. "Charity?" Henry questioned.

Charles spoke up and said, "That's how Mama looked that day she saw Two Feathers, in the clearing!"

Without saying a word or acknowledging Henry in any way at all, Charity walked to the center of the cavern; she then crossed her legs, and sat down. Charles went to his mother's side; then, he too, crossed his legs and sat down just as she had. Henry looked over at Undgadihi who was also watching them.

Speaking a stream of Cherokee words, Charity made fluent motions with her hands until her words turned into songlike chants that matched the motion of her hands. Charles sat quietly beside her with his eyes closed.

Henry started toward them, but Unegadihi stopped him.

"It is not for us to know," he said; his voice, lowered to a whisper.

Henry was confounded; he wanted to go to her, but did as

Unegadihi said and kept his distance. After about ten minutes, Henry sat down and leaned against the wall. Whatever was going on went on so long that Henry had fallen asleep; but not Unegadihi. Unegadihi was fascinated by the Spirit-World; therefore, it was an honor for him to witness a Passageway at work.

As each spirit came forward to sit in front of Charity, they told her their 'tsunigayvliiyvli'stanv,' their line of descent, their ancestry, and then told how they came to be waiting in the Spirit Cave.

Because there were so many of them, it took a long time for her to guide them past Wudeliguhi, the Darkening Land, or the Land of the Dead, and into Galv'lati, the Heavens. By the time she finished, she was weak and tired.

When she opened her eyes, she turned to see that Charles was sitting beside her. He had discovered that if he sat close to his mother during her trances and closed his eyes and relaxed his mind, that he, too, could see the spirits. However, he could only understand some of the Cherokee language.

"What happened to them?" he asked his mother.

"They were old and too weak to follow their people when the soldiers forced them to leave, so they came here to this place. They called it, the Place of the Spirits Song. It is where the, 'adonvdo, nvyu, daganogeda,' the Spirit Stone Sings. The Spirit Stone makes the flutelike sound we hear.

"They came here to die," Charity explained, "Without a

guide to Galv'lati, they could not leave- they were lost in the Darkening Land."

"That must be why we came here, huh, Mama?" Charles questioned.

"Yes, Son, I am sure we were called here so that we could help them continue their journey to the Unequa Adanvdo, the Great Spirit. We would not have found them on any other day. The entrance to this place is only visible to mortals on the day of the Equinox- and there are only two of those in a year."

"Wow," said Charles, asking, "What is a mortal?"

"A mortal is an undead person," she replied. "Now, let's go- I can rest and await the birth of your brother."

"Another brother!" exclaimed Charles. "How do you know Mama?"

"I just do Charles, and he won't be the last," she said with a sigh.

✳✳✳

A cold wind, moon rose in the month of November that chilled them to the bone. Henry was glad they had stockpiled firewood, preserved berries, made jellies, and canned all they could from the garden. The only thing left growing were collard greens, which thrived in cooler weather, and a few beds of potatoes, which they needed to dig before the ground froze or they'd be ruined. The boys and Henry gathered scuppernongs from thickets along the river and near the creek, where the vines grew wild and in abundance- from these, they made juices and thick, dark jelly.

The previous month, Henry and Jeremiah had managed to kill several deer, one wild boar, a few squirrels, and some rabbits, which they'd smoked to preserve the meat. All they had to buy in town was flour, meal, sugar, and lard since none could be rendered off the wild game, which tended not to have fat. Charity, although big with child, wanted to make a Thanksgiving feast along with special treats for the children, and since it was nearly Christmas, she had asked Henry, to buy some ginger and vanilla.

The boys had found an old sassafras tree, about a half mile from the cabin and had been watching it. As soon as the leaves had fallen, and the sap settled down, they had dug a good supply of roots and let dry in the sun. She was sure it'd be enough to last for months.

Saving the precious chickens, for a chicken and dressing dinner for Christmas, Charity opted to cook a ham off of a wild hog Jeremiah killed. That, along with a pot of snap beans and potatoes and a cake of cornbread was what they had. It was plenty and everyone seemed to enjoy it.

***

The second week in December, the weather turned even colder; Charity was reminded of crispy South Carolina mornings at her grandparent's cabin. While they made gingerbread and gingerbread men, using dried huckleberries for their eyes, she told the children stories of her Nokomis.

Preserved huckleberries, were also used to make a cobbler, and she made the berry-bread they always looked forward to.

Unegadihi, who was a frequent visitor, had showed them how to pop dried corn, which they seasoned with salt and butter. He also told her how to make fry bread, which they all found to their liking. Charity hoped she was making wonderful memories for her children that would stay with them long after she was gone from the world…

* * *

They were all grateful when Unegadihi brought in a large, wild turkey that he had killed, the day before Christmas.

"Now, we can have turkey and dressing for Christmas dinner," Charity told him happily. "This is going to be a wonderful Christmas!"

Over the warmer months, Henry and Jeremiah had managed to make enough money to buy each of the children and the adults a new pair of boots, which they were sorely in need of. "I'm sorry I couldn't afford to buy toys or candy for the children," he told Charity.

"It will be alright," she smiled, adding "we've got plenty of food and love; that's all that's important."

34

A Georgia Mountain Christmas

Cherokee Co, Georgia Country
Dec 25, 1843

Christmas morning, 1843, dawned cold and blustery.

"I do believe it might just snow," Jeremiah said to Charity as she came into the front room. He and Unegadihi were sitting at the table drinking coffee.

"It may as well snow," she said, as she poured herself a cup of coffee. "It's too cold to do anything."

The only thing Charity liked about cold weather was that she could cook things ahead of time and store them in the shed outside and they'd not ruin.

***

In mid-December the weather turned extremely cold. And, since Charity could not stand the thought of anyone having to sleep out in it, she had convinced Henry to let Unegadihi stay in the cabin with them.

(Ever since meeting Two Feathers, years earlier, her thoughts always went to his story of the winter he lost his sight when she thought it might snow.)

At first, Henry rejected her idea. She promptly put her hands on her hips, gave him a stern look, and said; "I declare Henry; if I didn't know any better, I'd swear you are jealous!"

"I reckon I just might be a little jealous," said Henry. "The two of you seem mighty cozy since that day in the cave."

She smiled and kissed him square on the mouth and then whispered in his ear, "You know you're the only man I'll ever want in my bed, Henry Elijah Gullege." Turning every shade of red imaginable, Henry blushed.

✳✳✳

"On second thoughts, I believe you are right- It'd have to warm up some ta snow. I ain't seen it this dang cold since I was knee-high to a grasshopper- and that were a mighty long time ago," he replied.

"It will snow," Unegadihi said firmly.

"See, I told ye!" exclaimed Jeremiah.

"Told her what," asked Henry, as he came into the room.

"That it's gonna snow," Jeremiah replied.

Henry chuckled and said, "Well, I believe you're right, Jeremiah. Just look at all that snow falling out there." Jeremiah turned to look out the window.

To all their recollections, it was the first time it had snowed in probably seven or eight years.

"Henry, would you fix me another cup of coffee, while I go

get some things I need to put under the tree."

"Yes, Ma'am, I sure will."

Unegadihi never spoke much unless spoken to- he was a silent type of person and took a little getting used to. Therefore, when he quietly stood up and opened the door to go outside, no one questioned him as to his plans or where he was going, or even if he planned to return. However, once Unegadihi was outside, Jeremiah could not contain his curiosity. "Now, jest where in the world do you reckon he be off to," he wondered aloud.

"I don't know," Charity responded. She too, was curious, but understood him- she would never ask him about his comings and goings.

She left the room and then returned with three rag dolls she had made for the girls; she'd made them from the rags of old clothes, flour sacks, and a few buttons and ribbons Mrs. Finley had led her to several months earlier that were stored in a box in the loft area. Henry's smile, showed pride in his wife for her devotion to her family, and for her craftiness.

Unegadihi returned shortly thereafter with a blanket rolled up and tucked under his arm; after shaking off the cold and snow, he laid it on the table and partly unrolled it. Without trying to appear nosy, she, Henry, and Jeremiah were all trying to get a look at what was inside the blanket.

After he unrolled it some, Unegadihi stood up straight and then turned to face them. He looked into Charity's eyes as if asking for her consent to give the gifts- smiled gratefully and nodded her assent.

Inside his partially unrolled blanket, there were two, carved, wooden flutes and two, bows and arrows. He picked them up and placed them under the tree near the rag dolls. The children had decorated the cedar tree with strung- together holly leaves, berries, and popped corn.

After placing those under the tree, he returned to the table and finished unrolling the blanket. In his bedroll, he also had a beautiful beaded necklace, which he handed to Charity- she admired it and then thanked him for being so thoughtful. He also had in the roll, two, carved, wooden smoking pipes; one for Jeremiah and one for Henry. They graciously accepted the gifts, admiring the construction of them.

Eyes twinkling happily, Jeremiah stated, "Don't cha think we need to roust them young'uns up out of the bed?"

"You do the honors," said Henry, puffing on his new pipe that he'd promptly packed with tobacco and lit.

Already trussing the turkey, getting it ready to roast, Charity wiped her hands on her apron and joined the men by the table so that she could watch the children's faces, when they saw their gift under the Christmas tree.

Of course, the three older boys were the first ones down: they were so excited about seeing the snow through the window that they didn't even notice the presents under the tree. However, when they turned from the window, the gifts were the first thing they noticed; probably because Jeremiah was bent over pointing at them, grinning. Jubilantly, the boys rushed toward the tree. From the look on his face, thought Charity, Jeremiah seems to be enjoying this more than the children are at the moment.

"Let's wait for the little ones," Henry said firmly, stopping the boys before they reached the tree.

Charity looked up to see that all the other children, except little Mary, were climbing down from the loft. She looked around room, double checking to see if maybe she just did not see Mary brought down. She looked back up, just in time to see a poised to jump Mary, yell, "Catch me," and then jump.

The older children usually assisted her down, but in their excitement had left her in her bed - momentary flashes, of Henry, standing their children on the table or other off the ground surfaces and telling them to jump, flashed through her mind. He'd always played with the children when they were small toddlers- they'd jump and he'd catch them, and then swing them around before putting them back to jump again.

It was unexpected- but, luckily she caught her before she hit the floor! Her heart pounding out of her chest from visions of what could have happened had she not caught her, she scolded Mary. "Don't-you-ever-do-that-again!"

Realizing she'd spoken a little too harsh when Mary pouted up to cry, Charity hugged her lovingly, and then told her, "You can be hurt very bad jumping from way up there; it's too high. Mama does not want you to be hurt." After hugging her youngest a little longer, Charity pointed to the Christmas tree and told Mary to go look under it for her gift.

"Wee," said Mary, "a baby for me!"

"Yes, pumpkin," Charity said, smiling happily as Mary picked the littlest doll. "It's a baby just for you."

Then, just as Charity hoped while she was making the dolls, Nancy chose the middle-sized doll and Martha chose the largest. It was now the boys turn to choose their gift. Since he was the youngest, Aaron picked first; he chose a flute. Charles was next. He stared at the gifts for a long moment because he had wanted an Indian made bow and arrow, ever since the first time he heard the story about Dancing Rabbit Creek. If he picked one of those, he could be a great warrior like Kawa'ha… In the end, he picked a flute, saying that he'd wanted one ever since hearing the flute played by Two Feathers' son at his camp. John and Uriah were both pleased; they both had wanted the bows and arrows so they, too, could be warriors like Kawa'ha. When Henry passed out the children's new winter shoes, they were as pleased over the new shoes as they were the other gifts.

Having waited until the children settled down some, Jeremiah grinned a toothless grin as he produced a handful of licorice whips that he'd kept hidden for weeks in his special *hiding place*- there was one for each child.

As the aroma of roasting turkey stuffed with sage-filled dressing filled the air, they all settled in to weather the storm and enjoy their first Christmas as a newly blended family on a snow-

When the Yellow Mocker Calls

covered Georgia mountain.

Lila M Beckham

35

Interlude

On the 20th day of January, 1844, Charity gave birth to her and Henry's eighth child; a son, whom they named Jackson Lane Gullege after Doctor Lane who helped deliver him. Jackson's birth was as an easy, uneventful birth. She and Henry were pleased that all went well and the baby seemed healthy; they could now make plans to leave as soon as spring came. By mid-March, they had the wagons packed and were ready to roll.

The night before their planned departure, Charity went out onto the front porch to smoke her grandmother's pipe, which she enjoyed and had grown quite accustomed to. She sat out there with Mrs. Finley and had a long conversation, going so far as to invite her to travel with them, but Mrs. Finley said that her place was there, where her life had been.

Although Mrs. Finley was departed, she was still a great conversationalist. She and Charity talked at length about many things- Charity ended by asking her to watch over Unegadihi, for although they had tried their best to get him to travel with them, he said he wanted to stay near the Spirit Cave. He told Charity that he needed to be on his own, and that he would always be thankful for the kindness that she and her family had shown him.

The morning they left Canton, he told her that when he died, his spirit would seek her out so that she could bless his crossing into the next world. He said his goodbyes to her and her family and then, just as Tokola had done, Unegadihi walked off into the forest before they pulled their wagons away from the Finley cabin.

The next several years, they made their way slowly but surely toward Alabama. When they found a pleasant place to make camp and stay a while, they would do so. When they were near a town, the men took odd jobs to support them. Several times, they spent upwards of six months a place, but something was always lacking; the appeal to keep going to new and better places, was strong.

They wintered the last Christmas they spent in Georgia, living in a small overseer's cabin, on a plantation near the thriving railroad town of Marthasville. December 29 of that very year, 1847, Marthasville changed its name to Atlanta.

Henry and Jeremiah had taken jobs on the plantation, Henry as the overseer, and Jeremiah, since he was skilled in so many areas, was hired to teach the slaves the owner bought in Atlanta to be wheelwrights and farriers. A man in his mid-thirties by the name of Jacob Clark owned the plantation. Right off, Jeremiah noticed that Jacob Clark had him an eye for the ladies. Clark was unmarried and all but one of his house slaves, were young women.

Taking the plantation jobs was the easiest way they could make repairs to their own wagons and save enough money to go on to Alabama.

"We need to make sure the Bossman don't get a good look at your wife, Henry," Jeremiah said, adding, "Men like him, they think they can just take whatever they want from poor folks."

"Yeah, I can tell that he fancies himself a ladies man, but he'll play hell getting that one in yonder to pay him any mind," Henry replied. "She done told me that he put her in mind of a strutting, bandy-legged rooster - she said they think they own the barnyard- all fluffed up and feathered- they're pretty to look at but have no sustenance; especially around a bigger, stronger rooster."

Jacob Clark had partially inherited his plantation from his uncle, who had built it, then had the misfortune of dying before he could enjoy it. His aunt, a Virginian by birth did not want to stay in Georgia once his uncle died; she sold the house and land to him, for pennies on the dollar; even letting him take ten years to pay it off so that she could return to Virginia.

Charity's family lived and worked on the plantation for a year and a half; the longest they had stayed in any one place since leaving South Carolina.

Henry was relieved when he thought they had enough money saved to leave; he had decided that farming cotton was mighty hard work, and to make it profitable, took a lot of land and a lot of folks working a lot of hours.

They left the plantation of Jacob Clark and traveled four hours west of Atlanta before they crossed into Alabama. Then they traveled several more hours before coming back into the mountains. Once there, they begin the year of 1848, living in a small, rented house in the township of Jacksonville, which was located in Benton County, Alabama.

Jeremiah was getting older and more crippled; Henry left him at home with Charity and the younger children, while he took Uriah and John with him to work. He worked for Benjamin Easley as a Ditcher, while the boys worked as hirelings, doing whatever work Easley needed them to.

With Henry and the boys away during the week, Charity settled into a routine of sorts, being a homebound mother. She didn't particularly like being stuck in the small town at all; she would much rather have been stuck in the small cabin in Canton…

36

Paint Me a Mountain

Jacksonville, Benton Co, Alabama
Nov 1849

Awakening from a wonderful dream in which she dreamed about her grandfather, Charity felt wistful. In the dream, she was still a young girl. She had discovered a set of pigments in a trunk under her grandfather's bed. The set contained all the colors of the rainbow. Each color was rich and vibrant when mixed with linseed oil and smeared onto her hand. They were intense, deep, colors… simply beautiful…

In the dream, her grandfather turned to her and said, "Paint me a mountain, Child- paint me a mountain like the mountains in my homeland;" after which, she began outlining a scene on the back of a tanned deerskin hide. As she sat up in bed, she wondered what the dream meant. And, as she sat there and thought about it, she remembered the painting that hung over the mantle in her grandparent's cabin. Her grandfather had told her that his mother painted it for him before he left his country to come to America. *Why did I not take it me when I left- even when we stopped there on our journey here, I left it there…*

Just sitting here wondering about it, is not going to bring the painting to me, thought Charity as she got up out of bed. Dreading the thought of facing another day of the same old same, she took her time.

She had never felt exactly this way before, however, she sort of felt similar to this after Jane's abduction and desecration by Wheeler- and yes, it was a desecration. Wheeler had taken Jane's innocence without her consent... Wheeler was like a black bile that had settled in her soul and was eating away what was left, causing her to feel filthy, immoral, and unsound.

Charity felt that if she didn't get a grip on herself and find something to soothe her soul, she was going to wither away, she dressed in going out clothes; her naturalistic soul felt stifled, weighted, smothered down into a lump of blackened coal tar. Shaking off the melancholy feelings, she went into the front room and put on a pot of coffee.

Later that morning, she left Martha and Jeremiah watching the children and walked to the Mercantile to inquire about the price of a set of pigments like the ones in her dream. Mr. Aderholt, the store proprietor, told her that he didn't have much call for painting materials- but stated that a good set of pigments and brushes would cost her a pretty penny.

"Well, Sir, exactly how much is a pretty penny," she asked, her tone showing that she was a bit perturbed by his uppity attitude. "It really doesn't matter," she told him, "I intend to buy a set, no matter the cost. How much?"

"Well, it depends. If I can't find a set in the storeroom, I'll have to order them from Montgomery or Mobile, and that'll cost more money, probably upwards of five dollars or more."

"Like I said, Sir; I want them. I will wait until you have searched the stockroom. Then, you will know whether or not you will have to order them."

It bothered her that he acted as if he thought she didn't have two nickels to rub together, much less, the five dollars or so he thought the set of pigments would cost to order.

While he was in the back looking for the paints, she looked around the store and picked out a few things she needed while there. She picked up a writing tablet, a pen, and an inkwell; she wanted to write a letter to Eli and Nancy, back in Carolina; she hadn't written them since leaving Canton. Mr. Reed had lent her the materials in order for her to write them before they left there. She needed to let them know where they were and how they were doing.

Shortly, Mr. Aderholt returned; he was toting a 2x2.5 ft oblong wooden valise of sorts; she wondered it held painting supplies. "Well, Miss, this is your lucky day," he said, "I found that I did have one in stock." He grinned. "The missus said she ordered it for some young man that never did return to pick it up." He laid it on the counter and opened it up.

"This one comes with what they call a palette- to smear your paint on, real horsehair brushes, and an assortment of dry pigments that you can mix with either linseed oil or water. It has little metal cups that hold the paint mixture.

The whole thing unfolds to stand on four legs; it has an attached easel and these drawers open up to hold your materials. It has directions, if you'd like me to read them to you," he offered.

"Thank you," she said, "but I'm capable of reading them myself."

"How much do I owe you, Mr. Aderholt," she asked, after laying the other items she intended to purchase on the counter.

"With the stationary, the pen, ink, and the sealing wax, that'll be six dollars and two bits," he replied, and then said, "Ma'am, if you don't mind me a asking, what are you, going to paint on," he asked.

"What would you suggest, Mr. Aderholt," she asked politely.

He smiled and said, "As a matter of fact, the missus also ordered an assortment of canvases. I can sell those to you for two dollars."

"I'll take them," she said, pulling a ten dollar gold piece from her purse. She smothered a smile at the look on his face, as he reached for the money. After she received her change, he asked, "Do you need some help getting these things home? I have a delivery boy that can carry them for you." Being eight months pregnant with her ninth child, Charity accepted his offer.

The boy toted her packages right up to her door, and then into the house and set them on the table. For helping her, he received ten cents.

"Thank you, Ma'am!" the boy exclaimed excitedly, as he turned and rushed out the door. She smiled. She knew she had given the boy a tip he wasn't likely to forget for a long time.

"What you got, Mama," asked the children when they saw her packages.

"I bought me a set of paints," she said, adding, "as soon as I can, I am going to paint my grandfather a mountain."

"A mountain," Mary said. Charity could hear the disappointment in her voice. "I want you, to paint me a pony," she exclaimed. "I want a white one!"

"I will, but first, I have to paint grandpa's mountain."

"Why?" several responded.

"Because he asked me to," she told them.

"But, Mama; your grandpa is dead- you told us so! How could he have asked you to?" the children wanted to know.

"He came to me in a dream and told me to paint him a mountain. I won't know why he wants me to, until I paint it," Charity explained. She then told them that her grandfather's mother, her great-grandmother, had painted a picture of a mountain for him to bring to America with him.

"It hung over the fireplace," said Martha. "I remember seeing that painting when we stayed there the night after we left home…"

"Yes, that was it… I wish I had brought it with me… I still don't know why I did not get it off the mantle- I knew his mother had painted it…"

"I still want a white pony," Mary pouted.

"I want a picture of a deer," Aaron chimed in.

"Soon," she promised. "Now, y'all run and play; I have chores to do."

Jeremiah, who had just walked in the back door, looked at Charity's packages spread out on the table. "Didn't you tell me one time, that your granddaddy had a painting in that old cabin you were raised in?"

"Yes, I did. I wish I had thought to get it; it just never crossed my mind… He brought it with him when he came here; he said his mother painted it. It was of a snow capped mountain, in his homeland. I believe he called it, the Puy-de-Dome." - "That sounds French to me," said Jeremiah. "I don't know," Charity replied. "I'll have to paint it from memory… I've seen lots of mountains, but I've never seen a mountain like that one."

"If'n you are an artist, it'll come to you," assured Jeremiah. "Artists ain't like everyday folks, they's different. Painters, paint things they've never seen before; maybe, sometimes, they paint from memory. Sculptors, sculpt things they imagine in their heads- and writers, they write about things they ain't never seen or done, afore either - imaginary things mostly," said Jeremiah.

"I reckon I understand it…" Jeremiah noticed that Charity

seemed to not really be paying attention and when he looked at her, her saw her wince and hold her stomach.

"Little feller kicking pretty hard, huh," he joked. When she didn't respond right away, and then suddenly took a deep breath, he asked, "Are you all right, Missy?"

"No I'm not - I think it's time, Jeremiah," she told him. "I reckon since Henry's not here, you're going to have to help us deliver this baby, Jeremiah."

"Oh, no, Ma'am- old Jeremiah don't really want to have to do that."

"Well, I don't know any of these women around here, Jeremiah!" she snapped, I'm going to need a little help."

"Well, I know a few of 'em- I've been talking to 'em; they're nice ladies, they won't mind a lendin' a hand. I'll run and get Mrs. Jenkins, next door ta come over here, or see if she'll let Maybelle, come help us."

"Okay; before you go, will you put on a pot of water, please- they'll need plenty of hot water. I still got a little ways to go, but this one is early- don't tarry. I'm going to go lay down. Martha Jane, you keep watch over the little ones and keep them occupied somehow so they don't get in the way."

"Yes, Ma'am- is there any way I can help you, Mama," Martha Jane asked.

"The best way you can help is by tending to the little ones."

"Yes'um,"

After an hour or so, she knew that something was wrong.

Drenched with sweat and writhing in binding pain she attempted to get up, thinking that maybe if she walked a little, it would help with the delivery; however, she barely made it to a sitting position before she had to lie back on the bed. Sometime later, she vaguely remembered Jeremiah and a Negro woman, standing over her in the bed.

"Helps me put her on her back- Mista Jeremiah," the woman was saying, "and let me see, if I can turn this here Chile 'round- his head ain't in da right place and she ain't even a opened up fer it, yet!"

Drifting in and out of consciousness, Charity heard Jeremiah say, "Please Doc, don't let her die…"

"Oh, Lawdy; no, sir- not today, Lawd, not today!"

She remembered hearing her children crying and Martha trying to console them… Then she tasted something bitter that someone spooned into her mouth; she tried to spit it out. They spooned it into her mouth again - she was so tired and weak she gave in and swallowed it. If only I could walk the wind, she thought to herself, I would feel renewed.

She tried to leave her body, but could not move… then, as if from a far away distance, she heard a voice speaking Cherokee. After a moment, she knew the voice was talking to her!

"Come to me, Usdi Saquo," called the familiar voice. "Do you hear me, Little One," he asked. It had been a very long time, but she knew his voice.

"I have tried, but failed," she answered.

Lila M Beckham

"Tsiayauwayi," he said firmly. "I will take you by the hand."

She reached out to take his hand and was lifted out of her body; the pain went away. Everything became clear when she looked into his eyes; eyes, the color of falling snow.

37

Purgatory

Somehow, Two Feathers had reached out for her from wherever he went after he died and took her by the hand, then pulled her soul out of Purgatory- He pulled her soul out of her body and away from the pain.

"Am I dead," she mumbled. After opening her eyes, she saw that she was in a place of total darkness. There were no trees, no clouds, no water; only his hand and his eyes; he was the only person she saw; the only *thing* she saw.

"Dideyohvsgi," she asked.

"Did you see the Yellow Mocker, Little One; hear him call your name?"

"The wh-" suddenly, she remembers him speaking of the Yellow Mocker when they were in his camp along the Yellow River. "No," she responded.

"No, Utaluli, It is not time," he answered.

"Will the time come soon?"

"Tala- not today, Little One; it is not the wish of the Great Spirit."

"Why is it so dark," she asked. "Are you sure, I am not

dead?"

"Utaluli, Usdi Saquo," he replied, firmly. "I not speak two-tongued; I mean what I say and say what I mean- not one thing and then another."

"I'm afraid," she said. "It is so dark here- are we in Wudeliguhi, the Land of the Dead?" Charity feared the land in between- she did not want to be there.

"Little One, I speak the truth, tsiwanihu toeu, Usdi Saquo!" he exclaimed. She knew he was angry with her for doubting his word.

"When you return, you will become Duyugodv Ayosdi, A Seeker of Truth. You will ride the wind and become as Akilvdiha'nole; he who rode the wind. You will seek and learn many things, Little One. Dideyohvsgi, you will be the teacher of not just your children, but to the generations that follow. You are my Sogainisi, my son's grandchild. I am your Enisi-egwa, your great-grandfather. Gigahai, my blood, flows through your body. One day, you will be Agigau, a beloved woman. Now you must return to your body, Little One, for it is time; your stesi needs you to push and bring her forth into the light and air."

Charity had listened intently and understood everything he told her. "Enisi, gvgeyu, I love you, Grandfather," Charity told him.

She felt him turn loose her hand; in the blink of an eye, she was back in her body, the pain of labor bearing down on her.

"Push, gosh darn it woman, I said push!"

When the Yellow Mocker Calls

She opened her eyes to see a strange man, bent over, reaching between her thighs. She bore down and pushed as hard as she could; the baby burst forth from her womb. The strange man held the baby up by her feet and swatted her bottom, but the baby did not cry! Cry, baby, please cry, her heart screamed!

When the baby still did not cry, the man placed his mouth over her mouth and nose. What the heck, thought Charity. What is he doing - is he sucking the air out of her?

The man, who she now realized was a doctor, raised the baby up by her feet and once again slapped her across her bottom. This time the baby made a noise, faintly at first, but then, her cries became stronger.

The doctor wrapped her in a blanket, and then gave her to Charity, who smiled weakly. "Once in a while, newborn babies need a little help to start breathing," he said. "For a while there, I thought I was going to lose you both."

Charity was exploring her new daughter's face with her fingertip. "I reckon if you hadn't a fainted the way you did, I never would've gotten that baby turned around- You didn't know what you were doing, but you were fighting tooth and nail to keep me from turning that child. When she finally came out, she wasn't as big as I thought she was going to be- she's a mite small. I'm thinking she was a month or so early. That's a blessing you're holding in your arms; eight month babies, don't usually make," he said.

"Who are you," Charity asked.

Lila M Beckham

"I'm Doctor McAdams," the old man said. "Your grandfather, come and fetched me after him and the niggra woman couldn't get the baby turned."

"My grandfather?" she questioned; her mind going to all her grandfathers, even Two Feathers... They were all dead!

"Yes, Mr. Jeremiah. He came and got me."

Charity nodded- she wasn't going to deny Jeremiah as being her grandfather- after all, he was very much like a grandfather to her.

The doctor examined her and then said, "Everything looks fine- no hemorrhaging; the baby seems to be doing well. You two get some rest, I'll check on you later," he said, and then gave her a strange look. "Are you sure you're okay, miss- you seem a little out of it."

"I'll be all right," Charity replied, adding, "I'm just tired."

Patting her on her shoulder, he said, "I'll be back in the morning to check on you and the baby." As he gathered his bag, he said, "You've got some good folks to look after you. Now, don't go a jumping up too soon and trying to do too much. All that childbearing you've been doing, is taking its toll on your body," he said gruffly. He then got a stern look on his face, and said, "After what happened today, I wouldn't recommend you having anymore children."

His last words broke her heart; she loved her children, very much. They were conceived of the love that she and Henry shared.

Just then, Jeremiah poked his head in the door. "Did you call me, Doc?" he asked. The worry was visible on his old face.

Doctor McAdams said, "No, Sir- but I'm done here if you want to visit."

"I'm going to be fine," Charity told Jeremiah. However, he did not look convinced that she was.

The other children nudged past Jeremiah and were gathering around their mother's bed; they wanted to be near her and take a look at their new baby sister. Jeremiah was relieved, but during the birthing when he thought she was going to die, he had experienced the same feelings of helplessness that had driven into a bottle, when his wife and baby died, all those years ago. Charity smiled at him and squeezed his hand, thanking him for getting help for her.

Later that night after things settled down a bit, Jeremiah brought her a cup of coffee and asked if he could visit with her for a while. She appreciated the coffee, it was calming. She was happy that he'd come in to check on her.

"You know, if we had been livin' out in the wilderness, you could've died today, Missy," he said. "I didn't know what to do for you…"

"Quit beating yourself up, Jeremiah," she scolded, "everything happens the way it's supposed to happen- if I had been meant to die, I would've died… Certain things happen to touch certain people or maybe so that someone will learn a life lesson from what took place. Now, you quit your worrying and look at our newest family member; our beautiful little girl," Charity said, as she uncovered the baby's face.

"What are you going to name 'er?"

"I don't know," Charity replied. "I haven't even considered a name yet."

Clearing his throat, Jeremiah offered a suggestion. "What about Cynthia? That was my baby girl's name. Although my little girl never had a chance, because of the fevers, this 'un here done proved she's a fighter."

"Cynthia Ann…" Charity said, thoughtfully. "I think that would be a fine name, Jeremiah. We'll tell the children that we are naming their new baby sister, Cynthia Ann. I think Henry will like it, too," she said, smiling.

Later, when Jeremiah brought her a bowl of soup and a glass of milk, she could tell that he still was not alright, so she brought up what the doctor said.

"The doctor said that my grandfather came to get him." She smiled at Jeremiah and said, "You know, you really are like a grandfather to me, and even more so for the children. Some of them haven't ever met Henry's parents, and some don't really remember them because they were so little when we left Carolina; my parents and grandparents are all dead…" she said softly, "You're the closest person to a grandfather, they'll ever know, Jeremiah."

"You and Henry and them young'uns of yourn, is the nearest thing to a family, this old man has had in nearly fifty years. I just hope to be around long enough to see 'em grown; that ain't likely to happen though…" he said sadly.

"Don't say that," she scolded. "I know for a fact that you'll be around a whole lot longer than you think."

Having lived in purgatory for so many years, Jeremiah had let the devil convince him that he was worthless. He knew they loved him; he couldn't deny that- but what if he had let Charity and the baby die, the way he'd let his own wife and child die? He knew that Henry would never have forgiven him if he had let them die- he would no longer be his friend… the children would have hated him too, if he'd let their mother die… He knew that Henry and his family cared a great deal for him; however, he also knew that Henry loved his family more than anyone or anything in the world…

I ain't worth a damn no more, thought Jeremiah as he sat in the backyard puffing on his pipe that Unegadihi made him- I can't even do a decent days work I shake so bad," he thought to himself as he lifted a glass of water to his lips, and it's a getting worse and worse… he thought as he sat the glass down with a thump, nearly dropping it. Maybe a good drink of whiskey is just what I need- it ought to stop these shakes… I may as well, he thought to himself as he got up and headed toward the saloon.

Lila M Beckham

"What's your poison, Mr.," asked the barkeep.

"Whiskey," replied Jeremiah.

The barkeep sat a shot glass on the bar, then reached and pulled a bottle of whiskey from under the bar and poured him a shot.

"Leave it."

"That'll be two bits, up front," said the barkeep in a gruff manner.

"Keep 'em coming," Jeremiah said, dropping a silver dollar on the table. The bartender gave him a long look, set the bottle down, and then busied himself behind the bar.

It was about dark the next day, when ten-year-old Aaron reached the saloon- he bent to look under the doors before pushing them open and walking in. Jeremiah's rheumy, old eyes raked over him like a fine-toothed comb. The blueness of his eyes, shined through their whiskey clouded lenses.

His glance, sized the boy up and then cast him aside, as he picked up his glass and chugged back another swallow.

Slamming it down on the bar, his palsied hands shook as he picked the bottle up to pour himself another shot. After tossing it back, he said, "No doubt, your Pa sent you to fetch me home."

"Yes, Sir, he did."

"Well, you can tell him that I said he can mind his own damn business- Now, go, get yourself on back home; I don't want you in here!" Jeremiah slammed down his glass, picked up what money he had left, and the bottle, then staggered toward a table and sat down, turning his back to the boy, leaving him staring at his feet, feeling uneasy and self conscious.

"Please, Jeremiah," begged Aaron. "Please come home with me."

The old man ignored him.

Shuffling his feet, the boy stood there a moment or two, and then turned to head toward the door. As he reached the doors, he looked back over his shoulder at the old man; tears welled up in his troubled eyes. He started to say something, but then thought better of it. Pushing open the doors, he left. After hearing the, swoosh-swoosh of the saloon doors; the old man took another swig of whiskey, this time, straight from the bottle…

37

Jeremiah's Demons

With a fractured heart and sympathetic understanding, Henry set the cup of coffee he'd gotten from the bartender, on the table in front of Jeremiah. He looked upon his old friend a moment before he spoke. "Old Man, you haven't had a drink in nearly six years; what possessed you to pick up that bottle again? I'd a never figured you for falling off the wagon after all this time.

"When I thought Missy was gonna die, it was like all my old demons jest come a running at me, full force," said Jeremiah, slightly belligerent.

Henry could tell that Jeremiah was still slightly tangle-eyed, as he used to call it when he was drunk. "You can't do this to yourself, Jeremiah, or to our friendship. My family loves you; we want you to come home. Hell, old Man, I wouldn't know what to do without you around. You've had my back ever since we was, locked up," he said quietly. Jeremiah's hands shook so badly, as he tried to raise the cup of coffee to his lips, that he spilt about half of it.

"See!" Jeremiah yelled, "I done got to where I shake so

damn bad that I can't even drink a cup of coffee! I jest ain't worth a damn to nobody no more!"

"You may not realize it, old man, but you mean a lot to me and my family," said Henry. "And, you might not know it, but we need you, and you need us, too. Now, come on and drink that coffee so we can get on to the house and get you cleaned up. Charity and the young'uns are going to get worried if we don't get there soon."

At the mention of Charity and the children, a heartbroken look came across the old man's face. "I done recollect that Aaron, well, he already be a mite worried about me. I remember seeing him a standing right yonder. Such a sad look on that boy's face," mumbled Jeremiah.

"Now, don't go to fretting about that, old man. That boy loves you, and there ain't nothing you could've said or done that's gonna stop that love- all of us love you; we're not going to shame you just because you got drunk."

"I hear what you is saying, Henry, but it won't be easy for him to shake his mind free of the sight he done seen me in, nor the way I spoke ta him; I'm plumb ashamed of myself..." After looking up into Henry's calm and gentle face, Jeremiah said, "I don't know if'n he'll forgive me, but I hope he do."

Jeremiah's first attempt to stand and walk toward the door, failed; he plunked back down onto his chair. However, he did not give up on the first try; and after another attempt, he made it to his feet. He stood there a moment before his shaky legs would carry him to the door.

Shortly before supper was ready, Henry returned home, bringing Jeremiah with him; Charity was quite relieved to see him. She loved the old man and so did the children. Henry took Jeremiah to his room and helped him get himself cleaned up. During supper, Charity and Henry both tried to make everything seem normal- no one mentioned Jeremiah's absence of the previous two days and all of them tried to carry on normal conversations- Several times, Charity saw one of the children sneak a peek toward Jeremiah; she figured they were curious about his absence. Aaron did not say anything at all during supper, but did walk over and hug Jeremiah's neck when they finished supper; she smiled at the look on Jeremiah's face. When she stood to help the girls clear the table, she too, hugged Jeremiah, and whispered that she was glad he came home.

Later that night, when she and Henry had gone to bed, she broached the subject of moving out into the country. Speaking her heart to him, she told him that they needed to move from where they were living, not just for her, but for Jeremiah and the children too.

"Our family does so much better when we're further out in the country; we all seem happier too- I've already talked to them some about it; neither me nor them is cut out for this city life." Listening quietly, Henry lay there and let her talk without interrupting.

"The next county up is called Cherokee County. Today, I

heard that there is a majestic waterfall at a place called Little River Canyon. With all my heart, I want to go live there. Please take us there, Henry," she begged, snuggling her head against his shoulder.

How could he not resist her pleading? "We will pack the wagons and leave as soon as you and the baby are able to travel," he said, pulling her near. She hugged him tightly and then snuggled back down into the crook of his arm, molding her body into his.

"You keep that up and I will have to go bunk down with Jeremiah."

She giggled, and then turned serious as she spoke. "I truly have been worried about him. He has been on the brink of purgatory lately... he has always had such a great sense of wisdom about him, and yet, he remains fragile in so many ways... Much of it is because he is getting older and his health is not so good; he shakes badly and much of his strength has left him; however, he is also fragile mentally- everywhere he goes, he carries the burden of guilt with him- he also has horrible memories from his childhood that he carries with him. Did you know that he remembers when he was a child of two to four years old- I cannot remember past the time I was eight or so- only little flashes earlier than that. I wish I could remember my parents the way he does his; however, I would not want to remember them dying... Nokomis told me that her brother brought me to her and Grandpa's cabin after finding me in my parent's home- they had been dead for several days… many people from the tribe died that year… I'm glad that I do not remember that…" Charity was quiet for a moment before speaking again. "I'm going to ask Doctor McAdams if there is something he can give Jeremiah to help him with his physical ailments, or if there is something we can do to help him… I honestly do want this for him and the children, Henry; I don't just want to move for my own needs, but for our family as a whole," Charity explained. "You know that, right?"

"Yes, honey, I know you do; you don't have a selfish bone in your body." Charity felt a little guilty because at times, she did feel selfish…

✳✳✳

While sitting at the table drinking a cup of coffee, the next morning, Jeremiah apologized to Charity; she assured him that her feelings toward him had not changed and that she loved him and wanted him to stay with them.

"When you've lived in Hell as long as I has, your scar tissue gets so thick ye can't feel thangs like ye ought to and the guilt ye feel, it jest lingers in your mind a eaten away and a eaten away until ye can't shake it. Guilt makes a fella feel so worthless that even when folks is a telling him good thangs about him, he still can't feel 'em his self," Jeremiah said.

"I'm sorry that you've been through so much heartache, Jeremiah; but you must be strong- if not for yourself, then for us.

We all love you very much!"

"Ma'am, I'm gonna try my hardest ta keep myself straight. I might've fell off the wagon, but I got back up, didn't I?"

"Yes, sir, you sure did."

"And, I'll keep a pickin' myself up as long as I has y'all ta lean on."

"You know we'll be here for you… as a matter of fact, I talked with Henry last night and we have decided to move up to Cherokee County. I heard that there is a majestic waterfall at a place called Little River Canyon- I want to live near it," she told Jeremiah. "Doesn't that sound like a great place to live and raise our family?"

"Yes'um, it do, but what the heck is it with you and the Cherokee name? Missy- is it because you are part Indian," he asked.

"Well, I am three quarters Cherokee and although I might not live amongst my people, I feel close to them when I'm in the places where they have lived. Their sweat is soaked into the soil and their spirits linger in every blade of grass and each grain of sand… I can feel them… Does that make sense?"

"Yes'um, I reckon it makes a whole lot a sense; least ta me it do."

"Everything is going to be fine once we get settled up there."

"I sure hope it do, Ma'am. I know you and them young'uns is going ta like it better than a living in this here town. I can tell ye don't like the city-life."

"Its way too confining for me," Charity admitted. "I feel as though I'm being smothered alive... I was raised up in the mountains until me and Henry married, then I lived in a valley along the Savannah River. Before I married Henry, I'd never been further that a mile away from the cabin I was raised in; even after we married, we only went into town; well actually, it was a fort, not a town, maybe once a year, and then, I didn't get to go every year."

"Sounds good ta me," said Jeremiah.

"It's a much simpler life out in the country. I don't like looking out the window and into my neighbor's kitchen; and, there are not enough trees! Most of the trees are in the town square. I love going outdoors to use the toilet; here in town, everyone knows when you go to the toilet. I love trees, grass, vines, creeks and rivers. And the air is so much cleaner smelling in the country! It smells like a mud hole full of dung, is nearby when you step outside. And when it rains, its even worse," Charity laughed.

Jeremiah was glad to see her so happy; his spirit was lifted and it made him happy too.

It would be three months before they moved, but the months seemed to fly by. Charity assured Henry that she and little Cynthia were ready to travel. The nearer the time came to leave, the more excited and high spirited Charity felt. Her excitement and good feelings turned into anxious ones as the time neared for them to leave. When they were loaded and finally on their way, she felt a tinge of fear of the unknown- however, spring was in full-bloom; she enjoyed being out in it and smelling the fragrance of spring!

Riding on the wagon seat beside Jeremiah, Charity said, "These days, my moods seem to be as varied as the colors of the sunsets."

"Yes'um, I noticed... We ought to be to them falls, in another day or so."

"I wish Henry and Uriah hadn't left ahead of us, but I understand he needed to find a job and a seeing about a place for us to live."

"That be a good man you got there."

"Yes, sir, I know he is... I just hate him being separated from the rest of the family. Hopefully, we'll all be together once we get there. And, to tell the truth, I really miss not having John here with us..."

Hearing the sadness of her tone, Jeremiah said, "Now, you know John be a good boy; well heck, I reckon he be a man now that he married and is a settling down with Sarah -"

"But, he's only seventeen," Charity said, cutting off his words. Jeremiah could not help but snicker at her.

"What do you think is so dang funny, you old coot," asked Charity, giving him a hard look because he irritated her by laughing at her.

"Now, don't go and get yourself all twitterpated," Jeremiah chuckled.

"You're enough to cause someone to be constipated!" Charity snapped at him. "Why are you grinning like a jackass eating briars, as Henry would say?"

"How old was you and Henry when y'all got hitched up?"

Seeing where he was going with that question, Charity stuttered, "But that's different," she stammered.

"How's it different?" asked Jeremiah, "You thought you was grown up enough ta get married at fifteen. Heck, John is older than you and Henry was. He'll be fine- you gotta cut them apron strings and let 'em go when they is ready ta fly solo; ye caint keep 'em in the nest forever."

They rode along in silence, for a mile or so and then Jeremiah asked, "What'd Henry say the name of that place they was going to look for work?"

"Gaylesville," Charity replied. "He said it's near the confluence of the Chattooga River and Little River. We were supposed to stay due north when we left town. He said we'd have to go around a lake, cross the river, and then come back down some."

"Well," said Jeremiah with satisfaction, "I believe we has made it to the lake he told us we'd have ta go around."

"I believe you're right. Its getting late in the day- I think we should make camp here for the night."

"I'm gone get closer to the water first," Jeremiah said, "I

believe I might jest go a fishing today and catch us some fish for supper."

"Fish sounds good. I hope you can catch some."

39

Noccalula Falls

Black Creek Falls - Noccalula Falls,
Cherokee Co, Alabama
March, 1851

After a supper of fried fish, grits, and biscuits, the children's bellies were full and their imaginations were running wild- they hadn't completely forgotten living on the trail- The same as when they were younger, they wanted Charity to tell them a story before they went to sleep. She smiled at their eagerness, remembering all the stories she had told them at night while they were on the trail from Sandersville to Canton. It seemed that once they were settled in a house and not camping under the stars, the need for her bedtime stories were no longer necessary. Living on the trail seemed to bring her children much closer to her; she missed living that way...

"Please, Mama!" begged Nancy and Mary, "We want you to tell a story," they said in unison, interrupting her thoughts. Then Martha joined in, wanting a story too. Charity scanned the faces of her boys, but they were busy, whittling on pieces of wood. Aaron looked up; probably because he could feel his mother's eyes on him. Charity was remembering when they, too, use to beg for all the stories of her ancestors that were passed down from generation to generation. She had hoped that they, too, would keep this tradition going forth into the newer generations to come.

"I'm listening, Mama," said Aaron.

"Me too, Mama," said Charles.

She then looked at Mary and Nancy; both, were lying on their stomachs with their faces propped on their elbows, anxiously awaiting a story. She smiled and began telling her story.

"Long ago, on a mountain summit, within sight and sound of a rushing waterfall, lived a great Indian Chief, whose young daughter, Noccalula, was famed far and wide for her extraordinary beauty and loveliness of character." She smiled when saw the girl's eyes light up. Then the boys raised their heads, looking at her questioningly." She continued telling her story.

"Many gallant braves sought the old chief, asking for the hand of his daughter, Noccalula, but only one was favored by the girl's father; a rich chief of a powerful neighboring tribe. He was favored because he had much to offer in exchange; he had wampum, horses, and blankets.

"Noccalula pleaded in vain; telling her father that her heart was already given to a young brave of her own tribe. This young warrior, though noted for his skill and valor, possessed little in worldly goods.

"The old chief refused to listen to Noccalula; he ordered his daughter to make ready for the marriage he had arranged! What was a maiden's silly fancy, against many horses, much wampum and a union with another strong tribe? The girl's lover was driven from the tribe and a marriage agreement was settled upon by the neighboring chief.

"The wedding day arrived and a great feast was prepared. In silence, Noccalula allowed herself to be arrayed in the festive wedding robes. To be sold to a stranger by the father she loved, filled her heart with incredible sorrow." Charity paused to let them absorb her words, and then continued her story.

"Her chosen lover was forever banished. Overcome by grief, Noccalula quietly slipped away from the merrymakers. The soft, rhythmical rush of the waterfall's waters, called her to come to them. After reaching the top, she stood poised upon the brink of the vast chasm, staring below. One leap and her troubles were over…" She heard the children's sharp intake of breath.

"Heartbroken, the remorseful father, gave the great falls his daughter's name. Since that day, the waterfall has been called, Noccalula Falls."

"She jumped," asked Martha, disbelievingly. Charity nodded her head. She had read the short story, "The Legend of Noccalula Fall's," while she was looking through Mr. Aderholt's mercantile for things she may need. The story was written by someone named Mathilde Bilbro.

"How come you've never told us that story before, Mama?" asked Charles, his face screwed up in disbelief.

Charity smiled; she told them that she didn't know the story before- that she had read that story while looking through some newspapers at the mercantile in Jacksonville.

"Blue blazes!" Charles exclaimed. "I can't believe she would just jump because she was gonna have to marry some rich Indian chief! That's stupid!"

"No, it's not!" Martha said vehemently. "I'd jump too, if I was her! She was in love with someone else." Then, Martha looked at her mother, and in a very serious tone, asked, "Y'all ain't going to make me marry somebody I don't love; are you Mama?"

"No, of course not," Charity laughed.

"Good," she said.

Jeremiah chuckled and said, "All these stories catch your fancy too, don't they Missy. That'd be how come you wanted to come up here. You're hoping ta get a chance ta talk to that there Noccalula, ain't cha?" he asked.

"Well, you'd know I was lying if I said no; so, I may as well admit to it. Of course, that's the reason I wanted to come- I hope her spirit still hangs around there so I can meet her!" Charity was smiling.

"Well, jest between you, me, and the gatepost," Jeremiah winked, "I hope she be a hanging round there too."

Charity had to laugh. She liked seeing Jeremiah with a gleam in his eye, and a little spark coming back to him.

They all went to bed with a full belly, smiling and happy. Charity could feel her body and spirit, being renewed from the fresh air and sunshine; and from being off the plains and up into the lower Appalachian mountains. She slept a peaceful sleep that night and awoke refreshed and ready to continue on their quest.

"We should be able to get in quite a few miles today," Jeremiah told her as they climbed aboard the wagons.

"I hope so," she replied; adding, "I'm getting more and more anxious to get to those falls."

They skirted the lake, the next several days, following the well-traveled road. And, they met nary a traveler for those two days, either. Jeremiah grew worrisome; he thought that they might have missed a turn somewhere; however, Charity assured him they had not and told him they were going the right way because she could hear the spirits calling her. About mid-afternoon on the third day of March, they reached what they thought were the falls.

The river sung, calling Charity to its side. As she knelt down, she felt the mist of the falls on her face, moistening her skin to a sultry glow.

Jeremiah and the children watched as she kneeled at the water's edge. With face tilted skyward, and arms raised towards the heavens, she stayed.

"Is Mama praying?" Nancy asked.

"No, she is talking to spirits," Charles answered, then got down off the wagon and walked over to where his mother was and knelt down as she had. Charles closed his eyes to listen.

Nancy stood quietly beside Jeremiah for several minutes, and then, placing her hands on her hips, she stomped her foot.

"It's not fair!" Nancy said indignantly. "Why does he get to listen, and I don't- I never get to go with Mama!"

Offhandedly, Jeremiah said, "Sometimes, life ain't fair, Little Lady."

He wouldn't be paying too much attention to Nancy's tantrum; he was fascinated by the expression on Charity's face. He wished that he, too, could see what she was seeing. He thought that maybe it'd make dying a little easier to face, if he could see that there was something else to look forward to on the other side. Something real, something he witnessed with his own eyes.

Mary started toward Charles and her mother, and then stopped. She turned and went over to Jeremiah. With her eyes as big as saucers - she wrapped her arm around his leg and held on tight.

"What's the matter, Mary," asked Martha.

"I'm sacred of them," Mary mumbled.

"Who are you scared of? Is it Mama and Charles?"

"No, them," Mary replied, pointing a finger in her mother's direction. Everyone looked toward Charity.

40

Princess Noccalula

An aura emanated from Charity and surrounded Charles as he knelt down beside her, it nearly made them invisible to the others. The aureole seemed to have a life of it's own as it moved around them. In the midst of the invisible field around them, Charity could feel the spirits nearing, searching her out. She kept her eyes closed, until she could feel their presence in front of her; slowly, her eyes fluttered open. There were five ghostly apparitions standing there; what appeared to be a white family and a young Indian couple.

The first to come to her, were the three white people, which was a young man, a woman, and a small girl child. They said that when the government first opened the Louisiana Territory for settlement, they had left their homes in Virginia to travel to this new land and build a life there; the young father blamed himself for taking his family on the journey- as they were crossing the river, the oxen had been swept under and the wagon overturned, dumping them all into the swift current. They had three young children with them, but could only find the one that was with them now- their other two children were lost during the tragedy.

After searching for what seemed like hours, they saw the a bright light; and, although the light felt warm and inviting, the woman was afraid to go to it, and she did not want to leave her lost children behind. Avoiding the light, they ran away and continued their search for their other children; soon, they too, became lost. Since then, they had wandered until they saw the warm, inviting light again…

Gently, Charity explained to them that they no longer walked among the living, and that if their other children were not with them, either they survived the river of death or they went into the light; but either way, they would be waiting for them at the end of their journey. The man and woman wept tears of joy as Charity led them through the pathway and into the next realm.

Once she had done this, the young warrior placed his essence firmly between Charity and who she suspected was Noccalula. Trying to shield himself and Noccalula from her, even though it was they that sought her out, he puffed up his chest bravely. Charity knew he had to be the young brave from the story; the one to whom Noccalula had given her heart and her life for… Reading his aura, she learned his name was Edahi; "He goes about."

"Ga-do'detsadoa?" he asked gruffly- which meant, who are you.

"I am the passageway, "Eti, gasuyeu so qua, Ganenutlvi," she replied. "I will lead you out of the darkening land and into the light."

"How do I know to trust you?" he asked.

"Did you not seek me out?" she questioned. "You are in Wudeliguhi, the land of the dead. I am here to lead you to the light-"

"You lie!" he yelled, cutting her off. She felt Charles jump at the sudden explosion of Edahi's voice.

"Tali tsudulanayi degawanihu luwudi," Charity stated tersely. "I speak not, with two tongues;" she said gently, "the Great Spirit has sent me here to guide you." She could see disbelief still in his eyes.

"Can you touch me?" she asked.

"Can you touch the trees; the grass? Smell them? Can you feel the mist of the falls on your face? No, you cannot. I do not speak untruths, Edahi."

It was then that Noccalula stepped forward. "What you speak is the truth," she said. "I no longer feel these things."

When Edahi saw that she was talking to someone else, he turned, looking around. In that moment, Charity realized that even though they were there together, and he appeared to be placing himself between her and Noccalula, Edahi could not see Noccalula, nor could she see him.

"Tsiwanihu toeu, I speak the truth, always," she told Noccalula. "It is what I do. I am a Chosen One, a Passageway. I was sent to help those who are lost on a path into the light, "Eti, gasuyeu, so qua, Ganenutlvi," said Charity. "If you listen," she said, "You will hear the river's daganogeda; it's spirit talks to you; the river does not lie either."

"I know the river sings... I remember feeling a deep sadness. A sadness that overtook my spirit," said Noccalula. "My father broke my heart when he banished Edahi and said I was to marry the wealthy chief. My heart belonged to Edahi... I could not marry someone I did not love.

"The song of the river called for me to come here. I stood atop the falls and begged the Great Spirit to intervene and soften my father's heart- Edahi came and we argued... the river called and I jumped. I thought if we could not be together, I had rather be dead... We could have run away, but that would have caused disgrace to Edahi; he is a warrior. A warrior never runs away!"

Charity saw the bitter sadness on Noccalula's face and heard heartbreak in her voice as she revealed the truth of what happened that fateful day.

The morning of her wedding to the neighboring chief, she had found Edahi and tried to get him to run away with her; they had met at the falls. He had come to tell her goodbye. Even though his heart was also broken; he was a warrior- he had to keep his honor above all else, even Noccalula. He told her that he was leaving and going somewhere where he could never see her again. It was what he *had* to do. However, Noccalula was a woman in love. All her heart could see was the man she loved, turn and walk away from her. She again begged him to run away with her; and, when he refused to disgrace his father, she yelled that he did not love her, as she loved him. And then, she turned and leapt over the falls… During the telling of her death, she had become visible and audible to Edahi; he looked from Charity to Noccalula.

"She speaks the truth… it is what happened. Gvgeyu, I love you Noccalula," he said softly. "I am sorry for what I put you through… My father taught me that honor comes above all else. I could not dishonor my father before the chief and lose his respect. I did not want to hurt you- my heart was ripped from my chest- that is why I followed you into the Tsikamagi- the River of Death; it's spirit was too strong and called you away from me."

Noccalula turned to Charity. "If we go through this passageway you speak of, will we be whole again, be together again? Will we feel the other's touch again?" she asked.

"I do not know." Charity spoke truthfully. "It is not for me to know; I am only a guide. A Duyugodv Ayosdi, a seeker of truth. If you are ready and I will show you the way into the next world; I too, will learn new knowledge; knowledge of the unknown."

Noccalula and Edahi came together and joined hands- they stared into each others eyes a moment and then both said they were ready.

As Charity began the prayer to talk to the Great Spirit, peace came over her; it enveloped her and a circle of light surrounded her, Charles, and the young Indian Princess and her lover.

Jeremiah and the children watched the peace and tranquility

fill Charity's features as she chanted her lyrical song to the Great Spirit. Mary, who still clung to Jeremiah's leg, let go and stepped a step toward her mother to watch, her expression, intent. Raising her palms toward the heavens, Charity continued her prayer until the young couple walked into the light that appeared to them. After several minutes, Charity rose to her feet, as did Charles. He opened his eyes and looked into his mother's eyes.

"Where do they go Mama?"

"I do not know, son," she replied. "I would hope that they go to the Unequa Adanvdo, the Great Spirit in the heavens."

"I don't understand why they would jump from the falls and kill themselves, just because they could not marry- it don't make sense."

"I cannot answer that, Charles; however, I do know that some people feel desperate at times and desperation does strange things to a person's mind. Many times, human beings are faced with things that they cannot comprehend. They see only what is in front of them and not what can be. Instead of coping with whatever it is they are faced with they run away from it." She paused. Witnessing the confusion on Charles' face, she felt the need to explain further.

"Once we run away from whatever it is we do not want to face, the Nvnehidihi, who sowed doubt in our minds and began his deceitful lies way before our decision was made, becomes even bolder with his lies.

"The Nvnehidihi is the Pathkillers; they are many. Two

Feathers said a Pathkiller will do everything in his power to keep you from moving forward. He whispers lies in your ears that only you can hear. He causes you to doubt your self-worth, your abilities that the Great Spirit gave you. He speaks with two tongues; you must not listen to his lies; he wants to keep you from the Great Spirit. If you are careful and observant, you will know when he is near. Banish him from your mind- he can only hurt you if you let him. Now, we must go, our work here is done."

"Yeah, Mama, they're gone!"

Charity looked down at Mary's smiling face and she could not help but to smile too. She wondered if Mary would keep her gift of sight, or would she too outgrow it as she had, before it was thrust back upon her by Two Feathers.

Charity remembered that as a small child, she would sit in her mother's lap while she sang lullabies to her. When her grandfather realized what she was doing, he told her to quit pretending- there was no one there. But there was- her mother was there. Her grandmother always encouraged her to talk to her mother... She also remembered her little friend, White Doe. They would sit and play in the sand together. Grandpa would shake his head and say that she was imagining things. After a while, her mother stopped coming to see her and so did White Doe. Charity now realized that she wasn't imagining them; they did come see her, but not in the flesh as she visualized, she was interacting with their spirits.

That night, they camped at the falls. It was such a beautiful place. The girls begged for the story of Noccalula again, and Charity obliged after a little persuasion. When she lay down to sleep, a feeling she'd had all afternoon, grew stronger in intensity; she knew that someone needed her. While nursing Cynthia, she began to doze; almost immediately, her soul rose and floated away from her body. Her spirit rose high above the wagons, tree branches, brushed against her. Her Spirit Guide appeared and they soared along the night winds to where she needed to go.

From high above, she looked down and knew where she was; a familiar presence greeted her- almost comforting her. He lay alone, dying...

41

The Spirits Song

Lying on a bed of straw, Unegadihi had come to the Cave of the Spirits Song- where the, "Adonvdo, Nvyu, daganogeda", Spirit Stone sings. He had come there to die. When he saw Charity, he smiled weakly.

"Ga ga na?" he mumbled, asking who was there.

"I am here," she whispered.

"I knew you would find me. The Nvnehidihi has been lying, whispering to me that you would not come to guide me home."

As Charity looked upon his now frail body, which had once been so large and strong, hot tears stung her eyes.

"Do not cry for me, Sahani Dikata. I will walk the winds of the Great Spirit," he said. "I will go home to my people, my homeland. Return to the innocence of childhood, where my father now awaits me."

"I would not break my promise to you," she said, squatting down beside him, she took one of his large hands in hers. Distant drums sounded and began to beat a slow rhythmic tune.

She knew they were calling for him, but she did not want to turn loose his spirit just yet, at least not until she could tell him how much his friendship had meant to her; before she could speak, he raised a trembling hand and placed a serpentine finger across her lips, hushing her speech.

"It goes forth shining," he said. "We were meant to help one another. I help you- now, you help me. I cannot do this alone, Agigau-a ge ya," he said, calling her Beloved Woman. "You must show me the passageway; you are the Chosen One. Place me on the path to the other side, to the light. As the crow flies, so will I. Akilvdiha'nole," he said, smiling weakly. "I will be, he who rides the wind," he mumbled, closing his eyes.

"You surely will," she whispered and then kissed his weathered cheek. Taking his hands in hers, she began her prayer to release his spirit so that he could soar home. His eyes fluttered slightly and then closed for the final time. When he exhaled his final breath, she released his hands and watched his spirit rise. Her heavy heart lightened and her spirit sang with joy.

He looked back at her- smiled, then turned away to begin his mystic journey. The tears she had held back flowed softly down her cheeks...

✳✳✳

Some while later, she awoke. Cynthia's warm breath on her breast and Mary snuggled tightly against her back, caused her to feel sated. Suddenly, she had grown tired of roaming, moving from place to place. This spot, felt like home... When they left the Carolinas, she had followed Henry's dream of moving to

Alabama. Now that they were there, it was her time to fill a void. She loved this spot beneath the falls; and what a beautiful spot it was… It was the perfect place to build a home for her family.

She wanted to stay there; Henry could build them a cabin. It didn't have to be fancy or very large as long as it had a porch like the houses in town, where she could sit with her coffee and look out upon such a beautiful sight each morning… maybe even a window near the bed where she could see the falls as soon as she awoke. Charity sighed with longing.

When she eased out from under the wagon, Jeremiah was already up. He had stoked the fire and had coffee brewing. When she sat down beside him, he handed her a cup of coffee. She took a sip and looked to her left- her eyes rested on the falls; Jeremiah could tell that she had something on her mind.

"What's the matter, Missy? I know sumthin's eatin' at your craw."

Charity sighed before she spoke.

"Last night, Unegadihi called me to his side," she said sadly.

"So, old Uni passed on, did he," said Jeremiah, looking her in the eye.

"I know he was your friend- What else is eatin' at you?"

"I think you read me too well, sometimes, old friend," she smiled.

"I want to stay here," she said, "To stay here and look upon such beauty every morning would satisfy my soul."

"So you won't have to think about all the ugliness that's out there in the world or that might come your way…" he said knowingly.

"Yes," she said thoughtfully. "A great change is coming; much like when the Indians were driven from these lands; devastation the likes of which we have never seen in our lifetimes."

"I's seen a lot, Missy- don't know if'n it'll top some of 'em."

"All I know is that the soil will turn red with spilled blood- brother will be pitted against brother, father against son. Most will join this great war, without a cause other than they have been challenged to do so."

"I is sorry that you can see these things in the future, Missy; but in a way, ain't it a blessing?" he asked.

"You would think it would be, wouldn't you," Charity said, "but its not. When we were on the Yellow River, Two Feathers told me some of the things he saw happening in the future; it was as if he was reading my thoughts, because I had seen many of those things, too. He told me that Aaron would not live to give me grandchildren; he said that Aaron would die in a great war of the white man.

I did not want to listen to him, then. Now, I wish we could talk again… Aaron was so young at the time, but he is now fourteen. At best, we have only a few more years left with him. I want to live those years here among the mountains and in sight of the waterfall. I know that Henry will want to live nearer the town. Jeremiah, I want you to help me keep my children, my family, here in the shadow of the falls. Will you help me?"

"A 'course I'll help you, Missy, but you know me, I worry worse than an old woman. I'd rather be out here too," he said. "My soul seems less restless and more at peace. When you're stuck out in the woods, it's easier to avoid the temptations that them towns and cities has to offer."

"I know it's asking a lot of you, Jeremiah. You may want a life of your own. Maybe find a nice woman and settle down…"

"Oh, no, Ma'am!" Jeremiah quickly interjected. "I done got too old, for all those shenanigans! Y'all is all I needs- don't worry your head bout that, Missy. I'll do what I can, to help you persuade him to your way of thinking."

"I'm thinking of a way to go about that right now." Charity smiled and patted his shoulder. Getting up to start breakfast, Charity said, "We love you too; you know that don't you?"

"Yes'um I do- them young'uns'll be up afore you know it and a raring ta go. You can bet they'll be hungry, too," he chuckled. "At least the older ones are able to help care for the littler ones. That helps you out a lot."

"Yes, they are a big help," she agreed.

***

Henry and Uriah found work as hired help on the Plantation of a Mr. Samuel Haynes. A well to do gentleman, whose family originally came to the territory from Virginia. Although Mr. Haynes owned slaves, he had none that were skilled in various tasks that needed to be performed on a plantation- Henry had become quite proficient as a wheelwright and at Blacksmithing- he was hired to teach the tasks to several of Haynes slaves. Henry quickly realized that although the slaves acted as if they knew nothing about being a wheelwright or smithy, they did; they acted ignorant in order to fool the master. Henry said nothing of their deceit, but let them know that he knew of their deception and he would not tolerate it. The master was pleased at how quickly and how well they were learning the trade. Henry told them that it was always better to be honest- and that honesty was always rewarded with praise.

Haynes had a pretty daughter named Hannah that had been eyeing Uriah from about the second day they were there. The sideways glances they gave each other didn't go unnoticed by her mammy or Henry.

After a couple of days, Henry said the Uriah, "You need to watch out, Son. Her daddy ain't going to take too kindly to the two of you getting too friendly."

"But why not, Paw?" asked Uriah. Henry could tell from the look on his son's face that he honestly did not understand why he would not be accepted as a suitor for the hand of young Hannah Haynes.

"That girl is from a different class of folks than us, Son. They've got money and slaves; they've probably never wanted for anything in their entire lives."

"Well Papa, you ever think that some folks, no matter how much money they got, might just need a friend?" Uriah asked.

"You make a valid point, Son," said Henry, "but I don't want you to get your feelings hurt, or your heart broken."

"Well, it's my heart, Papa. I think I'm old enough to decide for myself if I want to risk it. People shouldn't judge other folks just because they ain't got as much as they have... You're judging them on account of their money, slaves, and the property they own- that's not right either, is it?"

"Yeah Son, I reckon you're right; maybe I am judging them unfairly. I haven't given them the chance to prove themselves worthy or unworthy."

"Mr. Sam seems like a fair man. I think he'll understand. If he don't, then he don't- I'll just have to wait and see."

"I just hope he gives you the proper chance to prove your self-worth to him... You know, we will be going to meet your mama and the children Friday. Maybe, we will get the chance to look around, explore some, and check out the town and the folks that live there before your mama and them get there."

"We'll talk about me and Hannah later," Uriah said gruffly.

"If the need arises, Son," Henry replied.

42

The Singing River

Gaylesville, Cherokee Co, Alabama
April, 1851

Charity, Jeremiah, and the children made it to the outskirts of Gaylesville on a Friday afternoon; it was the 18th day of April, in the year 1851. Already, she missed the peace of the wilderness; she also missed the soothing calmness of the watershed. Although Gaylesville was not nearly as large a town as Anniston or Jacksonville was, it was still a town. Charity disliked towns of any size; to her thinking, they seemed to brew trouble.

Henry must have been watching for them. They had no sooner stopped, than he came out to meet them; his face showed great joy and happiness. Charity's heart still melted every time he smiled at her. In the late afternoon sunlight, she noticed that he was starting to gray a little at his temples. It only served to make him even more handsome. He was no longer the young boy-man she had fallen in love with. His days of hard work in the sun, had turned him into a rugged, handsome thirty-seven-year-old, fully-grown man. When he wrapped her in his arms and kissed her deeply, her knees became weak…

"I missed you so much," he whispered softly.

"And I missed you!" she whispered back.

Suddenly, they were surrounded by their girls; all of them wanted their daddy's attention; at least, for a moment or two. Henry obliged by taking each, one at a time, and hugging them tightly and then he swung them around, as only a daddy can do. Aaron was the only one of the boys that clamored, along with the girls needing his father's attention; John, Uriah, and Charles stood back and waited until their father finished with the younger children and then stepped forward to shake their father's hand; naturally, they went in order from oldest to youngest.

Charles waited his turn and then stepped forward and shook his father's hand as his older brother had, however, he went one further by grabbing his father and giving him a quick hug. Proudly, Charity stood back and watched; then, suddenly, Time, confronted her, as she realized how quickly the years had passed-her sons were nearly grown men. The change of demeanor in his sons did not pass Henry's notice either; his sons were suddenly becoming men.

Jeremiah had stood back as Henry had said his hellos to his wife and children and once Henry had made his rounds, he stepped forward and gripped his friend's hand in a firm shake.

"It's good ta see ya, friend," said Jeremiah.

"And it's good to see you too, Old Man!"

"Look who's calling somebody old," exclaimed Jeremiah. "You're getting a little snow on the roof, your own self, *old* friend!"

"Just because there's a little snow on the roof, don't mean there ain't a fire in the fireplace," said Henry with a chuckle, glancing toward Charity.

Charity loved to listen to the lighthearted teasing between Henry and Jeremiah; she was thankful they had found one another and was close. She felt they each, needed the other in their lives for one reason or another. She was also thankful that she had never felt a need female companionship; else, she would have been a very lonely person.

Drawn from her reflections by the sight of Aaron hanging back away from everyone else, Charity went to him. Appearing forlorn and miserable, he was watching his father interacting with the other children.

"What's wrong, Son?"

"Papa don't even act like he sees me," he said sadly.

"I am sure your daddy didn't mean to ignore you, Son," she assured him. "We were all clamoring for your father's attention; he didn't know which way to look first! Why don't you go on over there and talk to him," she urged, but Aaron just shuffled his feet and remained in place.

After staring at Henry for a moment, he glanced toward her.

With her eyes, she begged him to come to her. Untangling himself from the other children, Henry came over to where she and Aaron stood.

"What's wrong with Aaron?" asked Henry, his voice showing his concern.

"He thinks you haven't noticed him," she said.

"Of course I noticed you, Son. But, to tell the truth, I didn't know who the heck you were! When I finally figured it out, I didn't know whether to give you a hug or shake your hand like a man because you've grown so dang tall!"

Aaron was now grinning from ear to ear and had his little chest puffed with pride over his father's comments. Charity smiled when, like a little man, Aaron stuck out his hand. Henry shook it and then pulled him to him and gave him a hug, too. "We men are gonna have to plan a fishing trip for tomorrow so we can catch up," Henry said firmly.

"Yes, you should. I think y'all men need to spend some time away from us womenfolk," said Charity, smiling at Henry and thanking him with her eyes.

Looping his arm around her waist, Henry pulled her to him and kissed her. While Charity fixed supper, Henry had the boys help him remove enough things from one of the wagons to make a spot just big enough for him and Charity so they could sleep in the wagon away from prying eyes.

After everyone was fed and tucked in, Charity and Henry

went down to the river and bathed- it was hard for both she and Henry to constrain themselves until they were in the privacy of their makeshift bedroom; but once there, she removed her gown and snuggled down into the strength and comfort of her husbands loving arms; thanking the Great Spirit above for sending such a wonderful man to be her helpmate in life.

A cool breeze blew across Charity's body, her nipples hardened. She giggled and pressed herself closer to her husband, not to hide herself, but to feel the warmth of his body against hers. Enveloping her in his arms, Henry hugged her to him; moments later, his lips found hers. A tender kiss led to his kissing her neck, which in turn, led to his lips traveling to her breast... She needed him as much as he needed her; he made love to her in his slow and gentle way...

After making love, they lay entwined, holding each other close. The breeze that flowed over the river before reaching them, cooled the rivulets of moisture their lovemaking had caused to form on their bodies- Charity did not know it yet, but they conceived their daughter Emmaline that night on the banks of the Little River Canyon.

After making love, they snuggled and talked about all the things he had missed while he was away working. She filled him in on their journey there to meet him, telling him about how beautiful the area around the Noccalula Falls was and how much she would love to live there.

"Yes, when we passed through there I knew you would fall

in love with it," Henry told her. "I've been checking into getting a piece of land near there."

"Really!" she exclaimed, hugging him.

He nodded his head, yes, then said, "It was my dream to bring our family here, and now that we are here, I want you to be happy too."

"It was both our dreams, Henry... I will be happy anywhere, as long as we are there together."

✳✳✳

Within minutes, Henry had fallen fast asleep. And, as she lay listening to the steady rhythm of his breathing, she sighed in contentment. However, she herself could not go to sleep. It wasn't because she wasn't tired, because she was extremely tired after the long trip, and she was very relaxed after their wonderful lovemaking; however, the later the hour became, the more strange she felt; something around her was definitely different than earlier in the day. Laying there listening, she heard the soft singing of many voices- after listening longer, she thought the singing was coming from the river.

She tried to ignore the low humming sound and go to sleep, but the voices refused to go away and leave her alone; therefore, all she could do was toss and turn. After about thirty minutes, she could stand it no longer; she pulled on her gown and eased out of the wagon. She was surprised to see her great-grandfather, Two Feathers sitting cross-legged in front of the fire.

"Enisi," she said in surprise. "I thought you had gone for good."

Turning his pale eyes to hers, he said, "Tla, Usdi Saquo; No, Little One; I was called here to the singing river by the Great Spirit. You must not listen to those who call from the, Tsikamagi, the River of Death. You must be strong of heart and a strong believer; resist them. They will seek you out and try to call you into the river- they want you to join them in death," he said, pausing to let her absorb his words. "They are the vengeful ones; the ones who carried their anger in life, into death. They seek to make all as unhappy as they was. They seek the purest of souls to corrupt and deceive. They will call you to them, but they will not leave the Tsikamagi, the River of Death.

"If you listen with human ears, the voices calling you sound like the voices of angels. If you listen long enough with human ears, you will unknowingly enter their world; it is a world that one cannot return from. You must listen with your soul's ear; it will hear what is true.

"You walk in the spirit world; when you walk with the spirits, it is easy to be deceived by them." He paused in thought before continuing his discourse.

"Do not trust all you see with human eyes, Little One- You see me as I was. The way you remember me- the way I taught you, through endurance. I am here in spirit- my flesh is not here- my flesh rots away in the soil of our ancestors and is carried off by maggots. In your mind, I sit cross-legged by the fire. In your mind's eye, I will always look the same…" He paused once again, letting his words sink into her thoughts.

"I would love to feel the heat of the flames as I reach toward them," he said with longing- they are not here in this world, they are in another realm.

"It is cold here, Little One. When your time comes to make your final journey into the spirit world, bring a warm blanket," he chuckled. After he chuckled, he disappeared, leaving Charity sitting there alone, with many questions on her lips.

In the quietness of the night, she heard the Singing River call for her to come to it; slowly, she stood and walked toward the whispering voice…

43

River of Death

Startled awake from her dreams; she found herself standing alone in the dark night. She had actually stood up and walked a few feet while in her trance- She wondered what woke her; was it something from her subconscious or... The fire had long ago burned out; not even an orange ember could be seen smoldering amid the pile of charcoaled rubble. Enisi was right, she thought to herself. His sitting there cross-legged in front of a fire is how he will always look to me, because I see with my mind's eye. Where moments before, he was sitting there talking to her, he was now gone and so was his fire.

Stirring the ashes and charred wood with a stick, she dug deep beneath the surface and scooped the pale orange embers up to the top to revive the fire. Fanned by the wind, several loose embers caught on the splinters of fat-lighter'd she'd placed in it and quickly blazed to life. After putting a stick of firewood on the fire, she put on a pot of coffee.

After talking with Two Feathers and learning about the Singing River of Death, there was no way that she would be able to sleep now.

Sitting by the fire, sipping a cup of coffee, she could hear the timbre of the river softly singing to her- The sound was so soothing that she began to listen. The voices were calling her to come to the river.

"You must not listen to them, Little One. The ones who call to you from the Tsikamagi, the river of death," she heard Two Feathers say. "They seek to deceive you into joining them. Listen with your soul's ears."

Feeling a presence near her, she stood up and looked around. Slowly, Charles walked into the circle of the campfire light. "You should be sleeping," she said gently.

"So should you, Mama, but I woke up a little while ago and couldn't go back to sleep because of the noise. Do you hear them, Mama?"

"Yes, Son, I do," she answered. "But we must not go to them. Enisi, my grandfather, Two Feathers, told me to listen with my soul's ear, not with my human ears. He said they seek me and others, trying to get us to join them in the River of Death.

You must not listen to them, either, Charles. They will use your tender young heart to get you near. They might even try to use you to get to me."

"It's hard not to listen, Mama," he said. "How do I listen with my soul and not my mind?" asked Charles, his tone serious.

She crossed her legs and sat back down by the fire the way Two Feathers always did. Charles followed suit and sat down just as she had.

"Close your eyes and breathe deeply," she instructed. "As you breathe, clear your mind of all thoughts-"

"How can I not think of anything at all," asked Charles, interrupting.

"You have to clear you mind to be able to listen to your heart beat. If you cannot hear it, breathe deeper and concentrate- let your mind enter your body and travel to your heart… you can see it in your mind, watch it pump blood through your body. Relax and breathe until all you can hear is your heartbeat."

"I'll try, Mama."

Both, relaxed, breathed deeply and listened. As they listened, the voices changed; they became deep, gruff, and raspy. No longer were the voices calm and soothing; they were plain scary sounding.

"Mama," Charles whispered.

"Yes, Son?" she answered.

"I can hear them with my soul's ears, now," he said. "Can you?"

"Yes, Son, I hear them. Enisi was right; they no longer deceive me. They do not sound angelic- they sound hideous and evil."

"Mama, what about Mary?" Charles asked.

"Unequa Adanvdo! I had not thought about Mary! She is so little. I hope she will fear them and not go to them. We must keep an eye on her, Charles. You will have to help me- we must protect her from the evil of the Nvnehidihi, the ones Enisi calls the Path-killers!"

"What's wrong with the two of you, tonight?" asked Henry, who had come out of the wagon without them hearing him.

"We couldn't sleep," Charity replied. "I might could now- I think I'm going to lay down for a bit. You need to try and do the same, Charles."

"Yes, Ma'am, I will," he replied, getting to his feet. "I need to get up early anyway. Goodnight, Mama, Papa."

"Goodnight, Son," they said in unison.

Taking Charity's hand, Henry helped her to her feet, wrapped his arm around her waist and nudged her toward the wagon. Lying with her head on his strong shoulder, she soon fell fast asleep.

Brushing the hair from her cheek, Henry watched her as she slept. A peaceful expression graced her features; he hadn't seen such a peaceful look on her face for a very long time. To him, she hadn't aged much at all; she was still the beautiful, young slip of a girl he had fallen in love with some twenty one years earlier. Laying there looking at her, it seemed as though those years had slipped by way too fast. They were still relatively young; they should have plenty of good years left to spend together. Henry wanted her to always look as peaceful as she did at that moment, and if getting a piece of land near the falls accomplished that, then he intended to do everything in his power to get that land for her, even if he had to work seven days a week to do so! He snuggled her close, closed his eyes and drifted off to sleep.

Lila M Beckham

Charity woke to the smell of frying bacon; she felt slothful for staying in bed past daybreak. She stretched lazily and reached for Henry; he was gone from her side. Reluctantly, she dressed and climbed out of the wagon. The bacon smelled so good. It had been a long time since they'd had bacon for breakfast- she wondered where it came from. Henry was busy as a bee trying to make breakfast.

"It sure smells good out here."

"I thought you might like it," Henry grinned and handed her a cup of coffee. "I was trying to surprise you."

"Oh, you did- I could certainly get used to this," she said, wrapping an arm around him and hugging him. Knowing he did not pluck the bacon from thin air, she asked, "Where did you get the bacon?"

"From the smokehouse on the plantation," he replied. "Mr. Haynes said that I could get a slab of it yesterday," he grinned, "I asked for it because I knew it was your favorite."

"Yes, it is, especially with buttered grits and biscuits," she said, looking around for the latter two.

"I'm trying, Hon. And, Jeremiah's been trying to find the grits, without having to wake you up to ask where they are."

"Oh, has he now," she giggled. "Have you got the water boiling yet?

"No," he replied, sheepishly.

"What about the biscuits?" she asked.

Again, he replied with a no answer. Charity could not help

but to chuckle as she walked over to the supply wagon, got out the flour, lard, grits and some butter. "I'll have a batch of biscuits whipped up in a minute. When you get the bacon out of the pan, you need to put on a pot of water for the grits."

"Yes, ma'am, will do!"

When she looked at Henry, he was grinning happily. The aroma of the sizzling bacon soon woke all of the children. The tempting smell had their stomachs rumbling hungrily.

"Y'all are just going to have to wait a few more minutes," she said when they all wanted a piece of bacon. "I was lazy this morning and overslept."

"But, mama, we're hungry," they whined.

"I can't help it," she told them, "good biscuits take a little time to cook, as does good grits; y'all will just have to wait."

Henry watched as she deftly whipped up a batch of biscuits, arranging them in the iron-lidded pot, and then placed them over the heat.

"You do that so well," Henry observed.

"Thanks to your mama," she said, smiling. "Nokomis never got to teach me too much, before she died and Grandpa, well, he just made sure I was fed."

"I know you miss him, Charity. I was thinking that if we have another son, I'd like to name him Robert after your grandfather, Robert."

"When we have our next son," she said, "I plan to name him, Robert Henry, after you and Grandpa" she said, kissing her husband's cheek.

Jeremiah spoke up and said, "That sounds like a mighty fine name."

"The one after Robert Henry will be named Jeremiah," Henry added.

Jeremiah grinned, and then said to Charity, "Missy, you a naming that last little 'un Cynthia, was enough to last this old feller a lifetime… I don't expect no more favors," he added.

Charity leaned over and gave him a kiss on the cheek. "It wasn't a favor, Jeremiah," she said firmly, "It was a pleasure to carry on your little Cynthia's name in one of my children- I just hope she never disappoints you."

"If she be anything like her maw, that ain't a gonna happen," he replied.

Doing a head count with her eyes, Charity added up the number of biscuits needed in her head- she hoped she had made enough; maybe I need to make another batch, she thought to herself. These men and the older boys can eat two or three a piece… Stirring an extra cup of grits into the pot of boiling water, she figured that making them a little thicker would fill everyone up better and stick to their ribs a little longer too.

"Mama, have you seen Mary," Charles hollered.

Charity's heart jumped into her throat! "She was here just a minute ago," she said, looking around for her youngest child. Suddenly, she wondered if she actually saw Mary while doing the head count or had she been too preoccupied with other thoughts to realize that she wasn't there. Lifting the pot of grits off the grate and hanging it on a pot holder, she began to panic. The nearby river, filled with the restless spirits of the Nvnehidihi suddenly entered her thoughts. Her fears were valid. "We must find her!" she hollered for all within earshot.

Henry, seeing the panic in her eyes, grabbed her and said, "Slow down Hon, we'll find her. Everything will be all right."

Charity jerked away, and started toward the river. "You don't understand, Henry; she see's them too!"

"Sees who?"

"The spirits- the ones in this river are called the Nvnehidihi! They're the unhappy, mean spirits that harm people!" Charity took off running toward the river, looking in all directions, screaming for Mary to come to her. Then, she saw her; she was standing at the edge of the river. Before she could call her name again, her tiny body disappeared beneath the water!

44

The Nvnehidihi, Path Killers

Suddenly frozen from the sheer terror that gripped her heart when Mary disappeared into the river, Charity collapsed to the ground; however, she quickly rose again to continue her run toward the river; the Nvnehidihi had her baby and she must rescue her from them!

Before she reached the river's edge, she saw the ghostly figures of the Nvnehidihi astraddle pale misty horses rising from the river, converging to the spot Mary disappeared. "No," she screamed as loudly as she could.

Bodies suddenly rushed past her, as Henry, Charles, and John sped past toward the river. Collapsing in relief, Charity sunk to her knees. Charles stopped running and came back to his mother's side to check on her. In one swift movement, Henry was waist-deep in the river. He swept Mary into his arms and carried her from the river and laid her on the ground.

Charity heard Mary cough several times and then start to cry, asking for her, but her eyes were on the Nvnehidihi, whom she knew were still a danger to her family. They now resembled paper-thin skeletons on horseback that she could see through.

They rode their ghost horses in a circle around Henry, John, and Mary, raising their spears up in the air.

Charles, kneeling at his mother's side, also saw the Nvnehidihi.

"What are they doing, Mama?"

"Showing me how easily they can subdue me by threatening my family."

"There must be a way to stop them."

 The Nvnehidihi looked toward her and laughed mightily, whooping and hollering as they left their circle and started toward where she and Charles kneeled on the ground; Charles covered his ears trying to muffle the ferocious sound they made. Galloping toward her, the ghost horses leapt over her and Charles and then turned back into the river and faded away. She jumped to her feet and ran toward Mary.

Henry was scolding Mary for going into the water, without him or her mother with her. Pitifully, Mary looked at Charity and said, "They gone bye-bye." She grabbed Mary into her arms and hugged her tightly, realizing how close she had come to losing her. Covering Mary's face with kisses and squeezing her tightly, Charity finally took a deep breath and sighed in relief.

Pushing to be released from her grip, Mary said, "I'm hungry."

"The biscuits- Oh my Lord, they're probably burnt to a crisp!" Toting Mary, astraddle her hip, she rushed back to the wagons.

"Don't cha worry," chirped Jeremiah, "I just checked on the biscuits and they is a doing fine. The grits is a mite thick, but they'll stick ta the ribs better that way. I ain't as fast as y'all is; I figured there were enough of you a looking for Mary, so, I stayed here to watch the grub."

"I'm sure glad you did," said Henry. "I worked up a fierce appetite, sprinting across that field like I was a young spurt."

Charity handed Mary off to Martha and told her to change her out of the wet clothes and not to let her out of her sight for one minute.

By this time, Charity's insides were trembling so badly, that she felt as though her bowels were wound into a tight knot.

"I don't know if I'll be able to eat a bite," she mumbled.

"Now you listen to me, Missy," Jeremiah said gruffly. "If'n you don't eat, your insides is gonna feel a lot worse than they do now!"

Charity, who was stirring the pot of grits, teared up when she accidentally splattered a drop onto her hand. Thinking he had made her cry, Jeremiah said, "Aw, now, come on, Missy, don't go ta crying. I didn't mean to sound so gruff!"

Smiling through her tear-filled eyes, Charity reached out a hand and touched his arm. "It wasn't anything you said," she patted his arm gently. "These grits are mighty hot- I like them that way, don't you?"

Just that tiny bit of tears she shed, released an enormous amount of strain; she felt better already. When the aroma of the bacon, grits, and biscuits caused her stomach to rumble, she knew that she would be able to eat and she did. Everyone said their breakfast was delicious; she thought so too.

***

When they finished breakfast, Henry and the boys began packing everything back into the wagons for the trip to the Haynes Plantation.

"Where are we going, Papa?" asked Charles.

"Mr. Haynes has generously offered us the overseer's cabin to stay in on his plantation. I figure that if me and Uriah are working there, then maybe you and John can help out a bit and make some money too. It will probably take us a couple of years, but if we hang on to every spare penny we make, we might be able to buy that piece of land your mama wants, down there by those waterfalls she is so fond of."

"We can do it, Papa, I know we can," Charles replied.

And, so it was that they moved onto the Haynes Plantation, in upper Cherokee County, Alabama in the summer of 1851.

When Henry told her of his plans, Charity smiled and tried hard not to show her disappointment in having to wait longer to live by the waterfalls, but disappointed she was and disappointed she would stay, at least for a bit.

The Haynes Plantation wasn't nearly as large as the one

Henry worked on in Georgia, but it was reputable and Mr. Haynes was well respected in the county. The cabin they were to live in, was of timberwork construction and set a good half a mile back of the main house, a quarter-mile west of the slave quarters, and, the best thing of all was that it was about five hundred feet from the river; close enough to fetch water from, but far enough away that the constant timbre of the Nvnehidihi could not be heard.

For months, Charity scanned the river for signs of the Nvnehidihi; she was thankful not to see any, especially when the long hot days of summer came upon them and the family went there to swim and bathe. The river was the saving grace of the plantation that summer, and the next five or so after that.

When it was nearing time for the birth of Emmaline, Charity couldn't help but feel a little anxious, especially after what happened with the birth of Cynthia.

Mr. Haynes owned approximately sixty slaves; several of them were skilled midwives- When her time neared, he sent a woman named Annie to stay with her during the day while Henry was working.

With the reassurance of having Annie there with her, Charity relaxed; the birth of her tenth child, Emmy, turned out to be an easy one. And as one day rolled into the next their first year there slowly passed.

Most days, after she and the younger children finished their chores, she would spend several hours teaching them how to read and write and do arithmetic, as she had done with the older children. After their lessons, Charity and the children would explore the river banks to keep boredom from setting in; they had quite a collection to show for it. They had found numerous arrowheads, a few unbroken pieces of pottery, and many beautifully patinated sticks of driftwood. Also, during that first year, she had become friendly with several of the slave women that worked in the main house of the plantation.

One day, while they were doing laundry and talking, she asked them if they had ever heard the river singing. Pinky, who was every bit of fifty and the daughter of Mr. Haynes old mammy, Gracie, said that when she was about little twelve, she had heard it- saw it too! She said it happened alongside the river, down in Gaylesville.

"I's ain't never heared nuthing like it, and I won't forgit it either," Pinky said. "I's was accompanying Miss Essie Haynes to a picnic she was invited to down there and had slipped out after the white folks was in bed so's we could has a little picnic too- when the noise begin. The ones of us that heared it, thought it was beautiful singing and we was a wondering where it was coming from. When we figured out it be coming from da water. We was about to go down there and see, but Thomas, an old, gray-headed man, even way back den, told us not to go down in that water unless we don't wanna ever come - He say that a band of Injuns' that lived there a long time ago, had been drove off into the water to drown, by a tribe of they enemies, that wanted they land! Ain't that terrible? That's just terrible, ain't it...

"Well, Thomas, he say that once them Injuns knowed they was gonna die, they gathered up all their chillren, big and little ones, and they walks in that water, all on they own. They was a holding they babies to them tight and a singing to keep 'em from being scared. Why, they just willingly walked in that water and drowned theyselves, Miss Charity. Thomas says, some of 'em rode in on they hosses and drowned them hosses, too! That's why you can still hear 'em a singing. They died like that, and they sing to keep the chillren from being scared... Has you heard 'em a singing, Miss Charity?" Pinky asked.

"Yes, I have, Pinky. I have also seen them."

"Oh, Lawdy, Miss Charity, you sees them! I think I'd be plumb scared to death if I see them, too," Pinky exclaimed.

"It can be scary Pinky, but I want to thank you."

"What you wanna thank me for, Miss Charity- I didn't do nuthin."

"For telling me about how they died... Now, I can understand their distrust and anger... I can even understand them calling children to come into the water... death by drowning was probably preferable to what might have been done to the by the other tribe... Maybe they are not the Nvnehidihi, after all. Maybe they're just lost souls looking for the passageway..."

"Well, I can tell you one thang, I's don't want ta be round no mean, angry Injuns, lost or not, that's for shore!"

Lila M Beckham

Charity had to chuckle at Pinky's statement. Later, as she and Charles was exploring around the river, she told him Pinky's story.

"That's awful, ain't it Mama."

"Yes, Son, it is horrible to think of what they went through; but, I imagine there have been all sorts of horrible deeds done to people of every kind… Back in the thirty's, when they drove all the Indians from these lands and sent them out west to live on reservations; that was horrible too- I heard many died."

"Mama, I've been thinking," Charles said.

"About what, Charles?" she asked.

"Well, I've been wanting to go back to Georgia- go to the Yellow River to see if I can find some more of that gold we found," he said.

"Charles, I cannot tell you not to go. You have always been my explorer child. Remember that time in Sandersville when I told you to stay at the camp with the rest of the children while I went hunting for the first time."

He grinned and said, "Yes, ma'am, how could I forget - you shot that sucker graveyard dead. It was the best day of my life!"

"I knew right then that one day, you'd want to go off on your own- explore the world and so on- if it's something you really want to do, then you should go… If you go, I will miss you very much… You must promise to be very careful, and not to stay away too long at a time."

"I promise, Mama!" he said excitedly, then became solemn.

"Will you talk to papa for me- I know he'll be harder to talk to- he don't understand me the way you do?"

"Yes, son, I will talk to him- give me a little while to smooth things over. Let's head back to the house. About how long do you think it'll be before you'll want to take off on this adventure of yours?"

"I'd like to leave as soon as possible, Mama. I want to find some gold and buy you that land by the falls that you want," he said excitedly.

"You know your father is working on that- I just want you to return safe and sound; that's all the treasure I need."

After a week of discussions, it was settled. It was a warm, sunny day in August, 1853 when Charles left on foot, headed east to Georgia; he was just seventeen years old... Charity was not sad; she understood that it was something her son needed to do. She knew that he would eventually find himself and discover what he was meant to do with his life; more importantly, she knew that he would return.

45

Miracles

Alford's Bend, Lower Cherokee Co, Alabama
February, 1859

At forty two years of age and big with child, Charity had begun to feel her age. It had been nearly eight years since the birth of Emmaline, whose name had been shortened to Emmy. After several years, and she had not gotten with child, Charity thought her childbearing days were over- she was pleasantly surprised when she found herself with child again. This one would be the son whom she would name after her grandfather Robert and her husband Henry.

The little house they had built in the foothills of the Piedmont Region of the Appalachians was reminiscent of the Finley's cabin they had lived in on the Georgia Mountain. And, even though this one was a good mile from the river and the falls, Charity had made it into a home; however, she still held onto the hope, that one day, she would be able to rise each morning and be able to sit on the porch, drink her coffee, smoke her pipe and have the Fall's within sight.

The cabin that Henry, Jeremiah, and the boys built four

years earlier had two good-sized main rooms and a loft for the children; Jeremiah's bed was in a corner of the living area, near the fireplace where he could keep warm. He was pretty much crippled by arthritis and was not able to get around as good as he used to- it kept him bent over and hobbling whenever he moved around; he said that keeping warm helped with the pain and stiffness.

Since moving to Etowah County and building the cabin, Henry and Aaron had gone to work for Benjamin Easley down in Benton County, working as ditchers to maintain the city of Anniston's drainage system- they usually came home late on Friday evening or early Saturday morning, then returned to Anniston on Sunday afternoon.

Homespun Martha, met and married a man in his thirties, by the name of Oliver Henley, Ollie for short; they lived nearby. John met and married girl down in Jacksonville by the name of Sarah Lipscomb; they had a son they named John Jr. and were expecting a second child; they lived in Benton County near her folks. Three years earlier, Uriah had finally given up hopes of marrying Hannah Hayes when she married a planter from Virginia. Two months later, he met a pretty girl named Mary Moore, at a church picnic; they married and also lived down in Benton County; they had given her and Henry their first grandchild, a son they named William. Charity could tell that Uriah was hankering to live nearer her and Henry; she hoped that he would soon be able to buy a piece of land nearby.

Whining because she thought she was an old maid at the age of eighteen, Nancy was constantly complaining that if they lived in town instead of out in the woods somewhere that she might at least have the chance to meet someone. Quiet, motherly, fifteen-year-old Mary was blossoming into a real beauty; she was a homebody and did not seem to be in any hurry to marry. Even though Cynthia had been named after Jeremiah's daughter, Emmy was his favorite of her daughters. Both girls were growing as fast as weeds; Cynthia, who was already as tall as the older girls, threatened to get even taller- she favored Henry's mother, Nancy, but did not have Nancy's calmness about her- Mary had inherited that quality; and little Emmy was the spitting image of Charity. And, it would seem that she had also inherited some of her unique abilities.

Charles had returned home four and a half years earlier, bringing what money he had earned panning for gold and working. That money, along with what Henry, Uriah, and John had earned working for Mr. Haynes was how they bought the twenty acres of land from Jefferson Alford, in Alford's Bend.

They had not heard from Charles but once in the last four years- she received a letter from him two years earlier saying that he and his wife Emma, whom they had not yet met, was living in Canton in the old Finley cabin; they were expecting their first child. She did not want him to know, but she had kept an eye on him by walking the winds to find his spirit; he seemed content.

She had appeared just long enough to caress her granddaughter's cheek…

She would love to walk the wind to see him and his family, but it seemed she had lost her ability to walk the wind; that always happened when she was with child. She could still see troubled, restless spirits that had become lost on their journey. One would think that living so far away from town, they would be few and far between but it seemed they were everywhere.

Their youngest son, Jackson, turned out to be the spitting image of his older brother Charles. In fact, the two of them were so much alike that she often caught herself calling him Charles. Maybe it was a blessing; it helped her not to miss Charles so much.

Just as she and Charles used to do, over the last three years or so, she and Jackson had explored every crack and crevice of every cave, for miles around! She missed going on their explorations, but she had gotten too heavy with child and a little too clumsy for the agility needed to climb rocky ledges; here lately, Jackson had taken to exploring by himself. That happened to be what he was doing that day in February, that she would look back on, as a miracle day.

Charity was seated at the kitchen table, peeling potatoes, when Jackson burst through the door and said that he had been bitten by a snake.

"What kind?" she asked hurriedly.

"I don't know; it was too dark in the cave to see what kind it was."

She looked at his hand; it had already begun to swell, which meant the poison was spreading. As calmly as she could, she said, "We need to get the poison out; come here and give me your hand."

Using a dishrag as a tourniquet, Charity tied it around his upper arm, stuck a wooden spoon handle through it and twisted it as tightly as possible. She then got her sharpest knife and cut an x across the bite marks, and then sucked all of the poison she could out of it. After which, she rinsed her mouth thoroughly. She was too big with child to go traipsing through the woods looking for Echinacea to make a poultice to place on the bite, so she washed it with lye soap and then poured turpentine on it, hoping to draw out the rest of the poison. She had just finished doctoring Jackson when she experienced the first pains of labor.

"It's time," she told Nancy. "Ride over to Martha Jane's house and get her to come and help me." When Nancy started to whine about going, Charity said, "I cannot go myself or I would, and Jackson is in no condition to go either. Now, please do it and hurry," she said, as another pain squeezed her midsection.

"Yes, Ma'am, I'll be back as soon as possible."

After Nancy left, the pains came faster; and, in a short amount of time, she could feel the ooze of bloody flow that sometimes accompanied childbirth.

"You're not wasting any time getting here, are you Robert

Henry," said Charity, rubbing her stomach as it tightened in another contraction.

When Nancy arrived at Martha's house, she was pleased to see Jefferson Alford there visiting Martha's husband Ollie. The two of them were friends and spent a great deal of time together. As Nancy was going up the steps to the front porch, Jefferson winked at her; he knew he would make her blush by doing so- that was why he always flirted with her. Nancy knew that Jefferson was married, but she couldn't help how she felt about him.

At thirty five, Jefferson was a well developed, handsome, and self-assured man. From what Martha told her, he was married to a woman that was a least twenty years older than he was. Martha also told her that Ollie had told her that Jefferson's father forced the marriage to secure more land. They already owned most of the land around there; it was even named after them!

Having almost forgotten why she came, Nancy lingered on the porch to flirt with Jefferson. "Mornin' Nancy," said Ollie, "what brings you over?"

Dang it, she thought to herself. "Mama needs Martha," she muttered.

"Martha's inside; go on in," Ollie told her. She glanced at Jefferson and blushed; he smiled, as his eyes examined her red-cheeked face.

"Martha!" she called aloud as she entered Martha's kitchen. "Mama needs you to come quick; she said it's time for the baby."

"It's a little early isn't it," Martha muttered, wiping her hands on her apron. "Let me get a few things I might need. Go and tell Ollie to hitch the wagon for me," Martha instructed.

Nancy walked back out onto the porch where Ollie and Jefferson were standing, smoking cigars. At the sight of Jefferson standing there, leisurely leaning against the railing, she could not help but blush again. He was just so danged handsome with his blazing blue eyes, that always seemed to be twinkling with mischief.

"Ollie, Martha said for you to hitch up the wagon. Mama needs her to come; its time for the baby," she said, relaying Martha's instructions.

"Dang, girl; your mama is still spitting out babies at her age- good Lord, how many does that make now, got to be at least a dozen," Jefferson said, amused at his own pun.

Nancy felt a twinge of ire rise up, because she felt as though he was making fun of her mama; but when he added that she could have stopped after she was born because she was perfect, she looked into his twinkling blue eyes and she could not be mad. And his saying she was perfect, caused her to smile.

"Oh, there's so many of us that I done lost count," she said cheerily; although she in no way felt cheerful. She was not sure if he was just making conversation so that he could talk to her or if he was making fun of her family. When turned to go back inside the house, she heard him chuckled, as he followed Ollie to the barn.

Lila M Beckham

***

When Martha and Nancy made it to the homestead, Jeremiah and the younger children were waiting outside. Martha noticed how worried Jeremiah looked. She patted him on the shoulder and told him that everything was going to be all right; she was there to help. By the time Martha was fifteen, she knew more about birthing babies than many grown women did.

"Y'all jest take care of your maw; don't worry bout me; I'll be all 'ight."

Flushed and taunt, Charity's face clearly showed that labor pains could be extremely painful. "I'm worried," Charity told them as soon as they entered her bedroom. "Something is wrong- this delivery feels much like it did when I was delivering Cynthia. I know he is a few weeks early- I don't think he's in the right position. All the excitement over Jackson being bitten by the snake must have caused me to go into labor too soon."

"Snake bit!" exclaimed Martha. "Nancy, you didn't tell me about that," Martha said sternly. "Is he alright?" she asked.

"I sucked the poison out, the best I could," Charity told her, adding that his hand had already began swelling, which meant the poison was already spreading in his blood and tissues.

"Mama," Martha said sternly. "You should not have done that, especially with you being pregnant! Some of the poison always gets into the person doing the sucking; which means, it gets to the baby too!"

She wasn't telling Charity anything she didn't already know- but if it meant saving Jackson's life, she'd do it again. After a couple of moments of silence, Martha asked, "Has your water broke, yet?"

"No, it hasn't," Charity replied.

"Nancy, go look in the medicine cabinet and find that bottle of laudanum we had left over from when Uriah's foot was nearly cut off," Martha instructed.

"That stuff has probably done turned into syrup by now," said Nancy.

"Just do like I said, and go it quick!" Martha snapped.

"Martha, don't snap at your sister like that," said Charity, in a calm manner, and then asked, "What are you planning to do with the laudanum?"

"When me and Ollie first got married and were living in Double Springs with his brother, I was helping with the delivery of my sister-in-law's baby and we ended up having to send for the doctor. He gave her laudanum; he said it was to slow her labor. He said that it eases the pain which in turn caused you to relax. I figured that if you take some, it might slow yours down and give the baby time to turn into position."

"And if it doesn't help- what then?"

"I'll do what he did; I'll massage your stomach and try to turn him. Now, try taking deep breaths, relax, and try not to push!"

When Nancy returned with the laudanum, Martha gave

Charity two spoonfuls. When the pain had not eased any after five minutes, she gave her another dose. The pains started to ease and Charity relaxed. Soon, she started to get sleepy and began to doze; Martha left the room to check on Jackson.

46

The Longest Day

In darkness, Charity lay. No longer in pain, she tried to sit up. Voices droned in her ears, but she could not open her eyes, nor speak to respond or ask them to speak plainer- Struggling, she finally sat up and then stood; however, she was in a void of total nothingness except the black space surrounding her. Every direction she looked, all she could see was the same shade of black. Suddenly, a brilliant, yellow bird appeared; it landed in mid-air upon a branch that blended with the blackness surrounding her; she knew he was the yellow huhu Two Feathers had spoken of. The yellow mocker was about to speak to her when a snowy, white owl suddenly landed beside him, shooing him away. Charity stared at the owl- she wondered why he had come.

The owl puffed up his feathers, then started to speak. "Do you hear me calling, Usdi Saquo? Little One, I am here."

"Enisi, egwa; is that you, Grandfather?"

"Yes, Little One. I have come to meet you. It seems you have left your body and lost your way. Come to me."

Trusting him implicitly, Charity stepped forward toward him- as she did, she stepped from the total darkness and into the light of a clearing, where her grandfather, Two Feathers, was sitting cross-legged behind his fire, sprinkling different powders into it that made it flare different colored flames. After he finished, he turned his pale, snow-colored eyes toward her and said, "You are not supposed to be here, Little One."

"I feel comfortable here, Grandfather- why can I not stay here with you?"

"You should not be here- you belong in the land of the living."

"But, I cannot return. I have forgotten how to walk the wind... I have failed your teachings, grandfather. I am so ashamed," she said. "I no longer search for wisdom; and, when the spirits beckon me, I avoid them- turning the other way as if they do not exist..."

"You have not failed, Little One," he said.

"I have failed, Grandfather; I don't know what to do to make it right- please talk to me, Grandfather; tell me what to do to make it right," she begged.

"You walked the wind, to get to me. You are asking me for my wisdom. I gave it to you long ago; you have misplaced it. When we walk so close to death, it is easy to become afraid. You must learn to trust your soul's ears- you have not trusted your soul's ears, since the River of Death. The spirits there were not the Nvnehidihi, only the misguided ones that had died before their time, and were confused. You knew that, but still did not trust what you knew. You will not renew your spirit until you confront your fears, Little One."

"But, Grandfather, I still have so many questions. Please let me stay here for a while and teach me," she begged.

"I have taught you, Little One. I have given you the answers. Seek and you will find them. The little one inside you is safe; his heart is open; he will give you joy with his coming. We must face the bad and overcome it, before we can find the good. You must return and face what you know soon comes. Now, go away; I am sleeping."

"But, you called me to come to you, Grandfather-"

"Yes, Little One, I did. You were coming to me, and lost your way. Now, go away and let me rest," he said, throwing more powders into the fire. Suddenly, she was again in the darkness; however, when Charity opened her eyes and saw Martha sitting beside her bed with a worried expression, she knew she was back inside her body.

At first, trying to speak was a struggle, but she finally managed to speak. "I will be fine," she told Martha.

"I know you will- I think the baby is turning... but, I'm truly worried about Jackson; he is burning up with a fever."

"You must cool him down," Charity told her. "I am positive that I got most of the poison out of his hand; but, some of it had time to get into his bloodstream... I don't know how long it took him to get here from the cave he was exploring. Mix a teaspoon of the laudanum with a teaspoon of the ground up sacred bark of the cinchona tree and put it in a half a cup of water and get him to drink it. The two, mixed together should lower his fever and relieve his pain. I will be fine. Now, go tend your brother," Charity told her.

As she lay back and tried to relax, so that little Robert Henry could finish turning into position to be born, she wished that she knew what kind of snake had bitten Jackson. Some snake bites were more toxic than others...

Jimsonweed, she suddenly thought - *that's what we need for him.*

"Nancy, come here!" she called. Nancy came running to see what she needed. "What's wrong Mama; is it time?" she asked.

"No, I'm fine, but I need you to go find some jimsonweed for me; we need it for Jackson. I've been raking my brain trying to remember the old remedies."

"Mama, I don't know what jimsonweed is!"

"Yes, you do, you just have to remember it. When we lived on Hayes Plantation, you went with me several times to search for herbs, and every time, you would point it out to me, especially when they were blooming, because you liked the trumpet shaped flowers- some were cream colored, some were purple. I told you never to put it in your mouth. They had spiked, balled seed pods on them."

"Yes, Ma'am, I remember them now; but, you told me that they'd kill me if I even touched them," said Nancy, cocking an eyebrow.

"Well, I may have exaggerated just a little. I didn't want to take any chances, because you seemed so fascinated with them, but, now I need you to go find some. We need to cook some of it down until it's thick and syrupy for Jackson."

"What do you mean, we," asked Martha as she entered the room. "I'm sorry, but you are not getting up out of that bed, Mama. After Nancy finds whatever it is you want her to find, then you can tell me how to make it and I'll make it and give it to him," said Martha, placing her hands on her hips as if her mother was an unruly child that needed instruction. For the time being, Charity let Martha's bossiness slide- she would deal with that later.

"Alright, but you must be careful," said her mother. "Jimsonweed is best if it is seeding, those would make the strongest mixture. If not, you will just have to use the leaves and flowers. Crush them up really well, and then put about a quarter cup of the crushed Jimson in a quart of water and boil it for about twenty minutes, and then pour a half a cup of sugar in it, mix it, bring it back to a boil for another fifteen minutes, then remove it from the heat and let it cool. Be sure to tie a rag around your face while you're working with it. Don't inhale the vapor; it can cause hallucinations and make you drunk."

"If it's that bad, then why in the world are we going to give it to Jackson?"

"In low doses, the poison can help strengthen your brother's resistance to the venom that is already in his system."

"It looks like adding more poison would make it worse."

"Yes, but it's a different type of poison," she told Nancy. "When a snake bites a person, the venom causes the passageways to the lungs to swell and close up. The jimsonweed tea will open up those passageways to his lungs. If you give him too much of it, it can cause those hallucinations I was talking about or worse; too much can be toxic and kill him."

"Good Lord, Mama!" Martha exclaimed, "If it's that bad, then I don't know if we should even give it to him!"

"We have no other choice, Martha. It is the only thing I can think of right now, that is always available that will help him to breathe. You have to give it to him- It has been used as a medicine, for hundreds of years by native people."

"Alright, Mama- I will make it and give it to him," said Martha, ceding to her mother's wisdom.

To Charity, it seemed as if hours passed before Nancy returned; however, it had only taken her twenty minutes to go find some and return. She had pulled up and entire plant and brought the plant to Charity to ask if it was the correct plant.

"Yes, that's it. Now, take it to Martha. Tell her to take several of the flowers and mash them up in a bowl until she has a quarter cup. Tell her if she needs further instruction to come tell me. After she has made the tea and let it cool, she needs to give him a teaspoonful every three to four hours."

"Yes, Ma'am, I will," said Nancy, then left the room to find

Martha so she could prepare the Jimson tea.

The longer Charity lay there, the more restless and fidgety she became. No longer in pain, she did not see any sense in staying in bed. Finally, she could stand it no longer. She got up and went into the front room of the house. Poor, old Jeremiah, still had the younger children occupied outside, trying to keep them and himself out of the way. She eased over to where Jackson lay on a bed that Martha had fashioned for him with a straw-ticked mattress and several quilts. His breathing sounded a little raspy. She sat down on the floor beside him and took his hand, raising it to her lips, she kissed it softly.

"Mama," he mumbles.

"Yes, Jackson," she whispered, picking up a washcloth Martha had in a pan of water, she wrung it out well and then sponged his face, forehead, and neck- she then leaned over and kissed his cheek, saying, "Mama's here."

Martha saw her mother sitting with Jackson; she sighed. There was no use in arguing with her mama about staying in bed; she had done well to stay there as long as she did.

"Mama," she said, "I think this has cooled enough to give him some."

"Bring it and a teaspoon over here," Charity instructed.

Raising his head and shoulders, Charity slipped closer and laid his head in her lap. She dipped the spoon in the liquid and encouraged him to take it. After he had sipped the liquid off the spoon, she handed the bowl back to Martha, telling her to be sure and put it where the children could not get a hold of it.

She knew that she should move out of the way because Jackson could experience hallucinations, or worse; he could become unruly and thrust about; however, she was not about to leave him.

It only took a minute or two for Jackson to begin to feel the effects of the Jimsonweed tea; it is absorbed rather quickly through the mucus membranes of the mouth and stomach. Soon, he was hallucinating. She imagined he was seeing all sorts of horrors, when he began slapping at his hands and face, and trying to get up off the pallet.

"Quick, y'all help me hold him down," she yelled to Nancy and Martha, who seemed to have turned into stone statues, standing there staring at Jackson. Suddenly, Jackson jumped to his knees, flailing about, pushing this way and that- eventually shoving Charity away from him as she was trying to get up so she could hold him better- she landed hard on her rump. A jarring pain ran through her lower midsection.

Martha and Nancy wrestled him back down onto the pallet as Charity scooted out of his way. She wanted to help him, but realized that she was in no shape to do so. Crawling on her hands and knees, she managed to get back to her bed. A trail of bloody fluid followed behind her as she crawled...

Seeing the blood, Martha screamed, "Mama, are you okay!"

"Don't worry about me," she yelled back, reaching for the bottle of laudanum - the pain was so bad that she took a swallow straight from the bottle. "Just take care of your brother," she said, lying back and closing her eyes. As soon as it entered her stomach, the laudanum soothed her- almost immediately, her pain eased. However, she felt immense pressure build as her womb contracted. Taking deep breaths, she resisted the urge to push; she was able to do this through several labor pains. The shadow of a person loomed over the bed; she looked up to see Cynthia is standing at the foot of her bed.

"I'm alright, Baby," she said to her.

"Mama," Cynthia questioned.

"Yes," Charity answered.

"Is Jackson going to die?"

"No, Cindy Lou," Charity said firmly, trying to keep her fear abated. "He will be better in a little while. Can you hand Mama a cup of water?"

"Mama, you're bleeding…"

"I know I am, baby; it'll be all right. I'm going to have your new brother, real soon."

"I'm scared, Mama," said Cynthia; her voice was trembling.

"Don't worry about Mama; you go and help Jeremiah; I'm okay."

"We're all hungry, Mama. We haven't had anything to eat since this morning. Jeremiah says we have to wait- I don't think I can wait any longer, Mama; my stomach is growling something fierce."

As if on cue, Cynthia's stomach grumbled loudly.

Lila M Beckham

"Of course you are- I know you're hungry, I can hear your tummy grumbling. If you can wait just a little bit longer, until Jackson gets better, Nancy and Martha can fix y'all something to eat."

Suddenly, a blood curdling scream came from the front room, and then Nancy yelled, "Jackson is dead!"

"No," Charity yelled, "he's not dead. He has just unconscious. If his fever doesn't break, you will need to give him another dose of the jimson tea, in about an hour; after that, every two hours- and Nancy…"

"Yes, Mama," Nancy asked.

"Please, do not scream like that again unless your life depends on it… Jeremiah and the children are hungry. Get those biscuits and ham we had left over from breakfast this morning out of the larder and take them out to them," Charity instructed.

"Yes, Ma'am," Nancy replied. "Give me just a minute; I'll see to them as soon as I get this floor mopped up." She was helping Martha by mopping up the blood trail that Charity had left behind.

Hearing Jeremiah's familiar shuffle as he came through the front door, Charity called him to come to her. When he entered the room, she smiled at him and said, "Come here, Jeremiah." When Jeremiah reached her side, she reached out and took his gnarled, trembling hand and squeezed it tightly.

"You have been like a father to me these last fifteen years or so, and you are the only grandfather, most of my children have known. I just want you to know that I am going to be fine, and so is Jackson," she said, firmly, emphasizing her assurance with a squeeze of her hand. "I appreciate you always helping me with these young'uns, too," she smiled.

Jeremiah's eyes welled up with tears that soon ran over and were spilling down his wrinkly old cheeks. He was so choked up and overcome by emotion that he couldn't speak; however, he wore his thoughts on his face. She, Henry, and their family meant the world to him. She was the daughter he never raised and Henry was the son he never had.

"I want you to relax and try not to worry- I want little Robert Henry to remember you as his grandfather too," she said firmly. The old man bent further forward; his teardrops fell on Charity's face as he kissed her cheek. "Now, you go in there and eat something so you can keep your strength up, and remember, don't worry; all will be well, soon."

She, herself, had to hold back tears as she watched him shuffled toward the door. Turning once, he looked back at her, smiled and nodded his head.

I wish it was Saturday, she thought to herself. *If it were, Henry and Aaron would be here and that would be a comfort to me. But, no, it's Monday, the 14th day of February. They sure have a big surprise coming when they return home on Saturday!*

The dose of laudanum had eased her pain, however, she knew that she was definitely in labor, especially now that her water broke and she was bleeding. The contractions that started earlier were getting closer together and harder- when the next pain came and she felt the pressure of the baby's head bearing down on her bladder, she knew that it was time to start pushing. She called for Martha and told her that it was time.

Because of the laudanum, she barely felt any pain- it was mostly pressure. After several more forcible contractions, she bore down and out he came. He was all pink and wrinkled and had a head full of black hair!

"Well," said Nancy, when Martha handed the baby to her to bathe; "he not any bigger than a good-sized loaf of bread!"

"She's right, Mama," said Martha, packing a towel between Charity's thighs. "He might just be the smallest baby you've ever birthed."

"Well, I, for one, am glad that he wasn't any bigger. If you're through bathing him, bring him to me," Charity told them. Nancy had cleaned him up and wrapped him in a receiving blanket. Martha took him from Nancy, and, after staring at him for a moment, she placed him in Charity's arms.

A few minutes later, Mary brought in Cynthia and Emmy in to see their new baby brother. They didn't pay him too much attention though; they just wanted to see their mama and see that she was okay.

After a minute or so, Mary took little Robert Henry from her mother and sat down on the foot of the bed to hold him- glancing her way, Charity could see that Mary was quite taken in by her new baby brother; their bond would be a bond that was hard to break…

"He is just darling, Mama," said Mary, her voice showing her excitement.

"Well, I'm glad you think so highly of him," said Nancy. "He can be your responsibility to look after instead of mine- I have enough on me already!"

Watching Mary holding the baby, cooing and smiling at him, Charity had a vision into the future. The vision brought heaviness in her chest.

Noticing her mother's expression change, Martha asked, "Mama, what's wrong? Are you hurting is-"

"Nothings wrong- I reckon I'm just wore out."

"I imagine so," said Martha. "I'm going to get you cleaned up and then go and check on Jackson. You need to try to get some rest."

"I will, as soon as I feed the baby."

Jackson seemed to be breathing normal and easy, when Martha knelt down to feel him to see if he had a fever. He was cool to the touch and sleeping soundly; she went back to give her mother a report.

Charity was thrilled that he was doing better.

"Are you hungry, Mama?"

"I finished peeling those potatoes you started peeling this morning and put them on. What do you want me to fix besides those?"

"I was going to heat up the beans from yesterday, cut up a chicken to fry and make cornbread fritters to go with it- but," she said, glancing out the window, "Its starting to get dark out- I hate for you girls to have to cook all of that, and I know you need to get home to your husband."

"Ollie is not helpless; he can fend for himself for one night," said Martha. "Besides, Elizabeth is here with us; she is the one that counts!"

"Thank you, Martha; you have been a big help to me today; you and Nancy both have."

"What about me," asked Cynthia?

"Yes, you too, Cindy Lou!" she laughed. And then, Emmy caught her eye- she was standing quietly back, watching all that was going on. Emmy reminded her of herself when she was little.

"Now, y'all let me feed little Henry; I need to get acquainted with my new son." They all left the room. As Charity nursed the baby, she became groggy; she tried to stay awake but couldn't - she couldn't help but go to sleep.

In her sleep, she heard someone call for her; she tried to respond, but couldn't- And, as she looked around for them, she heard them call again. This time, she realized that they sounded far away. She was walking through a canopied forest- stopping, she searched for them with her eyes, but she did not know which way to look or which direction to go. Why was she so confused? Was it one of her sons calling for her? She could hear him calling, but could not find him! She would look for Enisi, maybe he could help her. No, maybe not - what were his last words to her? "You still must face what you know will come soon." That was what he said.

"But, how, Grandfather? How do I face something like that? Please tell me?" Something he had told her long ago came to her mind.

"Endurance," was what he said. "Endurance, Little One, you will learn, that it is essential to life."

"Mama, can you hear me," her son called.

Charity struggled to see who was calling her. They stood in front of her, but they were a blur- her vision wasn't clear. Then, she felt a hand on her shoulder and opened her eyes.

Nancy stood beside the bed, holding a plate of food.

"Mama, I brought you some supper."

Charity eased the baby out of her arms and onto to the bed beside her. Scooting up in the bed, Nancy propped several pillows behind her and then handed her the plate of food.

She really wasn't hungry - she was just tired. She wanted to go back to sleep and finish the dream she was having... She took a bite of potatoes, trying to stir up an appetite.

"Mama, you need to eat more than that or you're not going to have enough milk for the baby," Nancy observed.

"I know I need to eat more and I will when I feel better. I'm just too groggy and tired to try to eat. Please, just let me rest a bit longer. That's all I really need right now," she told Nancy.

"I will put it up for you." Nancy took the plate and left the room. A feeling of complete and utter sadness came over Charity. Tears welled up in her eyes and overflowed her sadness.

Slipping down under the covers, she closed her eyes and drifted away. Looking down into the Tsikamagi, what the Indians called, the River of Death, the bridge sighed in unison with the river below that was singing loudly.

Opening her heart, Charity listened with her soul's ears. One of the singing voices raised mournfully above all the others. And as she listened, she heard her say, "All the memories I have, they are beautiful within my mind, but they do not feed this hunger, deep inside my soul."

As she gazed down into the river, she heard her grandfather speak.

"You know what you must do, Little One."

47

Beneath the Bridge of Sighs

Knowing what one must do and actually doing it, are on totally different ends of the spectrum, especially when faced with the reality that the time is nigh. Charity had never really been afraid to face anything that was put before her- Yes, she was shy as a young girl, but never afraid; and, she had outgrown her shyness when she became a mother. However, what Two Feathers was asking her to do, scared her- she was afraid that she would not survive it…

"I cannot, grandfather," she cried aloud. "I will not; it is not yet time."

The skies rumbling overhead drew her eyes upward- the skies darkened angrily and lightning bolted out of the clouds and streaked toward her. Just before the bolt of lightning reached her, she woke. When she opened her eyes, the darkness of her bedroom greeted her. She felt around on the bed looking for the baby; instead, she felt another body lying beside her. She drew her hand back, not yet fully awake, nor trusting her senses.

"Mama, are you awake?" the body asked. That was when

she realized that it was Martha lying beside her; she breathed a sigh of relief.

"Yes," she muttered. Her mouth was, so dry, she could barely speak. "I'm thirsty," she mumbled, "Can you get me a glass of water?"

"Yes, ma'am," Martha replied, getting out of bed. She lit the bedside lantern and then went to get her mother something to drink. She came back with a glass of water and a cup of buttermilk.

"You need this more than you do the water," she said, handing Charity the cup of buttermilk first. I didn't think you'd mind me laying down with you awhile. I've gotten too fat to be climbing up into the loft; especially carrying Elizabeth with me," Martha explained.

"It is fine, Martha. I didn't even know you were there, until I woke up." Charity asked, "Where is Elizabeth?"

"I was going to put her in the crib and put Robert Henry in a dresser drawer, but you were restless, so I let Mary take Elizabeth to bed with her and left Robert Henry in the crib. She'll be fine; she sleeps through the night and Mary is a very fine babysitter."

"Yes she is; she loves little ones…" Charity's heart ached again.

"You were talking in your sleep, Mama. You kept saying something about grandfather and that it wasn't time…"

"Did I?"

"Yes, ma'am, you did. Which grandfather was it?" she asked.

"It was Enisi, Two Feathers," Charity told her.

"Why were you telling him no, that it was not yet time. Time for what?"

Charity took a swallow of the milk, and then said, "He told me that I must face the spirits in the singing river. He said that I will have to set their spirits free so that they will be at peace and be in harmony with all beings. He said that I must be strong of heart and a strong believer in the Great Spirit's power... I do believe, but right now, I feel very weak and unsure of my ability to free them."

"Mama," Martha said firmly; "you are the strongest person I've ever known- in many ways, you're much stronger than Papa is."

"No, I am not strong," Charity protested. "I don't feel strong enough- I want to wait until my ability to walk the winds returns..."

"Ever since I was a little girl," said Martha, "I have wanted and hoped to be just like you... I remember so much that you seemed to have forgotten."

The passion and admiration in her daughter's voice, moved Charity to tears as Martha talked of her remembrance's, such as her mother's first hunt, and how she always made sure they were safe and never let them go hungry. She talked about how she admired her storytelling ability when she told them all the stories of her ancestors. She even spoke of her teaching them how to catch dewa's and tame them, and she talked about the night the spirit lightning visited them and how brave she was then. And, how brave she was when the whirlwind flipped the wagon over and scared them; "but it didn't scare you, Mama; you were always fearless!" Martha exclaimed.

Charity smiled. She, too, remembered those times past...

No, it wasn't that she was never afraid. She had just always done whatever it was that had to be done to protect those she loved- However, she had never felt this weak and vulnerable before.

Lying there thinking of her childhood and what it was like when she was growing up, she wondered why she was afraid to face them now? She remembered asking her Nokomis, Shadowy Moon, why she smoked a pipe? Nokomis told her that one day, she too, would smoke the pipe, just as her mother before her, had smoked it.

"The "tso la, tsalu, gatvlati," Nokomis said to her, it will soothe your mind and settle your stomach. You will be, "dohi, tohi", peaceful within your mind and spirit," Nokomis assured her.

"Martha, can you pull my trunk out from under the bed?"

"Sure I can, Mama," Martha replied excitedly. She had wanted to get another look in her mother's trunk for years!

Charity never would let them mess with it when they were

growing up; however, she used to pull the trunk out about once a year, take everything out of it and tell her children the story of each and every item in the trunk; especially what each item meant to her. Martha remembered there being a beautiful buckskin dress, boots and a big patchwork quilt in the trunk…

After much pulling and tugging, Martha finally managed to pull the trunk free of the bed.

"Open it up," Charity instructed.

With bated breath, Martha did as she was told.

"You must promise that after I am gone, you will keep my trunk safely put away. Protect it from the elements and from anyone that may wish to take it or anything out of it. Other than my family that shares my blood, these are my most precious possessions."

"Don't talk like that, Mama! You're talking as if you're going to drop dead at any moment; I won't hear of it!"

"Some things have to be talked about; I want my wishes known before the time comes for my passing- that way, there won't be any decisions that have to be made or fighting over who gets what and so on." Charity lifted the quilt that Nokomis referred to as her, "Seasons of Life", from the trunk.

"This Yegali was woven and sewn by Shadowy Moon's own hands; she was my Nokomis, my mother's mother. Each of the scenes she's sewn represents a season of her life while here in the Gadawahi Tsalagi, the Land of the Cherokee." Charity then picked up the smoking pipe.

"This was her kununawa; now, it is mine. One day, it will belong to one of my children- I don't know which one yet, but I am sure it will be the chosen one- the one appointed by the Great Spirit."

Next, Charity took her mother's hairpins and comb out of the trunk.

"This gilusti hahl ta wo ja, hairpin and comb, belonged to my mother; they are all that I have left of her…, her name was Gige'sdi, she was so named because of her violet-colored eyes." Charity then reached in and pulled out her Asani, which was a deer-skin dress, and her tsulawas, which were her moccasin boots. "On the day I met your father - my grandfather said that I could not wear these into the white man's world…

I have kept them in this trunk, and in here," she said, placing a hand over her heart. With tears in her eyes, she looked into Martha's eyes and said, "I want to meet the Great Spirit, dressed in these."

"Mama," Martha said sternly. "Please stop talking as if you could drop dead at any moment- I don't want to think about that!"

"But you must think about it- I am going to die, my agwetsi- my daughter. Everyone dies; I am just dying a little sooner than you expect." Charity smiled. "Do not be sad; we still have time."

Neither of them noticed that while Martha was tugging on

the trunk, trying to get it out from under the bed, Emmy had slipped into the room and sat down in a darkened corner- She had heard all they said, and watched intently as Charity took the items from the chest. *Almost*, eight-year-old Emmy, had fixated on one thing her mother said- to keep the trunk and items in it, safe.

"I want to be buried near that stand of junipers by the falls," she continued. "What Grandfather would call the place 'the water rolls over the rocks there.' One day, after my body has nourished the earth and the earth has absorbed all my blood and my body turns to dust- my dust shall rise and spread across the earth the same way the mighty, Tsulehisanvhi, the mighty Phoenix rose from his ashes and was reborn; and, I will be dressed in these," she held up the boots and deerskin dress. "Because, Tsitsalagi - I am Cherokee! And I am proud of my ancestors, as you and your siblings should be."

Martha leaned over, hugged her mother, and said, "I will do as you wish, Agitsi," she said, calling her mother in Cherokee. "Just please stop talking about dying- you worry me with all that talk." Charity smiled and nodded her head.

After handling the objects in the trunk, Charity felt a stronger connection to her ancestors- her birthing-pains had also eased- she sat up and then got out of bed. Wrapping the quilt around her, she picked up the pipe and pouch of tobacco and then walked out onto the porch and sat down in her rocking chair that Jeremiah had built for her when they built the cabin.

Lila M Beckham

With only a candle for light- because it was still dark out, she carefully packed the pipe with tobacco and then lit it.

Lighting it, took a little more effort and determination than she figured it would, but she accomplished the task after holding a lighted match to it and puffing it several times. Once she was sure it was lit, she sucked on the pipe stem and then inhaled as she had seen people do when smoking.

The first few puffs, made her cough; however, she was determined to learn to smoke the pipe the way her grandmother had.

Inhaling the smoke, came easier with each puff she took. Once she mastered it, she leaned back in the rocker and relaxed, letting her mind drift back through the years, back to living in different places and the days and nights when her children were little and they'd lived on the trail. And then, she let the visions and memories of those she loved that were now gone come to her. Soon, her spirit was riding the night winds as if an eagle's wing carried her.

First, she found Henry, lay in his arms and held him tightly; but only for a moment. Going back the way they'd come, she flew at the speed of light, soon reaching her old home in the mountains of the Carolinas - her grandparents and Tokola had long since passed into the next world, but in her mind, she could see them there… After a moment, she soared along the watershed of the Savannah River to where Nancy and Eli were still living; both had grown old and gray… When Charles came into her thoughts, her route changed back in the direction she had come. Soon, she was over lands she had never seen before; sparsely populated, beautiful lush lands that begged to be tended.

Unexpectedly, she came alongside a great, muddy river; *this must be the mighty, Mississippi River that Jeremiah speaks of*, she thought, searching for a sign of her beloved son. Glowing embers from a nearly burned out campfire caught her attention as it glowed beneath the twilit sky; she knew it was Charles. Swooping low, she landed gently beside him. She sat and watched him sleep for awhile; his face was peaceful. Softly, kissed his cheek and whispered in his ear that she missed him and wanted him to come home.

Martha had not followed her mother onto the porch; instead, she had gone into the kitchen to make a pot of coffee. When it was ready, she fixed Jeremiah a cup and then fixed her and her mother a cup and carried it to the front door. Thinking Charity asleep, she stood there a moment watching her. A movement out in the field caught her attention. When she looked toward it, she gasped and dropped both cups of coffee!

48

Kagali

What had so startled Martha was a riderless, pale horse that came galloping across the field running straight toward the cabin. It ran up to the porch and stopped in front of where Charity sat. Martha breathed a sigh of relief when she saw that it wasn't a ghost horse; at first, it had seemed to be see-through and ghostly white…

Charity opened her eyes and looked directly into the horse's eyes; she sighed. "Alright, Enisi, you win," she said softly. She stood and then stroked the horse's face and long thick neck.

While petting the large horse, she asked Martha to get her a cup of coffee, and to bring her the length of rope that hung on a nail beside the fireplace.

When Martha returned with the coffee and rope, Charity looped the rope over the horse's head, cinched it around his neck, then told Martha to lead him out to the corral and put him in with the other horse.

"He sure is a beauty - you reckon someone will come looking for him," asked Martha.

"No, he is mine," Charity responded matter-of-factly.

"Yours?" asked Martha curiously. "When did you get him?"

"I got him just now, when grandfather sent him to me. He doesn't want me to stay cooped up inside and thinks I need a way to get around."

"Oh, of course," said Martha, leading the horse away.

Charity was sitting, drinking coffee, smoking her pipe and enjoying the sunrise, when they heard the baby crying.

"Sounds as if someone woke up hungry," clucked Martha.

Charity smiled at the sound, then asked Martha to bring him to her.

"Out here on the porch? Don't you think it might be a little too cool out here for a newborn, Mama?"

"How many babies, have I raised?" Charity asked tartly.

"A bunch," Martha responded.

"So, don't you think I'd know if it was too cool," Charity asked.

"Yes, Mama, you would," Martha did as told and went to get the baby out of his cradle.

Jeremiah, who was lying in his bed listening to them talking, had to chuckle to himself at their butting heads. *Martha ought to know better than to try and boss her maw around*, thought Jeremiah as he sat up on the bed.

"Alright, you old coot!" said Martha. "I hear you over there chuckling- Don't you be a making fun of me!"

"I taint a making fun over you, Miss Smarty Pants," he laughed. "Don't ye know by now that your maw is gone do whatever it is she wants to do?"

"I ought to, I reckon," Martha replied. "But that don't stop me from trying, now, does it!"

"Nope, don't reckon it do," Jeremiah agreed.

✳✳✳

A few weeks after the birth of Robert Henry, Charity felt like learning to ride the beautiful horse her grandfather had sent her. She didn't own an extra saddle, nor even a bridle for that matter; Henry and Aaron had the two sets they owned, on the horses they rode to Anniston to work each week; therefore, Jeremiah took it upon himself to make her one. He measured the horses head and fashioned a halter and reins out of strips of buckskin leather he'd tanned himself several years earlier intending to make a buggy whip out of.

"This here ought to be plenty sturdy," he said, showing her how to put it on the horse. "Now, you learning to ride this here horse bareback, now that might jest be another matter…"

"I'll manage; don't you worry about me," Charity grinned, using the porch rail to gather enough height to get onto the horses back for the first time. She had on a pair of Jackson's britches she'd cut down to fit her, because his were the smallest pair they had, and one of Henry's older shirts for a top; it was baggy and hung half-way to her knees, so she tied a length of rope around her waist, to control the way it fit better. And, after much consideration, she had decided to name the horse, Kagali, which simply meant, February, or the month of the bony moon.

After the first day of riding, Charity found a nearby stump to use to mount her new horse. She would lead him up to the stump, stand on it, grab a hold of his mane and then swing up onto his back.

The first few times she rode, she let him have his head to just go wherever he wanted to go; she wanted to learn to balance on his back without the luxury of a saddle to hang onto. He seemed to read her thoughts; all she had to do was hold onto the reins and onto him. And, after a few minutes cantering around, they were flying across the valley toward the river- his mane and tail, and her long, dark hair flowing in the wind behind them as they went.

Riding Kagali across the fields and up to the falls was more enjoyable than she had ever imagined it would be. When she was on his back, she felt young and vibrant. She soon learned to relax and became one with Kagali. Racing across the valley, they were one body, one flesh, one soul… she was so happy, she let out a whooping yell that even surprised Kagali. He jumped up in the air, landed gracefully without hardly breaking stride- this was to become a regular routine between the two.

Charity sewed and fashioned a papoose and saddlebag, so she could take Robert Henry and other things she wanted to carry with her on her rides; oftentimes, she took Emmy with her, too.

Emmy quickly learned to mold her little legs around Kagali's back.

Several years earlier, Jeremiah had made her a folding stand to hold her canvases and pigments, encouraging her to paint- that was before his hands had become gnarled with arthritis. And, now that she had Kagali to ride, she could easily take her children, the stand, her pigments, canvases and such as that with her, find something she wanted to paint, and spend all day outside. And that was what she usually did, except laundry days, which meant she was tethered to home; she grew to dread the days she had to stay confined to the home place. However, she used them to teach her girls how to keep a good clean house, the way Henry's mother, Nancy had taught her when she went to live with them. And, it was paying off- Nancy, Cynthia, and Mary were getting better at managing the chores and laundry without her help.

Several weeks earlier, while riding above the falls, Charity saw a mountain in the far eastern distance that sort of reminded her of the painting that hung above her grandfather's mantle, except that it didn't have any snow atop it; however, she figured she could easily add snow to the painting; that was where she planned to go on this day.

When she reached an area that offered a good view of the mountain, she placed the baby on a blanket in the shade, along with their lunch and asked Emmy to help watch him so that she could paint a portrait of her grandfather's mountain. The baby seemed to be content to lie there on his belly and play and Emmy picked wildflowers, asking a million questions about everything she saw; Emmy's chatter did not annoy Charity at all- she actually enjoyed it. And when she finished the painting and stood back to look at it, little Emmy stood beside her. "What do you think of it?" she asked Emmy.

"It's very pretty, Mama- but…"

"But, what?"

"The real mountains don't have any white stuff on top of it."

"I used my imagination to make the snow on top," Charity told her. "If you use your imagination, you can do that."

"Really!" exclaimed Emmy.

"Yes, baby, you can."

"Then, I'm going to use my imagination, too. The next time I see that old Indian man, I'm going to pretend he is not there…" Charity immediately knew that Emmy must have seen Two Feathers.

"The old Indian man is no one to be afraid of- I'm surprised you saw him."

"Oh, I'm not afraid of him," replied Emmy. "But, sometimes, he comes into my dreams- I don't like him to be there- so now I can make him go away."

"Okay, baby, you do what you want in your dreams. After all, they are your dreams and no one else's.

Charity decided not to pursue asking questions about Two

Feathers- If he was visiting Emmy in her dreams, then he had a reason. Remembering her first encounter with him, and every meeting since then, he trusted him explicitly- which meant, she trusted him with her children.

Gazing at the finished painting, she wished her grandfather could be there to see it - she wondered if he would approve of her snow-capped mountain. When it was good and dry, Jeremiah framed it for her. Proudly, she hung it over the fireplace, as had her grandfather, his painting in his first home.

Later that summer, she painted a scene of the children playing amid the willows that encircled a small pond that was not too far from the cabin; they were tickled to be in their mama's picture. She also painted Kagali grazing in the meadow; she managed to catch his tail, mid-swing, which, according to Henry, made it real to life. Henry did not say is aloud, but he was glad she seemed to be coming out of the sadness she had right after the baby was born.

Indeed, Charity was feeling much better, and she felt stronger, but she did not know if it would be enough; she still had a task to face- a task that still scared her- she was reminded of it every time she looked toward the river. She knew that she must eventually go back to the River of Death, to the singing river and help the lost souls that were stuck there, to cross over...

About mid-April, Charles made it home. After staying with them for a week, he took a job in Gaylesville, as a ditcher for Mr.

Long. Later on, Charity made a decision. She decided that as soon as the weather cooled down, about October, she would seize the opportunity to face going back to the singing river; she would accompany Charles back to Gaylesville after one of his visits.

When October came, she readied herself, both physically and mentally, for the trip. She let Henry and Aaron leave for Jacksonville, without telling Henry of her plans. She knew that he would worry and she did not want that- Two Feathers had told her what she needed to do- she had to trust his wisdom. When Charles found out her plans, he insisted that he go with her; she was grateful for his help. The trip to Gaylesville took all Sunday afternoon to get there and then it took them thirty minutes to set up a camp for the night- it was dark by the time they finished and she gathered her courage to go to the river. She almost laughed at herself for being afraid as she sat there having a conversation with the spirit of a Koasati woman, named Lá:na Nilahasí, which in English, meant, Yellow Moon.

49

Yellow Moon of the Koasati People

Cherokee Co, Alabama
October 1859

When Charity called out to the spirits, Yellow Moon was the only one that understood Charity's words; she had spoken both Cherokee and English when she called out.

"How can we understand each others language?"

"Because, we are the same," Yellow Moon responded. "We see what is."

"Tell me what happened," Charity spoke calmly, not wanting the others to be afraid of her.

"In my visions," said Yellow Moon, "I saw that death that was coming. I tried to warn my people, but they would not listen; they say I am a woman, not warrior- women are born to farm, cook, and raise the young.

"The Miko, the name we call our chief, he was very old and set in ways long past. My people, the Koasati, were here long before the Principal People, *your* people, the Cherokee, came here. Our small, village is only forty or so people. Our Ná:ni, our warriors, were on a hunt when your people attacked. Miko was very ill, not of great strength… The month of the Cold Wind Moon had come- food was scarce- the hunting party had to go far for food - there was only us women, children, and the elderly left in the village.

"Even when Miko and the elderly warriors mounted their ponies, the attacking warriors knew he was infirmed and not much threat to them- they drove all of us into the river…"

After listening to Yellow Moon's story, Charity exclaimed, "How horrible that must have been for you and your people!" Yellow Moon politely waited a moment and then continued telling her story.

"A yellow mocker came to sit on a limb above my head; he sang loudly, trying to calm all that could hear his voice. After I saw the mocker, I knew that to resist the enemy was futile, our time had come. I picked my child up, and held him close, I sang him a lullaby as loudly as I could to drown out the noise of those who were screaming and the yellow mocker's song- I wanted to calm him as we entered the water.

"When the other women heard me singing and saw that I was holding my child tight to calm him, they did the same. And then, the elder warriors and Miko, who had mounted their ponies, joined us in song as they rode their ponies into the river.

"The Principal People, not believing their eyes and ears, stopped their attack to watch and listen; but my people sang louder and joined those that had already died in the river…

"Before that day; I had only known beauty and the love of my family- the memories I have, are beautiful within my mind, but they do not feed the hunger deep, inside my soul. I did not mind dying- dying is a part of living, but I cannot find my soul mate to join him. He was away on the hunt- but did not return. If he had returned, I would feel him… Others here wish to find their soul's mate, too. We stayed here, waiting, singing, and watching for their return from the hunt, but…" quietly, Yellow Moon stared off into the distance.

"Why did those riding the ponies, try to scare us away?" Charity asked.

"That was Miko and the elders; they, too, wait for the return of our strong, young warriors to lead us," Yellow Moon answered.

"They should not have scared us like that!" Charity exclaimed.

"They were afraid of you. You could see them and they feared you would see us- they did not understand that you were not going to harm us."

"How long ago did this happen?" Charity wanted to know.

Yellow Moon appeared thoughtful before she answered.

"Time as you know it is not the same here. We are the same as the day we went into the river. I know not, how long, or when- only what is. My thoughts are the same. I am here, there is no other time."

"Have you seen the passageway?" Charity asked her.

"There is a great passageway opened into a strange bright land, but we our Miko says that we cannot leave the darkened land or the water to enter into this land- we cannot go without all our peoples," Yellow Moon answered.

"Yes you can," Charity said earnestly. "The ones you wait on, they are there in the bright land!"

"Are you certain of this?" Yellow Moon asked, wanting to believe that it was true. "If you are certain-"

"Of this, I am certain," Charity said, explaining, "You have been here a very long time- your bodies have not aged- but people living out here in the world, those you were waiting on to return- they have grown old and died while you remain the same."

"Then I will go," Yellow Moon said, looking toward the bright land. "I wish to see my husband again- I want to lie in his strong arms once again.

"Then you will have to help me! You have to convince the others to cross into the bright land," Charity told her.

"They will not listen to me-" Yellow Moon sounded disheartened. "I am but a mere woman. I do not have a voice other than to sing the song of return."

"What if I can convince them to go forth shinning into this new land, would you help me?" Yellow Moon, nodded her head.

"Good, then, it is settled," Charity said firmly, "we shall begin. All you have to do is watch me and do as I do," she instructed.

Charles built a fire on the bank of the river, in the place his mother had instructed him to; he had been watching his mother, patiently albeit anxiously waiting for her to bring the spirit to the fire. When his mother began walking toward him, he became sensitive to the spirits. The young Indian woman following his mother was beautiful. When they reached where he and Jackson waited by the fire, the four of them, Charity, Charles, Jackson, and Yellow Moon knelt down forming a circle around the fire.

Charity began to chant while sprinkling a fine powder into the flames; the flames leaped higher and spewed into brightly colored plumes of smoke. She then raised her face and hands toward the heavens, calling to the Great Spirit.

Yellow Moon also chanted, raising her face and hands toward the heavens. Charity could feel the presence of Yellow Moon's people as they neared her- they formed a circle around them and the fire. She and Yellow Moon continued to chant, singing a song of praise unto the Great Spirit, asking Him to reach down and save those who had lost their way.

Jackson could not see the spirits; however, he saw a fine smoky mist rise from the river and slowly move toward where they were- it soon surrounded them. He looked at his mother and brother's faces.

He could not see, nor hear whatever it was that they saw and heard, but he could surely see the mist and feel the coldness surrounding them. He was nervous, in fact, plumb jittery, he wanted to cut out and run away, however, with the mist surrounding them, he felt it was safer to stay put- therefore, he closed his eyes so that he could not see the mist...

With Yellow Moon's voice raised in joyful song, the others were soon singing too; not the sad mournful lullaby of the river, but a song of joyous, harmony and peace. Charity knew they surrounded her; she could feel their presence. When she felt their presence diminishing, she opened her eyes to watch them ascend into the light.

Yellow Moon, who was leading her people- going forth to the light, stopped and turned to look back at Charity. She hugged her child to her and smiled before turning to continue her journey. Charity looked at Charles. He had tears of joy running down his cheeks.

"I could see them, Mama. As they left, they were no longer sad and angry; they were happy and filled with joy."

"Yes, I know son; they are happy now that their spirits will join their families in the lands of the Great Spirit- they will rest now."

"How come I can't see what y'all see, Mama?" Jackson asked.

"Son, I do not know why some can see and others cannot. My grandmother could see the spirits of the dead, and said that her grandfather could too. Charles can see them sometimes- even your sister Mary saw them when she was little; but then, as she grew older, she lost her vision of the outer realm. I am pretty sure that Emmy also sees spirits- she may retain the power to see them or she too, may lose it. Mine has always been. Your brother did not start until he was about your age."

Charles looked at his brother and said, "I was with Mama at a clearing, when we lived up on the mountain in Canton. I saw that she could see something that I could not. When I sat near her, closed my eyes, and opened my heart, and mind, I began to hear them. You have to tune your soul, to become one with the Great Spirit; then, it will come."

"I don't know if I want it to come, if it's going to make me cry."

Charles laughed; "It didn't hurt me- I cried tears of joy and happiness. It's hard to explain, but it is just a beautiful and joyous feeling that comes to you."

"Yes, it is," Charity agreed and then said, "Charles, I need to speak to you alone. Can you follow me down to the river," she asked.

"I ain't gonna stay here by myself!" Jackson exclaimed.

"We will be right here- you'll be able to see us- besides, the spirits are gone, nothing or no one will hurt you."

"Are you shore, Mama?"

"Yes, Son, I am sure," Charity replied.

"What do you want to talk to me about, Mama," Charles asked, as they walked toward the river.

"Charles, a great, upheaval, caused by a mighty war is coming."

"Yes, Mama, I know," he responded.

"You do- but how?" she asked, surprised.

"You forget that I have visions- I think I've always had them, but thought they were just dreams when I was younger."

"Yes Son, I remember, but I don't know if what I see happening, is what you see," she said. "When this war starts, your brother Aaron will die because of it. Two Feathers told me that when Aaron was little- now, I see it too."

"Not if I can help it, Mama. I intend on being there with him, so that I can look out for him. I saw the same thing in my mind, several years ago. I saw and heard him calling for you; and, when I went to him, he lay dying," Charles's voice drifted off, wondering if he had said too much.

"That was the same vision I had," Charity said solemnly.

"Mama,"

"Yes, Charles."

"I have seen other things, too."

She looked into her son's eyes; saw the anguish in them and said, "Some things are better not shared."

"But, Mama..." Charity placed a finger across his lips, to hush him.

"I would rather not know, Charles," she said calmly.

Changing the subject, Charity brushed his thick black hair away from his forehead and said, "What I do see in your future is that you and Emma will eventually give me another beautiful granddaughter."

Charles looked into his mother's eyes. Seeing her attempt to appear expectant over forthcoming events, he could not help but to try and smile. He wanted to please his mother; however, his heart ached for what he knew would come. He hoped his visions were wrong, but, that was not likely. And, if Emma was to give him another daughter, he longed to raise his family in Finley's cabin in Canton; he'd only uprooted them to come to be near his mother during what he knew was an unavoidable event…

50

War

Cherokee Co, Alabama
April, 1861

"War?" asked Nancy. "What are you talking about, Aaron? Why haven't heard about this before?"

Aaron looked at her as if he was wondering if she were dense or just plain stupid; then said, "The war with the Yankees, of course- have you had your head under a rock!"

"No," Nancy yelled. "I just haven't heard about it and wondered why."

"Prolly because y'all stuck out here in the wilderness and men folk didn't see no use in filling you women's heads with talk of war," stated Aaron. "Anyhow, it was just talk until now!"

"I want ever get a husband now," Nancy suddenly wailed. "They'll all be off playing war! Why do they want to fight anyway?" she asked, and then remembered hearing something about freeing slaves. "Why don't they just set all the darkies free and be done with it," she said smartly.

"Don't be so snide to your brother," Henry reprimanded,

adding, "Besides, there's more to it than just slavery that's starting all this war talk; it's about the government trying to nullify states' rights, and other stuff that's over your head. Besides, it'll all blow over soon and things will be back to normal."

"Normal; what's normal," Nancy huffed. "I'm stuck out here in the middle of nowhere helping Mama with a passel of young'uns!"

"You need to watch your tone, Nancy Ann Gullege," said Henry sternly.

"I'm sorry, Papa-"

"I'm not the one you need to say sorry to-"

"I'm sorry, Mama; I do apologize," Nancy said quickly, seizing the opening to bring up what she had wanted to ask her parents for awhile. "I want to go and stay with John and Sarah in Anniston. It's boring out here and there is so much excitement in town- Please let me go, Papa" she begged.

Henry looked to Charity for help.

"Sarah is expecting again. If John is running off to war like Aaron is, then maybe it would be best for Nancy to go stay with Sarah for a while- I'm sure Sarah can use the help. I'll still have Mary and Cynthia to help me."

Nancy yelped with excitement, ran to her mama and hugged her.

"Hold on now," said Henry teasingly. "I didn't say yes, yet."

"Don't tease me, Papa; please say yes," Nancy begged.

Wistfully, Charity smiled. She knew that Nancy, who was now officially an "old maid" at the age of twenty, was still very much infatuated with Jefferson Alford and that the reason she wanted to go stay in Anniston with her brother, was because she figured she would get to see him more often. Charity did not approve of the match and would rather Nancy meet a nice, younger, unattached man; however, she knew how stubborn her daughter was and that come hell or high water, Nancy would end up with Jefferson, regardless of her druthers. She had learned there were many things of which she had no control over and one of them was another person's heart. Accepting that knowledge, gave her peace. Therefore, it was with mild acceptance that she nodded her head...

"When are you leaving?" she asked Aaron.

"I'm leaving right away, Mama. I just came home to grab some stuff and say goodbye. I'm supposed to meet up with the rest of 'em in Jacksonville. We'll be heading off to join up as soon as we can."

"Make sure you give them our names and where we live when you sign up." Charity told her fourth-born son, hugging him tight.

"Jeez, Ma, you act like I'm still a little young'un."

"You are still my little son," she said, smiling. "You always will be."

As Mary helped Nancy pack to leave, Nancy said, "It'll be fun living in town; don't you want to come, too, Mary?"

"No," Mary answered quickly. "I need to stay here and help mama; with you gone, she's going to need me. Nancy, please don't stay away too long," Mary added. "With you gone, it will be lonely around here."

"Don't be silly," said Nancy. "You'll still have Cynthia and Emmy, to keep you company. Besides, I plan to stay as long as it takes to find a husband."

"That's what I figured," Mary mumbled.

"Mama," Nancy suddenly yelled, asking, "where's my blue dress that you were letting out the hem on?"

Charity had been listening to them talking; her heart went out to Mary. Mary had always had an older sister around... she hoped that Mary would be content with just her younger sisters there... her vision of Mary's future was not as clear as it was for some of her other children, but she did not feel that anything bad was going to happen to her. Her stubborn little mirror image, Emmy, worried her more than any of the others did. Shaking her head, she smiled sadly as she finished putting the final stitch in the hem of Nancy's dress just as Nancy appeared in front of her; she handed the dress to her.

"I wish I had some new dresses- this old thing used to be Martha's before she got too fat to wear it-"

"You need to be thankful for what you have- it's still in good condition... Nancy, you behave yourself down there in town," she instructed, not going into detail of what was running through her mind but wanting to warn her to guard her heart.

"Don't be such worrywarts, Mama," Nancy replied. "I will be fine- I know what I'm doing."

I'm sure you think you do, thought Charity, wishing she could stop her- she said a quick prayer that all would eventually work itself out.

✳✳✳

When Henry told Jeremiah that he was going to stay home for a week, so that he could get some of the planting done, it surprised and delighted Jeremiah- he missed having Henry around.

"It's already mid-April," said Henry. "Before this war gets to going, if it gets to going, I wanted to plant a good vegetable garden for y'all to eat out of come summertime."

"Yep; you wait too much longer and the crops won't make anything and it'll all be for naught," Jeremiah said, somewhat sadly, as the talk of war caused him to remember what Charity had told him years earlier, about Aaron dying in a great war- he wondered if she had also told Henry, and if that was why Henry was staying home- just in case she broke down once Aaron left.

He wanted to ask Henry if she had told him, but reckoned it'd be best to keep his mouth shut and wait and see- he'd know soon enough, because that day had come… Thinking himself all grown up, Aaron was going off to war...

When the Yellow Mocker Calls

***

After Aaron and Nancy had left, Charity dressed in her riding britches, packed her paints and canvases and then mounted Kagali and rode off to be alone. She could not stand all their questioning eyes on her, watching her as if they were waiting for her to implode.

Riding across the meadow, she talked aloud to Kagali, "What do they expect from me? I know they think I can, but I cannot fix everything!" Sometimes, I need to be alone- just to be by myself even if it's just for a little while, she thought. I need to find inner peace with this. I've consoled myself to Nancy's destiny- now, I must console myself to Aaron's destiny- He is so passionate about this war... There is nothing I can do but pray that when that time comes, we will get through it...

What bothered her so much was the passion that Aaron exuded when speaking of fighting in this war... she would never have thought it of him when he was little... If put toward something positive, that passion of his could move mountains! However, the passion he felt, she knew, would be short lived, and that he would be dead in just a few short months.

She would gladly give her own life to save his, or any of her children for that matter; but, she knew it was not possible. Everyone has a role in life, an allotted amount of time that they will reign on earth. Each person has a necessary function, a fate in life that they are destined to play out...

Lila M Beckham

She knew could not intervene in what was already predetermined by the Great Spirit, even if it was her own son that was to die; she had learned that when her grandfather, Tokola, and Unegadihi died- she was helpless to do anything to stop their dying. Aaron was no longer a child; he was a man who has made his own decisions in life. If she had told him when he was six that he would die when he was nineteen, he would have been afraid to live his life; he would have missed living…

Taking her paints, pencils, and accessories from her haversack, she outlined *her* vision of the hills in the distance- filled with the pungent smoke of a war that was on the horizon. As soon as she finished the outline, a vision of her son lying in her arms, staring into her eyes as he took his final breath was more than she could bear. She grabbed a handful of paint and smeared it across the canvas, and then fell to her knees and wailed, "Why? Why does it have to be like this?" she asked the sky above.

Warm tears stung her eyes as she looked at the small tintype photo of Aaron he'd had made while in town. Staring across the haphazard hills to the northeast, she had a vision- from there, they would come.

***

Days turned into weeks and weeks turned into months as the war among the states built momentum. Charity tried to keep her families' spirits up, even though it was getting harder and harder to keep up her own.

With the war going on, the man Henry worked for wasn't able to work him, but two days a week. Charity, the younger children, and Jeremiah were glad to have him home more, but things were getting tight as far as keeping food on the table, clothes on their backs, and shoes on their feet. Besides having the garden for fresh vegetables, a few farm animals for milk, eggs, and occasionally as a meal, Henry's hunting supplied enough meat to get by. However, in the larder, the staples of flour, meal, sugar, and coffee was running extremely low- The army's requisitioning of those things had taken its toll on everyone in the county, so they were getting even harder to come by.

John's wife Sarah had lost the baby she was carrying when she slipped and fell on the porch, during a thunderstorm; she had gone out to get some clothes off the line to keep them from getting wet. Charity's heart ached for her loss. And, since John, too, had gone off the fight in the War Between the States, Nancy was still staying there with her; Jefferson Alford was still courting her every chance he got to steal away from his elderly, ill wife.

A young man named Phillip Christopher that Henry had nicknamed Dan because he wore a coonskin hat like the great woodsman Daniel Boone, had taken an interest in Cynthia when Henry befriended him at work and brought him home with him several weeks after Aaron left. Of course, this young man had also joined the war effort as was most young men in the county; however, Charity had seen in her visions that Phillip would return from the war and marry Cynthia. They would have a large and loving family and be surrounded by grandchildren when they were well into their old age…

About the middle of October, the weather began to turn cool; by November, it had turned back to near summertime weather again. As she and Henry sat out on the porch enjoying one of their rare cups of coffee that they allotted themselves, she could tell that Henry had something on his mind so she asked him what was bothering him.

"Charity, do you ever wish we could turn back the clock to before we left Carolina and maybe not have left there to come here to Alabama?"

Charity thought back through the years and the journey that had brought them to where they were, and then said, "No, Henry; I don't have any regrets- our life is as it was meant to be; I would not change any of it. We have our children and our grandchildren- and, if we had not come, where would poor old Jeremiah be now?"

"Yes, you are right. Where would he be if we had not come into his life- Where would I be?" Henry said thoughtfully.

51

Saying Goodbye

Culpepper, Virginia
November 15, 1861

When the call of the Yellow Mocker woke her, Charity raised up to look out the window- perched on a limb in the tree near the window, the mockingbird set, singing his bothersome tune and staring in at her.

Looking over to where Henry lay sleeping beside her on the bed, she longed to cuddle up beside him and shut the outside world away, but the mocker's beckoning call stirred her to action. For months, she had dreaded this day coming; no mother should ever have to watch their child die. Rising slowly, she did not know if she had the strength to face what she knew she must.

Listening with her soul's ears, she heard him… Aaron's calls for her, reached through the night and across the miles; she could not ignore the powerful force of motherhood. Her child needed her; she must go to him.

Entering the room of the makeshift hospital, she heard him- looking around, she saw him lying on a sweat-soaked cot.

"Mama?" she heard him call, then again, "Mama… Is that you Mama? Please don't leave me, Mama," Aaron's voice, then trailed off as he gave up the effort to keep calling for her.

"Who the heck is he talking to, Sarge," asked a young private lying on a cot across from where Aaron lay.

"Hell, son, I don't know," the grumpy sergeant snapped. "He's been at it ever since they brought him in here last night. I wouldn't a thought he'd a made it this long," the sergeant added.

Standing over her son, watching the pain and anguish etch across his face as he struggled to breathe, was almost more than she could bear; she wanted to float away into the night and run away from it all- to run away from Aaron, but when images of him at birth, taking his first steps, toting a sack as big as he was and so many others quickly flashed through her mind, what she saw lying there was not a full-grown man, but her child. Letting her spirit flow around and through him, she wrapped him in her embrace. She lay beside him, kissed his face and stroked his dampened hair.

"Mama's here, baby," she said softly. "Mama is right here and I am not going to leave you." Aaron opened his eyes and looked at her.

"Would ya just look at that," the young private said in awe.

"What is it now?" the sergeant asked gruffly.

"Look at him, Sarge! He looks just like he see's somebody right there with him. Ain't that strange, Sarge?" the private asked.

"Don't nuthin' strike me as strange these days, son- I have seen enough strange stuff in the last few weeks to last me a lifetime! Don't nuthin' surprise me anymore- I think it's all in their heads- they just think their maws are there with 'em- he ain't the first one I saw do that, and prolly won't be the last.

"If I had to take a guess, I'd say he's delirious with fever or something and thinks he's a talking to his maw. Now, don't keep a hollerin' at me every time he moves or mumbles - there ain't a damn thing I can do for him, or you neither- it won't be long, he'll be gone," the sergeant said sternly.

The young private looked back over toward Aaron, and then shook his head, saying to no one in particular, "Yep, that is mighty strange. Looks just like somebody is there with him, and he see's 'em."

Holding Aaron in her arms, she stroked his hair and whispered softly a song that she sang to him when he was a little boy. When she finished the song, she felt his body go limp in her arms…

"It's alright, Mama," he said. "I don't hurt anymore."

"Come, take a walk with me," she said, standing and reaching out a hand to him; he took her hand and they left the makeshift hospital and walked out into the death and destruction that was War- Then, Charity gathered his spirit and walked the night winds into a bright sunlit meadow. As they walked and talked about life, Aaron asked, "Mama, did you know that I was going to die?"

"Yes, Son, I knew," she said softly. "Do you remember when you were a little boy and we were on our way to Cherokee County, after leaving the farm where the nice lady fed us and gave us supplies." he nodded his head

"When we reached the Yellow River, we met up with Two Feathers and his tribe; he was the old Indian man with eyes the color of falling snow."

"Yes, Mama, I remember him. He said that he could see us, but his eyes were blind," Aaron replied.

"Yes, that's right," she replied, "He was Two Feathers, my great-great-grandfather. That day, he called for each of you to stand in front of him so that he could "See" you - you didn't want to go… After seeing you, he told me that one day, I would hear the Yellow Mocker call- that day, you would one day die, in a great war of the white man. So, yes, Son, I have known all these years that this day would come," Charity told him.

"You could have told me, Mama," Aaron said.

"No, Son, I could not- it would not have been fair for you to know - If I had told you, you would have lived your life in fear and anger," she said.

"It wasn't fair to you either, Mama- He should not have told you! You could have been happier; lived a happier life if you had not known."

"Maybe, Son," Charity replied, "however, I am glad that he told and that I knew this day was coming; if not, I would not have been listening when you called for me to come- you would have…" she couldn't bring herself to say it.

"It doesn't matter, Mama, I would have come anyway. If it was my destiny there was nothing that would have changed that."

"Maybe Aaron, but I still question why. You are so young, as are most of the men that lay here dying... all of them far away from their homes and families... It's just not fair!" she said angrily.

"I have to go now, Mama," he said weakly. "The time has come for us to part- don't be sad... I know I haven't said it much since I was a little boy, but I love you, Mama; you're the best mother a son could have..."

Suddenly, Charity was standing over his bed. She stared into his lifeless eyes... Bending down, she took his hand and kissed his cheek.

"I love you, too, baby," she whispered, clinging tightly to his hand, willing him to stay- not wanting to turn him loose- but, he was already gone.

As her tears began to flow, she thought, at least his spirit is free...

She awoke, crying. Henry turned over, pulled her close, and wanted to know what was wrong. She told him of Aaron's death and how she had known it was going to happen and had kept it from him. She could feel the pain he felt, as he tried to be strong and begged his forgiveness for keeping it from him.

"I cannot blame you for not telling me- if I had known and you didn't, I would not tell you either; however, I wish you had told me, so that we could have borne it together and you would not have had to bear the burden of knowing alone." She lay in his arms, clinging to the strength she felt with him that she herself did not have. She did not want to leave his arms nor the sanctuary of her bedroom.

"We must tell the family..." said Henry, pausing, "You know- we probably will not be able to lay Aaron to rest, here at home. Several men from our area have been killed in this war, and their families did not get their bodies back. Mr. Driskell, who lives down the road from where I work, lost her son, Benjamin last month- so far, all he has gotten is a few belongings- he didn't even get what pay he had earned."

"Oh, Henry! I hadn't even thought about a funeral. What will we do?"

"There's not much we can do. If they have already buried him, then we will have a ceremony of our own and place something of his in a grave and mark it. It will have to do..."

"Maybe we can go and get his body and bring him home-"

"Charity, we cannot do that- it is too dangerous with all the fighting that's going on out in Virginia and places like that- we have our family to think of."

She knew that Henry was right; they would have to let it be. That did not make the thought any easier to cope with. The thought of Aaron buried in a place that she did not know its whereabouts, did not sit well with her. Rising, she got out of bed and went to put on a pot of coffee; she and Henry was setting on the porch drinking a cup of coffee when the sun started to rise over the hills to the east. It was then that Charity could see how pale and haggard Henry looked; her eyes moistened and her heart ached for him; his loss was as severe as hers was.

At least, she had gotten to hold Aaron in her arms, to talk with him and to say goodbye. Henry hadn't had that luxury; this caused her to feel even worse about not telling him. But, she was only trying to protect him from the pain of knowing… She could tell from his expression that he would not have the same type of closure she did, and that worried her; she worried about what might be going through his mind while watching his expressions change…

The next few weeks were a nightmare as they waited to hear the official news of Aaron's death. Finally, Henry had to ride down to Anniston, Alabama to find out if Aaron had been listed on the lists that came in weekly. (A list of dead and wounded was sent to the county seat of each county in each state and posted so that everyone could read it to find out about their loved ones that were fighting in the war; folks gathered weekly to read the lists.

Since Aaron had signed up in Calhoun County, that is where his name would be listed on the list of dead or wounded. Also worried about his other two sons that were off fighting in the war, Henry wanted to check for their names too, just in case Charity was keeping something from him again… All his sons had joined the war effort thinking it'd be over before it even got started good; however, that had not been the case- the war was raging, intensifying, with no clear end in sight. Henry hated to admit it, but he was grateful that Uriah had the accident that nearly cost him his foot when he was young, or else, he'd be out there somewhere too.

After reaching Anniston and hearing all the talk of war and of the battles his and other men's young sons were fighting and getting killed in, Henry became extremely angry. The news had come of heavy tolls in certain battles and that the North was bottling up the South's port cities and not letting supplies get in or out.

"They trying to starve us out- trying to keep our boys from getting supplies, too - Damn'it, come wintertime our boys are gonna be barefoot," said Jackson Teller as they waited for the list to be printed, spitting an angry wad of tobacco juice on the ground by Henry's feet to show his disgust.

Thinking about all the bad news he'd heard and seeing Aaron's name written in ink on the list of dead and wounded in combat, a worried, angry Henry did something he hadn't done in years, not since he and Jeremiah were arrested on drunk and disorderly charges, back in Georgia; he took, when Jackson Teller offered, several big swallows of whiskey! The hot liquid felt good sliding down his throat and into his stomach; it also calmed his nerves. And, even though he could have drank more, maybe even wanted to drink more, he didn't; he knew what that could cost him…

After standing around talking for a while, he decided it was time to go; he also needed to stop and visit with Nancy and John's wife, Sarah, and tell them about Aaron's passing before heading home. When he got there, Nancy's "fella" was there visiting. Henry thought that Jefferson came off a might uppity, but reckoned it was because his folks had owned half the county while alive. Henry didn't like his daughter having anything to do with a married man; however, he knew that was what was going on. He'd heard from somewhere, maybe it was from Martha, that Jefferson's wife was much older, and that she had never been able to give Jefferson any children. He understood a man wanting children of his own, but it didn't have to be with *his* daughter and he darn sure didn't have to like or respect the man and he made sure Jefferson knew how he felt. It was a hard day and Henry was a sad man as he made his way home…

52

Contemplations

Etowah Co, Alabama

Aug 1862

The Noccalula Falls area was once a part of Cherokee County, but it had been taken in as a part of Etowah County. Etowah was a Creek Indian name that meant, "Tribe." Standing on the rim of the falls with the cool water rushing around her bare feet, Charity looked down into the swirling pool of water eighty feet below and wondered if she was standing where the princess, Noccalula, had stood all those years before when she jumped into the swirling abyss and took her own life... Feeling the rocky, earth shift beneath her feet, she thought how easy it would be just to slip over the rim and into the depths of the pool below. All she had to do was to ease a little closer to the rim...

Even though she stood there and contemplated it, she couldn't do it; she loved Henry and her children too much to take her own life. She could not leave them- she didn't want to leave them, but it felt as if some spell had come over her as she stood there staring down.

She had hoped coming there would renew her spirit and

make her feel better. The ever encroaching danger of war caused her to be edgy and irritable. When Henry suggested they go up and spend the day, she had hoped going to the waterfall would relieve some of her stress; and, in a way it had. Making her way back down and around to the bottom, where Henry and Jackson waited, she could not help but revel in the beauty of the Great Spirit's handiwork.

"It's beautiful here," Henry said, reaching a hand out to help her down the last large flat rock.

"Yes, it is," Charity agreed. "But, it does not feel the same here now as it did the first few times I came here. The first time I came, I wanted to stay here forever- I still love it here, but our lives have changed so much since then."

"Maybe, one day, I will be able to buy land here at the falls and build another small cabin just for you and me in our old age," Henry said hopefully. Charity nodded her head and managed a weak smile; she knew that that day would never come; she could feel the Wind of Change in the air…

"Let's go home, Henry."

"Already; are you sure? We haven't even eaten the picnic we brought."

"Yes, I'm sure," she replied. Her meaning of *going home*, had gone over his head- At that moment, she longed for the security of the Carolina cabin she'd grown up in and the comfort of her grandmother and grandfather's spirits and having Henry's parents nearby. "We need to get home before dark. It's getting too dangerous to be out and about these days- I heard cannon fire yesterday morning- that means the fighting is close by."

Disappointed, Jackson drug his feet when they were ready to go, asking her to tell him the story of Noccalula again. Apparently, Henry was not ready to leave either because he, too, wanted her to tell the story. She was surprised that Jackson even remembered the story she had told them about the Indian Princess, Noccalula, for whom the falls had been named; he was very young when she told it to them. When she said that she was not in a storytelling mood, she could see the disappointment on both their faces; she felt bad about it, but not bad enough to stay and tell the story.

Ever since, Aaron's death, Henry had been moody and brooding- she knew it was because he was worried and felt helpless. The war that he and everyone else thought would be over before it started had now been ongoing for a year and a half...

At first, the Confederate Army had managed to keep the fighting above the Mason Dixon line; however, Northern troops would slip past them and come deep into the Southern states; battles were occurring all around. They had heard of battles in a place called Shiloh, Tennessee, also in New Orleans, Yorktown and Richmond, Virginia. They'd even heard of a battle over at Fort Pulaski, which was located at the mouth of the Savannah River causing them to worry about Henry's parents.

When they heard about that one, Charity had spoken what

was on her mind- "I sure hope your mama and daddy are alright," she'd said and then regretted saying it when she saw the look on Henry's face.

It had been nearly twenty years since they left the Carolinas. Nearly twenty years since they had seen Nancy and Eli... They exchanged letters several times a year, but that was not the same as visiting with them.

So far, they had been lucky that only a few small skirmishes had taken place in northern Alabama; however, people were warned not to go out into the areas where Northern patrols may happen along.

"It's like being held prisoner in your own home," Jeremiah fumed. "You can bet, if'n I was able bodied, I'd be right out there amongst 'em," he said.

"Yeah, I bet you would, Old Man," said Henry. "After all of those battles you were in when you were a young man, I would have figured you'd had enough warring to last you a lifetime?"

"I didn't say that I ain't had enough!" Jeremiah bellowed. "Just that if I was able to get around better, I'd be out there with them boys, a helping 'em whup them damn Yankees and send 'em packin' - That's what I meant."

"You're getting a little feisty in your old age, Old Man. Gosh dang it; just bite somebody's head off, would you." Henry couldn't help but to laugh when Jeremiah spit and sputtered some more- throwing more profanities at him.

When the Yellow Mocker Calls

"You just want something to bellyache about, you old coot; it doesn't matter what it is, you'll find something to gripe about," chuckling under his breath, Henry turned and walked out the door and headed to the field to finish plowing the fall garden.

Charity sat back and smiled. She didn't dare let Jeremiah see her smiling, though. If he did, he'd be mad at her too. Poor old feller, he wasn't handling growing old graciously. He was miserable from the arthritis that had him all bent and twisted and he couldn't hear as well, nor see as well as he used to.

Everyone in the house seemed grumpier than usual. Charity figured that everyone was on edge due to the war and because of being confined to the house; she, herself, was a veritable fountain of emotions, but figured it was because of what Henry's mother had referred to, as going through the change of life- Nancy had told her that all women go through the change when their childbearing years are over… If she didn't know any better, she'd think she was expecting again.

"You might be a going through the change of life," Jeremiah offered one day when she was all jittery and flustered. Charity knew something was changing, but she didn't think it was her- it was the people around her…

War does something to people, she thought. It will make people do and say things, they'd never dream of doing at any other time.

Nancy and Sarah had come out to get some fresh vegetables

and told them about all the horror stories that were circulating through town, about women and girls being raped and murdered. They talked about homes being pillaged, by marauding soldiers and freed Darkies that were looking for food and shelter. When they happened upon lone, unprotected women, they'd do whatever they wanted- the womenfolk couldn't stop them, not with their men folk gone off a fighting in the war.

"Mama, y'all need to move into town," Nancy said earnestly.

"I'd rather take my chances against the Yankees, than to have to live in one of those pig sties again," Charity said.

"At least let Mary and Cynthia come and stay with us," she begged. "They'll be safer."

"I don't want to go and stay with y'all!" Cynthia said, stomping her foot.

"Me, neither!" Mary exclaimed.

"You just want us to come so we can do all the hard work," said Cynthia.

"That's not true-"

"We both want to stay home with Mama," said Mary, not letting Nancy finish her sentence.

"But y'all are going to miss all the excitement- they've been planning a spring dance at the end of the month," added Sarah.

"They who," asked Charity.

"Why, the Ladies of the Confederacy, of course!" said Nancy, in a superior manner, which made Charity want to smack her.

"Oh, of course- why, we wouldn't want to miss that, now would we girls," Charity said.

"Quit being sarcastic, Mother," Nancy said. "I know it's not something you'd like, but it would be fun for Cynthia and Mary.

Charity, herself, did not want to get anywhere near town, if she didn't have to, but she didn't consider her daughters might want to go. She looked at Mary and Cynthia and raised an eyebrow, wondering if they wanted to go.

"We still don't want to go, do we Cinthy," Mary said. "We're going to stay here with Mama and Papa- they need us to help them."

"Yes, they do," said Cynthia, in a not so pleasant tone- "Especially since we're the only ones that think about others before ourselves."

Charity could see the fire fly between Cynthia and Nancy's eyes and thought for a moment that they were going to attack one another the way they used to- however, Nancy quickly gained her composure- she did not want Jefferson to see her bad side, especially since she was trying to woo his heart. From the look in Nancy's eyes when she looked at Jefferson Alford, Charity could see that she was still very much infatuated with the charming Jefferson Alford, who had so kindly driven them out to the farm in his fancy buggy.

After Sarah and Nancy left heading back to town, Henry

said, "It must be nice to have all that money," referring to Jefferson's fine horse and buggy.

"He ain't a gonna have it long if the Yankee's get a look at it," said Jeremiah, spitting a stream of tobacco juice off the porch.

"From the looks of things, they're going to take everything they can get from us Southerners anyway," said Henry. "They may as well take our money too; what little we have- which ain't much a'tall these days…"

Aaron had been dead for over a year and they still had not received any of his personal belongings, nor the pay he had coming, for his service to the Confederacy. Henry had decided to file a claim to see if they could get Aaron's personal belongings and what pay he had earned; if they had not heard anything by the end of summer, he was going back to file another claim.

John and Charles had both, at separate times, came home on leave. Both, had only been allowed a week to plow and plant their families a garden, before having to go back, or else be charged with desertion.

Henry, Jackson, and Uriah had helped both of them as best they could, and poor Henry was stretched thin as it was, trying to make sure that all were taken care of properly. He and Charity had talked about building another room onto their cabin and moving John's and Charles's families all into their home.

"It would definitely make it a lot easier on you," Charity said. "But, honestly, Henry, I don't know if I could handle that many women in the same house with me."

"Well, don't worry about them," said Henry. "I'll just keep doing the best I can for them; but the rest will be up to them- or maybe their own pa's can help them some. It seems like when a girl gets married, all the upkeep of them and their home, falls on the husband's family!"

"Your family took me in when Grandpa died... I- "

"That was different. You didn't have anybody left- those girls do!"

Charity snuggled Henry's back and held him close, wanting nothing more at that moment than the comfort of his nearness.

"I love you," she mumbled into his shoulder.

"I love you, too," Henry replied, unraveling himself from her arms and turning to face her...

53

Hard Times

Calhoun Co, Alabama
March 4, 1863

The fall and winter of '62 had been hard on folks living in the South, especially in the North Alabama Counties where Charity and her family lived. Snow, wind, and rain had pounded them for weeks- Snow, which was rarely seen in the South, had been heavy the early part of January- and then the winds and rain had come- upsetting the early spring planting season. Being able to buy most of the things a family needed to survive, was as hard to do as it was to get the money needed to buy them with; and, it was getting harder by the day.

Now nearing the two year mark, the war was still going on- and, they still had not received any of Aaron's belongings, nor the money due him for his six months of service; the family was in dire need of that money.

When Henry told Charity that he'd be back in a day or two, she nodded her head- she too, had plans to leave the cabin. Now that spring had come, she was going to take the children and go out looking for fresh greens- she was sure she could at least find some pokeweed and harvest the edible parts to cook- it would also be good for Jeremiah's arthritis. Henry said he was going down to Anniston and see about filing another claim for the payment that was due Aaron and hopefully, he could get some supplies on his account at the mercantile.

"If we can get Aaron's pay we'll be able to buy some flour and meal; maybe, we can even afford a bag of sugar."

"It would be good to have sugar," said Charity, wistfully. "I could make some sassafras tea…"

With assurances that he would be careful and that they would be all right without him, at least for a few days, Henry rode off in the early morning light of the fourth day of March, 1863. As she watched him ride south, away from the cabin, Charity had a sinking feeling in her chest. For months, before the bad weather set in, Henry rode back and forth to Anniston several times a month looking for work and doing odd jobs to make money or bartering for the food staples that his family needed- why should this day be any different, thought Charity? It took her several attempts before she was able to shake the bad feelings she had.

Having made good time, Henry arrived in Anniston about noon. The town was bustling with activity; he wondered what was going on; he soon found out. Word had come that on the first day of January, the Northern president, Abe Lincoln, aware of the publics growing support of abolition, had issued an Emancipation Proclamation declaring that all slaves in areas still in rebellion, were, in the eyes of the Federal Government, free!

Henry had no objections to freeing the slaves; however, he could understand why folks were concerned. Other than the obvious concerns of former slave owners fearing revenge from their former slaves, people wondered where would the newly freed slaves stay and how would they take care of themselves? Most slaves knew nothing of the world other than the life of a slave. There was also a ruckus stirred up over something called the First Conscription Act. The Act had been passed up North because of recruiting difficulties. It declared that all men between the ages of twenty and forty five were liable for military service and had to come when called; however, service could be avoided by paying a fee or finding a suitable substitute to go in their place. The act was seen as unfair to the poor because they could not afford to pay the fees; riots had broken out in the working class sections of New York City and other large cities in protest of the Act.

A similar Conscription Act passed in the South, was provoking a similar reaction amongst Southerners. Men were grumbling about and wondering how in the world could their families get by without an able-bodied man there to plow the fields and plant crops- it just wasn't *doable*, they said.

"All of us with sons old enough, done had to give them up for the cause and now they want us to abandon our wives and little ones- what the hell are they thinking!" That's what Henry heard all around him. Drunken men were arguing; some, outright fist fighting in the streets.

The Confederate Army's recruiters were making it even harder by offering incentives to any man that signed up. They were given seeds and assured two weeks to finish planting their crops - They'd also get a cash sign-up bonus, plus a month's supply of flour, meal, fatback, beans, and a 20lb sack of sugar for their families to live off of until their crops came in; it was a mighty tempting offer to many of the men gathered there that day; including Henry.

After standing around and listening a while, thinking of what his best course of action was, Henry decided his first order of business was to file another claim for Aaron's belongings and the payment due him. When he reached the adjutant's office, he was informed that because of numerous claims filed by families and by wounded soldiers, the government was running behind in making payments to the families of the fallen soldiers. It was pretty much as Henry expected. After finishing in Anniston, he made his way over to Jacksonville Township to visit with Nancy, John's wife, Sarah and his little grandson, John. When Johnny saw him on the porch, he came running to him, yelling, Paw Paw, Paw Paw!

Nancy offered him a glass of cool, sweetened sassafras tea, which he eagerly accepted; he was parched, after the long ride.

"How did y'all manage to get a hold of sugar," he questioned.

"Jefferson brought it," Nancy said quietly. "He's good to me, Papa."

She knew how her father felt about her relationship with Jefferson; Henry did not like Jefferson nor did he like her keeping company with him.

"He's a good man, Papa. I swear he is, and as soon as we can, we are going to get married- I promise."

Henry busied himself playing with little Johnny and talking with Sarah, he was not in the mood to discuss Nancy's affair with Jefferson- he'd just wind up getting mad and alienating Nancy even more.

Nancy wished her father wasn't so hardheaded and that he would listen to her about Jefferson, but she could tell by her father's manner that she may as well give up on getting him to change his mind about him.

It didn't escape Henry's notice that in addition to sugar, the girls also had flour. Sarah and Nancy offered him biscuits and a slice of sweet bread to take with him; Henry refused the offer. Thinking of Charity and the children at home, knowing they hadn't had flour or sugar in months, he couldn't have eaten a bite either one.

When Henry passed through Jacksonville proper on his way out of town, Henry made a decision. He stopped at the recruiter's office and signed up for the duration of the war. He received his sign-up bonus and the supplies they promised. He was told to report back there in two weeks to start his training.

He made one more stop before heading home; there were a couple of things he wanted to get from the mercantile. One of them was an early anniversary present for Charity, since he would be gone for their anniversary.

Although he knew he shouldn't be spending the money frivolously, he had seen something there a while back that he wanted to buy her. He looked through them, going over them several times before deciding which one he should buy. Finally, he narrowed it down to two and then decided to buy both. He also bought ten pounds of coffee, because he knew how much Charity loved it. And, he bought candy for the children and a plug of tobacco for Jeremiah.

Once he had these things to take home with him, Henry felt a lot better about his decision. And, even though he knew it was going to get dark on him, he did not camp for the night, instead, he rode straight home, not arriving until nearly nine o'clock. He had expected to find everyone in bed, but Charity was sitting out on the porch smoking her pipe and waiting for him. When he saw her sitting there; even though he was loaded down with a bounty, Henry started to regret his decision. Not because he was afraid of fighting in the war, because he wasn't. It was because he would have to leave her in two weeks, and that was going to be a very hard thing to do.

"I was beginning to wonder if you had been waylaid,"

Charity said quietly. "I knew you would not stay overnight."

Henry could tell that she was measuring him up- reading him. After nearly thirty years together, she could read him pretty well.

"Did you file the claim," she asked.

"Yes," he said, "but they said they were way behind in processing claims because there are so many of them being filed."

"Henry"

"Yes?"

"I wish you would have come and talked with me first, before making a decision that affects us all."

Chagrined, Henry looked down at the floor.

"I know that I'm supposed to respect your decisions because you're my husband; but I sure wish you would have talked it over with me first. That's all I'm going to say," she said. "Now, tell me, how long do we have before you have to leave us?"

Dumbstruck, Henry wondered if Charity really could read his mind...

54

Mustered In

Alexandria, Calhoun Co, Alabama
March 11, 1863

When Henry came home with all those supplies, she knew the only way he could have gotten them was to join the Confederate Army; Nancy and Sarah had already told her what the Confederates were doing to raise an army. Charity could not be mad at Henry; he had done what he thought was best for his family. They needed the money and the supplies, but those material things would not replace her husband's presence in his absence, nor would they stop her fear of losing him- war destroyed more than the earth it was fought for; it tore apart and destroyed families' lives.

The same feelings of dread that Charity remembered from when she was a young girl and set off on an adventure with her grandfather, settled in her heart- She had neither visions nor premonitions of things to come, only the horrible feeling that she would never see Henry again. She wanted to beg him not to go- beg him to stay there with her and the children, but she knew she could not do that- she would not cause him to feel guiltier than what he already felt- she knew it had not been an easy decision for him to make- sacrificing himself for them- she would have done the same thing if she could have…

Night after night, she held Henry tight and made love to him as if it would be the last time she held him. Always a gentle lover, Henry took her to soaring heights of passion and then gently and lovingly brought her back to earth...

The day Henry left, they all stood on the porch to watch him ride away; poor, old Jeremiah cried like a baby as he, Charity, and the children watched him ride away in a wagon driven by Uriah, who was not fit for duty because of his foot. When the wagon turned toward the trail leading to Alexandria, Henry looked back once and smiled and waved; even at the distance he was from them, Charity could feel how heavy his heart was.

"When will papa be coming back?" Emmy asked sternly, worry lines creasing her brow. Charity looked down at Emmy, her own heart heavy in her chest, she could not make light of his leaving to lessen her youngest daughter's worry. Taking a deep breath, she answered honestly, "I don't know, Honey." And, sadly, she did not know. It was one of those times she wished that she could see the future, see Henry coming back up the road toward their home.

Charity watched them leave until their wagon disappeared from sight. She then went inside, poured herself a cup of the wonderful coffee Henry had sacrificed his freedom for, and then went back out and sat down in her rocker. After several sips of coffee, she lit her pipe and inhaled a long, strong, puff, hoping it and the coffee would soothe her frazzled nerves.

Jeremiah and the older children moped around the house all that day; several days actually, but they weren't alone. If not for having to continue doing chores and cooking, Charity feared she might have gone crazy; she could not shake her feelings of dread; however, she knew that she would have to stay strong because they all looked to her for their strength. She could not let them know how weak she felt.

Lying in bed that night, fingering the pages of the two books her thoughtful husband had bought her, loneliness washed over her, consuming her. Without Henry by her side to share in her joy after reading them, she found no comfort in the books. Laying them aside, she blew out the lamp; her mind was too full to even attempt to read.

Lying there, she tossed and turned, then finally drifted into fitful sleep. Running alongside the river, she found herself looking for someone; someone that she knew could help her make peace with the dreadful feeling that filled her heart. Stopping to listen, she heard a distant voice chanting a singsong melody. Sitting on the lower limb of an ancient willow tree, she leaned back and closed her eyes; listening comforted her. The old willow cradled her body, its weeping boughs whispered, endure.

Suddenly, she was a young girl sitting in front of Two

Feathers and his fire, outside the walls of Fort Charlotte- he said, "Endurance, Little One - you must be strong and endure."

"Grandfather, please help me," she pleaded. "I don't know if I can endure this!" Silence greeted her pleas; Two Feathers and his fire were gone... Turning, she saw Henry and his parents setting up camp- Henry smiled and waved - her heart melted for him. "Yes, I must endure for your sake," she whispered.

Waking, she turned toward the window; it was still very dark outside. Faintly, she could make out the limbs of the oak tree nearby- there was no yellow mocker there; she lay there staring a moment and then dozed, but fitful, worrisome dreams did not let her rest. Before daybreak, she was sitting on the front porch drinking coffee and smoking her pipe. At daybreak, Jeremiah joined her. Watching him hobble out, his back bent and his feet shuffling, she felt a distinct form of pity for him.

Looking up at her, he said, "My old back is giving me hell this morning; must be gonna rain soon," he complained.

After he seated himself in his rocker he asked, "What are we gonna do, Missy," and then looked out toward the hills. The first light of day had just begun to filter through the trees.

"I really don't know what we're going to do, Jeremiah," she replied. "But I do know that we have to make the best of it, whatever way we can."

"It's gonna be mighty hard on you and them young'uns with Henry gone, having ta do all the chores and plantin' all by yourselves," he said. "I ain't gonna be much help to ya-"

"Don't talk like that, you know you help a lot- you keep the children occupied when I need you to." Jeremiah nodded, but didn't respond to what she said, he seemed to have other stuff on his mind.

"Youse need ta start hidin' everything out yonder in that little cave, that's out back of the barn; Henry said that he'd heard the Confederate Army was a commandeering folk's excess crops and such. And while I don't want ta see our fightin' fellers a going without something ta eat, I'd a whole lot rather it be them than you and them young'uns a going without!"

"I hadn't even thought about hiding our food, Jeremiah. That is a great plan," Charity told him. "Glad I am that you have the forethought to think of it. We need to move stuff out there as soon as we can," she said, thinking of the supplies and money Henry had brought home and given her. That would be something; if the army showed up and took it back- they knew that Henry would be gone. "I'll get the children to help me move everything we can spare out there this afternoon. Just in case they find the food, I'll bury the money he gave me somewhere else. I will tell you and Mary where it is, in case… We don't want all our eggs in the same basket, do we?"

"Noam, we don't," said Jeremiah, a grin creasing his old, wrinkled face.

***

Over the next several months, she and the children worked

hard in the garden; luckily, the army had not shown up to confiscate any of their food or money; however, she was not about to relax her vigil and be caught off guard. When the crops came in, she and the children harvested, canned, and put every extra morsel in the cave for safe keeping. So far, she had only received one letter from Henry- Nancy and Sarah had brought the letter to her; Henry had addressed it to them, knowing it would be easier for them to get it since they were in town. In his letter, he said that his battalion was in Memphis, Tennessee, but that they had gotten word that they were to march toward Mississippi in the next several days… Charity looked at the date of the letter- it was well over a week past- *they are probably well on their way to Mississippi by now*, she thought. *They may already be there…*

As soon as Charity finished reading the letter, she slipped it in her pocket, immediately, Nancy started in on her about her and the children leaving the cabin and moving into town with them. "Please Mama, y'all have to- it ain't safe for y'all out here," Nancy begged. "Jefferson says there are freed nigras, stragglers, and Yankee deserters looting and robbing folks that are in unpopulated areas- out here, is about as unpopulated as it gets!"

"You already know how I feel about that," Charity stated flatly, adding, "If we need anything, Martha and her children, along with Ollie's parents, are not that far away - and it's not much further to Uriah's; I can ride there in twenty minutes."

"What if you don't have twenty minutes to spare, Mama,"

protested Nancy. "If you're in town, you'll hear the news about what's going on in the war sooner," Nancy added, hoping that it would urge her mother to move to town; however, she could see that Charity wasn't changing her mind.

"I don't want to know what's going on," Charity replied stubbornly. "I'm sure you'll come and let me know everything I need to know."

"Well, of course we will, Mrs. Gullege," Sarah interrupted, hoping to stop the argument.

"If things keep getting worse, we may not be able to! Jefferson might not be able to bring us out; what then, Mama," Nancy exclaimed.

"Why isn't he out there fighting like everyone else?" Charity asked angrily, pulling her pipe out of her pocket and lighting it.

"He does his part, Mama- he has given the army a lot of money for the cause- why do you think they haven't come out here and confiscated your crops and animals- Jefferson is the reason!"

Unfazed by Nancy's determination, Charity said, "I am sick to death of all this war talk; let's drop it, and maybe for once, have a normal visit."

Saying anything against Jefferson always drew a sharp tongue from Nancy. Charity knew that Nancy was in love with him- and, if indeed, he was looking out for Nancy's family, then maybe he loved her as much as she did him. Charity hoped that one day, Nancy would find happiness, whether with Jefferson or someone else; everyone deserved to be as happy and in love as she had been with Henry all the years they'd shared…

* * *

On the day he left, before he was even out of sight of the house, Henry regretted signing up with the Army of Virginia; however, he had thoroughly enjoyed seeing the looks of happiness on the faces of his children and Jeremiah when he gave the children the candy and Jeremiah the tobacco; his family needed the money and supplies. And, although Charity seemed pleased to get the books, she had told him that she would much rather have him home with her, than the books. However, Henry was a man of his word, he would have to live with the decision he made…

He was even more regretful after learning that he would not be going to Virginia like he thought he would- he had hoped to find where Aaron was buried and maybe that he would get to see Charles and John who were somewhere up near Pennsylvania last he heard.

After a brief week of training in Talladega, he was assigned to the 30th Alabama Infantry. His unit marched out, headed southwest toward Tuscaloosa, to join with the rest of the 30th Alabama Infantry; however, they were soon rerouted to Memphis, Tennessee.

After marching about ten miles, feeling blisters form on his tired feet, Henry wished he'd kept the horse and joined the Calvary; he hadn't considered all the marching he'd have to do when he joined the army. He thought it better to leave the horse home; figuring his family could use it more than he could.

After marching a week, they reached Memphis, Tennessee. Henry was assigned under General, Carter L. Stevenson to Co. E 30th Regiment, Alabama Infantry. As soon as they arrived, they were ushered into battle; agog, Henry stared out over the intense battle playing out before him, mesmerized, until a cannon boomed and a cannonball came whizzing through the crowd and mowed down several men, breaking limbs and nearly decapitating one sergeant. Quickly scampering out of the way- an alert Henry looked around with a different set of eyes. The wounded sergeant was nearest him, so that was who he ran to help. Grabbing him up, Henry threw him over his shoulder and ran toward the medic tents at the back of the line. Once he deposited the sergeant, he headed back to help the others.

During the next three days of non-stop fighting, Henry did more toting of wounded soldiers than he did fighting- at least he felt useful. Resting briefly beneath a sweet gum tree, Henry thought of his sons- they had endured months of this carnage and as far as he knew had survived it… "God be with them," he whispered, closing his eyes, hoping to get a few minutes sleep.

When the battle was over, his unit was told to march southwest; they were to join the rest of the 30th Alabama Regiment in the Southern, Fortress City of, Vicksburg,

Mississippi. From what he'd heard, Vicksburg dominated the last Confederate controlled section of the Mississippi River; however, they were badly in need of more soldiers to defend it. It was to be a long march; approximately 350 miles. One of the officers told them that it would take them 10 or more days, marching morning to night to reach their destination… The only good thing about the roads to Vicksburg was that they were well traveled and easy to follow. Luckily, they did not encounter any enemy forces as they made their way there- They made it to the outskirts of Vicksburg, on the afternoon of the 25th of March, 1863. When they were within five miles of the city, they began to hear cannon fire. Getting in, was going to be dangerous…

55

The Siege of Vicksburg

Civil War
March 25, - May 26, 1863
Co. E 30th, Alabama Regiment

After crossing the Black River Bridge, Henry's regiment was given orders to slip up into the Chickasaw Bluffs Region and join General Pemberton's forces. They were told that Vicksburg had to be held, regardless or how many Yankees showed up to fight for it. 'We can't let them Yankees get control of the city!' was the shout Henry heard all around him. And, since leaving Memphis, Henry had not even had to fire his rifle other than to shoot a jackrabbit or two for supper several times; but all that was about to change.

Perched high on the bluffs of the Mississippi River, Vicksburg was surrounded by bayous, rivers, and creeks. It didn't matter which way they marched, trying to find a place to cross, they always ran into some type of water; Henry had never seen so many tributaries in one place. In a three week period, they must have covered a thousand miles, marching here to there, trying to find a way through the Yankees and into the fortress; and, although they had not seen much action or gotten into many skirmishes, they knew the Yankees were closing in behind them and slowly surrounding them. Henry had overheard the officers talking, he knew the Yanks had twice as many troops as they did, and more gunpowder and cannons- he heard one of them say that the Confederacy didn't have a snowball's chance in hell of beating the Yankees! That did not sit well with Henry- he wished he was back home with his family… From one day to the next, Henry didn't know if they would be hunkering down or marching, and when they did find a way in, Henry sighed with relief- however, his relief was short-lived.

General Pemberton, trying to please Jefferson Davis, who insisted that Vicksburg and Port Hudson must be held, and also trying to please General Johnston, who thought both places worthless, militarily, had been caught in the middle- a victim of a convoluted command system and, his own indecisiveness- he'd kept his troops on the move for weeks, not going in but not leaving either. Finally, too tired and dispirited to think clearly, he chose to back his bedraggled army into Vicksburg, rather than to evacuate the city and head north, where he might have escaped to campaign again. However, when he chose to take his army into Vicksburg, Pemberton sealed the fate of his troops and the city he had been determined to defend.

Therefore, after a month of being ordered here and there, Henry's regiment was ordered into Vicksburg and told to keep

Sherman, McPherson, and McClermand out. The Yankees quickly surrounded Vicksburg; the Siege of Vicksburg had begun.

A week or so later, General Pemberton received word that General Ulysses S Grant was on his way with even more troops! By this time, the Confederate Army was lacking even the barest of necessary rations to sustain their soldiers; they were living off Johnnie cakes, Cush, and once a day, every other day or so, they got a piece of salt pork and maybe some goober peas.

What jerky, hardtack, and coffee Henry had brought with him was long gone… With each week that passed, he had to take up his belt a notch. The entire army was suffering from near starvation and dysentery…

Since the Union blockades meant no coffee beans, the Southern soldiers had been using whatever was available to make a replacement for coffee. The women of Vicksburg had conjured up a brew and distributed it among the soldiers that consisted of ground peanuts, chicory, wheat, corn, acorns, sweet potatoes and dried apples. The men were appreciative; at least it was palatable and better than what any of them had been able to put together.

On the 19th and 22nd days of May, General Grant and his troops, launched a series of frontal assaults on Pemberton's fortifications- South of Vicksburg, Henry and his fellow soldiers were caught in the middle of it; many succumbed to their injuries- And, as Henry gazed around at the death and destruction that surrounded him, he hoped that Charity and the children were safe; his mind conjured up so many images of the things that could be happening across the ever thickening dark blue line of Yankees closing in on them.

With each passing day, the fighting became heavier; Henry could not help but to worry about his family's safety; he hoped Charity, Jeremiah, and the children had moved into town or gone to stay with Uriah...

Several weeks earlier, to ease his aloneness, Henry had partnered up with a fellow who was from Mt. Polk, which was in Calhoun Co, Alabama; his name was Benjamin Phillips. He, too, had been born in South Carolina; and, the same as Henry had moved his family west to Alabama after hearing how fertile the land there was. Their path in life had taken a similar route.

Benjamin started moving his family to Alabama, about the time Henry and his arrived there. They, too, had eased their way across Georgia. Benjamin said that when he and his wife, Sarah, left Carolina, they had three children and that in the nine years it took them to work their way to Alabama, they'd had three more sons and a daughter. Having a lot in common, Henry and Benjamin hit it off right away. A likable fellow, Benjamin was long and lanky with a soft-toned slow drawl that reminded Henry of his father; Benjamin said he made a living for his family working as a sharecropper for a merchant in Mt. Polk. Henry found himself wishing that he had met Benjamin before the war.

The merchant, that Benjamin sharecropped for, liked to

grow his own crops to sell in his grocery store, and by renting tracts of his land to Benjamin and several others, who each gave the merchant a third of their crops in lieu of rent, the merchant accomplished his goal and Benjamin and the others were satisfied with keeping their families taken care of.

Late at night, when the fighting settled down and they were able to catch a nap, he and Henry would sit and talk about their families and their goals in life. Having grown close, they both agreed that if one or the other of them did not make it out alive, that the other would make sure to get their last messages, to the other one's family. Henry wrote a short letter to Charity and gave it to Benjamin just in case he didn't make it out alive; since Benjamin could not read or write, Henry wrote a letter for him to his wife Sarah and his children.

"You'll have to read it to Sarah;" said Benjamin, solemnly. "She ain't never learnt how to read nor write either."

During a lull in the bombardment, Henry and Benjamin exchanged their letters on a shake and a promise to fulfill their part should the need arise - that was on the 24th day of May, 1863. The next day, Union troops closed ranks and once more began firing upon the starving, bone-tired Confederate troops- that day, the cannon fire never lets up, even as night fell on the ailing City of Vicksburg.

Right before dark the next evening, just before reaching the Big Black River Bridge they were sent to defend, Henry and

Benjamin, along with a dozen or so others in their unit, made it to the high bluffs along the Vicksburg, Jackson, and Brandon Road; not out of cowardice, but rather out of sheer exhaustion, they took refuge in a deep cave cut into the side of the high bluffs behind a thicket of trees. They intended only to stay for a couple of hours, just to close their eyes for a few precious minutes; however, exhausted, tired, and sick, most of them immediately fell into a deep sleep.

As Henry lay there, listening to the boom of cannon fire, he thought of his family- for even as much as he loved them, in the last twenty four hours, he had not had the time to even think of his precious wife and children.

Closing his eyes, Henry envisioned Charity astride her horse Kagali as he galloped across the meadow near their home. The wind blew her long, thick hair out behind her and her lips smiled from the pleasure of being a free spirit as she sat upon his back.

When he called out to her, she turned toward him. When she saw him, her eyes lit with excitement and she turned and rode toward him. As she neared, her expression turned serious. Suddenly, she was in his arms, holding him; he could feel her soft, tender flesh against his as she kissed him. When their lips parted, she whispered words of love and encouragement. Filled with love and longing, her eyes examined his face. If only he could find the strength to wrap his arms around her, all would be well, but he was too weak.

Lila M Beckham

"Don't try to move," she whispered. "Just close your eyes and stay with me." Henry tried to stay there in her arms, but something was pulling him away. Reaching out, he tried to take her offered hand, but she slipped further and further away as a hand on his shoulder kept shaking him, telling him to wake up. It was Benjamin, telling him that they needed to go back out there and help the others defend the bridge. Breathing a heavy sigh, Henry got to his feet; he could still hear the cannons booming and the sound of rifles firing. He had no way of knowing that the Union troops had driven the others in their regiment, further back; he and the other men that had taken refuge with him, were surrounded by Union troops.

Everyone collected their useless rifles and walked to the entrance of the cavern and then began stepping outside the entrance to the cave. Henry heard a Yankee voice yell something. Being taken by surprise the way they were, their natural instinct was to turn and point their weapons in the direction the voice came from; it was a fatal mistake. Hot lead tore through Henry's chest with such force that it knocked him off his feet; the hot, searing pain was horrendous. He heard Benjamin say in disbelief, "I've been shot!"

A roaring sound in Henry's ears began to drown out the noise of the world around him; and then, the outside world began to darken. Suddenly, a bright light drew his eyes toward it- a shadow moving toward him, seemed familiar; it was Charity. He tried to call her name, but could not speak- His eyelids felt heavy;

the extreme pain he felt earlier, was lessening- suddenly, his soul was ripped from his body to rise above it and stare down at himself lying there. Then, he saw her- cradling his limp body in her arms; she was crying. In desperation, he tried to scream her name, but it only came out as a whisper... "Charity"

56

Lost

Bolting upright in bed, Charity stifled a scream. With the realization of what had just happened, the morbid reality of it brought the sting of hot tears to her eyes to her eyes. "Henry!" her mind wailed, silently asking, "Why" to the Great Spirit in the sky. "I tried so hard to get to him; why didn't you let me," she demanded angrily. "Why give me the gift of seeing, when I can do *nothing* to change what I see?" The sound of Henry's last whispered word, "Charity" rang loudly in her ears. Going into the kitchen, she grabbed a knife and poised it above her, wanting to drive it deep into her chest to stop the crushing pain she felt in her heart.

"No, Missy! You cain't do that; you has ta think of the young'uns- they still need you here ta help 'em."

Wailing miserably from the pain she felt in her chest, Charity fell to her knees, pulled her long hair around, and began cutting it with the knife. She was whacking it off so fast that she cut her head in several places before she finished. A million thoughts and memories rushed through her mind so fast that she could not separate them- even though the entire time, her mind kept asking, why? Why did he have to die? Why Henry and not someone else… Suddenly, someone jerked the knife from her hand and strong, comforting arms wrapped around her and stood her to her feet; it was Jeremiah.

"Shh, Missy," he whispered, "everything is gonna be okay."

"It will *never* be okay- *nothing* will ever be okay- *I will never be okay*- don't tell me that *it* will be okay," she whispered vehemently, even as Jeremiah hugged her close and began awkwardly patting her back. When she looked up into Jeremiah's pale, rheumy eyes, she saw that he, too, was in pain. *Henry was like Jeremiah's son…* Pulling him close, she sobbed into his chest.

"What in the world happened?" asked a shocked Mary, looking down at her mother's hair spread on the floor beneath her and Jeremiah's feet.

Charity could not answer her; she felt numb. Her body had lost all sensation. Without asking, Jeremiah knew what must've happened and why Charity wanted to kill herself before she cut off her hair; his old, hands shook more than usual as he tried to make a pot of coffee.

"Help your maw back ta bed," he told Mary. "I'm gonna make her some coffee." Without any questions, Mary led her mother back to her bed. Charity pulled the covers around her shoulders and just laid there and cried. Jeremiah knew what she was feeling; it was the same feeling that had driven him into a whiskey bottle for thirty years of his life.

Henry was like a son to Jeremiah; it broke his old heart to think that he would never again see his friend- never again would he talk with him; at least, not in this life. And, as bad as his old heart hurt, he knew that his loss and his pain was not the same as her loss and pain.

How she knew these things, was a mystery to him; but he had no doubt that she did. It seemed that this gift of hers was as much a curse as it was a blessing. Yes, she could walk the night winds and travel through space and time, but never back in time… if only she could go back in time, she could probably right many wrongs…

When the coffee finished brewing, Jeremiah took Charity a cup. She sat up and took the offered cup and took a sip of the strong, hot liquid.

"I have to go get his body, Jeremiah- I can't just leave him there; I need him near me."

"He *is* near you, Missy," said Jeremiah. "It's only his body that's there; not his spirit; its here with you."

"No, you don't understand," she said brokenly. "That's not what I feel - I feel that his spirit is lost; he can't find his way. I know he must feel lost and alone there, amid all the death that surrounds him."

"How in the world do you think you're gonna be able to find him? And, you can't just take off right in the middle of this war and go to wherever it is you think you're a going to. What you gonna do, Missy- march right through a dang army of

Yankees ta get to 'em!"

"I know where he is! He is near a cave, in a city called Vicksburg. I know I can find him, once I get there."

Jeremiah didn't have the heart to tell her how they deal with burying the dead in wartime. Sure, his body may lay there a day or two, but then they'll dig one big hole and dump all the dead in a mass grave. Finding his body, would be might near impossible. Was it really his body she wanted to find or did she really hope to find his spirit wandering around there somewhere and bring it home with her, he wondered... *By the time she travels across two states to get there, the latter is about all that will be left of Henry.*

After finishing her coffee, Charity got out of bed and woke Jackson; she sent him to get Uriah. Telling him to tell Uriah to come as soon as possible and be prepared to travel. She knew she would need Uriah to help her; she didn't feel that Jackson was quite old enough for what they needed to do- he was heartbroken when he learned why he was being sent to fetch Uriah. After he told Uriah, he was instructed to go by Martha's and tell her that her mother wanted her to come to her.

As she waited, many thoughts went through Charity's mind; one thought in particular stuck with her as she poured herself another cup of coffee and went out onto the porch to smoke; it was about the day she and Charles went to the river of death and talked with Yellow Moon. Charles had tried his best to tell her something, but she had stilled his lips with her finger, telling him that some things were better left unknown- she knew it was bad and did not want to hear what he wanted to tell her... She now wished that she had listened to what Charles had tried to tell her.

Would she have been able to change what was going to happen? She could have tried; even though, she knew in her heart that what was meant to be, would be, no matter what her wishes were. If she had known, it would have been the same as it had with Aaron- she could not have changed anything... she could not have enjoyed life with her love... She wondered if Charles knew that his vision had come to pass.

Charles

Charity had no way of knowing that Charles had also been there; when he knew the time had come, he tried his best to reach his father. Charles knew this day was coming; he had known for years... After reaching the cave and seeing his father lying there, he had stood in the darkness of the cave watching him sleep. He tried, but could not get near his father; there was a force between them; an invisible force that was stronger than his love for his father was. He knew then that his mother was there and the love she felt for Henry was what kept him at bay- her love was the only love that was stronger than his.

Jolted awake by an explosion near him, his spirit returned to his body so quickly that he lost bearing- he closed his eyes and tried to return to his father, but could not. After several minutes, he knew that his father's life on earth was over; he cried.

Upon waking, John also knew what had happened; the moment he saw his brother's tear-stained face, he asked, "Papa?" Charles nodded; that was all he could do. Later that day, they sat beside one another and reminisced over their lives and talked about how thankful and blessed they had been to have such a wonderful and loving father.

"Mama is going to take this mighty hard," said John.

"I know," said Charles. "I only hope she can hold it together- She and Papa have been together most of their lives…"

"Mama won't break- she is the strongest person I've ever known!"

"I know Mama is strong- but I also know how much she loves Papa; this is going to test her heart and her mind… I've had visions; visions that I hope don't come to pass…" Morose and depressed, Charles excused himself so that he could relieve himself at the base of a pine tree. When he returned to where John sat waiting on him, John said:

"We can only hope for the best."

"We need to go to her; but if we desert, they will come looking for us- we may end up dead, too; shot for desertion… Wouldn't that be something- Mama would surely break if that happened," Charles said, thoughtfully.

"Yeah, Little Brother, I know."

Charles had always hated being called "little brother", but

this time, it was comforting.

***

When Uriah arrived, Charity immediately informed him that she wanted him to go with her to look for his father's body or his grave if they had buried him by the time they got there.

"We can't do that Mama; there's a war going on," he replied.

"I don't care what's going on," Charity replied. "I'm going to get your father. You can go with me or I'll go alone," she stated matter-of-factly.

"I'll go with you, Mama," Jackson said excitedly.

"No, Son, I need you here to help Jeremiah and your sisters," Charity told him gently- "Jeremiah is old, your young and strong- you'll be the man of the house while we're gone."

"I can do that," said 15yr old Jackson. "And, when y'all get back, I'm gonna go and sign up and go kill them Yankees that killed Papa!"

Uriah immediately boxed his ear! "Don't go to talking like that- Mama has enough on her mind then to have to worry about you going off and getting yourself killed too! Now, you apologize to Mama."

His pride injured, Jackson said, "I'm sorry, Mama."

"Its okay, Son, I understand."

Turning her attention back to Uriah, Charity said:

"I thought I told Jackson to tell you to be ready to travel."

Uriah sighed in exasperation. "He told me, Mama, but I can't leave at the drop of a hat; I have a family to worry about- I need to make sure that Mary and the children will be safe while I'm gone- I'll see if they can stay with her folks- I'll have to take them over in the wagon... When did you want to leave?"

"The first thing in the morning," she replied. "That should give you time today, to take care of whatever you need to."

To be honest, Charity hated having to wait that long, especially knowing that it would take them nearly a week to get to Vicksburg. She could not relax knowing that Henry's spirit might be lost and that he could not find his way to her. She knew that if he wasn't lost, she would see him- he would have come home...

Uriah left, saying he'd be there as soon as the light allowed the next morning and they'd leave as soon as she was ready- "Don't worry- I'll be ready- you just be here," she said, hugging him before he left.

A long night lay ahead for Charity. She was so restless that she paced the floor for awhile and then when she did lay down, she tossed and turned for what seemed to be hours, and then, when she did close her eyes a begin to doze, she heard Two Feathers calling her.

"Do you hear me, Little One," he called.

"Yes, Grandfather," she replied, letting her spirit rise and drift to him. She wanted to talk to him, but did not want to talk to him; she was afraid of what he might tell her… and, she was also angry at him for not telling her what was going to happen to Henry. At that moment, she was extremely torn over her ability to walk the winds. If she could not walk the winds, she would not have gotten to be with her love. And because she could walk the winds, she was faced with the knowledge of knowing how vulnerable she was and how feeble her attempt to stop or to change what happened to Aaron and Henry. As she drifted through the Spirit World toward Two Feathers' voice, she hoped he could share some words of wisdom that might comfort her.

57

Keeper of the Sacred Flame

When her grandfather appeared before her, he appeared the same as he always had; he was sitting cross-legged by the fire, chanting songs of days long past, and every now and then, he would sprinkle a mixture of powders into the fire. And when he turned to face her, his eyes were still the color of snow, and as shocking as they were the first time Charity saw him all those years ago…

"There you are, Little One; I did not know if you would come."

"It's so dark and murky here that I could not find my way."

"It's not so dark when seen through different eyes," he replied.

"Does it appear that way to me because I feel dark and gloomy?"

"Only you can answer that, Usdi Saquo"

"Why are you always here in the Spirit World, Grandfather- is it because you're dead?" Charity asked, thoughtfully.

"Tla, no, Little One," he replied.

"Then why are you always here, always the same when I

see you?"

"I am the Keeper of the Sacred Flame, Little One. I keep the Sacred Fire burning to light the passageway for those who pass through on their way to the Great Spirit," he explained.

Her heart was suddenly filled with such pain that she could barely speak.

"My Henry was killed, Grandfather... I feel he is lost..."

"I know, Little One; that is why I called you here."

"I will be alone without him. I do not know if I can bear it, Grandfather. My heart feels as if it has been torn from my chest!"

When Two Feathers did not reply, she continued.

"I think his spirit has become lost- he wanders alone somewhere trying to find his way... I have to find him, Grandfather, I just have to!"

"Come here, Little One."

"Please, do not tell me endurance, Enisi! I do not know if I can endure this. Henry is my soul mate, we're one mind, one body, one heart, and one spirit," she explained.

"His earthly body has died, Little One. His spirit must now cross over and travel the path to the light."

"But I need him to stay! Please, Grandfather! Is there not something you can do to stop this- something I can do to hold onto him?"

"Tla. I am sorry, Usdi Saquo; his spirit must seek Unequa Adanvdo. The Great Spirit waits for him at the end of the passageway," he replied.

His words were alcohol poured into the gaping wound that was her heart.

"Your love is strong, Little One. If you interfere with his journey and prevent him from finding his passageway, he can become lost in the Ghost Land. You would not want that, would you; it is where the tormented go."

"No Grandfather, I would not want that," Charity replied. "But I must find him. I have not been able to find him, even when I walked the wind; I fear for his soul!" she cried.

"Do not fear, Little One. When the earthly body dies, the light is revealed. He will have to choose to go -"

"But I fear he will try to find me, and I did not know if he could!"

Charity could hear the frustration in Two Feathers' voice when he spoke.

"I know I cannot stop you from this journey, Little One; it has been laid out from your birth. I did not bring you here to stop you, but to warn you."

Suddenly, Charity was aware of other people sitting around the fire watching and listening to her and Two Feathers talk. Glancing around, she saw four or five men and a woman, the same as she, sitting cross-legged in a circle around the Sacred Flame.

"It is a very dangerous route you plan to take. In your haste to get where you are going and your mournful state, you will not be alert to those dangers. You must choose a new route, one that will take you to the Big Black River. Amotugwalvyi." The others around the fire repeated, "Amotugwalvyi."

"When you reach where the water rolls over rocks there, it will welcome you. You will be among, "yohvstianadvni," your kinfolk. They will guide you onto the safe trail to where your heart leads you."

"How will I know which way is the way you speak of?" she questioned.

"You will know, Little One. If you open your heart and listen with your soul's ears, you will hear them calling to you."

When Two Feathers finished speaking, he raised his pale eyes to hers and then faded away. When she opened her eyes she was back in her bed all alone. She lit the bedside lamp and took a pen and binder out of her trunk.

'*To wake alone; forsaken in this desolate world- no lover to hold my hand, kiss my lips, nor warm my bed on the coldest nights- no one to fill the abyss that is my heart, is the purest form of isolation. In the blink of an eye, our time together was over. It is with heavy heart, my Love that I say goodbye…*'

She wrote those words in a binder she had titled, The Seasons of My Life. Just as her grandmother had told her story on a quilt, Charity told hers with paper, ink, and pigments… All through the book, she had written of different occurrences in her life, sketched miniature scenes from the stories she told and scenes from memories of her travels- there was also portraits of certain people, or ghosts that others could not see with their eyes… Portraits filled many pages of the book; each labeled by name - Her grandmother and grandfather that raised her- Tokola, Two Feathers and his snow-white eyes- a portrait of the big, hawk-faced Indian, Unegadihi- A portrait of Jeremiah; also, one of what Mrs. Finley, whose cabin they lived in in Canton, looked like in life… there was even a drawing of the evil, Captain Wheeler…

***

Outfitting the old wagon with what he thought should be enough dry goods to get them through a week, Uriah was packed and ready; they could hunt or fish for what meat they needed. He was afraid to pack too much, for fear it would be taken from them on the trail. He arrived to pick Charity up just after daybreak the next morning. If everything went as planned, he figured they would make it to Vicksburg in about a week. He was very nervous about this journey. With all the battles that were taking place, it was dangerous to travel.

After they were loaded and leaving the cabin, Uriah asked, "Why don't we go down to Anniston and see if the army will send an escort with us?"

"They won't do that- they'll think me crazy for even attempting it. Besides, they don't have the men to spare; the Yankees have twice as many men fighting in this war. Haven't you noticed how starving and ragged our men are? We will make it fine by ourselves," she assured him.

They traveled through the first day without incident. About thirty minutes before dark, they stopped to bed down for the night. It would be another restless night for Charity; she was up and down all night. The sound of Uriah's soft snores, assured her that he was resting easy.

By the next afternoon, they had reached the outskirts of the small town of Jasper, Alabama. It consisted of half a dozen houses, a couple of two-storied buildings, and a combination jail and saloon; the town was almost deserted.

The mercantile had a sign outside the door, in big, red letters that said, 'Don't bother breaking in - it's not locked. Either the Yankees or the Confederate Army has taken everything!'

"Good Lord, Mama; it's getting bad ain't it?"

"Yes, Son, it is; and it's only going to get worse before it's over."

The third day out, they came to a river crossing. When they got down, they stretched their legs and refilled the fresh water supply; they saw that the river was teeming with small bream. The fish were spawning along the riverbank.

As he edged closer to the river and waited for the small fish to settle down, Uriah felt proud that he had thought to bring a fishnet. As soon as the fish settled, he made them run again, swooping about six of the hand-sized fish up with his net. We'll eat a good supper tonight, he thought to himself as he cleaned them and readied them for his mother to fry.

He knew how much his mother liked fried fish- he hoped

the fish would tempt her appetite; he had noticed that she wasn't eating much at all and it worried him- he also knew that she was not getting much rest either - the dark circles and bags under eyes told the tale. She wasn't talking much either, and that wasn't like her. He wondered what was going on in her mind. When he asked why she was so quiet, she had said, simply that she was listening.

"Listening for what?" he had asked.

"For the yohvstianadvni," she told him.

"The what?"

Charity had forgotten that Uriah didn't understand Cherokee- he hadn't heard her speak much Cherokee at all since he was a young boy... she felt a pang of guilt for not continuing their lessons after reaching Alabama- so much changed and they had grown old enough to work and to fall in love and want lives of their own... time just slipped away. So caught up in her own thoughts was she that she never responded to his question. Uriah did not know who or what the 'yohvstianadvni' were, but he was not going to pester her about it.

The further they traveled west, the less hilly the land became. One could tell that there had once been plenty of pine trees located in the area they were in, but the scars of war were everywhere they looked- the war had taken its toll on mother earth.

About four days out, they crossed through an area where a

recent battle had taken place- Uriah was surprised to see dead bodies lying on the battlefield... *Where did the other soldiers go? Did the Yankees kill all the Confederates and vice versa?* He thought that they would have at least buried their dead...

Glancing out the corner of his eye to look at his mother, it sort of surprised him to see the look of horror in her eyes. *She must be wondering if Papa is lying like this somewhere, exposed to vultures and scavengers...*

However, it was not the vultures and scavengers that horrified and sickened Charity; it was the emotion the souls of the dead were feeling as they wandered around lost and alone, not knowing how they came to be there- it was almost overwhelming. Sometimes, when life ends suddenly, the spirit can be thrown out into nothingness... Charity felt guilty for turning away from them, but they would have to wait; Henry was her only concern.

58

The Mother Mound

Early June, 1863

About noon, the fifth day of their journey, Charity told Uriah to stop the wagon. When he looked around, Uriah did not see anything in particular that caught his attention and did not know why his mother wanted to stop there; as far as he could tell, there was not anything they needed there. His mother had not asked to get down off the wagon and go pee or said anything about eating lunch. So, after applying the brake to keep the horses and wagon at a complete halt, he turned to Charity and asked, "Why did you want me to stop?"

"Shush!" she said quickly, "I'm listening."

Watching her facial expressions, Uriah wondered what she was listening to and why she looked so intense. After a minute, he saw her smile.

"What do you hear, Mama?" he asked anxiously.

"I hear an eagle soaring, a river running, people dancing, the moon rising, the sun setting- We are almost there!" she exclaimed, happily.

"Where, Mama?"

"We are near the Mother Mound; the land of our kin, the Choctaw. They will guide me on the right route. I heard a voice say, "Beloved woman, who see's a vision. Follow the ray of light over the red water. Keep going," Charity told him.

All afternoon, in silence they traveled. Uriah had not questioned her anymore; he could see that she was still listening for something and he did not want to bother her; however, when he saw that the sun was setting low on the horizon, he became worried that they would be caught making camp in the dark, so he turned to his mother and asked, "Don't we need to be stopping soon, Mama? It'll be too dark to make camp if we don't."

"Soon, but not yet," she replied.

About thirty minutes later they came to a high point of land, where, when they looked around, one could see for miles.

"We are atop the Mother Mound," she said, "Stop here." Looking ahead, they saw a river in the distance; the sunset turned the river red. At one point of the river, a bright, ray of light shone. "When we leave in the morning, we must go in that direction," she said, pointing to the bright spot on the river.

"We must find a way to mark that direction; it will look different in the morning with the sun behind us."

"That's easy enough," said Uriah. "I'll just point the tongue of the wagon in that direction, before I un-harness the horses." Charity smiled at his indulgent understanding of her wishes by not asking more questions.

After days of traveling and not sleeping well, Charity felt

tired and weak- she could tell that Uriah wasn't feeling too frisky himself- she hoped they would both get some much needed sleep that night. After a heavy supper, she did sleep, but it was not a restful sleep; it was sleep filled with many dreams. Dreams that caused her to feel even more tired each time she awakened from them. In one particular dream, she saw the lost, wandering souls, they'd passed on the battlefield and ignored; they were now haunting her dreams because she did not stop to help them…

Just after daybreak the next morning, they were again on the road. When they reached the river, they saw that the bridge had been blown up. After finding a shallow place to cross and crossing the river, Charity was once again at a loss as to which direction they needed to go to get to Vicksburg.

Sitting there in limbo, Uriah became slightly worried. The woman sitting beside him with a look of confusion on her face was not the same woman that had taken him and his siblings slap across Georgia on her own; that woman's propensity had always been to follow her instincts… He could see that his father's death was breaking her spirit- she seemed to be withering away…

"Why don't we keep going in this direction, Mama; the trail ahead is still clear; we can make good time."

"Alright," Charity replied. "I'll keep listening for directions."

Soon, they came to another river. This river was wider than the last one was and the water was so dark that it was almost black.

Sitting there, staring into the river, Charity suddenly remembered Two Feathers' words about the route that would take her to the 'big, black river'.

"We must follow the river down along the watershed and then cross it; that is where I saw your father- he should still be there."

"We need to make camp soon- we can travel another hour and then we have to stop," said Uriah, turning the team south to follow the snakelike river.

Early the next morning, as they prepared to break camp, the faint sounds of cannons firing, greeted their ears. Gazing off in the distance, Uriah asked, "What are we going to do, Mama?"

"We keep going," Charity said, sharply, seemingly without any concern whatsoever for their safety.

Thinking that maybe his mother was indeed losing control of her senses, Uriah said, "Mama, don't you think that it might be -"

"Dangerous," she snapped, cutting him off mid-sentence. "I know it might be dangerous," she said, "however, you need to understand that I have to try. When ya'll were little and we were crossing Georgia, there was danger every way we turned; we couldn't just stop, or turn around and go back home; your father was missing then, just as he is now. We have to try to get to him; he needs me!"

When he gazed into her eyes, Uriah realized that desperation was driving his mother, and the single-minded, determination, he saw on her face, was the same strength of mind he'd seen when he was a young boy. He had never questioned her judgment, then; so why should he start now? His eyes filled with compassion, Uriah gazed upon his mother's resolute face a moment longer and then geed to the horse to go. It would not be him that stopped her; it would be the Union Army.

They made it to within ten miles of their destination, Vicksburg, Mississippi, before they encountered their first obstacle. Union troops were blocking every access road into or out of Vicksburg. A burly sergeant, with a nasally sounding voice, stopped them and asked, "Just where you all think you're going?"

"My husband was murdered; we have come to collect his body, so we can take him home for burial," Charity replied.

"Have you now - don't you know there is a war going on; it's not safe to be in this area," he said.

"Of course, I know there is a war going on; that is why my husband is dead!" Charity replied smartly.

"Killed while fighting for the Confederacy, huh," said the sergeant with a slur as if the word Confederacy was poison on his tongue.

"It doesn't matter who he was fighting for," Charity told him, "he was my husband, the father of my children- I've come to take him home."

"Ma'am, it's not going to be possible; the dead have not yet been identified. As we get closer to Vicksburg, we're finding a good many soldiers dead; and, we've already captured many Rebel Soldiers that weren't able to run; they are being transported to another location. The dead are being buried, Ma'am," said the sergeant, talking to her as though she was dense.

"Where are they being buried?" asked Charity.

"Some are buried where they lay," he replied. "If they're not too badly decomposed, they're loaded onto wagons and taken to where the captured prisoners are held to see if they can be identified so that we can record their name before burial. We don't have the luxury of ceremony, Ma'am. Most confederates are buried in mass graves to keep down the spread of pestilence and disease their rotting carcasses are spawning."

"What does 'mass grave' mean, Sergeant?" asked Charity, confused.

"It means that we bury the lot of them, together; dump them in one great big old hole; it's easier that way," he said, grinning.

Charity knew that he was just trying to shock and provoke her. She also noticed how white Uriah's knuckles were getting, as he held tightly to the reins.

"I can't let you through, Ma'am; not until this siege is over, and we have captured all those Rebel Scabs."

"You must let me through! It will only take me a little while; I know where I need to go," Charity told the sergeant.

"How are we to you two are not Rebel Spies, sent here to-"

A younger Union Soldier, this one wearing a different style of uniform, interrupted the sergeant's rebut when he came over and asked, "What seems to be the trouble, Sergeant?"

"Well, Sir," said the sergeant, holding himself more erect as if at attention. "This woman here says that she is here to claim her husband's remains- he's one of those dead Confederates."

"Ma'am, I do apologize for my sergeants' rough manner. I am Captain Jonathon Brewer." Charity nodded her head.

"Ma'am," he said, his voice softening, "the sergeant is right; the city is under siege, we cannot let you go past this line. There is shelling going on; it is not at all safe for a woman, or any civilian for that matter," he said, glancing at Uriah who was still seated in the wagon.

"Please, Captain," said Charity, feeling the need to beg his mercy. "I know where he was killed- it won't take me long," she said, tears forming in her eyes.

"Now, how would you know that?" he asked curiously.

"I saw his death in a… in a dream," she stammered, knowing they would think she had gone mad; and, they did.

The beefy, Sergeant laughed aloud at her statement, while making an unpleasant face and then he twirled a finger beside his head, indicating that he thought her loony. Looking at his grinning mouth, she thought to herself that if she had a gun in her hand, she would shoot him right between his beady eyes!

"I guess you find that amusing, Sergeant," she said, adding, "I know many things are going to happen before they happen," she said, with a slight curvature of her lips as a vision of his arm being blown off, flashed through her mind. He stopped laughing when he saw the look in her eyes. He had never seen anyone look at him the way she did.

If looks could kill, I'd be a dead man, he thought to himself.

59

Ghostly Reckonings

Climbing onto the wagon, Charity said, "Let's go."

"I'm truly am sorry, Ma'am," said Captain Brewer, his voice flat and unemotional. "I cannot let you go through; you will have to go back home."

Uriah geed to the horses to get them moving and then turned the wagon around and headed it back in the direction they had come. Charity turned and gave the sergeant another hard stare before turning her head to look in the direction they were traveling.

In silence, they traveled; both feeling the sting of defeat. After they had traveled about a half a mile, Uriah stopped and turned to his mother. "What are we going to do," he asked.

With a heavy heart, Charity sighed and said, "I reckon we will have to go home and wait; however, we do have to make one stop for sure. I need to rectify my actions- by me ignoring all those dead soldiers we saw back on that battlefield, the Great Father above did not make a way for me to get to your father- I have to help those lost souls find their way, before the Great Father above will help me find my way to your father."

When the Yellow Mocker Calls

The battlefield was a day's ride back toward Jackson, Mississippi. When they reached it- a dozen buzzards circled above. Even in the light of day, scavengers were feasting heartily as Uriah pulled the wagon off the road and found a shady place to park. Wolves, coyotes, possums, and an assortment of birds eyed them as they alit from the wagon.

While Uriah unhitched the wagon and staked out the horses, Charity prepared herself to assist the half dozen lost souls that still wandered the battlefield; she knew that once they knew that she could see them, they would come to her. She wished that Two Feathers would come… she needed to talk to him. She had Uriah build her a fire at the edge of the battlefield about fifty feet from where he parked the wagon. Meanwhile, she let down her hair and braided it; then, she donned her Asani and positioned herself behind the fire. Crossing her legs, she sat down and began to chant a singsong melody; and, although the song was directed toward Great Spirit above it began to draw the souls toward her. She waited.

Unable to see what his mother saw, Uriah set about making camp for the night and fixing them something to eat, once he had snared a jackrabbit down by a thin, trickling creek while his mother was doing whatever it was she did to help dead people.

The first soul to come to Charity was that of a young Tennessean named Ernest Cobb- Ernest said that his family lived in Rutherford County, but he didn't know how to get there from where he was… Charity wanted to ask him if he knew where he was, but didn't; she did not want to traumatize him any more than what he already was.

When she informed him that he was dead and that he needed to go toward the light, he bowed his head and looked down. Then he told her that he accepted it, but that he would like to go and say goodbye to his folks. She told him to picture his home in his mind and concentrate on it; his thoughts should take him there, but not to forget about the light. He nodded his head and then faded from her sight.

The second soul that came to her was that of a man about Henry's age who told her that he was from Baton Rouge; the tone of his voice was pleasing to her ear. Although older, he was not as accepting of his fate as the young Tennessean had been. He tried to out talk her; told her that she needed to go back to wherever it was she came from, and that he was not dead. It took him standing by and watching several others come to her and learn their fate before he was willing to accept his. Once he realized that before entering the light, he could go home and in some way say goodbye to his loved ones, he moved on.

The last soul to stand before her was that of a boy of about sixteen years; but whose mind had been that of a much younger person. The sensations she received when he neared her, brought forth her motherly instinct- His uncharacteristic luminosity and defining gentleness brought tears to her eyes; he was much too young to die- She knew that his soul had lived a pure, unadulterated life. It was not that of some souls who she could tell had been around a long time- his soul was newly born… Assisting this young soul to move forward was heartbreaking and drained every ounce of energy she had- Charity hoped with all her heart that they did not run across anymore lost souls before they reached home…

✳✳✳

It took her and Uriah another week to make the trip home. When they arrived, Jeremiah and the children were glad to see them. Jeremiah wasn't a bit surprised when Charity and Uriah told him the details of their failed mission and how the Yankees had refused to let them pass.

"What are you planning to do, Missy," he asked, as they sat on the porch drinking makeshift coffee and enjoying their tobacco.

"I plan to go back as soon as the Yankees quit shelling Vicksburg; that's what I plan on doing."

"So you do, do you…"

"Yes, Sir, I do. That sergeant told us that they had them under siege. I know what *siege* means, so I know they cannot hold out much longer. With forty thousand men, women, and children there, I'm surprised they've lasted this long. Without a supply of food and other necessary supplies, they will have to surrender soon, or die of starvation," Charity replied viciously, her voice scathing; she could not help but be angry.

Another month would pass before the Confederates were

starved down enough to give up. By the end of the first week in July, the folks besieged in Vicksburg were in their final death throes; that was when the Confederate Army finally surrendered Vicksburg.

Lt. Gen. John C. Pemberton surrendered Vicksburg to General Ulysses S. Grant on the 4th day of July 1863. It took six days for news of the surrender to reach Charity; she quickly began making plans for a return trip to Vicksburg. They had received official notice of Henry's death, about mid-June; seeing the wrinkled parchment with Henry's name written on it, only renewed her resolve to go there and find Henry's body and bring him home…

After the disappointing outcome of their previous journey, Charity was determined that this time, she would not fail. Jeremiah doubted that she would find Henry; however, he kept those doubts to himself. He did not want to discourage her or to cause Charity more worry than she already had… The battle for Vicksburg might have been over, but the war was far from it.

Since Henry's death, Charity had lost so much weight that her family was worried about her; however, when they said something about it to her, she pointed out that most of them had also lost a significant amount of weight. Many times, she ate just enough to satisfy the hunger pangs in her stomach, hoping by doing so she could make sure that the younger children got enough to keep them growing; she knew their young, growing bodies needed more sustenance than she did…

While she and Uriah were getting ready to go back to Vicksburg, Nancy and Sarah came out with a letter that was addressed to her from Charles. Sarah had also gotten a letter from John.

In his letter, Charles said that he was writing to let her know that he and John were all right. He told her that in the middle of June they were sent to a place called Gettysburg, where they were involved in a large campaign and took part in a battle that took place the first few days of July. He said that in all the campaigns and battles he'd been involved in, Gettysburg was by far the most intense- thousands of men lost their lives there… He also told her that he and John knew about their father's death and that he was very sorry she had to go through the loss without her entire family around her. He did not want her to worry about him and John; he said that they would make it through.

Charity was glad that Charles sounded so positive. She often wondered why she could see some things and not others. Her ability to foresee events close to her had never been keen; however, it seemed that Charles had inherited that ability along with his ability to walk the winds… and, whatever other abilities he had… She would have to ask her grandfather, about this… Realizing just how little she knew of Charles' abilities caused her a pang of guilt; it had been years since the two of them had had a real heart to heart conversation.

After reading Charles' letter, she slipped it into her pocket and resumed packing what she and Uriah would need for the trip to Vicksburg.

Although she knew that Henry was most surely dead, for she had seen him die… The official report said that he was missing and presumed dead… It was easy enough to imagine that he was somewhere- maybe he was lost in the swamps around Vicksburg- maybe he was alive and trying to find his way back to camp… In her mind, she could easily picture his face when the two of them met again… she could almost feel the caress of his lips on hers…

60

Searching Vicksburg

Mid-July 1863

Following the same route as before, Uriah headed the old wagon toward Vicksburg. This time, there were no voices to guide her; this time, they did not need any guidance. Urgency fueled her to get there and find the cave she saw in her vision; however, it caused her to be anxious and fidgety; the week it took them to get there, seemed an eternity to Charity… The roads were not as deserted as they had been the first time they traveled there and that worried Uriah- he was afraid that someone would try and take the old wagon and team away from them… He breathed a sigh of relief as they passed the Mother Mound and entered the last leg of their Journey.

Driving down the main road into Vicksburg, after they passed the spot the burly sergeant and his men stopped them at on their previous trip there- it was Charity's turn to breathe a sigh of relief, somewhat relaxing her guard as they rode along the rutted, red-dirt road. Trenched deep from thousands of marching footsteps and mules pulling heavy artillery on them, the bumpy roads drove their tailbones deep into the rough sawn wagon seat, making the last few miles travel excruciatingly painful for Charity.

Trying to take her mind off of how uncomfortable the wagon seat had become, Charity began to look around at the scenery. It was the first time she noticed how lush, green, and beautiful the coniferous swamp they were traveling through was. The forest whispered soothing sounds to her from the tall cypresses and pines when a gentle wind blew through them. Abundant, dark olive colored kudzu vines twined upward from the earth, frapping the undergrowth and trees, forming giant kudzu castles that were soothing to look at and caused a cooling sensation as they traveled beneath the shade they created on that hot July morning. As they neared the Mississippi River, the breeze felt cooler, but had an unnatural odor to it. The ground changed from red clay to sandy loam and was not quite as hard and bumpy as the red clay had been. Charity told Uriah to take the next little road to the left; she said it would lead them to the cave. Uriah thought it more of a pig trail than a road…

After they traveled several hundred feet off the main road, a familiar sensation settled upon her and drew her attention to her right. "There it is!" she exclaimed, trying to get down off the wagon before Uriah could get it stopped. Once down, she ran up the hill, toward where she knew the cave should be, and then, stopped short. "He's not here!"

Slowly, Charity walked to the spot where Henry had been shot. There was not any blood on the ground, but there were drag and scuffle marks. Looking all around, there were no bodies or evidence of anyone being buried there.

"Maybe, they're in the cave," Uriah offered.

Charity nodded, but even as Uriah went to get the lantern out of the wagon, so they could look inside the cave, she knew that neither Henry's spirit nor his body was there.

Uriah searched the cave, but did not find his father's body.

Turning to face Uriah, Charity said, "We must go and talk to whoever is in charge. Maybe they can tell us where they buried your father."

Uriah nodded his head; however, his thoughts went to the day they were stopped by the brash sergeant and when he'd said about mass burials.

As if she could read his mind, Charity snapped, "Don't you even think about that, Uriah Gullege!" He wondered how she could do that- and voiced his thoughts before he could check himself.

"Because, the same thing crossed my mind, that's how."

Getting back into the wagon, they drove on into Vicksburg. Neither was prepared for the sight that greeted them. What they smelled and saw turned their stomachs; the stench of rotting flesh roasting in the hot July sun was unbearable. The dead were laid out; the wounded hobbled from one spot to another chasing the afternoon shade, and there were numerous spirits roaming the area.

Staring at the dead men, women, and children of Vicksburg,

laying out for the flies, maggots, and crows to feed upon, sickened Uriah. "Good Lord!" he exclaimed. "Why can't they at least bury them?"

In her mind, Charity understood why the dead were laid out the way they were; it appeared they had laid them out so folks could walk past and easily be able to identify them.

Immediately, she got down off the wagon and headed toward the bodies; a man's familiar voice stopped her. She turned to see Captain Brewer walking toward her. She had hoped never to have to lay eyes on him again- she definitely did not want to see that sergeant again; the thought of him angered her - she wondered if his arm had gotten blown off like in the vision she had.

Captain Brewer asked if he could help her. She had to admit that despite being a Yankee, Captain Brewer seemed to be a nice young man.

While pulling the notification letter she received out of her pocket, she told Captain Brewer that since she had been officially notified that Henry was missing and presumed dead, she had come back to try and find his body so she could take him home for burial.

The look on his face did not give any indication as to what was on his mind. He cleared his throat and said, "Ma'am, do you know when your husband went missing or was killed? I know it had to be prior to your last visit; am I right?" Brewer asked.

"Yes," Charity replied. "He- It was the 26th of May, Captain."

"Ma'am, I'm sure they've already buried the men killed in May," said the captain, his tone solemn.

"Where did they bury them, Captain?"

"I expect that most were buried in mass graves, before we took control of Vicksburg. Since taking command, we've had to bury over 12,000 unidentified soldiers and civilians. As you can see, we've laid them out in rows, trying to identify the dead; however, you must understand that they have to be buried. We have no other choice. If your husband is not among those lying here, then surely, he is buried with the others," he said apologetically.

Nodding her head, Charity began the task of walking through the rows of dead and looking at the soldiers that had been captured and placed in stockades. After doing so and not finding Henry, she went back to the Captain.

"Where are those mass graves, you spoke of Captain?"

"I can show you, Ma'am, however, I don't think it will help since they've already been buried- you have to understand that in this heat, over a month past- decomposition alone would prevent any sort of identification…"

Charity did not want to think of Henry as a rotting corpse, she quickly wiped that image from her mind as she replied, "Maybe not, Captain, but I'd still like to see the graves- if nothing more than my own self-examination."

Sighing, Captain Brewer told her the burial plots were about a half mile away and that they would fare better to take their wagon so that she would not have to walk it. "I'll get my horse and join you shortly," he said.

Climbing back onto the wagon to wait, Charity sat on the rough, hard wagon seat and looked around. Everywhere she looked, death and devastation greeted her eyes. Restless spirits wandered through the muddy, rutted streets appearing lost and confused. She knew they must be wondering why they were there, many of them, not understanding what happened to them. Some, she could tell, knew what had happened to them, but did not accept that they had died. Henry's spirit was not among those she saw...

While Charity was walking the rows of dead and looking at the men in the stockade, Captain Brewer had checked both the list of those killed in May, left by the Confederates, and Union's list of known burials; he did not find Henry's name listed on either, therefore, he had to assume that Henry was buried along with the thousands of others that had not been identified despite how they had tried to identify them... He felt bad for Charity's loss, but did not want to offer her false hope of finding him. To appease her, he was going to lead them out to the burial site. He hoped going there would at least offer her some closure...

Following behind Captain Brewer in their wagon, Charity realized something about her gift; many of the spirits that she encountered were not in physical form; however, to her, they appeared as they had in life, the way they looked before they died. This made her think of her grandfather, Two Feathers; he always appeared to her, not in his spirit form, but looking exactly as he had the first time she saw him at Fort Charlotte and as the last time she saw him alive, when they met along the Yellow River. Why? Wondered Charity... however, somehow, in the back of her mind, she already knew the answer; long ago, he'd given the answer to her...

The dirt road leading out to the burial mounds had deep ruts worn into it from the heavy wagons traveling on it after the recent rains. The jarring was hard on Charity's back; however, it did not dissuade her from going. When they arrived at the burial site, several dozen men were digging long trenches. Other men were rolling bodies down into them for burial; and there were more men whose job was to shovel the yellow clay earth of Vicksburg, atop the bodies in order to fill in the trenches and bury the dead.

The sensation of so many spirits around her had become overwhelming; Charity thought she was going to be sick. That feeling along with the stench of decaying flesh was almost more than she could bear- she said a quick prayer for the strength she needed to endure this leg of her mission. Images of Henry decomposing flashed through her mind; quickly, she pushed them away and pictured Henry as he looked before he left home to fight in this Godforsaken war. Henry's image was just as quickly pushed from her mind by the lost and restless spirits that were drawn to her- it was too much; she vomited over the side of the wagon... If Henry was among those there, she could not sense him.

Before they even stopped, she turned to Uriah and said, "I'm ready to go." Without question, Uriah turned the wagon around and headed back toward Vicksburg, he, too, was ready to give up. Not really wanting to drive through Vicksburg again, but having no choice, since it was the only route he knew, he urged the horses to a speed that was more than an amble and gripped the reins. He could tell that Charity was trying to control the nausea that must be rising in her throat again; he too, felt queasy. He knew that the sooner they drove past Vicksburg and left the area the better they'd both feel...

The young captain felt sorry for them as he watched them drive away.

"In one way or another, we've all been affected by this war," he thought to himself. Just the previous week, he lost his older brother, who was killed in the fighting at Gettysburg. It seemed to him that the North had many advantages over the South; especially when it came to burying their soldiers. *At least, most of our soldiers are buried in single graves...*

***

Traveling the now more than familiar path home, Charity's mind was full of thoughts; for days, she barely spoke. Uriah grew more concerned about her sanity. Charity knew that she was sinking deeper into the great abyss of depression; however, she could not find the strength to pull herself out. She wasn't sure she would ever want to leave the abyss; she felt safe there; Henry was there… And, as the war raged around them, Charity sat on the front porch, smoked her pipe, drank makeshift coffee, and relived the past over and over in her mind. Even though, Two Feathers had warned her not to let yesterday use up too much of today, she could not stop herself from living in the past… It was the only place she wanted to be- the only place she needed to be…

61

Limbo

Some people seek solace from the living, while others find solace in solitude…

Living in a self-imposed state of uncertainty, Charity did not want or need outside interactions; she just wanted to be left alone...

As the days drifted by, one melding into the next, winter came again; however, the change of days went unnoticed by Charity; to her, one day was the same as the last… She paid little attention to anything or anyone around her, even little Robert Henry who no longer tried to crawl onto his mother's lap and seek comfort there; he had begun to cling to his sister, Mary. It was only natural since it was Mary that took care of him and saw to his every need; she had done so since that day in May when Charity knew that Henry was dead. Mary had become a mother figure for four year old Robert Henry…

Charity was not the only one suffering from the loss of Henry; Jeremiah had also sunken into a great depression. Affected by age and crippling arthritis, suffering the loss of his old friend, and now having to watch Charity wither away before his very eyes, living life seemed just too much to strive for; Jeremiah felt lonely and alone. Even knowing that time heals all wounds, was no comfort to him; he feared he did not have the luxury of time on his side. If not for the sake of the children, especially Emmy, who had become his favorite, Jeremiah would have ended life on his own terms…

The winter of 1863 was a mild one. And while that was good for most, for others, it was not. It did not snow that year, however, the temperatures were up and down from freezing one day to near summertime weather, the next. The fluctuating temperatures took their toll on the weak and infirmed who developed pleurisy and other debilitating ailments; the changes affected soldiers and civilians alike. Jeremiah was among those that were affected the worst. He became sick just after Christmas, and within a week, he died.

At least Charity had come out of her self-imposed solitude, long enough to hold her old friend's hand and ease his passing into the next realm. Silently, she let her tears fall as they laid him to rest beneath the old live oak tree, in the spot where he had said he wanted to be buried. She knew that even though his body was buried deep in the earth, his spirit would search out those that had passed before him and seek those he had loved in life; and, she wasn't wrong- he sat on the porch for days, watching her, waiting for her to notice him… Why could not Henry do the same… why had he not come to her?

The only one that seemed to notice that Jeremiah had not crossed over was Emmy and she was extremely happy that he had not gone and left her, too. The two of them spent hours together, talking and playing- Emmy loved Jeremiah and was happy that he was no longer bent and twisted, no longer crippled. It didn't take long for them to develop a system of measurements to gage how far the appendage of Jeremiah's soul could travel from his grave as they took small trips exploring the lands around the cabin… When Jeremiah stopped, Emmy stopped and returned home; oftentimes, after encouraging him to go just a little further, pushing the limits of his tether.

***

Like the soul of an unbaptized child; an entire year passed while she existed in Lim·boplace; Purgatory to her, awaiting some sort of delivery from a life she chose not to live… A life she did not want to live… what was the use of living life without Henry by her side…

For months, day after day, she sat out on the porch, watching and waiting; her family gave up trying to tempt her back to life. After several more months, she took to her bed. Day after day, night after night, she lay there waiting for her life to end… With their father gone, their mother the way she was, and little in the way of provisions, the children still living there with her had no anticipation of the morrow.

When the Yellow Mocker Calls

On the eve of Christmas, there were no excited whispers wondering what gift they'd receive, no licorice whips for the little one to enjoy. This year, as the last, Christmas would not be a happy occasion.

With pity in their eyes, Mary and Cynthia watched their mother lay there, each, wondering if there was something they could do, someone they could call on to help. Uriah had ridden over every week to check on them; many times, bringing them what little he could spare from caring for his own wife and children. He, too, was at a loss as to what to do. Sitting beside her bed, he begged his mother to get up and take care of her responsibilities; telling her that when someone dies, life goes on for the living… she did not respond.

When Martha's husband, Ollie Henry was killed, she and her children had gone to live with Ollie's parents, therefore, she could only come on occasion; however, her mother did not respond to her either…

Nancy and Sarah had come out three times that year and brought them what supplies they could spare, but the same as with Uriah and Martha, Charity did not respond to them- she even turned over and stayed covered until they left. The only time she left her bed was to go out to the toilet, smoke her pipe, or to scrounge a small amount of food from the kitchen- never did she attempt to eat until everyone else in the house had eaten.

As she lay there on that chilly eve of Christmas in 1864,

snuggled deep within the comfort of her grandmother's season of life quilt, the last person she wanted to hear from was Two Feathers- What use was having the power to speak to the dead, if she could not speak to the one she wanted to speak to.

As she lay there, the ever elusive sleep evading her, from somewhere far away, she heard her grandfather's chant begin; she was not anxious to talk to him; not this time. "Go away Enisi and leave me alone!"

He did not stop; instead, his chants became louder and more insistent as he called her to him. Suddenly, she stood before him in the circle of the light of his Sacred Fire. "I don't want to be here! I don't want to talk to you," she said.

"Na hi yu ni hi, sge' u sti, soqua, awanihu!" he said firmly. "Then you will listen, Little One, for I am speaking!" he exclaimed loudly, sprinkling some of his powders into the fire, which caused multi-colored flames to leap higher than his head. "What are you doing?" he demanded. "U 'no le, 'ga no 'lv sga atsehi, eladi nvnehi. The wind, it is now blowing down a new path.

"You must be strong of heart, Little One- You are not dead! You lay around, waiting for death to claim you- You think death will end your loneliness. What of your life? What of those that live because of you? Your children are here, Little One," he said, pounding a tight-balled fist against his heart. "Think of them."

"Aya tla u du li ha, ganodu, Enisi," she said. "I want to die, Grandfather... my heart has died- I want to be with my husband!" Charity exclaimed.

"He wants you to live. He wants you to breathe life into your children. They still need you, Little One - Can you not see that they need you. Henry would not want your death," Two Feathers said sternly.

"How do you know, Grandfather? How do you know what he would want; have you spoken to him?" Charity asked angrily.

"Tla, I know because you love him so deeply that you want to join him. He must be a strong, brave man, for you to give him your whole heart," he said softly. Her grandfather's words were beginning to sink in; tears stung her eyes and she cried in shame. She was ashamed that she had let her husband down... So busy was she, wallowing in her own misery, she could not, did not, want to think about what anyone else was feeling.

"I don't know how to stop... What shall I do, Grandfather?"

"You will live- you will be strong. You will live for your lover- you will live for your children; and, you will live for me, Little One. When your earthly body no longer exists, you will become the Keeper of the Sacred Fire."

"I thought you died many years ago, but you once told me that you are not dead- are you dead, Grandfather?"

"Only my earthly body, Usdi Saquo," he answered.

"Where are you? How is it that I still see you, hear you, and talk to you?"

"We are one," he answered, beginning a short Chant.

"My life's blood, flows through your body. My breath breathes within your body. My soul, lives within your soul; I dwell within your dreams. We are one," he repeated. "Soon, I will take your hand; we shall become complete."

"Grandfather, you did not answer my question! Where are you? Where is the Fire," she asked, reaching her hand out to touch the flames.

"When my friend, the Yellow Mocker, called my name, my soul traveled to Skiahi. That is where it dwells- the Sacred Fires' Ashes, are kept there."

When she reached out to touch him, he was gone.

Awakening an hour or so before dawn, Charity felt rested and renewed. "Grandfather," she mumbled, a slight smile creasing her lips. *Was it a dream or did she really talk to him? No time to think about that; she had much to do.* Getting her old rifle out of the wardrobe, she cleaned it and then headed out through the back field toward the creek. That was when she realized that she had been immobile for far too many days. Her legs had become weak from nonuse. She laughed at herself for acting the way she had; Henry wouldn't want her to lie around being miserable. When crossing Georgia and they were separated, she didn't lie down to die- she fought hard to get to where her heart told her she needed to go- Her children were hungry and it was Christmas!

Hunkering down near a huckleberry thicket, she loaded her

rifle and waited. When the black powder cleared, the gobbler was still flopping around on the ground. She rung his neck and then headed toward home, collecting a few herbs along the way. Squatting near the huckleberry thicket, she spotted fresh rabbit droppings and she saw that a wild boar had been rooting under the bushes there, foraging for food. The Turkey would be enough for today; she'd come back for the rabbit and boar later. She stopped at the cave and got the tin she had stored several pounds of flour and meal in with bay leaves to keep the weevils out and took it with her- Her family was going to have Christmas dinner today!

Charity surprised the children when she came through the door toting the turkey she killed. They didn't get presents or candy that Christmas, they didn't even decorate a tree, but it would be a day they would talk about for years to come and pass down from generation to generation, much the same as the Christmas they spent on the mountain in Canton, Georgia.

The herbs she gathered along with onions from the garden and the turkey drippings made a delicious pan of stuffing and giblet gravy to go with the roasted turkey. Even though many family members were missing from the dinner table, the children were very happy to have their mother back to her old self. Love can be a powerful force. Oftentimes, it transcends time, space, and even death...

62

Acceptance

After another mild winter, March blossoms bloomed early, announcing that spring had arrived. Charity decided to give Vicksburg, one more try. Her hopes of finding Henry's body or at the least, his spirit, still had not been completely dashed. Uriah too, was ready to give it another try; he wasn't ready to give up just yet on finding his father's body. He held a faint hope of finding him alive somewhere; however, he did not share that with his mother; he did not want her to revert back into the shell of the woman she had been after their last trip to Vicksburg. Charity did not say anything, but she knew Uriah's feelings about his father; however, in her heart, she knew that Henry was dead; she had known the instant he was killed...

After Uriah finished his spring planting, they left Calhoun County headed back to Vicksburg. This time, their trail was full of obstacles, mostly of the human sort; there were stragglers everywhere. They saw many soldiers; both Union and Confederate soldiers roamed the roads. Most were on foot, which made it easy to outrun them, but many of them were of the mind to take whatever they wanted from whomever they wished. This didn't set well with Uriah, who was glad he had armed himself well for the trip.

The first real danger they encountered happened about two days out as they were crossing the Black Warrior River; two men wearing Yankee blue, tried to waylay them and rob them of their valuables. One of them, stood in the middle of the short bridge they needed to cross and the other man came running up behind them.

"Toss down your valuables," said the one that ran up from behind them.

"We have very little," Charity told him.

While she was speaking, Uriah pulled a pistol from under his coat. He told the men that what they did have, they would be keeping. One of the men raised his rifle and pointed it toward Uriah; Uriah shot him right between the eyes. A look of surprise and shock enveloped the other man's face and then turned and skedaddled out of there, real quick like.

"I'm sorry Mama, but I'm tired of trying to outrun 'em,"

"You did what you had to do, Son; that one there would have killed both of us and never given it another thought." Luckily, the rest of their trip went unchallenged.

When they reached Vicksburg, they were mildly surprised-The city looked a lot different than it did the last time they were there. A great many of the old homes and buildings that had been destroyed by the cannon fire, had now been torn down and what residents remained had begun to laborious task of rebuilding and cleaning things up. There were still several regiments of Yankees soldiers there; because the Union wanted to maintain its control over the city. However, the stench of death no longer permeated the air, hanging like a blanket over the town; both were glad as they made their way to the Union headquarters. Captain Brewer was no longer there; the man in charge was a gruff, burly man by the name of George Williams.

Charity showed him the second letter she received; it was dated the 21st of January 1864. It stated that Henry had been killed in battle, May 26th 1863.

Mr. Williams looked over the piece of paper and said, "Yeah, I sent this out, using the information from the Confederate comptrollers register. The date and cause of death was copied from the original report."

"Why can't you people tell me where my husband's remains are buried?"

"Ma'am, I am sure you understand that with so many dead, we had to bury the bodies. And as crude as it seems, mass burial was the quickest way to take care of this. With that many corpses lying in the heat of summer, it was a breeding ground for disease. I have no sure way of knowing exactly which grave your husband's body was placed in; however, I would think that it would have been in one of the first ones they dug."

She could tell that he was sincere and decided to use that sincerity to her benefit. "Would it be possible for you to direct us to those first graves?" she asked politely.

"Even if I do, Ma'am, there will be no way that you can find him- you cannot dig them all up and even if you did, he'd be too badly decomposed to make identification…"

"I understand that," she replied. "I just want to go there and pay my respects." Charity figured that if she got near where Henry was buried, his soul might be there or that maybe she would somehow sense his presence. Williams told them exactly where to go.

Climbing back onto the wagon they set out- she and Uriah did not have any trouble finding the burial site; however, they first had to pass by the place they were burying the men the last time they were there. It looked better than it had before; sprigs of pale green grass had even begun to grow over it.

It had been eight months since their last trip; most of the spirits had moved on, or crossed over; however, Charity sensed that a few were still there.

When they reached the end of the road, Charity could see the last burial mound; it was covered with thick green grass- She would have to pass two more burial mounds before reaching it. She got down off the wagon and walked the circumference of each mound, hoping for any sign of Henry.

After circling the first two burial mounds, she turned toward the last one- she was nearing the last burial mound when something drew her attention to the nearby willow trees; she turned and listened.

Lila M Beckham

Uriah watched her as she walked toward the trees. He thought that maybe she was going to relieve herself. He did not attempt to follow her; he stayed near the wagon, mainly to keep an eye on their supplies.

As Charity neared the trees, she was not surprised to hear her grandfather chanting. Making her way into the trees, she soon came to a clearing. Two Feathers sat at his fire, chanting; there was another figure there. His back was to her, but she knew it was Henry.

"Little One," said her grandfather, "I knew you would come."

"Henry," Charity said softly. But Henry did not turn to look at her. Looking at his features, she could tell that he was confused.

Charity wanted to cry out to him, grab him into her arms and hold him, but she knew that would be impossible; the Henry sitting before her was only there in essence, not in human form. Her memory of him was what let her see him as he had been in life.

Turning to her grandfather, tears welled up in her eyes. "Why doesn't he respond, Grandfather?"

"What you see sitting before you is what you have envisioned in your mind," her grandfather explained. "It is only the shell of who he was in life."

"Can he hear me- see me?"

"I do not know, Little One- the spirit is absent."

"Does that mean his spirit has already crossed over?"

"Perhaps- perhaps not- perhaps he shifted in death."

"What does that mean, Grandfather?"

"When his earthly body was of no further use, his spirit took up residence in another form, maybe human, maybe not- maybe his spirit rests with Unequa Adanvdo, the Great Spirit."

"I don't understand all of that, Grandfather! How will I ever know for sure whether he has crossed over or not?"

"You are a Truth Seeker, Little One; you will not rest until you know the truth. Your Henry's earthly body has died, Usdi Saquo; his spirit had to move on. Your life did not end; you, too, must move on."

Charity knew Two Feathers was right. The Henry she had known was dead. She knew that she would have to learn to live with the knowledge that things could never be the way they were before.

Sitting there in front of her grandfather and his Sacred Fire, she cried. Accepting that things could not be the way they were before and that Henry was gone from her life was the hardest loss she had ever known; she knew that if she survived the loss of her maternal grandparents and her son, Aaron, she could and must survive this; her children needed her.

When she looked to where the apparition of Henry had sat, he was gone. Saying goodbye to her grandfather, she left the clearing, wiping her tears away as she walked back toward the wagon.

"Are you alright, Mama?" asked Uriah.

"Yes, Son," she replied. "I will be fine... Your father's spirit has crossed over; we will have to accept that his body will remain here in Vicksburg."

Although he had held out a glimmer of hope that his father might still be alive, Uriah wholeheartedly accepted what his mother said was fact.

The trip home was a good one. They were more relaxed now that they had accepted that Henry was gone and not coming back. Uriah talked about his childhood and about the things he had not understood, but now, as an adult, had come to understand. She told him again of her childhood, her line of descent going as far back as she knew naming her ancestors- Telling him that the tradition of storytelling must be continued- she made him promise to remember their names and to tell his children and grandchildren.

"The ways of my ancestors are coming to an end," she said, taking her pipe out of her pocket and packing it with dried rabbit tobacco. "The people who were once the Great Cherokee Nation, are now treated no better than cattle; they've been sent out west to live on what they call reservations that are in unusable lands where they cannot prosper... I now understand where I could not as a child, why my white grandfather wanted me to live as white; he knew what was coming... My first born son, you must always remember that you have the strong blood of the, "A ni yv wi ya," the Principal People, and that your father's blood also flows through your veins. I am Tsitsalagi, Cherokee. Nothing will ever change that. You, too, are Tsitsalagi; your children are Tsitsalagi- the blood will remain no matter how many generations come after."

63

The Conclusion

Calhoun Co, Alabama
May, 1865

We should all hope to be measured by the strength of our character, not someone's perception of our weaknesses... Even the strongest among us have our weaknesses, but even the weakest among us will have certain strengths.

Charity's children only spoke of her strengths - Her strength of character- the strength of the love she had for her husband and children. The strength of the love she shared with those around her; and, the strength of the love she had for her Indian heritage... Those stories have been told and retold to the generations that followed.

After three failed journeys, during the height of the Civil War, traveling to Vicksburg in hopes of finding Henry alive or at the least, his place of burial, Charity conceded that her quest had no chance in succeeding. Upon her return home, she filed a claim with the Confederate States auditor for the benefits due both Henry and Aaron for their service in the Confederate States

Army- the claim was filed the 27th day of April, 1864. She had hoped to receive this money thinking it would sustain her family until the end of the war; she never received one red cent of the benefits her family deserved… however, they survived the war without losing anyone else in the family.

The War Between the States ended April 9, 1865. It took several weeks for word to reach them at the homestead there in Calhoun County. Charity's first thought was about her sons, John, Charles, and young Jackson, who had run off and joined the army in August of 1864 - she had not heard from him since…

Every day, after the chores were finished, she sat on the porch watching the trail leading to Anniston- Jackson was the first one to return home- he said he had been taken prisoner, along with the rest of his unit, when they were told to surrender to the Yankees in Meridian Mississippi; they were released via a pardon once they signed an Oath of Allegiance at a place called, Citronelle, Alabama, which he said was near Mobile. It would be another two weeks before Charles and John returned home- they had been imprisoned on Pea Patch Island, in a place called Fort Delaware the last six months of the war. Both were emaciated, each coughed short little coughs every now and then, as if they had something in their throats. Charles had been wounded; he said he survived because John carried him a mile on his back to get help for him…

Charles and John stayed overnight asking if there was anything she needed them to do before they went to check on their families; she told them that she and Jackson could manage, for them to see to their wives and children. Charity could tell that Charles was hesitant about leaving; when he tried to tell her something, she stilled his lips much the same as she had when he tried to tell her that his father would perish in the war…

"You boys have your own lives to live- go see to your wife an children," she said, kissing his cheek. "If it is meant to be, it will be."

After allowing Jackson several days to rest, the two of them began getting the ground ready for planting- it was backbreaking work, and at 50 yrs old, it was extremely hard on Charity's body.

A week later, she woke to the squawking of a yellow mocker outside her bedroom window. "Go away," she mumbled, before turning over to look out the window. The bird was perched on a limb in the tree near the window; his little ferret eyes stared in at her. "I hear you call my name, yellow bird," she whispered, "I'm not yet ready to go…"

About mid-morning, as she sat on the porch watching the trail to Anniston, a figure appeared. As he came nearer, she saw that he was riding a mule; she pinned her hair up and dusted the garden dirt off her skirt.

The stranger rode straight to the cabin. Dismounting, he introduced himself as Benjamin Phillips, saying that he had come to fulfill a promise. Charity knew why he was there; she had been patiently awaiting his arrival since the end of the war. She invited him in and put on a pot of coffee.

"I would've done been here, Ma'am, but I had to see to my family first."

"Of course you did," Charity said, smiling warmly at him. "I would expect nothing less out of someone my husband considered a friend - Henry would have done the same, Mr. Phillips."

"Please, Ma'am, just call me Ben- Mr. Phillips was my father," he said, his tone solemn.

Charity poured them a cup of the makeshift coffee and then suggested they set out on the porch- she wanted to smoke her pipe while they drank their coffee and talked. Hesitating a moment, Benjamin pulled Henry's letter out of his pocket and fingered it nervously.

Charity reached for it and then quickly pulled her hand back. Benjamin hesitated a moment and then handed it to her. She took the letter, brought it to her heart and then suddenly slipped it into her pocket. "Let's sit on the porch and drink our coffee- I'd like you to tell me about my husbands last days."

***

It was told down through the generations that she and Benjamin set on the porch and talked for nearly an hour and then Mr. Phillips left. After he left, Charity went into her bedroom and closed the door.

When she had not come out by the next morning, Mary went in to check on her. She said that her mother was lying in bed, and that she was holding the letter next to her heart. At first, she thought her asleep... The story is told that after reading Henry's letter, she went to join him.

Vicksburg, Mississippi
May 24, 1863

My dearest Charity, these last several months that I've been gone, have been the hardest days I've ever had to endure... In moments of silence, I close my eyes and picture your beautiful face and the faces of our children. My years with you have been blessed in so many ways that I dare hope for many more. The Yankees have us surrounded and the outcome does not look well- if I could have one last blessing, it would be that before I die I could lie in your embrace one last time... If you are reading this, it means that I did not survive this horror called War. So many good men have lost their lives, dare not I be spared. With my last breath, I will whisper that I love you...

Forever yours,
Henry

Be sure to check out these other titles by Lila Beckham

Emmy's Journey

(A Full length follow-up Novel featuring Charity's daughter Emmy and many other characters from When the Yellow Mocker Calls)

These Novellas are 160pgs or less

Annabelle's Diary

Orphan Girl

Tuesday's Gone

Deathbed Promises

Other Full Length Novels

The Joshua Stokes Series, which includes the following titles in order

1. Dumping Grounds

2. Fallout

3. Markers

Other Miscellaneous titles include;

The Empty Room (8pg short)

A Little past the Corner of Royal and Main (Short Story)

Darkling (a Samuel Parker Adams novella)

Lila M Beckham